David Blagrove

David Blagrove (1937 - 2016) grew up by the Thames in Abingdon and then Reading, where he became involved in the early efforts to save the Kennet & Avon Canal. After leaving school, he became articled to a London solicitor, whilst he and friends also operated a trip-boat business on the River Kennet at Reading. Abandoning a legal career, he and a friend then worked narrow boats for the Willow Wren Canal Carrying Company. Further employment followed as a lockkeeper for the Thames Conservancy, before marriage impelled another change of career, to that of history teacher.

David had contributed to the setting up of the Canal Museum at Stoke Bruerne while his pair of boats was iced-up there in the hard winter of 1962-3, and he developed a great fondness for the village during that time. He and his wife Jean moved to Stoke Bruerne in 1966, where he took up a teaching post in a nearby secondary school. David and Jean lived by the canal in Stoke Bruerne for the rest of his life, where he continued to be involved with the museum and with village events. Throughout the canal world, David was well-known for song-writing, performing, and relating his tales of the working boats.

He was a founder member of the Northampton branch of the IWA and served on the IWA National Council from 1981 to 1990; his appointment to Vice–President of the Association was made in 1991. Among his many commitments were other canal organisations, including founding the Commercial Narrowboat Operators Association (now CBOA). His ownership of various working boats continued, with the best-known being *Elton* and *Hesperus*. As well as teaching, he set up a boating business carrying coal for retail sale, and was later involved in other canal carrying businesses, notably South Midland Water Transport. His interest in waterways was not confined to this country; he had many friends in Europe and visited there often. Formal recognition was granted by his appointment to MBE in the Birthday Honours of 2014 for his services to waterways.

David wrote several non-fiction books; two on the history of the Grand Union Canal, at Stoke Bruerne and at Braunston, and more on another of his many interests, railways. He also wrote of his earlier life, in the autobiographies *Bread Upon The Waters* and *The Quiet Waters By*.

In the mid-1990s, David wrote a book of fiction, drawing on his knowledge of canals. It was clearly intended to be the first in a connected series, but regrettably no more books were written. *Ellison's Winter* was not published until 2020, about 25 years after it was written, and four years after the author died.

Ellison's Winter
David Blagrove

CANALBOOKSHOP

ELLISON'S WINTER
David Blagrove

Edited by Paul and Diana Monahan

Published January 2020
Canal Book Shop
Audlem Mill Limited The Wharf Audlem Cheshire CW3 0DX

ISBN 978-1-9160125-4-7

Editors' Note

I have known of this book for several years; indeed, David asked Diana and me to read it and comment - a task which extended into proof-reading and some editing. Unfortunately, further progress became lost among his many other interests and eventually his final illness. Some time after his passing, David's family asked us to seek publication of the book and at last we have been able to do so.

The book was written by David and originally intended to be published under a pseudonym. As the title suggests, it was also written as the first part of a series following the main character, Andrew. Unfortunately, the next volumes will not now be written. To us, the end of the book is clearly intended to lead into the second book of the sequence and as such, ends rather suddenly. In an attempt to remedy this, I have written a coda, or postscript, to bring the book to a more satisfactory conclusion. David and I were both brought up in Berkshire with a comparable education, although a few years apart; whether that has encouraged us to write in a similar style, I will leave others to judge. However, I hope that the coda will be seen as a fitting end to the book and as a warm tribute to a good friend, both to us personally and to the waterways.

Finally, I would like to thank David's family, who entrusted us with this task, and CanalBookShop at Audlem Mill who have been most helpful with the publication of the book.

Anyone who believes that they recognise any of the characters is surely mistaken; any resemblance is not intended and is purely coincidental. Of errors, I hope there are none; such as there are will have been a result of the editing process and are much regretted.

Paul & Diana Monahan
November 2019

Chapter 1
Preliminary Enquiries

John Watson was waiting in the visitors' car park when Andrew came from the Discharge Office. *There was no point in hanging about,* Andrew thought, even though he had rehearsed the scene in his mind this past year. *No demonstrations* he decided, *no looking back. Thank God that John was there as he had promised.* John was sitting there in the drivers' seat, his gloved hands resting on the wheel, somewhat greyer, somewhat balder than last time he'd seen him, thought Andrew, but still the old reliable John.

A small cyclone of brown leaves swirled round the car park, momentarily hiding the neatly printed Home Office noticeboard in front of which John had parked the Audi. The passenger window whined down.

John leaned across to release the door, "Well Andy! Is that all your luggage?"

Andrew glanced at the small grip in his right hand, "That's it. I'll sling it on the back seat. Don't bother to open the boot."

He opened the door, swung the bag in before him and flopped into the passenger seat. He yanked the seat belt round him and sighed. John pulled out a silver case, "Cigarette?"

"No thanks, I've got out of the habit and I won't start again."

"Fair enough, I'm cutting down myself. Where to?"

"For now John, anywhere, far away from here."

John pressed the starter, reversed out of the parking bay and headed out of the car park. Andrew did not look behind him as the car moved away.

Neither man spoke as John wove his way round the lanes towards Arundel. A watery sun was lighting the battlements of the castle, the trees in the park were bare.

As the car turned onto the A29, Andrew said, "Where are we

going?"

"My place for the moment. Jill's got a room ready for you."

"Well that's pretty good of you, but I really shouldn't intrude."

"Rubbish. Anyway, it's the least we could do for you. You know you're always welcome."

Andrew nodded. *Only so long as you're not an embarrassment*, he thought grimly, and said aloud, "A gaol bird's not always welcome, you know."

John glanced round at him. Andrew's face had a grimmer look than he remembered, and there was hardness in his grey eyes that he had not seen before. He said, "That's not true, and you know it."

"Sorry."

"Was it tough in there?"

Andrew laughed a short, bitter, bark. "Tough? Nothing like Basic Training, and nowhere near as bad as school."

He was silent for a moment, scanning the countryside as it fled past, then said, "Remember CSM Dunton?"

John chuckled, "Shall I ever forget. 'Yew 'orrible little men, you're gonna bloody 'ate me'. How right he was! What a bastard!"

"Well" said Andrew, "I can't say that I found a screw to touch him for bastardry. Nor did I come across a fellow lag as unpleasant as some of the boys I was at school with, and the food was better than at the Law Courts cafeteria. No, it was all right, as long as you kept your head down and kept to the rules. At least it was at Ford."

"What about Pentonville?"

"That, John, old pal, was different. Very different."

Andrew turned and looked out at the Sussex countryside, with its pastel colours, *like that watercolour artist, oh, what was his name? Warren? Warboys? Ward? Pamela liked his work; she always wanted one for the sitting room. She would, always liked something bland and precise, I suppose that's why she liked me to start with - the bitch,* "Damn!" he said suddenly, out loud.

"What's up?"

"Sorry, I just thought of something that I didn't want to."

John was indicating to turn off left onto a side road.

"We can cut across country from here. I need to call in at Guildford, and then the rest of the day's our own."

"Fine."

"Any plans for the immediate future?"

"I shall need to see exactly where I stand financially, then I shall move up country. I'm going to keep well away from Town."

"Well, you should have a little money to come. I've paid out Pamela, and you can see the account. A pity we didn't put Lipscombe on the market before the bottom fell out of it. Still, with the repayment of your little loan, her half share and legal costs, you've got just over ninety grand left. I've used some of the income from that to keep up the payments into your pension fund."

"And three years ago I was worth over two million."

"In total assets, yes, but not net, nor in income. Hence your problems."

"Don't rub it in. Did you recover anything other than cash?"

John was silent for a moment, and then said, "As a matter of fact I did or, to be accurate, Jill did. You know we went down to Lipscombe when the trial was still on?" Andrew nodded.

"I had the Power of Attorney that you gave me, and a key. Pamela hadn't changed the locks then. I went through your study and bedroom. That decent sergeant from the Fraud Squad was with me to see fair play. Jill did the rest of the house. There's two packing cases and three suitcases of your stuff, books and what-have-you, in our garage. Pamela suspected, but she never found how we got them out."

"Bloody Hell John, that was a hell of a risk for you to take."

"Andrew, you've been a good friend to me. It was the least I could do."

They had passed Alfold, and were back on the main road before Andrew spoke again.

"Are you in a great hurry?"

"No, not really, why?"

"Would you mind very much just pulling off the road for a few minutes?"

"Not at all, where? Here?"

"No, no, just a bit further on, look there. By that sign to Cranleigh. Off to the right."

John put his indicator on, pulled across to the centre of the road, spun the wheel and headed off down a side road.

"That'll do. Just pull up where you can. I'd like to look at something."

The Audi stopped. Andrew undid his seat belt, opened the door and stepped out. The low November sunlight played wanly in the nearly leafless trees. He walked a little way, towards some railings and stopped by them. John saw him cross the road and gaze for a long time at right angles to the road. He re-crossed and stared in the opposite direction. After some minutes he came back to the car, opened the door and got in.

"Are you all right?" asked John.

"Perfectly" Andrew slid the seat belt across and clicked it home. He smiled across at John.

"I know what I'm going to do now."

"So what were you looking at?"

"Something I read about inside. It's a derelict canal."

"You're joking," said Jill, her spoon half poised between the sweet plate and her mouth.

"No, I'm deadly serious", Andrew replied, sipping his Liebfraumilch. Dear old John, always tried to do the decent thing, even if sometimes it was not terribly stylish. Still, it could have been worse with a dessert, he'd come up with reasonable Bordeaux to go with the main course, and it was the first plonk that he'd tasted for more than three years.

"But you don't know anything about boats" said John. "You could never punt up the Cherwell without falling in."

"I can learn. Anyway, it will get me right away from the old things and ways. And I won't need to be a nuisance to either of you."

John began to protest, but Andrew cut him short,

"No, no John. I do appreciate what you and Jill are doing for me, but I must start getting on with my life."

Jill's blue eyes were wide, "But how can you live on one? It's lovely in summer, but it's winter now."

"You forget that I have had some experience of simple living conditions recently."

She blushed and averted her eyes. *She was still a stunner*, thought Andrew, *she's got a bit plump, but her figure's still good, even her face is not too lined, just a few crows' feet round the mouth. Lucky old John, pity she dyes her hair though.*

"I'm sorry, Jill. I didn't mean to lash out. You get that way inside you know. But seriously, a boat can be pretty comfortable. Not perhaps like this, but not bad either." He glanced round the dining room. 1930's stockbroker style originally, but they'd brought it pretty well into the present. *Good quality furniture*, he thought, *Harrods probably. I'll bet this table was on display there once.* John had always been quietly prosperous, and could be relied on for good, solid, *Homes and Gardens* sort of taste.

Jill reached across and picked up his sweet plate.

"Cheese and biscuits?"

"No thanks."

"Coffee?"

"Yes please, that would be lovely." Pity John hadn't got a drop of brandy about. He could have done with a little reminder of the good things. John offered him a King Edward cigar.

"Thanks no, I'm not starting again, besides which, I shall have to watch the cash."

"Well, if you're going to live on a boat, how are you going to make a crust? What do you propose living on? The DHSS? Plenty do you know, no shame in it, and you've paid enough tax and National Insurance anyway."

Andrew smiled, as Jill came in with the coffee tray. "I shall use my skills" he said, with a sardonic laugh. "That's what they tried to teach me inside. Rehabilitation they call it. So, what skills have I got, beside my redundant legal ones? I can run an infantry platoon and lead it in an attack according to the methods of the Korean War or Suez; I can debate a moot point; I know how equitable accounts are apportioned...."

"But you can't keep accounts" put in John, bluntly.

Andrew sighed and nodded, "Too bloody true, or at least, I can't keep them straight." He looked glum.

Jill leaned across and patted his arm "You can think positively, and there's nobody who can get round knotty problems like you can."

"Jill's right" said John. "Look at it positively. You can't practise as a solicitor again, but look at what you know, and what you can do. You were a damn fine advocate, and you know the criminal law inside out. You know what makes the police tick, you know how to deal with government departments, and you know how to set up business deals." Andrew toyed with his coffee cup and looked intently at the pattern. *Spode*, he thought, then said,

"You're absolutely right of course. That's what I'm going to do. But I'm getting right away from Surrey, right away from London. I'm going to live on a boat and be a trouble-shooter."

Next day, Andrew made an appointment with a bank manager in Northampton. He had decided before his release that he was going to make his base in the South Midlands. Handy enough to London just in case he needed to pick up any old threads, yet far enough away for him to avoid old associations. This had given him some sort of lodestar to steer for. Since John had looked after his affairs, the financial haemorrhaging which had led him to disaster seemed to have been staunched. Quietly and with his accustomed efficiency, John had settled his affairs and left him with a small amount of capital and some income. Discussing matters with John the morning after his release, Andrew found that he had sufficient in his current account to buy a second hand Volkswagen Golf. The next day he had headed his new acquisition round the M25 to the M1 and turned northwards. His plan was to set up a temporary base near Northampton. If he found somewhere reasonable, he would stay, otherwise he would move on. He had developed a deep-rooted distaste for staying in one place for long. Twelve months of looking at the same daily scene had awakened a long dormant nomadic instinct. Besides which, he thought, I'm pushing sixty now. I ought to see something other than offices and courts. There must be life beyond suburbia and a month in Dordogne every year. Hullo, wasn't that Junction 15? He pulled up the slip road and followed the sign for Northampton. It was an interesting feeling this. Into the unknown at Junction 15!

The girl in the Tourist Board office smiled as she looked up at the tall, quietly spoken man with a military bearing, who came into the enquiry office just before lunch. He looked a little like John Cleese she thought, and had an air of assurance about him that dominated the little front office. Although he was old enough to be her dad, she felt a little shiver as, with perfect manners, he took a piece of Tourist Board paper and wrote down the details she gave him.

"I want somewhere near the canal" Andrew said, so she gave him a brochure with a few names highlighted in yellow pen.

"You shouldn't have too much trouble this time of year" she said. "Would you like me to try some of the numbers for you?"

"That would be kind" he said. "This Mrs. Clarke seems a likely one."

"Yes, she's got an old farmhouse by the Grand Union Canal. Shall I ring her?"

"Please."

"It's about ten miles from Northampton, just off a main road."

"It sounds lovely."

Half an hour later, Andrew was sitting in a low-beamed sitting room whose square paned windows looked across a grassy yard.

Watercolour landscapes hung on the wall, a log fire crackled in an ample grate, its light flickering off polished brass ornaments. Mrs. Clarke, a petite woman in her early fifties, who looked as if she laughed a good deal, sat in a chintz-covered chair. Her ankles were demurely crossed above a neat pair of court shoes. She wore a heavy tweed skirt and a plain jumper. Andrew noticed a plain gold band on her ring finger. Convent educated, he thought, maybe a divorcee. She sipped a cup of coffee and said, "I can't tell you much about the boats, I'm afraid, but you can have a look in the magazines. I always take them." She rose and went to a table where the daily paper lay (*"Telegraph" reader*, noted Andrew) and produced two magazines with glossy covers, showing waterway scenes. "You can find all sorts of addresses and things in there". She handed them to Andrew. "Are you thinking of getting one to live on?"

Andrew nodded. "Yes. I've got this thing about it. I read a book recently by a chap who'd done it years ago, during the last War in fact. I'd like to give it a try."

"Oh, I know, you've read *Narrow Boat*." It's a classic. Everyone on the canals knows it."

"Really? I'd never heard of it before. I didn't think anyone knew much about the subject. Everyone I've talked to thinks that canals are industrial tips and that people who live on boats are hippies, or gypsies."

Mrs. Clarke laughed, setting her earrings dancing "That's what I used to think, before we came here. No, it's quite different. My late husband used to say it was a secret world. I'd say it was partly that, but more of an elongated village, stretching from London to Manchester."

"Have you been here long?"

"Here? In this house? About fifteen years. The children were tiny when we moved in. It was more or less derelict, and we renovated it. Took us five years to get it right."

"It looks lovely now."

"My husband was an architect. He was very good at those sort of things. Well, he made a living out of advising people over restoring old houses."

"You said 'was'?"

She smiled ruefully, "Nearly four years ago now. MS."

"Oh dear, I'm sorry."

"That's OK. You weren't to know. He was only 48, but the last year I had to nurse him continually. It was a relief when the end came." She took another sip from her cup. "And what about you? Are you on business or holiday?"

"As I said, I'm looking for a boat to live on."

"Yes, but are you thinking of living full time or part time on one?" Andrew smiled. "Just put it that I'm between jobs right now."

"Redundant?"

"You could put it like that."

Mrs Clarke laughed. "I see, and you're starting again." Andrew nodded. "Any family?" He sighed. "Not any more. I have two grown up sons and a daughter just finished University last summer. I'm divorced. The Decree Absolute came through three months ago."

Mrs Clarke said softly "I see. I think I understand. How long do you want to stay?"

"How long can I? Two weeks? Three perhaps?"

"No problem. It's my quiet season, and it's good to have a bit of company."

"No children then?"

"Like yours. They're grown up. Sally still lives at home, but she works in London during the week. It's cheaper to use Mum's place than pay for a flat so she's here weekends and dosses at a friend's place in the week. Tom, my youngest, is in the army?"

"Really? What's his line?"

"Royal Engineers. He went in from University and he's in Germany."

"So, you really are alone then. Well, you needn't worry, I'll behave myself. I have no interesting vices, but I enjoy a drink occasionally."

"So do I."

"Is there a decent pub near here?"

"Not in the village. It's become one of those ghastly eating-houses now with fizzy beer and a manager about ten years old. There's quite a good one about a mile in the other direction. It does food, bar meals, you know, but it's still a proper pub."

"Oh good. I was going to ask you about eating-places. Look, I've got to go to town again and do some odds and ends. I'll be back about seven. How about coming out for a drink?"

"I'd love to. But you must promise me one thing."

"Which is?"

"You must let me stand my round." Andrew's eyebrows rose slightly. She said firmly, "I'm not anyone's kept woman."

Andrew looked slightly surprised, and Mrs. Clarke laughed again "Don't take it amiss, but tongues in the countryside tend to wag over strangers."

"Fine. I'll let you stand as big a round as you wish!"

At the bank a young woman showed Andrew into an overheated waiting room. The room looked out onto a brick wall and was on the second floor. A plain panelled door labelled "I.C. Johnson, Assistant Manager" led out of the waiting room. They've relegated me to the Fourth Division, thought Andrew. I used to get the senior man at the Threadneedle Street Branch. After a wait of about five minutes, Mr Johnson, a balding man of forty-something, opened the door and came out to meet Andrew. They shook hands, and Johnson helped Andrew off with his short coat and waved him to a chair. Johnson settled himself behind his desk. "Excuse me, one moment" he said, and began tapping keys on a keyboard. He gazed enquiringly at a screen placed so that Andrew could not read it.

"I understand you are transferring here from our Threadneedle Street Branch," said Johnson. "Is it a current account?"

"Yes indeed" said Andrew, and there's also a Deposit Account" Johnson rattled away at his keyboard.

"Ah, I see. Yes. You have just over £5,000 on deposit with us, and

£3,753 in your current account."

"That'll be some two thousand less tomorrow, I've just bought a car."

"I see."

"You will receiving £750 or so per month from next month onwards. I want £600 to go to current account, and the balance to Deposit."

"I see." Johnson tapped more keys. "Any banker's orders or direct debits?"

"At the moment, only a small assurance policy."

"I see." More tapping.

"I shall use the current account for paying bills mainly."

"I see."

Perhaps, thought Andrew, *that's why his initials are I.C.* He said "I have a temporary address, for the next three weeks or so, you'd better send any statements and things there."

"Certainly. I'll just make a note" said Johnson, and tapped in Mrs. Clarke's address.

Andrew grimaced inwardly. Four years ago, bank managers would have come to him. At any one time he had over three million pounds in his Clients' Account, not to mention the Office Account, which never fell below fifty thousand. One tended to receive invitations to grand bankers' dinners and luncheons, whilst Jenkins, manager of the Threadneedle Street Branch had invited him to be godfather to their youngest. Now the wheel of fortune had left him with an under-manager who would doubtless never dream of asking an ex-convict to be a godfather, and probably would have an attack of the vapours if he knew that he was entertaining one in his office.

The two men shook hands again. Andrew found his way downstairs and out into the street. He asked the way to the Police Station, and was directed to a large 1930s concrete block near the bus station.

The duty constable raised his brows. "What? Here? I don't know.

Hang on a minute. Sarge!"

A uniformed sergeant came to the desk. "Yes sir?"

"I have to report for parole."

"Yes sir, you can do it here. Come through, and I'll take your details."

Andrew followed him into a small, bare interview room. Again he grimaced internally. The hours he'd spent in these places in other circumstances. The sergeant waved him to a chair and picked up a form.

"You've got a current local address?"

Andrew said, "Look sergeant. I may be travelling about the country, but I'll probably have a permanent address nearby. Can I always report here, or must I go wherever I am?"

"Well, sir. The thing is what was you in for?"

"Misappropriation of funds."

"Ha! We don't get too many of them round here. Was it a lot?"

"Half a million pounds. They got it all back."

"Worth doing time for, was it?"

"Not really. But I've learned a fair bit from it that I wouldn't have learned otherwise. Not all good I'm afraid."

The sergeant smiled sympathetically. "Put it this way, sir. It doesn't look like we'll be wanting to pick you up every time there's a rape, child molestation or mugging. But you'd best keep in regular touch for the time being. I'll have to report it further, and it'll be down to the Super to make the final decision about where you can report. What do you intend doing right now?"

"I'm hoping to live on a boat and do odd jobs. I can turn my hand to most things; at least I've still got my knowledge. They can't take that away from you."

"Solicitor were you?"

"That's it."

The sergeant smiled again. "Well, you ain't the first to come unstuck, and I don't suppose you'll be the last. Most of the ones I've come across end up selling things, or in estate agencies or summat like. I've only come across one who was dead rotten."

"You needn't worry about that. I'm not anxious to go inside again, although the open prison wasn't too bad. I prefer to be on the side of the law than against it. I suppose it's my upbringing."

The sergeant laughed. "I know what you mean, sir. Now, could I please see your Parole Certificate?"

"Anything doing here?"

The desk sergeant looked up to see one of his plain clothes colleagues, an inspector, closing the door into the reception desk.

"Not a lot. Just had a reportee for parole in."

"Anyone we know?"

"No, a stranger. Ex-lawyer from the Smoke. Moving down this way to live, on a barge I think he said."

"Oh ah. Let's have a look. You never know what's what."

The sergeant pushed the book of forms over the table. The inspector looked at it and stroked his chin. "That's interesting. I remember the case. It made the tabloids."

Walking back to the car, Andrew felt as if a load had been lifted from him. Deep down, he had been dreading seeing the police. Although the Fraud Squad had been most polite, and the officers from the City Police Station had arrested him in the nicest possible way, he had felt the disgrace of being in their hands most sharply. What had made it worse was that he had known many of them professionally, and had even cross examined the sergeant who formally charged him. Reporting for parole was one reason why he felt he had to get away from London. And now, the policeman had not treated him as if he were a real criminal at all. It would have been different I suppose, he thought grimly, if he'd been like old George. George's family was hard up, his wife was ill and couldn't work, one kid at nursery, one kid at school needing all the gear and money to go on school trips. George was a self-employed lorry driver, nice little business till the recession came, and he had been buying diesel from a contractor for his lorry - all legal, nothing shady about the deal. The trouble was, the diesel was untaxed, red diesel and he'd made a pound a gallon on his expenses and on his income tax returns. That was until the Customs and Excise caught him. He'd got a thousand quid fine and six months inside. Bad enough, but he'd been treated like dirt by the police, the children taken into care, wife put into a hostel by the Social Services and the home sold up. He'd done nothing worse than Andrew, but because Andrew was a solicitor, because he spoke grammatically and with a clear voice, and had been brought up to discipline at school and in the army, even the worst screws gave him some respect. The other cons caused him no trouble, except at Pentonville.... he shuddered at the thought, but George had had a hard time until he met Andrew. Anyway, he was lucky. Andrew doubted whether the police would be on his neck much. In fact that sergeant seemed as if he could be a useful chap to know some time.

The *"Rose and Crown"* was an undistinguished looking roadside pub, a stone building with a red tin roof at a steep pitch replacing its one time thatch. When Andrew and Mrs. Clarke walked into the bar, there were but two other customers in there, both men, sitting either side of a roaring fire on hard backed chairs. The landlord was sitting facing them on an old wooden settle. "Evenin' Anne" he said, rising and walking to the bar. He raised a flap and left it held up by a catch while he went to take their order.
"Evening Joe" said Mrs. Clarke, and nodded to the other two, who smiled at her in return. Andrew stamped wet off his shoes in the doorway, and walked across to the bar. Anne Clarke said "Joe, this is Andrew Ellison, who's staying with me for a few days."
Joe held his hand out "Pleased to meet you, Andrew. What are you drinking?"
"A pint of bitter please. Mrs. Clarke?"
"Anne, please, Andrew. I'll have a Cinzano and lemonade please."
Joe served the drinks. Andrew paid him, picked up the glasses and moved towards a table. The other two customers looked over their pint glasses as Joe went back to the settle.

"First time in these parts, mate?" asked one customer, a wizened, balding little man with darting, ferrety eyes set in a red, weatherbeaten face.

"Yes it is" said Andrew, "I've passed through on the motorway, and by train, but never stopped before."

"Ah" said the other customer, a bigger, younger man, with a fair beard and a generous waistline "that's what a lot of folks say, but there's more come here nowadays than there used to."

"It's that bloody Milton Keynes", said the older man. "Brought an 'ole lot o' people an' trouble, that 'ave."

"Oh no, Sid, you can't blame Milton Keynes for that. There's all sorts of people come into the country to live" said the landlord, "there weren't much doin' around here thirty year back, I know!" Sid snorted and supped his pint, but said nothing.

Anne said, "Andrew's hoping to come to live round here". The others nodded, but kept silent.

Andrew said, with a smile, "I know what you're thinking. Another London smartarse, come to force local prices up. Well, I'm not looking for a house, I'm looking for a boat." Something, which could have been relief, flashed across the faces of the two customers. The older one said,

"A boat eh? On the cut?"

"Sorry?"

"On the cut, the canal, you know."

Andrew laughed, "So they really call it that, do they? I thought that was just in books."

"O' course they calls the bloody cut 'the cut'" snorted Sid. "It's always been called that."

Joe, the landlord said "Sid here should know. He works on it."

"Oh, really" said Andrew, "What do you do?"

"They calls me a canalman these days" said Sid, "but I does anything. Mows grass, does a bit o' 'edgin', 'elps out lock keepin', moves dredgin' 'oppers, drives the tug. You name it, I does it."

"When the foreman's lookin'" said the younger man, "Rest of 'is time 'e sits in the mess boat readin' dirty books."

"You're as bad as that bloody manager" said Sid, "No idea of what a workin' chap does."

"You sound like the very chap I need to talk to" said Andrew. "Where do I buy a boat round here? And who do I need to see about licences and so forth?"

"I can't tell you too much about what's for sale mate, but you wants to talk to my boss at the office."

"Where's that?"

"Over at Braunston. He'll tell you all you needs to know."

"That sounds great. Let me fill your glass for you, and yours, and you too landlord. Anne? Then you can tell me how to find your boss."

Andrew parked his car in the grassy yard. The rain had stopped. Anne said "That was very pleasant. Thank you."

"Believe me, it was a real pleasure."

"How about a hot drink?"

"Thank you, I will."

They walked across to the porch; a bright light glared, making Andrew start.

"Oh, sorry. It's the security light."

"No problem. I think they're a very good idea. Works on a sensor doesn't it?"

"I think so; Tom made me fit it before he went abroad."

"You don't get any problems here do you? I should have thought this was a very low risk area from a crime point of view."

Andrew thought he detected just the faintest nuance of doubt before Anne replied "Oh, no. But better to be safe than sorry."

She unlocked the front door and stepped inside. *You get too suspicious, Ellison,* thought Andrew. *Too much association with the criminal classes.*

Inside the hall, Anne put the lights on. They were soft wall lights, which made the place look both warm and welcoming. In the carpeted hall a long case clock ticked slowly; there was a slight scent of wood smoke.

"What a lovely place to come home to."

"Thank you. I do love it, in spite of everything." They went through into the sitting room. Anne went into the kitchen beyond and began getting out cups. "Coffee or chocolate?"

"Chocolate, please. I haven't drunk it for years."

Andrew sat back in a chair and looked round. She had good taste, he thought. The ornaments were not cheap, nor were they overdone. In the window alcove behind the television was a plant stand with a flower arrangement on it. He called through to the kitchen,

"Do you do your own flower arrangements?"

"Yes, do you like them?"

"Very much. My wife does…er, did them. But not so artistically."

Anne came in with a tray. "So you are a flatterer are you? Trying to sweet-talk a girl?"

"Not at all. I really think they're good."

She sat in the chair across the hearth from him, placing the tray on the floor between them. "Help yourself. Biscuit?"

Andrew looked approvingly at Anne as she sat back in her chair. He suddenly realised how long ago it was that he had spent time with a woman. Her face was a bit lined, her hair rather mousy, but she had dancing blue eyes, with laughter lines in the corners, and full lips. She had changed from her tweed skirt of earlier and was wearing a plain grey one, with a necklace over her plain, high-necked jumper. Although on the plump side she had what looked like a good figure, with slim legs and neat ankles. Anne thought, *Ho! ho! my boy!* as she caught his glance. She shifted in her chair slightly, causing her skirt to ride up a little, and was gratified to notice Andrew's eyes widen slightly. He was, after all, extremely distinguished looking.

Suddenly Andrew said, "Please don't get me wrong. I'm home hunting, not scalp hunting."

"Well, you certainly come to the point" Anne replied. "Please Andrew, I know we've only just met, but you must realise that I have had dozens of men staying here, it's my livelihood. I don't rush into bed with any of them, but some are, well, easier to get on with than others."

For the first time for many months, Andrew felt himself smile unforcedly. Anne noticed that it was a soft, slightly crooked smile. He said, "That's fine, as long as we understand one another. I'm afraid that I am wary of women's company."

Anne leaned forward and poked the fire. Sparks whirled up the chimneypiece and reflected in her eyes. Andrew gazed at the blazing logs,

"I said 'wary', not 'weary', but I have to think things out. I've not yet come to terms with myself." He drank off the cup, rose and came over to her.

"Let me have your cup. I'll wash up."

Next morning was sunny and clear after the rain. Looking out of his bedroom window, Andrew saw that the farmhouse stood in a wide, low valley. Beyond the farmyard, at a slightly lower level, ran the canal, crossed by a hump-backed brick bridge. The towpath lay on the side away from the house, beyond its bare hedge fields sloped to a distant river. A tall spire reared above houses crowning the distant horizon. About a mile and a half away low sunlight flashed off the windows of a swiftly moving Virgin train. Andrew yawned and glanced at his watch. Fifty minutes to Euston, he supposed, watching it zip out of sight into a cutting. Fifty minutes away from that cat stalking a blackbird, from that tractor and trailer making their way sedately across the field from which the roar of the train was fast ebbing, fifty minutes from that heron, perched statue-like on a willow stump.

The scent of toast greeted him as he opened the bedroom door and padded to the bathroom in his slippers and dressing gown. Across the landing a bedroom door was open. He noticed an unmade double bed and Anne's dress from last night hanging beside a wardrobe.

"Is that you, Andrew?" came Anne's voice, "Breakfast in twenty minutes."

"Right oh!" he called back. He noticed that the cold tap was dribbling slightly. He went to turn it off, but it was down tight. Needs a new washer, he mused as he ran hot water for shaving. He rummaged in the suitcase of clothes that Jill had given him. It was one that she had salvaged from Lipscombe. Bless her! She'd pressed all his shirts and trousers. He supposed he'd better hang his trousers and jackets up, selecting a pair of faded jeans and a check shirt and jumper as he did so.

Anne had laid breakfast in the kitchen. He came into the low-beamed room, with its fitted kitchen, looked around and sniffed appreciatively.

"Smells good. I say, I thought last night, I do like your kitchen."

"Jim, my husband, designed it, just before he went down with MS. He was brilliant at that sort of thing."

Andrew opened a small carton of breakfast cereal in front of him.

"I'll say. Those units really set the kitchen off."

"What's the plan of campaign for today, then?"

"I thought I'd work my way north, towards Braunston, and call in at boatyards and things. Where do you think I ought to start?"

"Try Yardley Wharf just along the road. The chap there deals in boats and knows what's about. He's very helpful, they often send people to me."

Yardley Wharf lay just off the main road. It was another old farmhouse with the canal lying at the far side of another grassy farmyard from the house, but the owners had obviously taken the canal more seriously than Anne Clarke and her late husband. A number of craft were tied up beside the wharf; there was a drydock, a chandlery and a crane. A slight, bearded man in a boiler suit, carrying a pair of welding goggles, came from behind a gate as Andrew stopped his car on a gravelled patch near the crane.

"I'm looking for a boat", said Andrew.

An hour later, Andrew was driving out of the yard with a thousand arcane instructions ringing in his ears; where to go, what to look for, what to pay, how to get surveys, Certificates of Compliance, the merits of calorifiers, propane, long swims, traditional or cruiser sterns, air versus water cooling, teleflex versus mechanical controls, pump-outs, cess tanks, gas lockers and alternators. Also he had the offer of a job as a general labourer at £6.00 per hour. His mind whirling with information as obscure to him as emblements and estovers are to non-lawyers, he drove up, through the old village, onto the old coaching highway that was once the artery of the Romans. Today Watling Street hides beneath the number A5, and its traffic has been largely siphoned off by motorways, but it still strides, mile upon Roman mile, in a straight line though Northamptonshire. As Andrew drove north, the hills became steeper and the countryside changed to an undulating land with steep valleys. Not unlike a miniature Devon, he thought, that farmhouse near Honiton, which he and Pamela had rented for a month when the children were small, was set in country like this. Damn her! He snatched his mind back to the present as a roundabout loomed in front of him. Blast! Which way now? He caught sight of a direction indicator for Braunston and turned onto a bypass. A few minutes later he breasted a slight rise and saw in front of him a tall spire on a hilltop, with the sail less stump of a windmill beside it, and a cluster of roofs running down a ridge. As he dropped down a steepish hill he became aware, beyond tall brick buildings to his right, of the reflected flash of water, of sheds and more roofs and bright cabin sides peering out between hedges. Ah, there it was, a sign with a logo pointing to the Marina. He indicated right, pulled to the centre of the road and turned off.

Sid's boss was not in the office that morning, but a pleasant lady clerk listened to Andrew sympathetically. "We don't sell boats, we only run the canal. I can sell you a licence for a boat if you own one. But I'm sure the Marina next door can help you. It's just beyond where you parked your car."

"And what exactly are you looking for?" asked the man in the Marina Office.

"I think I need something built of steel, about fifty feet long, with a diesel engine."

"No problem there, plenty of them around. What sort of price range?"

"Do I have a choice?"

The man laughed; "Anything from ten to eighty K, but we tend to deal with the upper end of the scale. You generally get what you pay for."

"I see. So I ought to look at something more than ten thousand?"

"Yes, to be honest with you. Sure, I get more brokerage, but you can buy yourself a heap of trouble if you aren't careful. Anyway, take a look through these lists. We've got about five, I think, which might suit you."

Andrew was given a set of brochures, keys and instructions how to find the various boats, and courteously pointed in the right direction.

"Just shout if you need me" said the man, "I'll either be here, or in the Dry Dock just over there."

After an hour of climbing over boats and under tarpaulins, of unlocking padlocks and bumping his head in various cabins, Andrew was none the wiser. This was the oddest house hunting he had ever done. Every one was different, yet they all had features in common and, unlike houses, you only had to walk a few yards between each one. He glanced at his watch. It was gone midday, perhaps he could get something to eat and think things over. He had arrived at a point where the boats were all moored on a short branch canal, and strolled down to where an iron bridge straddled the water. Here the branch joined the main canal in a wide pool. A wizened old man was standing in the doors of a moored boat watching him incuriously. As he walked by him, the old man nodded solemnly and said in a reedy voice,

"Marnin'."

"Good morning to you."

"'Avin' a look round are ye?"

"Yes. I'm hoping to buy a boat."

"Oh ah!"

End of conversation, thought Andrew, and nodded politely to the old fellow as he turned onto the bridge. As he started to climb the slope, the reedy voice came from behind him,

"You wants to 'ave a look agin the Bottom Lock, mate."

Andrew stopped and turned. He felt ashamed at his apparent brusqueness.

The old man had bright eyes, which gazed out of his wrinkled, weather-beaten face with friendliness and honesty. Andrew smiled at him.

"I don't know" he said. "I'm running about for no reason. I've got no hurry."

The old man said "You ain't the only one as is in too much of an 'urry. But not all of 'em takes the time to speak."

Andrew was not quite sure whether this was meant as a compliment and asked, "What was that you said about 'Bottom Lock'?"

"That's where you wants to 'ave a look, mate. You just keep a-gooin' that road and you'll come to it."

"Thanks very much, I'll do that."

"You're welcome, mate" said the old man, turning to observe another person who had appeared from the other direction.

Andrew walked slowly along the towpath in the watery sunlight. There seemed to be boats everywhere: a sheet of water to his right behind a hedge crowded with them, more in front and tied along the bank. More sheds and buildings lay in front, to his left. There was a slipway where a longhaired young man was crouched amid snapping and crackling blue flashes as he welded a hull, there was a low brick building filled with chandlery, a bridge, and finally a lock with mellow brick buildings either side. For a while Andrew stood motionless on the lockside, gazing at the mellow brickwork and the green hills rising behind. It was as if he had stepped into another century, and he felt a sense of contentment that he had not known for years.

Into his reverie there gradually imposed itself a low-pitched chugging, which grew gradually louder. Andrew peered towards the source of the sound. Underneath the arch of the bridge, nosing its way into the chamber of the lock came a low set, brightly painted, boat's fore end. Behind the paintwork was a sort of short, green canvas tent and a long, open hold filled with neatly stacked bags. At the end of the hold was a bright painted cabin, with two chimneys ringed in glistening brass. A well-built man with a weather-beaten face was standing at the stern steering this apparition. He brought the boat to a stand, then swung himself up onto the lockside and pulled the lockgate up behind the boat. Andrew, seeing that the other gate was open, walked along to the end of its balance beam and pulled it. He was gratified to see it start to swing shut. The burly man waved his hand in thanks and cranked away beside the upper gates. Water began to bubble and spout round the bows of the laden boat, the bottom gates thudded shut and the boatman crossed the top gates and cranked the opposite paddles, loosing more water to burst and thunder below. Andrew walked up to him and smiled uncertainly. The boatman cupped his hand round a lighter, sucked at a hand rolled cigarette and blew out a cloud of blue smoke,

"'Ow are ye?" he asked.

"Oh, fine thanks", replied Andrew somewhat uncertainly, then asked,

"Going far?"

"Only down to Stoke and Yardley, this trip."

"What, Yardley Wharf?" The boatman nodded. "I was there earlier on this morning. I'm looking for a boat to buy." The boatman looked at him with new interest.

"What sort o' boat?"

Andrew explained as best he could, asking him if he knew of one.

"Could be. Tell you what, mate. Fancy a pint?"

"I was looking for somewhere for some lunch."

"There's a pub two locks up. You come up an' gi' us a 'and, and we'll 'ave a pint an' I'll tell you what I knows. 'Ow about that?"

"Seems fine to me."

"Right 'o then, shut this top gate be'ind me so's the lockkeeper won't come moanin', then walk up to the next lock an' shut the inside gate."

"The what?"

"The inside. The one nearest the towpath. Noo game to you is it?"

The pub by the third lock was another mellow brick building, with a bright coloured sign announcing that it was called "*The Admiral Nelson.*" While the boatman secured his boat above the lock, Andrew closed the two top gates. Together they walked into a room with exposed oak ceiling beams and whose windows overlooked the lock. There was nobody else in the bar, and only two couples eating lunch in the adjoining dining area.

"Mornin' Jim" said the boatman to the barman.

"Morning Jack", said the barman, drawing a pint of bitter, "And yours, sir?"

"The same please" said Andrew, drawing a note from his wallet. "And one for yourself?"

"That's kind of you" said the barman, "I don't think I've seen you here before."

"No. I've just discovered Braunston this morning."

"Well, I hope you like it. Good health."

Andrew noted that, as with the "*Rose and Crown*" last night, the prices were substantially lower than in London or Surrey. He ordered steak and chips then went and sat beside Jack, who had strategically occupied a window seat from where he could oversee his boat. Jack picked up his glass, squinted critically through its contents at the light, took a sip, licked his lips, and then took a long pull at the beer. When he set the glass down, thick froth remained where the beer had been. There was not much left in the glass. He sighed and grinned at Andrew.

"Ahh! That feels a lot better."

"What about this boat then?", said Andrew. "My name's Andrew, by the way, Andrew Ellison"; he held out his hand,

"Jack Turvey" replied the boatman, taking Andrew's hand in a massive paw and squeezing it.

Jack said "I knows this chap as wants to get rid of a fifty five foot cut down Josher, an' e' ain't arstin' a lot for it."

"A fifty five foot what?"

"A cut down Josher. An ole Fellers Morton boat what's been shortened."

"I'm with you. But if it's old, it must want work done on it."

"Not this 'un. 'E 'ad it sandblasted and rebottomed two year ago down Bottom Lock, an' you'll never wear an old Josher out. There's some goin' round over a 'undred years old."

"What's the accommodation like?"

"Pretty good. Back cabin, engine-'ole - got a bostin' good engine, a noo Ruston, bedroom, barfroom, kitchen, stateroom as'll sleep two if yer wants, an' a good bit o' storage up the fore end. Tell 'im I sent you, an' 'e'll take twenty five grand for cash."

"That doesn't seem an awful lot."

"Well y'see. 'Im an' 'is missus 'ave split up. 'E's took up wi' a bird on a Grand Union motor as needs ten grand spent on it. 'Is missus got a butty boat out o' the split an' wants anuvver five grand. Fifteen grand cash'll get 'er off his back and put 'im all right wi' 'is fancy piece. 'E's got it in the papers fer thirty grand, but 'ad no takers."

"So, where do I find this boat?"

"Not far. Oxford Canal at 'Illmorton, by Rugby."

After he had finished his lunch, Andrew watched Jack head his boat up the next two locks. He had pressed him to stay for another pint, but Jack had shaken his head. "Can't stay in the pound for long" he said. "It's quiet today, but summat could come along. Besides, I've got some drops to make top o' Buckby before it gets dark, an' if you wants to see that boat at 'Morton, you'd best make haste."

Andrew walked down the locks deep in thought. The old man was still on watch by the Marina, still leaning in the cabin doors.

"You saw Jacko didn' yer?" he said, as Andrew came down the slope from the bridge.

"Yes, I did. He was very helpful."

"Ar. 'E knows what's about."

Andrew bade him farewell, and returned to the Marina office. He handed back the keys and told the manager that he had not seen one he liked, but that he would be in touch.

Hillmorton was only six miles away, but it took Andrew quite a while to find the canal. Nobody that he spoke to on the main road seemed to know of its existence, but eventually a postman gave him directions to the locks. Even then he was not at first able to find the boat, but a man working in the dry dock told him that he thought there was a boat for sale below the locks.

"It's a cut down josser, or something like that, I'm looking for."

"Oh, ah. *Romford*. It's a Josher."

The short November afternoon was fading as Andrew walked round a curve in the towpath and saw his quarry. It was moored by a piled section of bank. A tall, dark man in his mid-thirties was chopping wood beside the boat and stacking his work in a neat pile on the foredeck. He straightened up as Andrew approached, and said, "How are you?"

"Fine, thanks", replied Andrew. "A chap called Jack told me you might have a boat for sale."

"What, him with the '*Burton*'?"

"A coal barge. I saw him at Braunston at lunch time."

"That's Jack. I'm Stu."

"Andrew Ellison." They shook hands.

"So this is it?"

"This is it. You'd better come inside. Oh, and if you want to buy one, you'd best not call them 'barges', they're 'boats'."

Andrew stepped across the foredeck and down to double doors, which opened into a cosy stateroom. At the forward end, logs crackled in a black iron stove. A settee and two armchairs covered in chintz were arranged before the fire. Stu sat Andrew down and walked past him to a small, but well equipped, galley. This was separated from the stateroom by a waist high partition serving as a breakfast bar.

"Tea?"

"Yes please. Milk, no sugar."

Over tea and biscuits, Stu came to business.

"I'll be honest with you. She needs some work. Not a lot, but some. The hull wants blacking, a bit of welding at the fore end, and the cabin needs painting outside. If you're really still interested, I'll show you over."

"Please don't think that I'm a time waster, but I'm a complete novice. I'm none too sure of what I want, yet."

"I'll tell you summat else", said Stu. "There's a load of people on the cut'll try and sell you anything, rip you off like, but I looks at it this way. You don't know me from Adam, and I don't know you. But I've got to live on the cut. I ain't leaving it tomorrow. I wants to stay here, and I got to get along with everyone else. If it gets out that I sold you a pup, it won't do me no good." He gazed steadily at Andrew, who noticed that his eyes were very blue.

"If you're going to live on the cut, to be one of us, like, you has to work like that."

Andrew found himself smiling. "Well Stu. Thank you for being so direct. I think we could do business."

Two hours later, after an exhaustive tour of the boat, and long explanations by Stu of how everything worked, from the Ruston Hornsby diesel to the pump-out WC, they stood in the stateroom, now softly lit by 12 volt bulbs disguised inside brass candle lanterns, and shook hands on a deal. Andrew would buy the boat, subject to survey, and it would be handed over in three weeks' time. In the meantime, Stu would have the necessary work done ("except the painting. You wants to wait and have it done when the weather's better, next spring.") and put the boat in dry dock for a surveyor. Provided there was nothing seriously amiss, Andrew would then pay in cash and receive a Bill of Sale.

"I shall have to sort the 'ex' out", said Stu. "She's been to a solicitor, and he's trying to stitch me up proper. Trouble is, I can't afford to go to one myself. If I ain't careful I can see everything I gets for selling this boat going up the Swannee. I had a letter this mornin' making out she's due twenty five grand and threatening me wi' the court if I don't pay up pronto."

"Really? What are you going to do about it"?

Stu shrugged his shoulders. "Don't see as I can do anything if she takes me to court."

"That's just where you're wrong. Look, Stu, you've been pretty straight with me, and I appreciate that. I used to be in the law trade myself before I, er, retired. Suppose you let me have a quick look at that letter."

Stu drew a letter, still in its envelope, from beneath an engine instruction manual on the breakfast bar. Andrew glanced through it. It was from a firm in Coventry and contained the most bloodcurdling threats couched in legal jargon. Written by an articled clerk straight out of university, I'll bet, he thought.

"Did you leave her, or she leave you?"

"Well, neither really. She got fed up with me not being interested in books and things, like. I got fed up with 'er being untidy and into things I didn't understand, you know, things like Animal Rights and that. We didn't fall out, sort of drifted apart. We'd bought a butty, so's we could do a bit of trading and contract work, but she moved into the butty cabin and I stayed on the motor like. Last month she told me she was going to move the boat to Stockton, and a chap came along and towed it away for her. That's when I decided to split for good. I said she could 'ave the butty and I'd give her summat out of the sale of this. Course, I've got to know this girl who lives on a full length boat, and she wants me to move in wi' 'er."

"So, really, she left you?"

"I suppose so. It don't make you feel very good to think of it that way though."

"Tell me about it", said Andrew, "I've been there myself. Anyway, the point is, if the boats were yours jointly, and she left you, she's entitled to half."

"I thought that's what we'd agreed," said Stu. "She's a pretty straight sort, then I gets this bloody letter."

"Quite honestly, this letter's a load of guff. I've seen them often enough. There's a lot of firms try this nowadays. Your wife goes to them to protect her interests, fair enough, but they put pressure on her to push for everything so's they get a fatter fee."

"The bastards."

"Quite. It's a game to them, and better than working for a living. It's your savings that are the stakes though."

"So what do I do then?"

"You play them at their own game. Once they see that you're going to fight, they'll know that she's not got unlimited means. I doubt she'll get legal aid, and they know it. If they want to get paid, they're going to have to advise her to settle. Meanwhile, you can have some fun with them. Got a piece of paper handy? I'll write down what you ought to say in reply to their letter."

Stu insisted on seeing Andrew back to his car. Although it was only just after six o'clock it was pitch dark outside. The night was beginning to be frosty, and leaves crunched underfoot along the towpath. Stu helped Andrew scrape frost off his windscreen, and, as he was about to drive away, gave him the number of his mobile phone. Andrew drove back to Mrs. Clarke's along the motorway feeling more hopeful than he had since leaving prison.

Chapter 2
Local Searches

John Watson leaned back in his armchair and lit a cigarette. He expelled a stream of blue smoke and looked at Andrew over his glasses. The pair of them were sitting in John's conservatory. Outside, a damp curtain of cloud hung over the Surrey Downs, which normally formed a backdrop to the view down the Watsons' garden. The garden itself looked drab, some leaves which had escaped Jill's daily assault with the electric sucker, were plastered damply on the soggy grass. The evergreens looked more miserable than ever, and the beech trees at the bottom of the garden dripped steadily. Inside the double glazing, though, it was warm and comfortable. Andrew had been invited for Sunday lunch with the Watsons, and the two old friends were having an aperitif while Jill added the last touches to the meal.

"It'll make a hole in your capital, old boy."

"Well, yes. I know that, but I've got to live somewhere."

"Um. Wouldn't you do better to rent?"

"It's not that easy to rent a boat, besides which I need some sort of semi-permanent base."

John looked doubtful. Andrew thought, I'll bet he thinks I'm buying a floating slum. Not quite this house, I admit, but still, it's not that bad.

John said, "Well, it's your money, and the Power of Attorney lapsed on your release."

"Look, John. Don't think I'm not grateful. Of course I am. I owe everything to the fact that you and Jill stood by me when the plug was pulled. You are my oldest friend, and about the only one who still wants to know me, but I know what I want, and what I need. In the last two days I've met more genuine people, the sort I would want to call friends, than in thirty five years in the City. Look at us. We didn't meet when we were well-off professionals. Remember Wolsey Barracks?"

"Shall I ever forget", said John feelingly. Andrew gazed at the log effect fire. They were both silent. They had both arrived at the barracks together that September morning, they had both got off the bus from the station. John had been upstairs, Andrew downstairs. They had both been directed to the Training Company office, and there they had found CSM Dunton. He was a guardsman who had been posted to the regiment towards the end of his service. He was sitting behind a desk, with a frightened looking soldier clerk beside him. He was red faced, with piggy eyes squinting at them from beneath the peak of his cap, which ran parallel to the bridge of his nose. On the left breast of his battledress blouse were two rows of medal ribbons. When he stood up, he was six foot three, with a backbone like a ramrod. He had looked at the pair of them as if they had been left behind by an incontinent dog. When he spoke, it was with a powerful rasp. The two gave him their names, and that was their first introduction. CSM Dunton was broker to their friendship.

"I wonder what happened to CSM Dunton", said Andrew.

John laughed. "Since we both know there's no justice in this world, he's probably a Chelsea Pensioner now."

Andrew chuckled. "At least he'll be among his own kind. To be truthful, he may have been a swine, but at least he was a straightforward swine and didn't pretend to be anything else. Not like some" he added, bitterly.

John grimaced, "Like Colin Shorland, for instance?"

"Like Colin Shorland" said Andrew grimly, and fell silent again. That was a name he did not want to hear. Shorland had been a partner in the firm, junior by two years to Andrew, but an able, if thrusting lawyer. He had also taken an instant shine to Pamela. It's always the cuckolded one, thought Andrew, who is the last to believe the gossip. He's always the fool who refuses to see the horns in the looking glass. She had fallen for his charm and flattery, had been encouraged by him in her high spending ways.

Until the children came, she had always seen herself as a career woman, and Andrew had encouraged her. Even when they were young, she had continued with her career as an architect, and had brought home a substantial salary to pay for what she wanted. But then, when the children went away to school, she suddenly decided that she wanted to be a countrywoman. That was when the dogs, the horses and the Range Rover came. That was when he had been persuaded to buy Lipscombe. Andrew was then the senior partner, business was good and expanding, property was ever increasing in value, the moon was made of green cheese and it was now or never for buying a small country estate. It was the mid-eighties.

"Get as big a mortgage as you can, Andrew" Colin had urged. "The market's got miles to go yet." Thank God for John's advice, thank God he hadn't heeded all the siren songs, but had taken a much smaller mortgage and made up the balance from the sale of their house in Wimbledon and some of the shares his father had left him. No thanks to Colin that he had not ended up far worse off than he was.

And of course Colin was there. He was there for the shooting, with his hand made Birmingham guns and his Barbour and his green wellies and his designer labradors and his silver hip flask. And he was there for Pamela's Dingley Dell Christmases, and for the summer barbecues and for the harvest supper, which they put on to raise funds for the Church. So often it seemed Fiona, his wife, couldn't make it. She was at a conference, or on a business trip, or seeing the children at school. Funny that.

Then, when the crash came, in '87, and Andrew's investments had plummeted overnight, it was Colin who suggested that, if he was strapped for cash, an advance from the firm might tide him over. All Andrew's instincts were against it, but he made the one great mistake of his life, he never ran it past John. Meanwhile, the children were going to university, Pamela wanted improvements to the stables, the Range Rover was exchanged for a newer model. There was never any end to the demands. In the end he gave in.

The bank was threatening to foreclose. Unfortunately Colin was not around at the time, he was at a conference of lawyers in Washington DC. Andrew had drawn the cheque himself. Only his signature was on it. When Colin came back, he denied all knowledge of any arrangement. He continued to deny it when the Law Society's auditors, and later the Fraud Squad, came round. It was Colin who formally dissolved the partnership before Andrew came up at the Old Bailey. When Pamela came to visit when Andrew was first allowed visitors, it had not surprised him to hear that she was leaving him for Colin. It still shattered him though.

"I suppose you wonder how it was that a successful City lawyer made such an ass of himself" Andrew said at last.

"I might have done once," said John, "but I'm older now. Believe me, it's amazing how blind successful people can be. Look at all the MPs who get caught cocking their leg. It doesn't make you a worse human being for getting found out. In any case, you know yourself, yours was more of a technical offence than a criminal one. Bad luck the judge had a down on solicitors."

"Well, it's behind me now. I've got to look ahead, not behind. Some day I've got to make peace with my children, but I'm not ready to face them yet. I will pick up those things of mine that you've been looking after for me, though."

"How's the 'trouble shooting' going? Were you really serious?"

"I suppose I wasn't really, but oddly enough, I've already found a client."

"You're charging him? Isn't that a bit dodgy?"

"No, I'm not charging him. But I've got a deal, and I wouldn't have such a good one if I hadn't given him free advice. What do you make of that? Don't tell me it's VAT-able."

John smiled, "No, I don't think you'll be liable for VAT at this stage."

Jill came to the conservatory door,

"Lunch is ready, you two. I suppose you hadn't thought to pour me a drink."

By folding the rear seat of the Golf flat, Andrew was able to squeeze in the three tea chests that the Watsons had kept for him. They were very heavy.

"Mostly books, you'll find" Jill had said, "but there are a few pictures and papers and things." The remaining suitcases went in the passenger seat. The car was low on its springs, so when Andrew turned off the main road into the lane which led to Mrs. Clarke's he took it slowly to avoid the potholes, with which the lane was liberally endowed. The lane ran between hedges, a narrow strip with wide verges, typical he noted of that part of the countryside. It was perhaps half a mile to the house from the road. In daylight it was possible to see the house from half way, where the lane suddenly tipped over a brow. At night one could see the house lights, and he found himself looking eagerly for them.

As he bumped through the puddles, his windscreen wipers flicking, Andrew caught a glimpse of something moving towards him. Suddenly he became aware that it was a car coming fast in his direction, with no lights. He braked hard, his headlights reflecting off a windscreen. The oncoming driver had a close-cropped head and a face contorted with rage as he swung the steering wheel and swerved left on to the grass verge. Andrew heard him yell abuse as he shot past, was aware that the car was black or dark blue, that it was a four door model and that someone was in the passenger seat, then it was gone. He opened his window and craned his neck backwards. The brake lights of the car showed for an instant, and then were gone. Andrew felt a surge of anger and thought of giving chase, then remembered that he was facing the wrong way, and that the made up track was only one vehicle's width. By the time he'd turned round, the car would be at the main road and away. He climbed out and saw the brake lights once more as the driver reached the main road, then it turned left and vanished.

"Christ!" he suddenly said aloud. Perhaps they had done something to Anne!

He jumped back into the car and set off towards the house. As he came over the brow, he saw the house with its outside floodlight glaring. He pulled into the grassy farmyard, leaped out and ran to the front door. He had a key; he threw the door open and called Anne's name.

"Andrew! Oh, thank God it's you" came Anne's voice. She came into the hall carrying a poker, put it down, seized Andrew's hand and burst into tears.

Andrew steered her into the kitchen, his arm round her shoulders. He gently sat her in a chair and put the electric kettle on to make tea. He found a packet of cigarettes on a worktop, offered her one, and went to light it. She fumbled in her handbag and produced a lighter. She stopped sobbing, took a deep draught and expelled smoke gratefully.

"Oh, Andrew, what must you think of me. Carrying on like that, so hysterical." She laughed nervously.

"Not at all. Just take it easy and drink your tea. Take your time and tell me about it."

She puffed her cigarette, then said, "I'm not sure where to begin. It's a bit difficult really." She paused, looking embarrassed.

Andrew said quietly "We all have skeletons in our cupboards. Sometimes it helps if we talk it through with a third party. Don't worry about shocking me. I'm used to hearing all sorts of secrets. I used to be a solicitor."

"Used to be?"

"Used to be. I'll tell you all about it some time. I'm retired now."

Anne drew on her cigarette, blew out a cloud and stubbed out the rest. "I've been very good since I gave up, but I needed that one. Sally must have left that packet behind this afternoon." She looked at Andrew. His grey eyes were mild, his expression invited confidence. "Promise me you won't tell me off for being stupid."

"If you knew just how stupid I have been, you wouldn't have the slightest hesitation. Take your time."

She sighed. "All right. You see, just before Jim, my late husband died, we got very short of money. We'd taken out extra mortgage to cover the renovations, then Jim fell ill. He was self-employed and so there was nothing coming in apart from my salary, but I had to give up my job to look after him, so then there was nothing except what the DHSS let us have. We sold everything we could, but towards the end I couldn't bear to worry him, poor thing. He was so ill at the end, and so brave."

The tears started in her eyes again, Andrew patted her hand. She blew her nose and went on, "After he died, I found he had an endowment policy which covered the mortgage, and a bit more, so I paid it off. That was when I started taking guests in, I didn't feel like going back to teaching, and I felt I needed to have some time to myself. Both the children had left home, and I thought I could cope. I didn't pay much attention to the other bills, but then I suddenly found that I was in debt again, a big overdraft at the bank, right up to its limits and electricity, telephone, water bills all due. Tom had just been commissioned, and I had promised to help him buy all the things he needed, mess kit, No.1 uniform and all that. I didn't know what to do. I know, if I had taken my deeds to the bank they would have helped, but I had had such a row with them over my overdraft that I didn't want to deal with the stuck up little squit of a manager again."

She took a sip of her tea, then went on. "One day, I was in town shopping and I saw this sign offering unsecured loans." She saw Andrew's eyebrows rise, and said, "You promised you wouldn't." "Of course I did. Carry on, pay no attention to me."

"Well, I took it out for five years. No questions asked, just fill in on the dotted line."

Andrew said, "How much was it for?"

"Ten thousand. At twenty-five per cent."

Andrew thought to himself, one born every minute, but kept a mask-like countenance.

"Well, it was a struggle, but I managed to pay at first. I'd got the bank off my neck, and for two years I managed. The bed and breakfast business was doing well; I have a little coming in from what I managed to invest out of Jim's endowment policy. You see, I thought I would be able to sell up here, find a smaller place and if necessary go back to teaching. I wasn't worried about repaying the loan because there was bags of equity in the house, but then the property market dropped. I advertised this place, but had no takers. Except for silly money, that is. I felt they were taking me for an even bigger fool than I was. This autumn the visitors suddenly dropped away and I got behind with the payments. I wrote to the firm explaining and received this horrible letter back saying that the payments must be kept up, or they would claim the whole sum and get a court order against me."

"Have you got a copy of the letter?"

Anne rose. "I've got all the paper work in the hall bureau" she said, "I'll go and fetch it."

She was soon back, with a blue cardboard folder. She opened it, foraged inside it and handed Andrew a piece of paper.

"Let's have a look at the agreement."

She gave it him. He took out his spectacles and read through both documents briskly. "Um. I see." He laid them on the kitchen table and smoothed them with his hands. "Got any receipts, or statements?" She nodded. "OK. I'll have a look at them later. Carry on."

"Well, then I went to the office. There was a nasty piece of work in there. Not the man that I arranged the loan with, but an older one. Greasy and sharp suited I think would describe him. He was really threatening. Said that if I didn't keep my part of the bargain, they had ways of making me pay. I told him that you couldn't get blood out of a stone, and told him to take me to court, but he said that the Court would only make an order in accordance with the Agreement and made awful remarks about what the bailiffs would take. Apparently they've privatised the bailiffs or something."

"Yes, they call them 'debt recovery services' or some such name. They work on a percentage."

"Two weeks ago, I started getting these odd 'phone calls. At first it was someone, usually a man, but sometimes a woman, asking for the money. Then it would ring and there'd be just silence. It would be all times, sometimes at two in the morning. I can't change my number easily, or go ex-directory because I need people to be able to find me, so I put in an answerphone. I still keep getting threats on the tape, or long silences, but it's better than keep being woken up. The day before you came I found this note in my door when I came back from the village."

She pushed a piece of paper across the table. It had been printed by a laser printer, noted Andrew. It read, *"Time is running out. We know where you live. £5,250 in seven days, or else."* There was no signature.

"Have you spoken to the police?"

"I did, when the calls started. They said they couldn't get involved in a civil matter."

"Demanding with menaces is hardly a civil matter. Anyway, what happened next?"

"Earlier on today, just after Sally went back to London, I thought I saw someone in the lane. I didn't take a lot of notice, but just after dark I heard a car pull up. I thought that maybe Sally had forgotten something, she is a bit scatter-brained. I looked out and saw that the car had no lights, but it triggered the security light. Two men got out of it. One was the nasty piece of work that I'd seen before; the other was a burly looking object. He had close cropped hair and was carrying a baseball bat. I could see tattoos on his bare arms. They got out and banged the door. I had put the lights out, but the tattooed one shouted that he knew I was at home. I went to 'phone the police, but the line had gone dead. I've got a car 'phone, but it's in the garage, and I was too scared to go out and get it. The thuggish one shouted that he knew I could hear and that I had a week to pay up, or they would do serious damage, and here was something on account. Then he smashed the downstairs loo window with the bat; they both got into the car and cleared off. You must have missed them by five minutes."

"Not even that", said Andrew, and told her about his meeting in the lane. "I can't say I got a good look at either them or the car, but I would agree with your description of the two charmers. The whole thing seems very crooked to me. I've heard of loan sharks using strong arm methods, but this seems a little more than just unsavoury debt collectors. They sound as if they are part of a larger racket."

"They're certainly pretty horrid."

"Well, let's see what we can find out about them, and think what we can do. The most important thing is to get them off your neck legally. We've got to get this debt cleared. I think I can see a way round that, especially if you have the deeds to this place. What I should like to do is to give them a nasty fright into the bargain. I know two wrongs don't make a right, but I fancy they may be deterred from trying their nasty little racket round here. I suspect that they are a bunch who've taken an assignment of certain debts from the loan company. I dare say it was part of some other shady deal, and no doubt someone else is leaning on this lot for money."

"Andrew, you aren't going to do anything violent?"

"Not me, Anne. Thirty-five years in the law teaches you that there are more ways of killing a cat than strangling it. Meanwhile, I think we ought to let the police know about what's been going on here this evening, let's go and get that mobile 'phone of yours."

Together they walked across the yard to the garage. Andrew took her hand as they did so. She gave it a squeeze, and Andrew felt himself strangely elated. For the first time for years he felt himself to be a protector of someone he wanted to protect. They recovered the 'phone and Anne spoke to the police. Then they returned to the kitchen and brewed another pot of tea while they waited.

The police car was in the yard within five minutes. There was one man in it, a cheery, red-faced young man, who said that he knew Anne. Andrew let him in. He stamped wet off his boots in the porch and came into the sitting room. Anne came in from the kitchen, where she had taken the cups.

"Are y'all right, me doock?" asked the constable.

"Yes, thanks. Mr. Ellison here turned up soon after they had left, and he's been a real help."

"Well", said the policeman, pulling out his notebook, "Since the incident's been reported, you'd best tell me all about it."

When Anne had finished, the policeman said, "I think this is going to have to be reported to the CID. I ain't too sure as we can do much ourselves. The car'll be well away by now, even if it could be identified. Someone'll come and see you in the mornin'. If Mr, er", he looked at his notebook, "Ellison, is stayin' here, I should think you'll be all right. There ain't a lot we can do, but I'll put summat out over the radio, an' Control'll tell all patrol cars to keep a look out. There's a patrol car along the main road at least every two hours durin' the night, more often durin' daytime."

After he had gone, Andrew went upstairs to change and shower. Anne put some logs on the fire. She rang her daughter, Sally, in London on her mobile 'phone, and felt better after speaking to her. Sally was all for coming straight back home, but Anne told her not to. "There's nothing you can do", Andrew heard her say as he came downstairs, "And anyway, Mr. Ellison is staying here tonight, thank goodness."

She rang off as Andrew came into the room. She smiled at him and waved him to a chair. She sat in the one in which she had interviewed Andrew when he arrived. *It hardly seemed that it was only three days ago,* thought Andrew; *my life is shaping along unexpected lines. Perhaps it was time to ride with the current. What did Shakespeare say? 'There is a tide in the affairs of men, which taken at the flood, leads on to...'* He snapped himself back into the present. He wasn't superstitious, but even so, he knew that it was unlucky to quote *'the Scottish Play'*. He sat down, and smiled across at Anne. "You know, there's something I should tell you about myself that you ought to know."

"You don't have to. I am most indebted to you, just for being around when you were. I'm not one of those people who believe that women should swoon around and let men do the tough stuff, but I was really glad to see you tonight. I've kept things going since Jim died without having to be the poor little defenceless woman, and I feel I've let myself down by being all female and tearful."

"Look, Anne, anyone, whatever their sex, would have been upset by what happened tonight. I think you coped marvellously. Just because you were tearful means nothing. If I had been in the same situation, I probably would not have cried, but I'd have sworn horribly and probably broken something. We all react differently. It's because I have seen that you are someone that I can respect, that I need to be honest with you. Besides which, I'd rather you heard it from me than from the police."

"Police! Andrew, what on earth have you been up to? I'm sure you aren't a villain yourself."

Andrew told her. He told her of how he had found himself in financial trouble, of how he had been advised to get himself out of the mess, of how he had made things worse, of how he had been found guilty by the Old Bailey jury and sent down for three years. He said little about Pamela, and nothing of Colin, nor of his time in prison, other than to tell her that he had earned full remission and been paroled. That was why he would be known to the police. It was inevitable that the CID would check on him and would soon find out his record.

After he finished, they sat in silence. Then Anne said,

"You poor man. You didn't have to tell me anything of this, and now I've made things worse for you by involving you in my problems."

"I said earlier, it helps to talk to a third party. That's why the Church encourages confession. It's good for the soul. As far as my getting involved with the police, it was entirely my choice, but I feel I would rather you hear it from me than from them."

"Well, I still think you've been treated shamefully."

"I didn't want you to know, I didn't want anyone round here to know. I'm trying to start again, but perhaps I'd better move on."

Anne's eyes glistened. "If you really want to move on, then you must, but I'd like you to know that I wouldn't want to be the person who made you. To tell you the honest truth, I didn't want you to know about my trouble. I was scared you'd leave and go somewhere else if you found out."

Andrew smiled again "I'm glad you feel that way. I'm not scared of two thugs who feel they have to pick on someone who is alone, and in the dark as well. I'm sure there is a way out, and I'd like to help you find it."

"You're sure?" He nodded. She rose, came over to him and kissed his cheek.

"Thank you, Andrew. Let me get something to eat and we'll put our heads together. You know those nasty little men have seriously annoyed me."

Andrew sat thinking while Anne clattered things in the kitchen. There was a very simple way out of this. He grinned to himself, John Watson would grumble, but that was typical John, and then there was Joey Caroni. He chuckled. He hadn't seen Joey since before his troubles, but he was one person who was not going to worry about criminal convictions. In fact it gave one more street cred as far as Joey was concerned. Meanwhile he'd better do some homework. The police could do nothing about the legal problems, but they could possibly be useful. There were always more ways than one of killing a cat. He called through to the kitchen "Have you got your deeds handy?"

Anne came out of the kitchen, wiping her hands, and went into the hall. She came back carrying a small black japanned steel box. She put it down, searched in her handbag for her keys, selected one from a key ring and opened the box. She took out a bundle of papers in an envelope, which she passed to Andrew. "I must dash", she said "the steaks are nearly ready. How do you like yours?"

"Eh? Oh, medium rare please."

Andrew shook the papers out of their envelope. There was a fat abstract of title tied in faded red ribbon, some handwritten parchments and some typewritten on stiff paper. Hmm. A typical farm title, he thought. Sifting the dusty papers, he read the social history of agricultural England in the twentieth century. The abstract showed that it had once formed part of a large landed estate. Sold up after the Great War, I'll wager. Ah yes! Here it was, auction particulars of 1920, and a Conveyance to a farmer, probably the sitting tenant. Here was a mortgage to a farming mortgage corporation in 1930. Hard times, borrow to see it through. On the back of it was the discharge in 1945. War had its winners, as well as losers! Here was a probate granted to the farmers' two children, a son and daughter, in 1956. He was a farmer, still farming the family land; she was a teacher, not enough in it to support two families, the girl must make her own way. On the bottom of the 1920 Conveyance were memoranda recording the sales in the 1960s of land for building plots, and of 255 acres to a neighbouring farmer. Sell off the family silver, and get out while the going's good! Finally there was the sale in 1979 of the farm to Jim and Anne, the young hopefuls. The farm was no longer a farm, it was a home, and the old peasantry were gone. The new couple came from North London; the old family tradition was broken. He glanced through the parcels on the 1979 deed. The Clarkes had bought the house and five acres for £45,000, and had mortgaged it for £40,000. Those were the days! Mortgage interest relief would have been considerable. The discharge on the Mortgage showed that Anne had paid off the debt in 1992.

Anne put her head round the door. "Do they tell you anything? All those bits of paper mean nothing to me."

"Oh, yes. But in fact they are mainly of academic interest. This is what really matters"; he held up a small piece of typewritten paper. "Your registration certificate with the Land Registry. All the rest is really superfluous nowadays, but very interesting to dry-as-dust lawyers. The point is, you have no incumbrances."

"Sounds as if I ought to see the doctor. What on earth are they?"

"Mortgages and the like, giving someone else an interest over the land. It's yours to do what you want with, unless the planners say otherwise. You redeemed your mortgage to the Building Society in 1992."

"That's when I got the deeds back."

"Right, so you can easily raise enough to get these creatures off your back. I have an idea how you can do it quickly and cheaply."

"Tell me over supper. It's ready. Would you mind uncorking the wine?"

Anne had laid the table in the kitchen. Two glasses were set out, a candle was burning in the centre of the table, and two soup plates were set out with rolls beside them. Andrew hoped he would be able to do justice to what she had prepared after Jill's lunch, which had, as always, been ample.

As he spooned up the soup, Andrew explained what he had in mind. He would negotiate an advance that would clear the loan to the sharks, she would find herself paying slightly less than half of what she currently was paying in interest, and repayments would be made by means of a bond. In ten years, this would repay everything and leave her with a nest egg.

Over the steak, which was served in a delicious sauce and with a side salad, he put the next part of the proposal. If she would let him moor his boat at the end of the farmyard, he would pay her each month a sum sufficient to cover the interest on the new loan. In other words she would be no worse off, she would be making savings, and she would be free of hustlers. Anne lifted her glass, and looked hard at Andrew over the top of it.

"It sounds too good to be true. But what if British Waterways won't let you moor there? I know some people further along the canal have had awful trouble over moorings."

Andrew gave his crooked smile. "Dry-as-dust deeds have their uses sometimes. You see, it looks as if you own the rights to your land right up to the waters' edge. I think your predecessors here must have had a wharf."

"Yes, they did. An old chap from the village told us that his father used to take coal round the parish from the boats, and that his grandfather used to bring hay from all over the estate to be taken to London for cab horses by canal."

"There you are then. Those rights were certainly conveyed to your predecessors, and it is arguable that you acquired them in 1979. I'll need to check with the Public Record Office what the provisions of the Canal Act of Parliament were."

"You've certainly got the bit between your teeth. You must have been a very good lawyer."

"I was," said Andrew with no false modesty, "one of the best. But seriously, any solicitor worth his or her salt could tell you the same. The only difference between me and most others in the profession was that I never specialised. You see, I loved general practice, you know, conveyancing, probate, divorce, litigation, criminal work, company law, the lot."

"Do you - did you - have any other interests besides the law?"

"No, apart from reading good literature and the theatre, I suppose I didn't. I took a lot of interest in my family when they were children, and while they were growing up, but once they were adults, I had less interest, and I've had no grandchildren, as yet. I like my children as people, but they are no longer everything to me. Just as well really. They've got nothing to thank me for now. I suppose it was my single-mindedness that drove Pamela and myself apart."

"She sounds an awful gold digger to me."

Andrew was silent for a moment. There was a deep hush in the old house. In the hall the grandfather clock ticked slowly and loudly, a log in the sitting room fire burned through and settled in the grate.

"There's always two sides to a quarrel" he said at last, "that's why there are lawyers."

Later that night, Andrew lay on his bed trying to read. Anne had appeared to have recovered from her experience by the time they finished the meal, and he had made his excuses and gone upstairs. He was sure that she would have liked him to stay up with her, he suspected even that she would not be averse to physical friendship, but he was not ready for that, yet. Twenty four months of monastic seclusion, on top of nine months of waiting beforehand, the break-up of his marriage and the estrangement of his family, had seemingly destroyed any wish that he might once have had to get close to any female; yet here he was, tonight, comforting Anne, whom he had only known for a few days, and unburdening himself of some of the demons that tormented his soul.

He had picked up a paperback copy of '*Vanity Fair*' in a bookshop in Northampton, and fully intended to read it, for one thing that he planned was to catch up on some of the classics that he had missed, but somehow he could not get into it this evening. It was no fault of Thackeray's, either. In prison he had at last managed to read '*War and Peace*', and by comparison Thackeray was simplicity itself, but his mind kept going back to Anne. He told himself grudgingly that he fancied her, but that he must keep his sights on his new life and not be side-tracked, then another voice told him that she was indeed part of this new life. In exasperation, he laid the book aside and lay in the dark gazing at the ceiling. He began to mull over details of his new campaign, and gradually the excitement of the chase overcame his doubts, and as it did so, he quickly drifted off to sleep. At the end of the corridor, Anne had cried herself to an uneasy sleep long before.

Sunlight reflecting off water woke him about seven thirty next morning. He looked out again at the scene that had so pleased him the first morning that he had looked on it. He felt a surge of anger at the thought that obnoxious characters should sully this place, then thought of the grinning skull in paradise. "*Et in arcadia ego*", he muttered to himself as he shaved. Once more the cheerful smell of grilling bacon came to him as he came downstairs to find Anne, in jeans and tee shirt, bustling about in the kitchen.

She greeted him with a smile and said, "Was I too clinging last night? I'm awfully sorry."

"Not at all. You had a bad experience."

"Did you really mean all those things you suggested, about a mooring and everything?"

"Of course. I would like nothing better. This would make a superb base for me when I get my boat."

She turned away, scooping up pieces of bacon and egg on to a plate. When she turned, she said "I'd love you to do that."

Soon after breakfast, the CID arrived. Andrew was just about to get in his car to go up to the village to the telephone box, when he saw their car come bumping down the lane. They turned out to be a woman Detective Sergeant and a man Detective Constable. The sergeant took Anne aside into the sitting room while the constable took photographs of the broken window and the tyre marks in the yard. Later on, all four of them went up the lane to find the place where Andrew had met the other car. It was not hard to identify. There were skidmarks on the road surface where Andrew had braked, and tyre marks on the grass verge where the other car had swerved. The constable took more photographs; the sergeant was not forthcoming beyond nodding at Andrew's opinion of the men's motives. The pair then climbed in the car and drove away. Anne looked enquiringly at Andrew.

"I don't think they can do much" he said, "all they can really do at this stage is to log the information against the next time that the bright pair misbehave. There's not enough hard evidence to connect them with demanding with menaces. You could have broken the window, they could have been lost and asking the way, their headlights could have failed. You know, I know and the police know they are nasty villains, but try convincing a jury. Anyway, I think the sharp dresser is the one who runs the Loan Company office. I think I'll go and see them later on. They don't know me, so I'll go to the office and have a good nose round on some pretext or another. If you're game, we could set up a little playlet for their benefit."

Andrew found the telephone box in the village near the green. It made a change, he thought, to find one that was not plastered with prostitutes' cards. This one merely had a crudely Tippexed message, "Gaz 4 Emma", on the board behind the handset. He rang John Watson's number and explained briefly what he had in mind. John was incredulous and the line crackled with disbelief. Andrew however, was adamant, and gradually John calmed down, promising to ring him later at Anne's to tell him how the land lay.

The next call was to an East End pub. After some delay, Andrew was put through to Joe Caroni. A suspicious voice said "Yus. Wot d'ye want?"

"Joe? Andrew Ellison!"

The tone of the voice at the other end changed. "Andy, boy! Good to 'ear from yer! 'Ow are yer doin'. I fought you was inside!"

"I was Joe, but I'm out now. I'm fine, how's yourself and Fiona?"

"Bleedin' good, both of us. What can I do for yer pal?"

"I'd like to come and see you as soon as possible. I don't want to say much over the 'phone."

"OK pal. Look, I'm stuck today, what abaht termorrer dinner time?"

"Just the job. Say half one, still at the 'Caroline'?"

"Yus pal. See yer." The line went dead as Joe rang off.

Andrew grinned to himself. Joey sounded just the same as he had that September day over forty years ago when he and John Watson had first entered the barrack room behind the orderly corporal. It was a long, bare, lofty room, with iron beds, not unlike school he had thought. A youth in civvy clothes, with a quiffed haircut was lying on a bed by the window smoking. The corporal had roared, "SHUN!" and the youth leapt off the bed.

"Yew 'orrible man! Yew don't lie on the bleedin' bed wiv your shoes on!" The lad had looked poker faced and removed his shoes, but as the corporal turned his back gave the newcomers a broad wink, then, when they were alone again had said "Wotcha mates, I'm Joey." That had been the beginning of another friendship that had endured. It ought to have. They had been through a good few things together since.

The Loan Company's office was in one of the main shopping streets in Northampton. Anne slipped away to do some shopping after pointing it out to Andrew. "Give me twenty minutes before you make your entrance", he had said to her. The office had a small window plastered with enticing advertisements for the facilities it offered. Andrew pushed open the door, which led into a small, but comfortable, reception area. There was a blonde girl reading a women's magazine behind the desk. She wore a ring through one nostril. She looked at Andrew with contempt and said "Yes please."

"I'm looking for a loan."

"Yes, how much?"

"Fifteen thousand." The girl looked at him with new interest. "Secured or unsecured?"

"Unsecured. I'm in a hurry for it."

"Just a moment, please, I'll have to see the manager." She went to a glass door behind her, knocked and went in. Andrew amused himself by looking at the various advertisements and working out the true rate of interest offered. The girl came out again, "The manager will see you now", she said.

As soon as he saw the manager, Andrew felt like shouting, "Tally-ho!" There was no doubt that this was the person he had briefly glimpsed last night, and who answered Anne's description. He was late forties, rather paunchy, with thinning black curly hair, a pencil moustache, brown eyes set close together, medium height. He wore a dark double breasted suit with a bold chalk stripe, a paisley tie, and gold rings on his pudgy fingers. He stood up as Andrew entered and proffered his hand. A notice on his desk said *"J.K.Willis, Area Manager"*

"How do you do Mr. Er?"

"Watson" lied Andrew.

"Watson, what can I do for you?"

"I need to raise fifteen thousand in a hurry."

"What security can you offer?"

"What would you want?"

After some more verbal enquiries, the manager pulled out a sheaf of forms and began to fill one in. "Name?"

"John Philip Watson."

"Address?"

"5, Lloyds Avenue, London EC3."

"Occupation?"

"Chartered Accountant."

The manager stopped writing, and looked suspiciously at Andrew, "What?"

"A chartered acc....." began Andrew, and stopped as upraised voices began to penetrate the room from outside. Anne's voice was raised in protest

"I demand to see him, at once. If I don't see him I'll call the police!"

The manager said, "Excuse me, I think we have some trouble", jumped out of his chair and ran to a door leading to a passage. "Mark!" he called, "We've got a problem" and then went into the reception office. Anne's voice became louder "That's him, that's one of the swine!" Running feet sounded behind Andrew and a burly, crop headed man in his late twenties wearing jeans and a leather jacket came running past him. "Out the way, mate!" said he by way of introduction and ran after the manager. "That's the other one!" came Anne's voice as he emerged into the front office. Quickly Andrew pushed the door shut behind him, dashed behind the manager's desk and riffled through his papers. There must be some information here, ah, here was something, an envelope addressed to J.K.Willis in the waste bin. He swiftly pocketed it and listened to the rumpus outside. Anne was evidently enjoying herself. The girl was yelling abuse at her and the men were obviously having difficulty in getting near her to throw her out. Time to ring down the curtain, thought Andrew and opened the door.

"Shall I call the police?" he asked innocently.

The two men swung round just as they were about to grab Anne's arms, and she slapped both their faces hard. "Madam!" shouted Andrew, she broke free and ran to the door, the receptionist shouted "No you don't, you old cow!" and tried to head her off. Anne dealt her another ringing blow to her cheeks as she ran past. "Keep a civil tongue in your head, you cheap little bitch!" she called and was gone.

"Leave it!" called Willis to Mark, who was about to start after her. He nodded and inclined his head slightly to the rear door. Mark rubbed his cheek and marched to the door with the same angry expression that Andrew had seen in the lane. A thug who doesn't like being worsted, he thought. Willis was all apologies. "Very sorry about that, some of these people can get very hysterical, I expect it's her age."

Andrew said, "I don't think we can do business. Good afternoon", and strode out of the office. Willis stared after him, then shrugged his shoulders and returned to his office.

Anne was waiting in the car park round the corner.

"You were absolutely magnificent" said Andrew, "I could hardly keep a straight face."

"I was absolutely petrified when I went in, but when I got going, I really enjoyed every minute of it. All three of them, they were the ones who've been making my life a misery."

"Well, now it's your turn. They'll be off your back tomorrow, and they'll have a lesson they won't forget. You see, now I know where they live, or at least where Willis, the manager, does."

Andrew found a message waiting on Anne's answerphone when they came back to the farmhouse. It was from Stu, wanting to speak with him urgently. Andrew rang him back on Anne's telephone and got through to him, evidently in a dry dock. Stu's voice was interrupted from time to time by thunderous bangs.

"What the hell's that row?"

"I'm 'avin' the boat de-scaled for you."

"De-whatted?"

"De-scaled. She's on the dock. I managed to get her in early, and me and my mate's goin' round 'er checkin' for any scale, rust like."

"That's very good of you. Does that mean you may have her ready earlier?"

"I can 'ave her ready for you by Friday. She's ready for the surveyor now. You could get the report by Friday mornin'."

Only four more days, thought Andrew. I shall have to get a move on with the other matter.

"Tell you what, Andy mate."

"What?"

"You wants to get away from 'ere Friday if you can, there's a stoppage starts at Stoke next Monday mornin', for four weeks."

"Sorry?"

"They're closin' the locks, for repairs, at Stoke Bruerne for four weeks. You won't be able to get 'er to where you wants until nearly Christmas."

"So I'll have to bring her straight through then?"

"You will, unless you wants a month at Stoke. I'll give you a 'and if you like. You know, show you how to go on. If you can give us a lift back to Braunston before Sunday night, that is."

"No problem, Stu. When shall I pick the boat up?"

"We'll float 'er off about eleven o'clock. We can be away by dinner time and go to Braunston. We can be down your place by Sunday mornin'."

After he had put the receiver down, Andrew turned to Anne.

"Things are hotting up. The boat's going to be ready ten days before I expected. There's a stoppage, as they call it, at Stoke Bruerne next week and it lasts till nearly Christmas, so I've got to go and get her on Friday, if the surveyor will make his report in time. Stu'll help me bring it down to here."

"Stoke's only a few minutes' drive from here" said Anne "if you wanted to leave it there for a few weeks, "Waterways" are usually pretty helpful. I've had guests here before who've done that sort of thing."

"I'd rather get it here if I could." Was that pleasure or

disappointment that flashed across Anne's face? Andrew wished he could fathom.

She said "Anyway, I can run you over to Hillmorton on Friday morning. I'd love to see the boat. You can always get your surveyor to fax his report to me before then."

Because the farmhouse lay between two village rounds, Anne's mail was delivered before 8.am each day. The postman lived in the last village, so he was wont to pop into home and have his breakfast before returning to the Head Office and clearing the post boxes en route. If she or her guests were quick about it, they could receive a letter in the morning and get a reply away by the first post outwards. Andrew was able to put this useful rural facility to good use next morning when, as he ate his breakfast in the guests' dining room, Anne came in with a large envelope addressed to him, bearing on it the frank of John Watson's office. Andrew opened it, drawing out a typewritten document, which he read through to Anne. It stated that Anne Janice Clarke was thereby mortgaging the property known as Willowleaze Farm in the County of Northampton to John Eric Watson of Phoenix Buildings Guildford in the County of Surrey Chartered Accountant, for the sum of ten thousand pounds at a fixed rate of seven per cent per annum interest for ten years. It also contained a clause by which Anne agreed to pay ninety pounds per month into a bond account for the same period.

"That's saving me a hundred pounds a month!" exclaimed Anne.

"It's doing more than that. I shall pay you well over half of what you have to pay out, and in ten years' time, you will have a nice little nest egg to pay the mortgage off with."

"So, what do I do?"

"You sign here. Not yet though, I'd better not witness it. Best to get a third party."

"Jane, my help, will do that. She's due any minute, it's her day to work here."

Andrew had not met Jane, Anne's part time help and general confidante, before, but she came bouncing down the lane a few minutes later in a battered Fiesta. She was a jolly, wiry little woman, who greeted Andrew in a pronounced Northamptonshire accent,

"Woy oop me doock! You the noo lodger then?"

Andrew explained to her what was required. She witnessed Anne's signature, writing in a neat, italic script, before bustling off upstairs to set about cleaning the bedrooms.

"All you need to do now", said Andrew, "is to give me the Registration Certificate. You can keep the rest of the deeds."

Anne brought the deed box from the hall. Andrew selected the document, wrote a brief note to John and slipped it, with the mortgage deed, into a stamped envelope and licked the flap.

"Only one more thing for you now", he fished in John's office envelope for a piece of paper, which he passed across to Anne. She turned it over and gasped. It was a bankers' draft for ten thousand pounds.

"Pay it in this morning, then we'll draw one for what you owe the loan sharks on Friday. We can drop it in to our friends on the way to Hillmorton."

He did not see fit to tell her that John had advanced the money out of the funds he was holding on Andrew's behalf.

The Princess Caroline of Brunswick' stood on a cross roads on the edge of Limehouse and Whitechapel. Andrew arrived in the East End, via the M11, within half a mile of its doors. Once upon a time it had been a proud East End gin palace, all frosted glass windows and iron curlicues. It had dispensed liquor to the grateful throats of the toiling myriads of sweatshop workers, dockers, tailors, cutters, pressers, draymen, vanmen, market traders, flash coves and prostitutes, who were its staple customers for decades. Discreet booths with mahogany and glass partitions had screened off the respectable matrons and middle class clerks and managers who needed to avail themselves of the *'Caroline's'* hospitality. Now it was different. The brewery had gutted the place of its old mahogany, glass and brass, and had replaced it with new, fake, mahogany, glass and brass. The ground floor was now one huge room, filled with the insistent thumping of amplified music, above which the customers shouted desultorily at one another, or bawled orders to the bar staff. Cross looking youths of indeterminate gender slammed down plates of food at the tables ringing the central area, and the thronging crowd shoved and pushed like a monstrous Rugby scrum into which someone had introduced glasses. Nobody in the crowd seemed to be over 25, most seemed to be teenagers. Although Andrew felt himself to be very conspicuous, his presence was in fact barely noted by the clientele and bar staff alike, most of whom were far more concerned with looking at one another. Eventually a bored looking barman deigned to ask what he wanted.

"Mr. Caroni" shouted Andrew.

The barman picked up a telephone and mouthed into it, then put it down and said, rather more respectfully, "Come this way, mate." He lifted a flap in the bar and led Andrew through a doorway. He pointed. "Up them stairs and to the left", before dodging back into the bar.

As Andrew climbed the long, somewhat threadbare carpeted staircase, Joey Caroni came out onto the landing. He held his hand out, seized Andrew's right hand and clapped him round the shoulders with his left.

"Andy, me 'ole pal. Bloody good to see yer!"

It was twelve years since Joey had been found Not Guilty of murder at the Old Bailey, and five years since they had last met. He was fatter and balder, but looked just as prosperous as ever. He wore a well-cut grey suit, a silk shirt and tie, hand-made shoes. His fingers were gold-ringed, he smelt of lavender water and cigars. His teeth flashed with gold when he spoke.

"Bloody marvellous to see yer again" he continued, steering Andrew with one hand over his shoulder, "come into the office."

The office was a large, square, room, comfortably furnished with leather easy chairs and a small bar. There was a computer screen, keyboard and printer at the far end, a few locked cabinets, a couple of desks with a Madonna incongruously perched on one, and a bookcase filled with almanacs and directories. The walls were covered with framed signed photographs of boxers and footballers. Next to the computer screen was a tall glass display case filled with silver trophies and several boxing belts. It had not changed much in five years, thought Andrew, not even the petite, dark haired girl sitting by the computer screen, who whirled her chair round, and exclaimed in cut glass tones, "Andrew! Darling!" She leaped out of the chair, rushed up to him, and planted a smacking kiss on his mouth, letting her lips linger while Andrew grasped her in a bear hug.

"Fiona, you look younger than ever" he said when at last he was able to disengage.

"Oi! Break!" called Joey. Fiona stood back and smiled. "Still the handsomest man in London", she said, "You don't look any the worse."

Joey poured a large malt whisky and proferred it to Andrew.

"Straight, 'ole pal, that's 'ow yer likes it, ain't it?" Andrew nodded. Joey poured another for himself and a Martini on ice for Fiona.

"'ad some grub 'ave yer?" he asked.

"No, no, I'm fine" lied Andrew, realising that he was in fact very hungry. "I couldn't eat a thing."

"Course yer bloody could" Joey picked up the internal telephone and ordered lunch for three to be brought up. He waved Andrew to a chair and said "A bit better grub 'ere than in Pentonville, I reckon, and better'n in the Troodos Mountains."

"It'd have a job to be worse" said Andrew.

"Pentonville was bloody awful when I wuz in there."

"I can assure you, it's hardly the Ritz now."

When the food arrived, brought by a mini skirted girl with alarmingly shapely legs, it turned out to be a beautifully tender sirloin steak with sauté potatoes and broccoli spears, accompanied by two bottles of Medoc and three glasses. When the three of them sat round the table and began to set about the food, Andrew was delighted to note that neither Joey nor Fiona were unduly concerned with dietary fads, and tucked in with vigour. After a sweet course, Joey ordered coffee and brandy, offered Andrew a cigar, which was declined, lit one himself and sat back in his chair puffing with contentment. Fiona excused herself and went back to her keyboard, kissing Joey on his forehead as she passed him.

"Best investment I ever made", said Joey, nodding after her. "She runs the 'ole business nah. I don't do nuffink wivvout arstin' 'er first."

It must be nine years now, thought Andrew, since Maria Caroni had died of cancer. Joey had been completely devastated, for although they had no children, he had worshipped her from the moment they had met as children. It had been a marriage of convenience, Maria's dad had been in the ice cream parlour business, Joey's was a fight promoter, yet in spite of the obvious pushing from both families, he had genuinely loved her. When he rang Andrew at his office, sobbing his heart out down the 'phone, Andrew had immediately taken charge. He had done everything, from obtaining the death certificate to booking the crematorium and paying the priest. Maria had held the reins in Joey's empire; she had kept the books and run the bank accounts. It seemed that there was nobody who could replace her. Joey had carried on without her, but had got himself into more and more of a muddle. Eventually he had had more than a spot of bother with HM Customs and Excise over VAT returns and the Inland Revenue over taxes, and Andrew had got John Watson to try to sort him out. John sent Fiona, his up and coming graduate assistant, fresh from university with a double first in science and business studies, along to Joey to unravel the mess. Fiona had been with him ever since, and while he was inside had run the business for him. Fiona had been to see him on visiting days, and it was Fiona who doubled his investment income in the eighteen months that he was away. Joey's release had coincided with Andrew's arrest, but word had come to him that Joey and Fiona had moved in to a large house at Chingford, and that she'd presented him with a baby girl. Joey had been beside himself with delight. Even with the child, Fiona had continued to keep the accounts of boxing promotions, pop groups, pubs, restaurants, betting shops and football clubs that formed Joey's business empire.

"So, what's yer problem, pal?" asked Joey, drawing on his Havana.

"I need the frighteners put on someone."

Joey's eyebrows rose. "I don't believe I'm 'earin' this", he said incredulously. "You, of all people, wantin' frighteners put on. Ain't yer got no friends left in the law trade?"

"Not to speak of", said Andrew with feeling, "anyway, the matter is somewhat outside the law. You see I think a mob has moved in round where I'm based, and a friend of mine has got caught up in it, quite innocently. I mean to say, I wouldn't ask you if it was someone who was a villain, or thoroughly deserved getting taken to the cleaners, but the local Bill can't, or won't do anything. You see, although there has been some strong-arm stuff, there's no evidence to stand up in court, and it's all over a civil matter originally."

"You'd better tell me what it's all abaht," said Joey.

Andrew told Joey the story of Anne's loan and the collectors. Joey listened intently, breaking in now and again to ask brief questions. When Andrew got to the bit about his encounter in the lane, and the two who had called at the farmhouse, Joey stopped him.

"'Ang on, Andy, that sahnds familiar. Let's try the ole' dog an' bone." He pulled out a slim mobile 'phone and punched in some numbers. The instrument buzzed and crackled, Joey said "Arfur? Joey." More crackling, then, "Listen pal, what's Jack Dooney up to these days? Ain't 'e moved up country?" He paused, listening to the crackle, "Norfampton eh? Yeah, I fought so, fanks pal."

He turned to Andrew. "Jack Dooney's lot. Got aht o' the smoke when Special Branch began takin' too much interest in 'is protection games rahnd the Irish clubs. Always was 'is style, send rahnd 'is local manager wiv an 'ard man before leanin' too 'eavy. Gentleman o' sorts, our Jacko. Colonel or summat in the UDA they reckon."

"So, what do we do about this 'Fiddler of Dooney'"?

"Leave 'im to me. 'E owes me a favour or two. Besides which 'e can be a nasty bastard if someone 'e don't know sticks 'is nose in. You don't want ter get yourself a spankin' at your time o' life."

"I've never been anxious to earn myself such a thing, at any time of life, it doesn't turn me on."

Joey laughed mirthlessly, "You wouldn't want one of 'is spankin's. You've eard o' kneecappin'? Well, 'e was the original importer o' the idea from Belfast. Still, 'e won't give me no bovver."

Andrew was silent. He knew Joey of old. He'd got where he had through mainly legal means, but he'd been on thin ice a few times. There was the time when a bent Detective Inspector and his team had nearly succeeded in fitting him up with a life stretch for murder. Andrew and George Ingham QC had got him off that, but it had been a close thing. Whilst Andrew had no doubt that Joey was quite innocent of that particular charge, and indeed several policeman did time themselves for attempting to pervert the course of justice, there was no smoke without fire. Joey certainly knew a thing or two about some unfortunate accidents that had befallen his enemies over the years. He had fought his way upwards out of the gutter, and he had fought hard, and you didn't fight such fights according to the Queensbury rules either. He had fought hard for his empire, and he fought hard to keep it, as several would-be protectionists had found to their cost. If Mickey Dooney owed Joey a favour, he would give no trouble.

Joey laughed loud at Andrew's account of the confrontation in the loan company's office the day before. "You ain't lost yer touch y' ol' rascal. There weren't anuvver brief ter touch yer. I'd like ter 'ave seen the ole' girl smack 'em rahnd the kissers."

"Not so much of the 'old girl', Joey" said Andrew. "She's younger than us, and not a bad looker either."

" 'Ullo! 'Ullo! Wot's this? You ain't got yerself smitten, pal?" Joey leaned back and leered at Andrew through the cigar smoke.

"Certainly not! Private Caroni, keep your opinions to yourself!"

"Yessir!" said Joey, grinning. "All I was wonderin' though, was where she's gettin' the blunt ter pay 'em orf?"

"Just say, she has private sources" Andrew replied, his eyes twinkling.

"Yer silly ole sod! Yer know what ole Solly Rubenstein the bookie always says? 'Friends is friends, and business is business'."

"Don't get me wrong, Joey. This is business. It's a deal where neither of us loses, and both are happy with the outcome."

"Well, good luck ter yer, pal. You're goin' ter pay 'em orf Friday mornin', right?"

"That's it, Joey."

Joey Caroni raised his brandy glass, "Cheers, then pal."

It was Thursday afternoon when the telephone on Mr. Willis' desk rang. Willis picked it up, and a soft voice, with a Dublin twang to it said,

"Willis?"

"Yes, who's this?"

"Jack Dooney." Willis felt his stomach muscles tighten.

"Oh, yes Mr. Dooney."

"I understand dere's been a little trouble wit' a Mrs Clarke, a widder woman."

"A little, Mr. Dooney. She's behind with payment."

"An' yez been round to her place wit' one of de boys?"

"Yes, Mr. Dooney."

"Somehow, I t'ink yez might just have overstepped de mark."

Willis was silent. Fear was beginning to grip him. He had heard the silky, soft tones before, and knew what happened to people who displeased Mr. Dooney. He suddenly needed to go to the lavatory urgently.

"Are ye still dere?" came Dooney's voice, quiet and menacing.

"Yes, Mr. Dooney."

"De widder Clarke's bringin' yez a bankers draft on Friday

mornin'. Yez better take it an' close her account."

"Yes, Mr. Dooney."

"An' don't go near her place again, yous or de monkey. Dere's certain friends of hers knows where you live."

"Yes Mr. Dooney." The urge to visit the lavatory was stronger than ever.

"And one more t'ing."

"Yes, Mr. Dooney."

Dooney gave him brief instructions and rang off. Willis made his way thoughtfully, and as slowly as he dared, to the staff lavatory. It would be expensive, but if the boss was paying...

Chapter 3
Some local investigations

Andrew sat in the passenger seat of Anne's Toyota as they threaded the western outskirts of Northampton towards the Harlestone Road. He had a briefcase on his knee, and two cases of his possessions in the boot. On the back seat was the most enormous bouquet of roses that he had seen outside a West End premiere. Although the day was dull and overcast, the smell of them filled the car. He had waited outside in the street when Anne took her Bankers Draft into the loan Company's office, for he had deemed it prudent not to be seen again, unless there was any trouble. Joey had said that there wouldn't be, and that was good enough for him. Anne was nervous though, but he had squeezed her arm encouragingly as she went towards the office. Less than five minutes later he had been astounded to see the nose-ringed girl hold the street door open for Anne, who had come staggering out bearing this huge bunch of roses and a bemused expression.

"I think they must have been flown in from somewhere" said Anne, "I just can't think how else they could produce these sort of roses in November."

Andrew looked at the label attached to the stems. It read "For Mrs. Clarke, with best wishes. M. Dooney Associates." It was, to say the least, an unusual feature of a loan repayment. "It's not what you know, it's who you know" he murmured, to himself.

It did not take Anne so long to find the locks at Hillmorton as it had for Andrew; he was able to pilot her directly to a small basin off the main canal, where Stu was waiting beside *Romford*. The hull glistened with newly applied black bitumastic paint, the brasswork had been lovingly polished, the white ropework and the bare wood at the stern end had been scrubbed. Thin streams of smoke rose from a stubby chimney near the fore end, and from a taller one at the stern.

"She looks superb," said Andrew, after introducing Anne.

"I think you'd best go through her and check everything before you take her" said Stu, so Andrew took Anne on an extended tour of inspection. He was glad to do so because he needed to be reminded of just what his new home consisted. He showed her the stateroom, with the fire glowing in the black iron stove; the spotless galley just behind; the bathroom and toilet ("Stu tells me he's pumped out and filled up with water"); the comfortable main bedroom; then the engine room with a gleaming green engine sitting in the centre amid clean, polished floors, with neat racks of tools fitted to the sides ("Stu's leaving me a complete tool kit for the engine, and a handbook"); and finally, the boatman's cabin at the stern, out of which they climbed onto the tiny, semi-circular stern deck. Just inside the double doors was a small black range, with polished brass fiddle rails, which was sending out a steady heat to warm the feet and legs of anyone standing and steering on the enclosed platform just inside the doors.

"It looks absolutely beautiful" said Anne when they had finished the tour.

"Not bad, eh?" said Andrew. "I shall have my work cut out to keep it like this. It's just what I've been looking for, though."

Stu was still standing on the dockside when they came up from the back cabin. Andrew smiled at him. "All right, Stu. I know what 'caveat emptor' means."

Stu's eyebrows raised.

Andrew said, "Sorry, Stu. Lawyers' language. It means 'let the buyer beware'. In other words, it's down to me if there's anything wrong with the boat after I've bought it." He glanced down at the briefcase, which he was still carrying. "Shall we go into the stateroom a minute? You can come too, Anne if you like."

In the stateroom, Andrew handed over bundles of fifty-pound notes in paper wrappers. There seemed to be a fearful lot of them, and they took some time for Stu to count. When he had done,

Andrew passed him a sheet of typewritten paper.

"If you'll sign this Bill of Sale, I'll give you a copy. Then you have good proof of your reason for carrying a lot of money on you if anyone wants to know, and I can prove title to the boat." Stu signed both copies, somewhat shakily, and the two shook hands. Andrew asked him what he intended to do with the banknotes. Stu said he was going to bike into Rugby to pay it in to his building society, but Anne said he'd do no such thing, she would run him into the town in the car.

Andrew took his two valises from the boot of Anne's car and began moving in while Anne and Stu drove into Rugby. By the time they returned, he had packed away his washing and shaving things and clothes for three days, he had extracted a jar of instant coffee, some sugar and a carton of milk, and had nearly boiled a kettle. The three sat in the stateroom drinking the coffee until Stu said, looking at his watch,

"We'd best make a start if we're going to tie up before dark."

Andrew went with him to the engine room. Stu had demonstrated the workings and how to start it when he had agreed to buy the boat; now was to be the moment of truth. Really, he thought, it's as logical as proving a title, and he forced himself to think clearly. Stu watched, half smiling, as Andrew gazed round the little compartment. Now, thought Andrew, let's get started. Switch on ignition... no, check fuel tank and sump oil levels first. He dipped the fuel tank and the sump, wiping the dipsticks on a piece of blue paper from a roll. Next he turned on the battery switch, followed by the ignition. Stu caught his eye and nodded. Andrew reached over his head for the throttle linkage and turned it round to increase the fuel supply to the injector pumps. "Not too far, now" said Stu. Andrew turned the rod back slightly.

"OK" said Stu, "off we go."

Andrew pressed the starter button; there was a loud clang as the starter engaged, then a crescendo of whirring which got faster as it grew louder, a cough, another, then a series of coughs getting faster in turn. Andrew released the button and the engine took up a steady, slightly muffled, beating. Andrew grinned through the open side doors at Anne, standing on the dockside looking in. He swung himself out of the doors and went to the stern.

"I think we're ready."

"Not quite," said Stu, "How are you going to steer her?"

"Oh, shucks", said Andrew," Where's the steering thing?"

"The tiller. In the cabin, hanging above the range. The pin's in the ticket drawer."

Andrew bent his knees and peered into the cabin. Ah! There it was, a brass tube hanging from the ceiling parallel to the roof. He unhooked it, drew it out and slid it onto the steel shank of the rams' head. There was a small drawer by the double doors, just inside on the left, above the range. Opening it, he found a heavy brass knob with a steel pin protruding from it. He dropped it through a hole in the brass tube to locate it on the steel shank, then looked inquiringly at Stu, who nodded.

"I'll loose off your fore end" said Stu, waking forward along the dock, "You loose your end."

Andrew looked at his feet; the mooring line was secured to a stout steel pin on the stern deck by a mysterious series of loops. He disentangled these with some difficulty and pulled the line inboard. He supposed he ought to do something with the line, so coiled it and hung it over the brass tiller pin.

"Roy Rogers boating!" said Stu reproachfully when he returned from the fore end. "That's 'ow cowboys do it!" He removed the rope, coiled it neatly and placed it on the sliding hatch in front of the steering position. Andrew realised that his learning curve was steepening already, and they had not yet moved from the bank. He looked at Stu, who said "Go on. Go for it. It's your boat now, and you've got to learn to control it."

Andrew stepped on to the stern deck and clutched the tiller. "Stand in the door hole", said Stu "and hold it by the wooden piece on the end." Andrew moved forward on to the step above the range.

"That's it. You'll soon get used to it. Now. Put her in gear and just let her paddle slowly forward." Andrew pushed the gear rod forward. The note of the engine changed as the propeller shaft engaged. A slight swirl of water came from under the counter as *Romford* began to move.

"Now hold the tiller over to bring the fore end round. Remember you pivot round the stern, not the fore end. It's not like a car with front-wheel steering" said Stu, stepping off the bank on to the catwalk. As Andrew pushed the tiller to the right the fore end began to swing to the left. A low arched bridge appeared dead ahead.

"Aim for the centre, and look out for the chimney" called Stu, making his way forward. Andrew wrestled with the range chimney and laid it flat on the cabin top as the fore end began to move through the bridge.

"Keep her going to the left. We're going that way" called Stu, pointing. Andrew realised that he was coming out of a branch onto the main canal. Stu had taken a long pole from the cabin top and was preparing to shove his end of the boat round, but realised that Andrew was going to make it with room to spare.

He called back "Wind her up a bit, and keep the tiller over."

Andrew turned a little brass wheel in front of him. The chugging of the engine increased in volume and tempo and white water spurted up beside the counter. Anne had run round to a flat-topped bridge, which was now straight ahead. She waved as the boat headed for her; Andrew was concentrating too much to notice, but Stu gave her a cheery wave as he passed through the arch.

"Ease her up now" called Stu, replacing the pole in a rest on the cabin top. "I'll get the lock ready." He stepped off on to the towpath in the bridge.

"You seem to be doing all right", Anne called down from above.

"So far, so good," Andrew replied, "but I've got some locks to deal with next."

Anne craned herself over the opposite parapet as Andrew passed underneath. Andrew suddenly found himself wishing that she were aboard with him. She waved.

"See you about Sunday lunchtime" and then was gone. Andrew waved absently after her and concentrated on a sharp turn, which had appeared in front of him, apparently ending in a brick wall.

There are three locks at Hillmorton, each one having a duplicate beside it. Since *Romford* had been moored in the stretch of water above the bottom one, there were two more to go. They were only just wide enough for the boat, unlike the locks at Braunston, but they filled quickly. Stu let Andrew steer into each one, showed him how to get off the boat and up on to the lockside, and how to let water into the lock by raising a paddle. The principle was the same as when he had helped Jack Turvey so he soon mastered it. Half an hour after leaving the dock they were clear of the top lock. Andrew glanced at his watch. It was already half past two. He had been master of his own craft for three hours already, and it seemed that the time had never existed.

Once they started from above the lock, Stu insisted on Andrew steering the whole time, so as to gain in confidence, but stayed beside him, sitting on the cabin top chatting and advising him what to do. Slowing down for bridges and moored craft, giving fishermen a wide berth, taking the outside of bends, Stu kept up a steady barrage of advice, until they reached the end of a long straight length crossed by a motorway bridge.

"I'll go and make some tea, you take her on round these turns" said Stu.

Andrew crouched over the tiller, revelling in the warmth of the range by his feet and the quiet, autumnal countryside, from which the light was beginning to ebb. Apart from one sudden lurch, caused by the boat touching the mud when he cut a corner, and which caused Stu to pop his head out of the side doors, he found he was managing surprisingly well on his own. Stu came up out of the side doors carrying two mugs of tea. He gave one to Andrew, placed his own carefully on the cabin top and glanced at his watch,

"Over half way" he said "you're making good time for a beginner."

By the time that Andrew had brought the boat through Willoughby Bridge and spotted Braunston's spire perched on its hilltop in front of him, the light was fading fast. He found though that his eyes grew accustomed to the gloom, even though it was quite dark when they came up to the junction where the canal to Oxford and Birmingham went off to the right.

"We'll need to go right up to Bottom lock", said Stu, "my new boat's laid just below it." Andrew nodded contentedly and carried on into a dark main road bridge hole. There were so many boats tied up here that he needed to concentrate. He suddenly realised that they were passing the Waterways office that he had visited what seemed to have been a lifetime ago, but which was in fact only ten days. A light showed in the window of a moored boat, which Andrew recognised as the one on which the old man lived with whom he had talked on his first visit. The silhouette of the old man's head and shoulders showed in the window, Stu called out a greeting, and the old man raised a hand as they passed. Then they were pulling in beside a pair of large boats lying abreast. Stu had taken a line from the fore-end, a young, fair haired woman came on to the stern and took Andrew's stern line.

"I hope he's behaved himself" she said, "I'm Emma."

Later that evening, Andrew took Stu and Emma to a pub in the village for a meal. They walked up through fields to the main street by the light of a half moon. By comparison, the village street seemed almost garishly lit. After the meal, Stu introduced Andrew to a number of people in the bar, and they fell into a convivial conversation. Andrew found himself deep in the topic of dogs with a well-set, red-faced man of about his own age, called Horace. Andrew had had little to do with dogs since his days in the Sussex

Weald, where everyone who lived in the countryside seemed to have Labradors or spaniels, or both. Anne kept a somewhat ancient black retriever, but apart from letting him in or out of the house, Andrew had not had much to do with him. The animal had been asleep in a barn when Willis and Mark the thug had called, and had taken no part in the proceedings.

"I allus says you wants a dug ter work" said Horace, "they ain't no use a-sittin' by the fire. It ain't natural for 'em. You look at Ben 'ere", he indicated the black and white collie which lay at his feet, his nose resting on his forepaws. " 'Es done 'is share o' work. Ten year old, 'e is."

Ben acknowledged his master's interest by slightly cocking an ear. "Poor ole chap can't move like 'e 'ad used to, but 'e can still get ship ter do what I wants. 'E ain't as quick as them yer sees on telly, but 'e ain't a bad 'un."

Stu said "You're dead right Horace. We has a dog on the boat, but his job's guarding' it. You'll see some on 'em though, soon as they ties up, off comes the dogs and craps everywhere, then they gets into litter bins, or fighting other dogs. I don't hold wi' bringing them into pubs neither, unless they behaves themselves, like your Ben."

"Ah, 'e's a good ole dug" said Horace, "'E be'aves 'isself. By the way, 'ave you 'eard any more about them pups as went missin' last wik?"

"Not a word" said Emma, "Joe's searched everywhere, and put notices in the Post Office, and on the locks."

"What's this?" asked Andrew.

"Old Joe Donnington", said Stu. "'He's got this pedigree Jack Russell bitch, had a litter five weeks ago. He'd put her to another pedigree Jack Russell, cost him a bomb it did, and then she come up with a litter of seven. He gets 'em to the vet, injections and what-have-you, which set him back a good few quid more, then last week he comes home and the lot's gone. Mother and the whole litter."

"If you arst me," said Horace "I reckon them 'ippies 'ad 'em. They was 'angin' around Top lock fer days at the time, then all of a sudden they ups and goes."

"They've gone up onto the Leicester Summit" said Emma, "Joe went over to Watford locks when they were going up, but he didn't find anything. Anyway, they may look scruffy, but I think they're straight enough."

"So long as they 'as plenty o' the ole wacky baccy" said Horace, and everyone laughed.

Andrew rolled over and sat up in bed. Light was streaming through a porthole covered by a piece of lace. It took him several seconds to fathom out where he was. He reached for his watch from the side of the bed. The time was 7.35. Swinging his legs out of the bunk he began to recall the night before. Gosh! Canal people seemed to have a limitless capacity for beer. Although by no means incapable, he had had quite enough last night, he must have gone out like a light when he hit the bed. He peered through the porthole. Outside it was just after sunrise on a bright morning, with new sunlight striking rippling water and reflecting onto the ceiling. He found some slippers and padded into the galley, filled a kettle and lit the gas. The sudden hum of the fresh water pump as he did so startled him for a second. The stateroom stove had gone out, so he raked out the ashes into a bucket while the kettle boiled. Then he made himself a cup of instant coffee, pulled back the curtains and sat by the breakfast bar looking at the scene outside. Someone was whistling loudly in the slipway opposite, then a radio suddenly blared into life, drowning the whistling. A moorhen swam past, its neck bobbing. Stu's voice came from somewhere overhead,

"Are ye ready yet? It'll be dark in eight hours."

Andrew pushed back the hatch over the side doors and put his head out. Stu was mopping down the cabin roof of the boat next to him. He grinned at Andrew.

"It were a good night, last night. How's your head this morning?"

"Better than it ought to be. I'm somewhat out of practice."

"We ought to be off by half eight" said Stu. "Emma's coming with us, and we'll kip in the back cabin tonight. We'll have to bring the dog, but he won't be no trouble. Is that OK?"
"It surely is. I'd better get moving."

Whoever said that boating was a leisurely occupation lied through their teeth, thought Andrew as he bustled about for the next forty minutes. In that time he shaved, lit the stateroom stove, raked out and drew up the cabin range, dressed and swallowed a quick breakfast of grapefruit, toast and coffee. He was carrying out his morning engine checks when Stu reappeared with Emma, who jumped across on to the foredeck carrying a plastic shopping bag. "Goodies for today and tomorrow" she said, "I'll put them in the fridge."
While Andrew started the engine, and Stu walked to the Bottom lock to get it ready, Emma transferred her dog, Snappy, a bright looking terrier and collie cross, to the bank, where he bounded off up the towpath, following Stu. She then released the fore end line, Andrew did the same at the stern and clutched in. The boat began slowly moving forward, edging slowly past the slipway and brick sheds that Andrew had looked at with such curiosity less than a fortnight before, and into the lock.

With Stu working ahead getting the locks ready, and with Emma helping him, Andrew found that he went up the locks at a brisk rate. Emma seemed just as expert and as keen as Stu. At the Top lock the lockkeeper told them to leave the top gate open as he was going to bring a boat downhill in a few minutes. Emma went into the cabin and Stu came back to the stern.
"We'll have summat to eat after the tunnel", he said, "Emma's getting it ready."
"Tunnel?" said Andrew, "What tunnel?"
Stu laughed, "You still got a lot to learn. We'll have to get you a guide book at Stoke."
"Now I come to think of it, I do remember something in "*Narrow*

Boat" about a tunnel at Braunston."

The hills rose up in front of the boat, and the banks of the canal became higher as they left the lock behind. As they rounded a slight bend Andrew saw the black mouth of the tunnel appear.

"How long is it?" he asked, trying not to sound nervous.

"About a mile and a quarter. It should take us about twenty minutes or so."

As the yawning hole drew nearer, Andrew offered Stu the tiller.

"No fear, mate. You've got to do it on your own. If you meet anything, keep right and slow down, but don't for Christ's sake stop. I'll just check the headlight for you. It's that switch there, that's right, above the side bed." Without waiting for a reply he worked his way along the gunwales to the fore end and stood on the deck gazing at the headlamp. Andrew pressed the switch and Stu gave him thumbs up before disappearing into the front of the cabin. The fore end of the boat swept into the dark hole, the noise of the engine became deafening, then Andrew himself was swallowed up in blackness. He felt around the doors for the cabin light switch and was gratified to see a burst of light round his legs when he pressed it.

There came a bang as the fore end hit the tunnel wall, then another. Andrew was dimly aware of sooty brickwork flying past his left ear, and desperately tried to correct his course. For a moment all was quieter, then he hit the opposite wall. Looking back at the receding entrance, he noticed that he was too far over to the right now, but the headlamp appeared to him to be so feeble as to be useless. Gradually though, his eyes became accustomed to the darkness, though he found it hard to believe that blackness could be so absolute, and he became aware of a distant white speck that marked the far end. Suddenly the front part of the boat appeared before him in a ghostly form, and he found himself passing beneath the vertical mouth of an airshaft. As he passed under it, he gazed up at the little circle of sky visible at the top, receiving a shower of water in his face as he did so. He brushed the drops away; the shaft rapidly receded, leaving a pale circle of water in his wake, and which soon disappeared.

He was controlling the boat better now. He took out a large torch that Stu had placed just inside the cabin and flashed it at the walls, which leapt into all manner of brick and ochre hues. He turned it off, then noticed that the white light at the far end of the tunnel had become both brighter and yellower. He realised to his horror that what he could see was the headlight of an oncoming boat. As it drew nearer he saw the oncoming light pick out the shape of the tunnel, with the bricks and their courses forming a continuous parallax towards the other boat. He saw Stu's head emerge from the cabin and look towards the advancing light, which now began to appear high above the water. Over the echoing thudding of his own engine, he could make out the higher note of an air-cooled diesel. Remembering to keep to the right, he turned down the throttle wheel and slid along the right hand wall. A high steel fore end appeared beneath the glaring light, as he heard the note of the oncoming engine change. Then the two craft were passing and he heard cheerful greetings being exchanged between Stu and the other steerer. As they passed he caught a brief glimpse of Jack Turvey's grinning face, with a cigarette clamped in one side of his mouth, heard an unintelligible shout; then he was gone, swallowed up in the clangorous darkness astern.

Andrew looked ahead; the end of the tunnel was now clearly visible. He passed under another shaft and crouched over the tiller, watching the opening in front grow ever larger, forming a vista of bare trees overhanging the water. Keeping in the centre was simple now, so he turned the throttle wheel to increase the engine revolutions. There came a tap on his shoes, he looked down to see Stu proffering a mug and plate. He leaned down to take them and was contentedly munching biscuits and sipping tea as they came out into the open. Emma came out of the engine room side doors and walked back to him.

"You did really well then. There's some breakfast in the kitchen. I'll steer if you want to go and have it."

Although Andrew was beginning to realise that hours spent in the open air at a tiller were capital instigators of a good appetite, he was still taken aback when he stepped into the kitchen. Stu was washing up cups and plates, behind him, on the breakfast bar was a packet of cornflakes and milk, while keeping warm in the grill was a plateful of bacon, sausages, eggs, fried bread and mushrooms. He had a momentary vision of Pamela lecturing him on cholesterol, then without a further regret worked his way steadily through the breakfast, finishing off with toast and marmalade. He helped Stu finish the washing up, then the two of them went out to the foredeck. Stu asked him how he liked the boat.

"Wonderful, so far. I'm still finding things out about it, and I wonder if I shall ever learn what I need to know about the canal."

"You don't want to worry about that, mate. I learn summat new about it every day, and I've been doing it all my life."

"All your life?"

"Yes mate. I was born on a boat. Our dad worked for Waterways when they ran a fleet, his dad worked for Fellerses - Fellows, Morton and Clayton that is. They was the firm as had this boat built."

"I thought that was someone called Josher",

Stu laughed, "Old Joshua Fellows started the firm off. His boats was all called Joshers after him."

"Really, when was that?"

"Now you're asking. Must have been well over a hundred years ago though."

Andrew was silent for a moment as he digested this. He knew the canals themselves were old and dated back to the eighteenth century, but what Stu had just told him made him feel as if he had suddenly met someone from a previous century. It was not quite as if one was living in an ancient house; after all Lipscombe had been pretty old, parts of it were Queen Anne at least, but there was no sense of continuity there. Here he was, sitting in his new home, talking to someone to whom history was not a dead thing in books, but a living tradition and part of his life.

Stu said "My mam's granddad, he only died five years back, and he were close on a hundred when he went. Still went boating when he were ninety-eight, and he used to say he learned summat new every time he went out. I don't think you can ever stop learning about the cut, not if you wants to understand it, like."

While Andrew was considering this philosophy, they came through a bridge. Beyond, the country opened out into a wide upland vista bathed in pale sunlight. In the distance, ahead of them, was a cluster of buildings and another canal crossing the fields towards them on a green embankment.

Stu looked at his watch. "We'll be at the Top of Buckby in five minutes" he said, "there's a whole lot more for you to learn now".

Stu and Andrew got off the boat in the bridge at Norton Junction, taking Snappy with them and leaving Emma to bring the boat down while they got the Top lock ready. Buckby locks are deep, slow, and the seven of them are spread out over a mile. They had been left in their favour by Jack Turvey, but some had leaked empty, so they took it in turns to go ahead "lock wheeling", as Stu called it , " 'cos you really wants a pushbike for this game, specially when you goes London Road, over the Cowroast like." Andrew's face showed his puzzlement, and Stu went on. "Tring Summit, mate. There's a pub by the top lock called *The Cowroast.*"

"Oh! I know it, on the old A41, Aylesbury Road" said Andrew, as he set about drawing the bottom paddles of the lock in the manner approved of and demonstrated by Stu, take the pressure on the rack first, then set the windlass at the top of its throw, then when you are ready to draw the paddle chuck all your weight behind it. The greasy, black paddle rack obligingly shot upwards, releasing a tumultuous cascade of water into the pound below.

It was by the fifth lock that they met the distressed lady.

Emma had walked ahead, Stu was steering, Andrew was closing up gates behind the boat and walking on the next lock. He caught up with Emma and leaned with her against the balance beam of the fifth lock. The gate swung slowly open and the pair walked backwards in a arc pushing the beam with their behinds. Glancing down the canal Emma said, "Mrs. Higgins looks as if she's lost something."

An elderly woman in slacks and a windcheater was moving slowly towards them along the towpath, peering into the hedge and calling out occasionally. She saw Emma, and asked, "Have you seen our Holly?" There were signs of tears on her cheeks.

Emma shook her head and said, "You haven't seen a black Labrador bitch, have you Andrew?"

Andrew said that he hadn't. Mrs Higgins blew her nose. "She's due for a litter in less than three days. I left her in the garden yesterday, when I went into Daventry to do some shopping. I was only away an hour and a half, and the gate was latched. Someone must have opened it and let her out. I was out till gone nine last night calling her and I've been out since seven this morning. Oh dear! I'm so worried she's got in a trap or something." The tears started to run down her cheeks.

"I'm so sorry, Mrs Higgins" said Emma, "If we see her we'll let you know. She could have run into the spinneys below the locks."

"She could have run onto the motorway," wailed Mrs Higgins.

"Have you reported to the police that she's missing?" asked Andrew.

Mrs Higgins shook her head, "I don't want no trouble with them".

"Where do you live?" asked Andrew. Mrs Higgins sniffed, then told him it was further back, by the canal. "Well, if you'll give me your 'phone number, I'll ring you immediately if anything shows up."

Mrs Higgins gave a watery smile. "That's very good of you, Mr. Er...?"

"Ellison, Andrew Ellison."

"Mr Andrew" said Mrs Higgins. "It's very kind of you." She

walked slowly away, still calling.

Emma said, softly, "Poor old soul. Her Holly's everything to her. She's always very kind to Snappy whenever we come past."

"That's a funny thing," said Andrew, "but it's the second missing dog I've heard of in less than twenty four hours."

At Bottom lock they chatted to the lockkeeper, who was working grease into the collars of the top gates.

"Poor ole mother 'Iggins is well upset" he said, "but I weren't on 'ere yesterday. There was only one boat come through, about this time yesterday. My mate said there was a couple on it 'e'd never seen before, but 'e didn't get the boat's name."

"I'll keep my eyes open" said Stu, "there ain't that many boats about now. I reckon me and Emma knows most on 'em."

"Wait a minute", said Emma, "there was one went up Braunston on Thursday, when you were over at 'Morton working on the dock, Stu. It went up soon after the hippy convoy, but it wasn't anything to do with them. There was a couple on it; the man was about Stu's age. I didn't see the woman too well, but neither of them spoke, which I thought was a bit odd. You know, I said 'good morning', or something, but they never replied."

"What was the boat's name?" asked Andrew.

"It didn't have one. At least, not one that I could see, but I'd know it again. It was a modern sixty footer, with the front clothed in, like a working boat, but dead scruffy. You know, tatty ropes, old bikes and rubbish all over the cabin top, dirty brasses."

"It must have come up from Warwick or Brummagem way" said Stu. "It can't have come down Napton, 'cos the locks there are shut, and it definitely didn't come up 'Morton."

The noise of the motorway was becoming more insistent. As they left the Bottom lock behind, it was visible on the left, a field away behind the bare towpath hedge. Andrew thought of the times that he had travelled along, in complete ignorance of the silent highway a few yards away. The roar of a train on the high embankment to his right brought more memories of travelling to Crown Court cases at Liverpool or Manchester on that line. He took the tiller from Stu, and the three of them chatted as they plodded through the countryside and into woodland, where the motorway roared but a few feet away. Gradually though, they moved away, and the motorway became a subdued buzz, barely audible over the throb of *Romford's* engine.

They stopped at Weedon for a beer and a snack lunch, meeting only one other boat on the way, then set off once more, winding through those same Northamptonshire hills that had so attracted Andrew that first day he drove north up the A5. Dusk was creeping over the countryside as they came through the brownstone arch of Banbury Lane Bridge, and Stu suddenly pointed ahead.

"Look there!"

A boat was tied up in the lonely stretch before the next bridge. It was on the towpath side looking across to where open fields rose up from the waterside to a distant ridge. Andrew could see that the boat had dark sheets covering an open hold in front of the cabin, and a jumble of things on the cabin top. Emma came scrambling out of the engine room doors.

"That's it, that's the boat. I'm dead sure of it."

Andrew slowed down to tick over as they passed. A face peered at them through a porthole, but did not acknowledge their presence.

"Funny lot" said Stu.

"Listen!" said Emma.

Over the quiet thudding of the Ruston Hornsby and the ripple of water round *Romford's* stern, came an unmistakable whimpering. Snappy, who had been dozing in the foredeck well, leapt up and barked sharply. A sudden chorus of barking sounded from underneath the black canvas cloths. A harsh female voice shouted something from under the black sheets, there came a smacking sound, and the barking stopped. The three on *Romford* looked at each other, but said nothing until Andrew had speeded up.

"There's more than one dog under them cloths" said Stu.

"Lots of people have dogs on boats" said Emma.

"They don't try to keep 'em quiet though."

"It doesn't make sense" said Andrew, "why would they want to keep them quiet?"

"I reckon they don't want to let anyone know they've got dogs aboard" said Stu.

"But why? I would have thought most people would want strangers to know they'd got a dog."

"Not if they'd nicked it."

Emma said "Mrs Higgins lost her Labrador bitch yesterday"

"I know that," said Andrew, "but why would anyone steal her?"

"Mrs Higgins breeds them. Holly's got a good pedigree, and she's in whelp."

"Hmm! That puts a somewhat different complexion on it. How much can you get for a Labrador pup?"

"A pedigree 'un 'll set you back three hundred quid" replied Stu.

"But they wouldn't have a pedigree certificate, so how could they be sold as pedigree pups?"

"If they're good ones" said Emma "they could still go for a hundred or more. 'Specially if you've got a market among the yuppies. There's more and more of them moving into this part of the world - you know, green wellies, Barbour jackets and four-wheel drives."

"I know only too well" said Andrew ruefully, "I used to be one myself. My wife was the one into dogs though. Retrievers, spaniels, Jack Russells, that sort of thing. Now I come to think of it, it was considered somewhat chic in Sussex to have a working dog. People were always after them, it made stockbrokers and chartered accountants, and city lawyers for that matter, think that they were taking part in a real life version of 'The Archers'."

"I'll bet those people were the ones who took Holly" said Emma, "they were certainly about at Buckby at the time she disappeared."

"Hey!" said Stu suddenly, "What about that bitch and litter of

Joe's what went last week? You know, the ones they thought the Hippies had nicked?"

"Yes, I'd thought of that" said Emma, "but that was over a week ago, and those people weren't around at Braunston then."

"But could they have been around with a car?" asked Andrew, slowing down for a bridge.

"I suppose they could have. Joe's place ain't right beside the cut. They'd be taking a risk though, bringing 'em back through Braunston on a boat" replied Stu.

"So what are we going to do about it?" asked Andrew "We can't very well board and search their boat. Excuse me a minute, Stu, while I shove the tiller over."

Stu eased himself out of the way as Andrew leaned out of the cabin doors to steer round a bend. Once they were straight, Andrew continued.

"We could inform the police, but it would have been better if Mrs Higgins had reported that she believed her dog was stolen, then they could act on information received. If we merely say that we have reason to believe that the dog was stolen, they can be accused of acting merely on suspicion. They don't always do much about things like that. Besides, we've no proof that any of the dogs we heard is Holly. We only have Emma's evidence, and that's circumstantial."

"What about the RSPCA?" asked Emma.

"Andrew considered for a minute, steering round an overhanging hawthorn and churning up mud as he did so.

"You wants to watch you don't get out of the channel" said Stu reproachfully, "we could 'a got farmed up there."

Andrew grinned "Sorry, boss. Still learning. Anyway, the RSPCA is certainly interested in cruelty. I think we all heard enough to warrant asking them to investigate, but proving cruelty is difficult. We'd need more evidence than three people hearing what sounded like a dog being hit."

"If it is Mrs Higgins' bitch" said Emma," We've only got two days or so to find her before she has her pups. She could even abort with the anxiety of being taken away from her home."

Andrew grimaced. "What's the RSPCA's local number?"

"Ah" said Stu; "you've got us there. Tell you what though. It's only another ten minutes to Gayton Arm End. We could find out at the yard there. I've got a couple of mates as works there."

As Stu had forecast, about ten minutes later they rounded a turn in the fading light and came through a bridge into a straight length of canal lined with moored boats. Before the next bridge the canal widened into a broad basin.

"Gayton Arm End", said Stu. "That's where you turns off for Northampton and the river. Pull in against the Sanny Station."

Andrew slowed down and steered towards a low quayside fitted with water taps and signs indicating that toilets could be emptied at the nearby building. When they were securely tied, Stu led the way into an adjoining boatyard. The manager was sitting in a lighted office. He greeted Stu and Emma, nodding amicably to Andrew.

"We'll soon find the number" he said, "I think the local inspector lives in Northampton." He rummaged in a file on his desk. "Here we are. We had him out a few weeks back over some kids air-gunning swans. I'll have a word with him if you like, we get on well." He pressed buttons on his telephone, which "bz-bzzed" a few times before there was a reply. The manager explained who he was.

"That's right. Fine thanks."

"No, not swans this time. Dogs."

"Yes, dogs. I've got some people here who think they may have uncovered some dog stealing, with cruelty thrown in."

After more buzzing and crackling from the instrument, the manager passed it to Andrew, who explained the story, pointing out its urgency.

"Well, if it's a bitch in whelp" said the Inspector, "I'd better go and check up. Look, you sit tight where you are. I'll go and take a look. Perhaps one of you would come with me to identify the boat. I don't want to go tramping round the countryside in the dark, looking for the wrong one."

"No problem."

"OK then. I'll be with you in under an hour. So long." The line went dead.

Andrew explained what had been arranged.

"I'll go with him" said Stu. "I knows the boat, and where she's laying."

The RSPCA Inspector was better than his word. He arrived in less than half the time expected, but even so, by then it was fully dark. The Inspector had a torch in his van, but Stu found a battery spotlight in the engine room and took that as well. He climbed in the van, which immediately shot off down the lane from the boatyard. Andrew watched its tail lights vanish over the humped bridge across the canal, and then turned to Emma;

"I think we'd best get some supper going. I'm going to be cook this time."

Cooking was not perhaps one of Andrew's greatest social skills, but he was nevertheless a competent plain chef. He had taken his turn in the kitchen when at open prison and had enjoyed the experience, he had often cooked for his family, especially while on holiday; so while Emma bustled about raking out the cabin stove and drawing up the fire, he set about creating a Bolognese out of odds and ends and a packet of spaghetti which he had brought with him. There was a bottle of Fitou to go with it, up under the fore end. He sent Emma to get it, uncorked it and put the opened bottle beside the stove, which, after a few minutes of drawing up clouds of smoke from the fresh fuel, settled down to a cheerful and warming glow which reflected a pleasing light into the saloon where Emma was laying the table for supper. He asked her how long she had known Stu.

"Just over a year now. Well, I've known him vaguely for three years, since I was working on the Hotel Boats."

"Hotel Boats?"

She laughed "Of course, you wouldn't have seen them, but they're all over the system in summer. Usually a motor and butty boat that carry a small number of passengers. Sort of cruise liners of the canals, you know."

"I see. And you used to work on them?"

"Yes. I did it as a vacation job when I was at University."

"Ah! I thought you were rather more than just a boat girl. Where were you at University?"

"Oxford. Lady Margarets. I read Ancient History."

"Really? Gosh, I was at Oxford years ago. Magdalen. I read law."

"Stu told me you were a lawyer."

"And how come you got involved with Hotel Boats?"

"Well you see, my parents live near Banbury, so when I wanted a vacation job, a friend of Daddy's told me about the boats. I went over to Braunston, saw the people who ran them and it just happened that they had been let down by an Australian girl who had been a stewardess, so they snatched my arm off. I did it every long vacation, then when I got my degree, I couldn't find anyone who wanted to employ a twenty three year old with a 2.2 in Ancient History, so I went back to the boats. When the season ended, they gave me a job in the boatyard, helping to clean up and paint boats. I enjoyed every minute of it, went out with the boats next season as mate, and that's when I got to know Stu. He was just breaking up with Karen, his wife you know, and was pretty down. I had been left some money by an uncle, and I'd just bought a pair of working boats, meaning to convert them to live on. Stu helped me do some repair work, and we never did convert them."

"So what are you going to do with them?"

"Well, Stu tells me that they need a fair bit of work done on the hulls, but he's got some money now, and he's going to help me. Then we're going to help out Jack Turvey with his coal business, and probably run as a camper in summer, you know, scout troops, girl guides and so forth."

"And do you feel it's worth an Oxford degree?"

"What's a degree worth if you can't find a job? At least I've never had to sign on. My parents grumble sometimes, but I've never had to sponge off them since I came down from Oxford, and I've never been so happy."

"You know, Emma, had I heard what you have just said a few weeks ago, I would have thought 'what a waste, what a drop-out', but I'm beginning to understand what it is about the life that attracts you. I hope you two can make a go of it. What do your parents think of Stu?"

Emma was silent for a moment. "They weren't impressed when I moved in with him. I had lots of grief from Mummy about going outside my class, and all manner of Victorian stuff, and she's only fifty for Christ's sake! Daddy was a bit better. I think he was hurt, but he has always said that I had to live my own life."

"I think I might have agreed with him. Does he get on with Stu?"

"Oh yes. I think he was a bit of a lad in his younger days. The family all say I take after him. And Stu's so sweet and natural. He's got no side to him at all. OK, I know some people might see him as rough and ready, but he's the best and kindest man I've ever met. His family are lovely, though I think they are a bit worried about me, but his old Mum took me aside soon after we had got together, and told me that although I was off the bank, she thought I'd do. That was really something to hear from her. Would you like the television on?"

Andrew was somewhat startled at this change of tack, but had not been a solicitor for nothing. He knew when a witness was getting tired of cross examination, so laughed and said, "I didn't realise that I had one."

"Oh yes. Stu told me he'd chucked the set in with the rest of the deal. We've got one on our boats anyway. I'll show you how to set up the aerial."

She rummaged in a cupboard and produced a small television set, and from outside the door an object like a skeletal football mounted on a stand.

"This goes on the cabin roof" she said, disappearing momentarily through the cabin doors.

"That's set it up OK now" she said when she came back, "but you must remember, never leave it out while the boat's moving."

"Why's that?"

"'Cos you'll lose it the first time you go under a tree. That's how Stu found this one. It was in the bushes near Brinklow, on the North Oxford."

Andrew thought the learning curve of this living afloat business was steeper than that of his first day at school, his first day in the army, his first day in articles and his first day in prison all combined. The television came blaring into life. Emma curled up on the sofa in front of the fire, while Andrew pottered in the kitchen and the Saturday football results poured forth into the cosy cabin.

Andrew finished his preparations and was sipping a glass of Fitou with Emma when they heard a car pull up on the wharf, the bang of two doors and the voices of Stu and the Inspector. Andrew went to the doors and invited them both in.

"Well!" said the Inspector, stamping mud off his Wellingtons on the wharf, "It wasn't a wild goose chase after all."

Stu was knocking the mud from his Wellingtons over the side. "Not much! What an 'orrible old cow!"

The two came into the stateroom and sat down before the glowing stove. Andrew offered them a drink.

"That's very welcome" said the Inspector, "a coffee if you could spare one, milk, no sugar."

"And me the same" said Stu.

Gradually the tale came out. They had walked along the towpath from Banbury Lane in the dark and had found the boat tied up in the same place. Jim, the Inspector had knocked on the side, while Stu remained some distance away, in the darkness. A chorus of barking had started, and a woman's voice was heard shouting at the dogs. After more knocking a side door was opened. A woman of about forty-five with straggly, dyed blonde hair had looked out. Jim explained who he was, showed his authorisation card and asked to see the dogs. The woman became abusive, shouting that she would report Jim for harassment. At this point Stu had stepped forward to show that Jim had a witness ("Good thinking, Stu" said Andrew). Eventually she grudgingly agreed to let Jim lift the tarpaulins at the stern end of the hold and climb in. The stench was ghastly, and he counted nine dogs, all chained down one side, most of whom cowered at his approach. He had noted a black Labrador bitch in an advanced state of whelp. Stu was not allowed to set foot on board, but got some idea of the conditions under the cloths from the smell and the whining.

The woman remained sullen and refused to give her name. Jim shone his torch round the evil smelling hold and noted that at least three of the dogs were verminous and that they and two more had running eyes. He took several flash photographs and came ashore, telling the woman that she would be reported to the police, at which her abuse reached new heights. Both Jim and Stu were left in no doubt that, had her man been with her, nobody would have set foot on the boat.

"So, let's see what we have," said Andrew. "We certainly have a prima facie case of cruelty, supported by evidence both verbal and, if your pictures come out, pictorial."

Jim looked at him keenly. "You talk like a lawyer. Well I'd agree that we've got evidence of cruelty, but I shan't get the police to move before tomorrow morning, and that's Sunday. What if our friends up sticks and move off before then?"

Stu said "They'll have to come by us if they do."

"What if they go the other way?" asked Jim.

"They won't"

"Why?"

"'Cos it's a sixty foot long boat, and there ain't nowhere she can wind between here an' Banbury Lane. Any road, if they're doing a bunk they won't want to go back on themselves. That'd waste two hours, time they'd turned round. No, I guess they'll either make for Northampton and hide down the river, or for Milton

Keynes and the bottom end."

Andrew said, "Where's the County boundary?"

"The what?"

"The County boundary. Where the canal leaves Northamptonshire."

"I dunno," said Stu, "Why? Is it important?"

"It is if you want the police to do anything."

Jim said, "If I remember right, the County boundary is the River Ouse, we sometimes get cases involving wild life down there. Yes, that's right! Of course it is. Milton Keynes is in the Thames Valley police area."

"It must be the aqueduct at Cosgrove" said Emma, "that's where we cross the Ouse."

"What we calls 'the iron trough'," said Stu.

"I know where you mean" said Jim. "I had a case of a swan which flew into the aqueduct some years back. If you go down the Nene from Northampton, it's miles before you leave the County, somewhere near Peterborough, I reckon."

"So, how long will it take them to get out of Northamptonshire going that way?"

Stu replied "it's a good three hours from 'ere to the river at Northampton. It's five mile an' seventeen locks. I ain't never been further than Wellingborough, but I'd reckon you'd need at least two days to get to Peterborough."

"What about Cosgrove?"

"Ah, that's different. An hour to Stoke, another hour down the locks, hour and a half to Cosgrove, another half hour for the lock and getting by all them tied-up boats. Say four hours."

"So if they are going to make a run for it, they'll make for Cosgrove. Once across the County boundary, they'll be reasonably safe. They'll be out of your jurisdiction" Andrew looked at Jim "and they can dispose of the evidence before the Thames Valley Police and your opposite number get their acts together."

"Let's hope it doesn't come to that" said Jim. "I must get home. I'll report the matter tonight, and we'll go and see them in the morning. If a valuable animal has been stolen, the police will act, but I'll leave that bit up to them. I'm only concerned with the cruelty, not the ownership."

"I'm sure the bitch is Mrs Higgins's Holly" said Stu, "but we could get her to identify it."

"Right-o. But leave the heroics to us and the police" said Jim. "You've done your duty. No, I won't have supper, but very nice of you to offer" he said to Emma, who was making plate laying gestures at him.

Supper was a somewhat excitable meal. People found it difficult to relax, although the bolognaise was washed down by two more bottles of Fitou from Andrew's cellar. The talk kept coming back to the dogs and what was to be done. It was decided that they would be better off staying where they were until tomorrow; although it was not very late when they finished their meal and washed up. They decided that they would be able to watch for the mystery boat and get some idea of where she was heading if they stayed overnight where they were, rather than pressing on to Stoke Bruerne for a drink.

By nine thirty, everyone was ready for bed in any case. Emma and Stu retired to the back cabin, while Snappy, after a brief run ashore, curled up in front of the stove and Andrew felt it would be unreasonable to disturb him. Andrew undressed and lay in his bunk, tired out, but with a combined sense of satisfaction and elation. After a few minutes he gave up listening to Radio 4, stretched out to switch it off and almost immediately plunged into a deep sleep.

Chapter 4
Requisitions on Title

The insistent whimpering of a dog woke Andrew from a dreamless sleep. Andrew sat up to make certain that he was not in fact dreaming. No, there was no mistaking the soft whimpering and scratching at a door. Andrew cursed Snappy. Damn dogs! Worse than some old men for wanting a pee at awkward moments. He threw on his dressing gown and slippers and shuffled into the stateroom. Flicking on the switch, he saw Snappy by the front doors whimpering excitedly. As soon as he saw Andrew, he pricked his ears, stopped whimpering and wagged his stumpy tail with excitement.

"What's up old boy?" asked Andrew, and was about to open the doors to let him out, when he felt the boat surge forward and lurch slightly as the mooring lines tautened. He had already learned that such a movement was usually caused by another boat moving in confined waters. He stopped, tensing himself involuntarily. Snappy was completely quiet now, his mouth slightly open, his ears cocked forward and tail still. Almost without thinking Andrew snapped the cabin light off, opened the top half of the cabin doors and looked out. From where they were tied, which was at right angles to the main line of the canal, he could just make out the dark shape of a road bridge at the end of the straight section of canal where the moored boats were. The underside of the arch seemed to be faintly lit. A long dormant voice at the back of his mind said "range, three hundred, sight on the middle of the arch." Suddenly a bright light glared in the arch, making him blink. He turned his eyes away, and as he did so, his ears caught a low, growling noise. The white light lit up the fore end of *Romford* and the buildings beside the canal, and then it was gone as suddenly as it came. Straining his eyes he could just make out a dark shape that had not been there before in the centre of the arch. Undoubtedly a boat was coming down the canal towards him. He ducked back into the stateroom to look at his watch. It was just before two thirty am.

He dodged back through the boat, tripping over an engine mounting as he blundered through the engine room. He tapped on the back cabin door.

"Whossup?" came Stu's sleepy voice.

"Stu, it's them. There's a boat coming down the cut."

There came a creak as Stu sat up in bed.

"What's the time?"

"About two thirty."

"Hang on. I'm coming."

Andrew padded back to the stateroom, watching the boat slowly approach. There was no moon, and the sky was overcast, but there was sufficient reflection off the water to see the ripples made by the boat's stem. The mutter of the engine grew louder. Stu crept beside Andrew.

"It's them all right, doing a moonlight flit" he whispered. "Keep shtum, they'll set off a security light in a minute."

It was now obvious that the boat was headed straight along the main line. The fore end crept into the wide water of the junction towards the main line bridge. Suddenly the scene was lit by a glaring light as the boat triggered the sensor of a floodlight on the wall of a house by the junction. The boat was most certainly the one they had seen earlier, and was being steered by a muscular, heavily built man with a beard. A woolly cap was drawn down over his ears. He did not glance in the direction of Andrew or Stu, both of whom nevertheless shrank back out of sight. Then he and the boat were gone, swallowed up into the darkness of the bridge. The security light went out, but the drumming of the boat's engine continued, fading steadily. As the boat reached the end of the line of moored boats, the listeners heard it accelerate.

"'He'll be going down Stoke by quarter to four, out the bottom by five, Cosgrove half six. Yes, he'll be over the trough before daylight, it don't start to get light before about seven. He's cutting it fine, but he should do it."

Emma came into the stateroom in her nightie, yawning and rubbing her eyes.

"What's all the fuss?" she asked, sleepily. Andrew told her.

"Well, aren't we going to stop them?" she asked.

"How?" said Andrew. We can't ram and board them."

"We don't need to," said Emma, "They've got to have water to float them."

Stu's eyes lit up "Yes! Of course we can stop 'em. Good old Emma! We knows how to stop 'em don't we! Ha! Ha!" he chortled.

"I'm sorry" said Andrew "I'm not with you."

"No, you wouldn't be, mate. No offence to you, but there's a few old boatman's tricks they won't know neither." He chuckled. "We'll follow 'em to Stoke and then nip ahead down the lane while they're in the flight. They ain't going to be too quick, because the short pound at the top runs off at night, so they'll have to fill it before they gets through it. We'll get by 'em and set things up for 'em."

"What, go after them now?" asked Andrew, astonished.

"'Course" said Stu, "then, when we've got 'em caught we gives Jim and the Ole Bill a dingle on the blower."

"That's all very well, but we've first got to stop them and then keep them until the US Cavalry comes. I'm not too worried about a rough house, I learned to look after myself in Penton- er, in the army, but I wouldn't want to see either of you get hurt. Also, you've got to be very careful making a citizen's arrest..."

"Who said anything about an arrest?" Stu interrupted, "They'll be glad of our help, time they're finished."

"All right. You win! I'm game if you are, but no rough-housing unless they start it first."

"They won't get a chance to start no rough house" said Stu, "what we does is this."

The others listened while he explained the plan. "We'd best get ourselves dressed, and give 'em twenty five minutes start. We don't want 'em to see our light behind 'em in the tunnel."

It was three o'clock when Andrew pressed the starter button. In the silent basin the muffled coughs sounded deafening. Emma slipped the fore end string aboard and Stu took the tiller.

"No offence, Andrew mate, but I knows my way in the dark."

"No offence at all. You're more than welcome." He chuckled. "I'll go and make some coffee."

Emma said, "I'm going to get some sleep in the stateroom."

Nobody looked out of either houses or boats as *Romford* drifted under the road bridge. By the time that Andrew had made the coffee and brought it to Stu at the stern, the boat's exhaust was raising the echoes under the high railway arch at Blisworth. Andrew noticed that Stu only put the headlamp on as he approached a bridge.

"Best way, mate" he replied to Andrew's question. "Just flash in bridges and on sharp turns, like the trade boats, or you blinds other people, and you gets to rely on it too much. You only really needs it in tunnels or coming into locks."

They drifted past a huddle of boats tied up at Blisworth Mill, then headed towards a dark hillside. The banks rose higher and bare trees arched above them. Andrew could only envy Stu's night vision. He had always prided himself on having good eyes for the dark, but this was something else. Stu seemed to have a radar in his head. The darkness in front grew ever denser. Andrew could just make out the shapes of trees high above them and dead ahead by the slightly paler night sky beyond. Stu shut the engine right down.

"We'll turn her off once we're in the tunnel and have a listen", he said.

Andrew slid into the engine room, whose light seemed all the more brilliant for the contrast outside. Suddenly the note changed into an echoing clatter and he became aware of brickwork sliding past, reflecting the light from the open doors and the boat's windows. He lifted the stop lever and the engine noise died away. There was utter silence, broken only by the slight ripple of water as *Romford* carried her way and, away from the reflected light, almost tangible blackness. There came a slight bump as the boat brushed the tunnel wall. Emma came through the engine room, she peered out of the side doors yawning and rubbing her eyes.

"Sssh!" said Stu.

Three pairs of ears strained to pick up any sound from ahead. There came a very low, distant muttering, barely audible.

"That's them. They can't be far off the far end" whispered Stu, though there was not really any need.

They listened for a couple of minutes. The muttering grew fainter, and then died completely.

"They're out." said Stu "Let them get clear, then we'll start. There's a bit of a turn in the cutting just outside the far end. They'll not see our light once they're round it."

"How long is it?" asked Andrew.

"The tunnel? Near enough a mile and three quarters."

Andrew stepped into the lighted cabin to look at his watch. It was nearly three thirty. It would be nearly four by the time they were through the tunnel.

"OK Andrew, mate, start her up" said Stu.

The starter motor engaged with a crash and the engine coughed again into life. Stu switched on the headlamp, causing the tunnel walls to leap alive. He shoved the gear lever in, *Romford* began to gather way, slipping swiftly, Andrew was ashamed to notice, down the centre line of the tunnel and not swinging either way.

Andrew went forward. Emma was once again curled up on the sofa, but he was far too animated to sit. He stood in the fore deck well savouring the curious dank and musty smell of the tunnel, looking forward into the converging lines of brickwork that the headlamp lit up. As the boat drummed through the echoing vault, he felt the old excitement that he remembered from his National Service days, when he and John had both been platoon commanders, and Joey Caroni had been his platoon sergeant. *There were those nights when they had escorted convoys through the Troodos Mountains; nights spent on patrol hunting for EOKA groups; and then there was the night when a grenade had shattered the windscreen and machine gun bullets had zipped into the canvas of the Bedford 3 tonner that Joey was driving. He could never forget the screaming from one of the overturned trucks as blazing petrol ran over two men trapped underneath, nor the look in Joey's eyes as the 3 tonner began to slide off the road into the bushes where he lay immobilised by a tree which had trapped his leg. The glare from the petrol fire made the whites of Joey's eyes seem huge.*

He shook his head violently as if to shake out the images that flashed across his brain. He consciously thought, bad things like that must go back into the memory cells. Christ! Cells! That was something else. *Cells, stored away like the others at Pentonville. Rows of them, rising up beyond iron galleries and suicide nets, behind clanging doors and the smell of disinfectant and excrement; and then the first sight of his cell mate, a shaven-headed youth with earrings and tattoos all down his arms, who snivelled all night. But there was the adrenaline-raising excitement there too, like when the three hard men went for him on the landing, with the screw accidentally on purpose looking the other way. He smiled grimly to himself as he remembered their look of surprise when they believed they had him cornered, and he had snapped the first one's wrist and chopped the second in his Adam's apple. Everything then had seemed to go into slow motion, except for himself, just as it had in Cyprus when he had got his rifle under the tree and eased it up to free Joey's leg. Two of the hard men had crashed down the staircase, leaving him the third, who he left writhing on the landing, screaming and clutching his genitals.* Some skills, like conveyancing, advocacy and unarmed combat had never left him. He found himself analysing whether or not he should use the latter if needed this morning. On balance he decided it would be better not to, as much as anything, he did not want his new friends to know that he possessed such an anti-social ability. It was a thing of the past and he did not want to resurrect it, his future lay here, among decent people, not in military adventures, or courtrooms, or prisons.

He had noticed cast-iron number plates on the right hand wall of the tunnel; rusting and indistinct, they appeared momentarily lit by the light streaming from the stateroom portholes and the afterglow of the headlamp. Now, to try and refocus his mind, he tried to see what information they bore. They seemed to be at regular intervals, he estimated a hundred yards or so, and timed the boat between the plates. Forty-five seconds. Well, if they were spaced at hundred yard intervals that would mean they were doing, what? He calculated mentally for a few seconds, four and a half miles per hour. In fact, Stu was exceeding the speed limit! However he did not suppose anyone would be about to report the fact. The boat had long left the modern concrete lined section of the tunnel and Plate twenty-six had disappeared astern, and he realised that they must be nearing the end. He strained his eyes forward. The brick walls still ran, dripping, to the end of the headlamp beam. Or did they? At the very far end of the parallax there seemed to be a darkness sharper edged than before. Plate twenty-eight passed by, and he was sure of it. The illuminated brick arch now stopped short in a hard, semi-circular outline. Beyond, the beam was picking up the branches of trees. In another two minutes they were out in the open, the echoing clatter of the engine changing to its more familiar thudding. They were in a wide, tree lined cutting, which disappeared as Stu turned the headlamp off. Andrew went back to the engine room and climbed out onto the catwalk. Stu's figure was just visible in the dark, a scarf pulled up over his face and round his ears.

"We'll tie up in a couple of minutes and go for a nose" he said, "I'll pull in the narrows, there's rings there. We don't want to be banging in stakes this time of the morning."

They entered a narrower section of canal, barely wide enough for four boats. Stu throttled right down and pulled out of gear.

"Take the fore end, Andy. I'll see to the stern."

They gently slipped beside a low quay wall, Stu reversed, Andrew stepped ashore and walked up the fore end, reaching aboard for the mooring line. They stopped.

Emma came to the front doors as Andrew tied the fore end.

"I've got some wellies here. Are they yours?"

"Thanks," said Andrew, "the grass seems a bit wet."

"I think it could rain before it gets light, so we'll need coats. I've found an old overcoat for you."

"I've got a waterproof in the engine room."

"Yes, and it's bright yellow. You can see it a mile off."

Andrew laughed "Fieldcraft, Emma. Of course, I should have thought." He took the old tweed coat that she held out. Once he had worn it to church on winter Sunday mornings at St. Giles, Lipscombe, and had chucked it, somewhat unwillingly, in the engine room on Friday, on Stu's advice. The coat held too many memories. He had been a sidesman and on the Parochial Church Council; those little matters had to go by the board with his conviction. He remembered the rector's letter of sympathy, which suggested at the same time that he might care to resign these offices. Well, at least he did not have to put on a solemn face with his overcoat any more, nor to put up with unctuous sermons on "Christian fellowship", a term which to him suggested glad-handing by the clergy, rather than the sort of true friendship he was discovering in his new life.

Stu shut down the engine and closed the side doors. He stood beside the others on the towpath, an indistinct mass in the darkness.

"We'd best get going. We wants windlasses and a mobile 'phone. Got 'em?"

Emma nodded, passing a windlass to Andrew.

"What now?" asked Andrew.

"I'm off to have a gander down by the bridge. You and Emma start down the lane to Bottom lock. OK?" The others grunted assent. "Right, see you." He vanished into the dark.

"Keep behind me" said Emma, and the two of them set off behind

Stu. There was a street lamp ahead, which showed buildings looming on either side of the canal.

They walked swiftly past the Canal Museum and the lightless cottages beside it. Another street lamp by the bridge lit up the Top lock, Andrew saw Stu's figure crossing the gates and padding down the far side. Emma led him past the lock on to the road that led down from the bridge. A lane led off beside the black mass of an old farmhouse, all its windows in darkness, but lit outside with a security light.

"This way." whispered Emma, darting across the road into the shadows beyond. Andrew followed her, his Wellingtons thumping on the road surface. Now he was in a lane between dark, bare hedges. Ahead the sky was lit with a distant reddish glow. Away to the left a line of orange lights glowed, probably the Motorway, thought Andrew.

Running footsteps sounded behind him. Stu came trotting down the lane; they stopped to let him catch up.

"It's OK" he breathed "They've only just left the second lock. I thought they'd be slowed up. They're in the long pound now, just across that field."

"So we're getting ahead of them are we?" whispered Andrew.

"That's it. We got to get down to the fifth lock, and we can hold them there till the cavalry come."

They carried on; trotting through the dark towards the distant glow, which Andrew calculated must be from Milton Keynes. Headlights suddenly gleamed ahead, and the roar of a lorry boomed out.

"That's the main road" said Stu. "We goes across it and cuts back, under the bridge."

They crossed the main road and walked swiftly along a wide, curving section of new road beyond it. When the new road bent sharply to the left, Stu led across a grassy patch parallel to the main road, which was now on an embankment beside them. Water gleamed ahead.

"Watch it!" hissed Stu, we turns right here, under the bridge. Here, have my torch if you like." He passed a small pocket torch to Andrew, who flashed it, pointing the beam downward. They were on the edge of the canal where it ran under a flat-topped concrete bridge. The towpath was on the opposite side, but a narrow brick shelf led underneath to a lock. Stu was already half way along the shelf, stooping to avoid hitting his head. Emma had disappeared.

Andrew scrambled under the bridge and up a ramp to the lock. In the blackness he could see Stu's form huddled over the paddle gear of the bottom gate.

"We wants to just get this 'un open a couple of turns," he said. "Chances are, they'll not notice that the rack's up in the dark. Luckily the pound above is pretty low. We'll get it well empty before they gets here."

He rummaged inside his coat and brought out a coil of thin rope. "Have a butchers through that rubbish over there. I needs a good brick."

Stu moved across to a pile of rubble lying near the lockside and kicked it.

"Let's have a look with the lamp. Careful! Don't shine it around! There! That'll do." He pounced on a couple of bricks, still cemented together, carried them under the bridge and then got Andrew to shine the torch on them while he tied one end of the cord tightly round them. He pushed one bottom gate open slightly and dropped the bricks in front of it. He jerked the end of the cord, grunted with satisfaction, then tied it off to the bottom of the gate handrail.

"Now we drops the pound off a bit more" he said, "Get that bottom paddle up, Andrew."

Andrew wound the bottom gate paddle up while Stu lifted the top paddle. Water gurgled and swirled in the dark recess of the lock. He walked up to Stu, who was standing by the top paddle post gazing intently into the blackness above the lock. Suddenly Stu tensed.

"Look there," he muttered. In the distance a pinpoint of light glimmered and flickered, moving from left to right. "They've got to the top lock of the Thick."

"Sorry?" said Andrew.

"There's three locks close together here. What we calls 'a thick'" Stu explained. "Only short pounds between them. We're emptying the second short one, they'll only be able to run the next lock into this short pound, but the water'll run out faster'n it goes in. They'll never fill this lock up." He wound his paddle down. "All we does is wait and see."

They walked back to the bottom gate. Stu carefully set the bottom paddle so that it was a few turns open. Emma came up the towpath and under the bridge.

"I've left all the paddles up a few nicks." She said.

"What for?" asked Andrew.

Stu said, "We could flood them cottages down below playing this trick, so Emma's been making room for the water that's coming down from above."

Andrew was silent. Commonsense really, all this, but quite arcane at first. Once it was explained it was simple, but he'd never have thought of this trick in a hundred years. He was quite content to be one of the troops and leave the generalship to Stu.

"How's the time?" asked Stu. Andrew flashed the torch on his wrist.

"Nearly five."

"We'd best get out of the road. We can go back to your boat and give Jim a bell. He told me he's up and about by six. That lot won't get into the Bridge lock in a hurry. Even if they do find what's up, they ain't goin' to get down to Bottom lock till daylight. Any road, it's coming on to rain. Let's go and get a cuppa."

"I cut some sarnies last night," said Emma, "I could do with one now."

The rain strengthened as they walked back up the lane. By the time they reached the boat it was coming down hard and cold.

"That pound above the main road'll be empty by now," said Stu as they ducked under the canvas cover at the fore end. He chuckled. The thought lent a pleasant piquancy to the tea and sandwiches.

Just after six, Andrew rang Jim's number. Jim answered almost immediately. He whistled when he heard of their quarry's escape, and laughed when Andrew explained what they had done to stop their flight.

"I'll call the police and get them over to the locks. Can you identify Mrs. Higgins' bitch?"

"Emma can, and I suppose we could get Mrs. Higgins over if necessary. They've got enough to hold the couple for questioning."

"OK. I'll be over there before seven."

"See you there," said Andrew, "'bye."

The rain had eased up, and there was just the faintest trace of daylight as they untied and set out for the locks with the boat.

"We'll just go down to the top of the Thick," said Stu, "I'll get the locks ready, and you two bring the boat down."

Before leaving the top lock, Stu wound up a few nicks of the top paddle.

"That'll start water coming down to make the pound back up," he explained. "The Waterways chaps'll be out in half hour's time, so we'd best start putting things to rights for them."

"They won't be too pleased if they find the canal empty," observed Andrew.

"Ah, but who'll get the blame? Them as been trying to fill a lock with the bottom paddles up" said Stu, setting off down the towpath to the next lock.

The first two locks of the Stoke Bruerne flight are close together, followed by a longer pound. By the time they had got to the third lock, at the top of the Thick, it was getting perceptibly lighter. They could see down to the main road bridge with the lights of a stationary vehicle beside it. They tied the boat up and walked past the lock. The sound of raised voices came to them over the trickle of water. Stu grinned.

"Sounds like a bit of bother down there."

At the next lock the three stopped and gazed, open mouthed.

"Fookin' ell!" said Stu in an awed tone.

The short pound between them and the next lock by the road bridge was empty. The top gates of the next lock were open and, in between them, completely stranded, was the boat that they had seen the previous evening near Banbury Lane. A group consisting of two policemen, Jim the RSPCA man and a woman were trying to help a mud covered man up the wall by the top gates.

Emma said, "I'd better pop down and close everything, before the whole flight dries out." She darted off with Snappy. The group by the lock hardly glanced at her as she ran by, but as Andrew and Stu followed her, the woman suddenly shouted,

"That's one of the interfering bastards!"

She pointed at Stu. Andrew looked at her curiously. She was forty-ish, with straggly, dyed blonde hair and plump. A shapeless sweater made her look even larger. Her voice was harsh and with a North London accent. She continued,

"That was anuvver of 'em, come stickin' their bladdy noses in larst night. Freatenin' me an' all."

One of the policemen said,

"Was this man the one that you allege assaulted you last night?"

The woman glared at him. "Why don't you mind yer own bladdy business? You ain't got no right stoppin' us."

"Shut up, yer silly cow!" said the mud-covered man, scrambling to his feet on the lockside. Andrew recognised him in spite of the mud as the figure he had seen steering the boat at Gayton. The woman lapsed into a sullen silence.

Next, Andrew recognised the policeman who had spoken as the red-faced Kevin who had come to the farm. He similarly recognised Andrew and nodded.

"All right then? What brings you here at this time o' day?"

"I'm bringing a boat down the locks."

"You're goin' to 'ave to find a set o' wheels for it then."

Jim nodded to Stu. "Morning, Stu. As you can see, we've got a bit of a problem here."

"I don't see one," said Stu.

"We've got to get to 'ave a look at that boat" said the other policeman. "Matey 'ere tried to jump on it and didn't 'ave a lot o' luck."

"Why can't you fill the lock?" asked Stu, innocently.

"'Cos the bloody bottom gate's jammed" said the muddy boatman angrily. "All the water in this pound's run out 'cos some silly bastard left a bottom paddle up, an' my missus didn't see it till it was too bloody late."

"Let's have a butchers" said Stu. He walked to the bottom gate and pushed it. It swung sweetly back against the sill.

"Seems OK to me."

The other man's bearded jaw dropped.

"It can't be."

"Try it for yourself."

Both gates met perfectly in the middle of the lock. Even Andrew was astonished. He stole a glance at Stu, who winked back at him. "It's still goin' to take ages to fill the cut back up. I'd best go back and do it," said the bearded man.

"No need" said Stu, "we got water coming down."

Even as he spoke there came a trickling sound from the lock above, water was beginning to run over the bottom gates.

"That next lock's full" said Stu, "If we runs it into this pound we'll have you floating again in five minutes."

"You really are an 'elpful bastard" sneered the muddy man.

"Thanks" said Stu, walking back to the lock above.

Water began pouring into the dry pound as Stu raised the paddles at the lock above; after a few minutes the lock chamber was half full, and water began lapping round the stranded hull. Two British Waterways men in overalls came clumping under the bridge with Emma and Snappy as another police car pulled up on the bridge overhead. It was developing into quite a party.

As the water rose, the two stranded boaters looked more and more anxious. At last Stu took a short length of line from Emma and flicked it over the boat's fore stud. He was soon able to draw the fore end into the bank. The bearded man looked relieved but the woman continued to glare at everyone who caught her glance. Stu and the Waterways men pulled the boat into the lock when the water rose sufficiently.

"Well now," said Kevin the policeman, "I have reason to believe that that you are concealing ill-treated animals aboard. Are you going to let me have a look, or do I have to send for a warrant?"

"Go on then, if you must" muttered the man. The woman continued to glare.

"Open sesame!" said the policeman. Jim and two other policemen began to undo the ropes holding the tarpaulins in position. It took a couple of minutes, then the covers were thrown back. A chorus of barking ensued.

"Phwoah!" said one of the policemen, holding his nose.

A vile smell of dog mess hit the company like a slap in the face. Jim jumped into the hold with a flash camera. He took a series of photographs then called Emma over. The dogs barked and whined, setting Snappy barking in sympathy.

"It's not very nice, but perhaps you could identify the missing dog."

Stu took Snappy's lead as Emma jumped down.

"This is definitely Mrs. Higgins' Holly. Look, you can see where her collar used to be. She had a black one, with brass studs and a plate with her name and address."

"Well, it ain't there now, you snotty bitch" called the woman.

"If I were you, me ole' duck" said Kevin, his face redder than ever, "I'd be a little careful what I said just now."

Emma stooped under a crossbeam. "Can you give us a bit more light!"

The policemen threw back another tarpaulin. It was fully daylight by now.

"This is Joe Donnington's Jack Russell. She's still got her seven pups" called Emma, "There! There! Good girl! It's all right, we're friends! No, she's not got a collar either."

"What a coincidence!" said Kevin, grinning. He turned to the couple on the lockside. "I have reason to believe that these two pedigree dogs are stolen. I must ask you to accompany me to the police station for questioning. I must warn you..."

"Bastards! Interfering bastards!" screamed the woman.

"I must warn you that you are about to be formally cautioned." And in front of Andrew, Stu, Emma, Jim, two other policemen and the two Waterways men, he administered a formal caution.

Jim then spoke. "I have sufficient evidence to bring charges of neglect and cruelty against whoever is responsible for these animals' condition."

One of the Waterways men said, "And I don't see any licence or licence plate on the outside of the boat, nor any name displayed, as required by the Byelaws."

"It looks to me," said Kevin, "that you two 'ave shit a serious pot full. Jack, can you take these two to the station? I think they'll 'ave quite a bit of talking to do."

"We'll get the boat down to Bottom lock for you" said the older Waterways man to the couple, "you can't leave it here."

"And you'd better give me the key" said Kevin, "I'd 'ate to 'ave to break in to search it."

The party began to break up. The couple went off with two policemen; Emma and Jim began feeding the dogs with food from Jim's van. Kevin scribbled in a notebook, and the Waterways men satisfied themselves that the canal was once more fully in water.

"Beats me 'ow they managed to loose all that water wi'out floodin' them 'ouses down the bottom" said one. "I says as much to your girl-friend when she told us what were up. Some boogger must a' deliberately left them paddles up. Still, all's well as ends well. Seems to me that we could do wi'out the likes o' them on the cut." He walked off with his mate, shaking his head.

"We'd best go and get the boat now" said Stu. "At least we know we got water for us to come down."

"Tell me," said Andrew, "how come the bottom gate shut so easily just now? I thought you'd jammed a brick in it."

"So I had" said Stu, "but Emma pulled it out while they was all talking to you and me. She chucked the brick away and give me the line back. That's what I used to pull the boat in. She's got a good head on her shoulders, that one."

"She certainly has" said Andrew.

Stu finished his last mouthful of bacon, egg, fried bread and mushroom with a contented sigh. He took a lengthy pull from a mug of coffee and said,

"That were bloody handsome, mate. I didn't realise how starved I was till you started cooking."

Andrew took his plate and put it in the sink. Emma slipped off a stool by the breakfast bar and went to wash it up. Andrew put out his hand to check her,

"No you don't, young lady! Chef's in charge here."

He took the plate, scraped off the rinds into a pedal bin and ran hot water over it. The clock on the cabin wall pointed to a few minutes to eleven. They were tied up below Stoke Bruerne bottom lock refilling the water tank with a length of hose from the nearby water tap. Just ahead of them, the mystery boat was being examined by the same two detectives who had called on Anne after her brush with the thugs. They had introduced themselves briefly and gone directly aboard the other boat while Andrew was cooking breakfast. Emma had made a statement in which she positively identified the dogs; an RSPCA van had taken away all the dogs, including Holly, who was to be reunited with her owner later that morning; the two suspects had been taken away for further questioning; the two Waterways men, with the assistance of Stu and Emma, had used *Romford* to move the boat down the locks to its present position. While all this was going on, Andrew set about cooking a breakfast worthy of the occasion. The day had developed into a clear, sunny late autumn day and a pleasant sense of accomplishment had settled over *Romford* and her crew.

Andrew thought that the woman detective, Sergeant Hollis, looked more like a successful lady horse breeder at a point-to-point than a policewoman. She was wearing brogues, well-cut jeans and a green windcheater jacket, topped by a ratting cap. She came walking back from her examination of the boat, leaving her assistant, DC Roberts taking photographs and scribbling notes. She accepted Andrew's invitation for a coffee and stepped aboard, looking keenly at Andrew as she sat down.

"I say, this is jolly pleasant. That other boat is a proper tip. The way some people live! I must say you've made this very comfortable. Was it you?" She looked at Emma, who coloured and looked embarrassed.

"N-n-no, not me. It's his boat." Emma nodded towards Andrew.

"Oh, I see. Haven't we met before? You weren't on a boat then."

"It was at the farm, last Monday" said Andrew.

"Right! The mystery intruders. We haven't got very far with tracing them."

"What a surprise! Still, as long as they leave Mrs. Clarke alone, that's OK."

"Is she alone down there?" asked the sergeant.

"Probably her daughter's with her now" replied Andrew. "She comes down from London at weekends."

Sergeant Hollis nodded. "Anyway, you've done a good job with that bright pair. It seems the RSPCA has been looking for them for ages, and so have the West Midlands Police. There's been some pedigree dog stealing in the Birmingham and Coventry areas that our friends may know something about."

An idea had been going through Andrew's mind for some time now, and he asked, "Tell me, did you find anything on that boat to connect the couple with Luton Airport?"

Hollis raised her eyebrows "And why should I have done that?"

"There's regular flights from there to Ireland and the Continent, both good markets for English dogs, and it's no distance from the canal further down."

Hollis smiled. Andrew thought she really looked most attractive when she did so. "I'm not saying too much, but you could just be right. Are you one of us?"

"No, not at all. I used to be a solicitor though, both defence and prosecutions, back in the days before there was a Crown Prosecution Service to foul it all up."

"Tell me about it!" said Hollis with feeling, "you say you used to be?" It was a question, not a reiteration.

"Retired" said Andrew, "I'm here for peace and quiet."

Roberts' voice came from outside, "Sarge! I'm finished."

Sergeant Hollis put down her cup. "I must dash now. Nice to meet you, and thank you for your help." Stu helped her up on to the bank "Maybe see you again." She walked back to her car talking to Roberts.

Emma was smiling when Andrew turned round from watching her,

"You old dark horse! She fancies you."

Andrew for once was lost for words, and then laughed. "Chance would be a fine thing. I'm old enough to be her father."

"If you'd been a teeny sex maniac when she was born" retorted Emma, "She's not that young. She hasn't got a wedding ring either."

"Thank you, the Sherlock Holmes Dating Agency" laughed Andrew. "I may be old and decrepit, but it's nice to know I can still pull."

Emma blushed for the second time that morning. "Sorry, but I think you're far too nice to be on your own."

"That's the best thing anyone's said to me this morning. Come on. We'll have to get started again."

Once Stu had shown Andrew how to roll up the fresh water hose without spilling water into the boat, they set off. Stu had said that the remaining journey would not take above an hour and a half, so they were in good time. Andrew steered, the other two stood either side in the pale sunlight. As they slipped quietly through the deserted countryside, Emma asked,

"What was all that about Luton Airport?"

Andrew eased the weight on his legs.

"My theory is that our friends were stealing dogs to order, so that they could be exported with false pedigrees and forged veterinary certificates. I'd be prepared to bet they had a contact in somewhere like Milton Keynes. If you think about it, a boat would be an ideal way to go about it. You've got plenty of space to keep the dogs, you slip around the country and hardly anyone sees you. Tie up somewhere near a town, near a road bridge, pinch the dogs using a van we'll say, and nip back to the boat under cover of darkness."

"That could have been what the chap were up to last night" said Stu.

"Think about it. Saturday night, people go out and leave their dogs. I'll bet they'd sussed out places days before, posing as reps for dog food firms, or animal welfare people or something like that. They'd never come under suspicion moving about the cut, and probably wouldn't have if they hadn't pinched Holly Higgins. After you and Jim went round last night, they decided to run for it, and might have got away if Snappy hadn't woken me up. That's what I think happened. Of course, the police will keep their cards close to their chests."

Stu was looking at Andrew goggle-eyed. "You worked all that out?" he asked.

"Look Stu, to me it's as simple as stopping that boat was to you two. It's horses for courses you see. I wouldn't have had the faintest idea of how to stop them. I'm not too sure that you ought to have done what you did, but it worked."

"For Chrissake don't ever let on to Waterways what we done" said Stu, "they'd go apeshit if they knew. Mind, it wouldn't have done if there'd been a water shortage on. I'd have had to think of summat else!"

It was nearly lunchtime when they reached the farm. Andrew

found a suitable place on the offside. There was a crumbling brick wall there, once, no doubt part of the farm wharf. Stu and Emma leapt off the fore end to take the mooring lines as Andrew nosed in, but years of passing traffic had washed mud up into the wall and, try as they might, they could not pull the boat closer than about three feet from the bank. Stu hammered in two stout iron stakes fore and aft, Andrew swivelled a plank off the cabin roof, and they managed to place it securely across the gap.

Anne came down from the farm with a young woman. Andrew had not met her, but he recognised her as a younger version of Anne even before he was introduced to her as Anne's daughter, Sally.

"You'll all come to lunch, of course" said Anne.

The three voyagers looked at one another.

"It's very kind of you, Anne," said Andrew, "but we are a bit mob-handed. I was going to take them to the pub."

"Nonsense. I guessed that you'd be here about now, and there's a joint roasting. You don't want my guests to have to eat cold meat sandwiches for a week do you?"

"All right, but on one condition."

"Which is..?"

"You let me supply the wine. I've got a couple of bottles of Fitou left."

"Fine. Shall we say half an hour? One fifteen?"

Over lunch, which turned out to be a beautifully cooked leg of lamb, with mint and red currant sauce, Anne and Sally heard the story of the dog stealers. Sally's eyes were like saucers. Eventually she could contain herself no more,

"You mean you actually let all the water out on the stinkers?"

Stu nodded, munching contentedly. Then he swallowed and said anxiously,

"Yes, but nobody's got to know about that. It's a sort of secret, like."

Andrew said, "Apparently British Waterways take a dim view of their water being wasted. At the moment, they think it was done accidentally by someone last night."

"Gosh!" said Sally.

"More parsnips anyone?" asked Anne.

Chapter 5
Continuing Inquiries

Stu was not a great reader, so the one thing that *Romford* lacked was shelving for books. Consequently on Monday morning Andrew visited a D-I-Y shop in the nearby town. He spent the rest of the day sawing, fitting and varnishing. There was space along two sides of the stateroom for some two hundred books and the rest fitted into his bedroom. He sawed and hammered until it was nearly dark, then swept up the dust and varnished the shelves. About six o'clock Anne brought him a cup of tea, sniffed the reek of drying varnish and insisted on him sleeping ashore in his old bedroom. Andrew was hoping that by morning the varnish would have dried sufficiently for him to set out all his books, for if there was one aspect of his old life that he missed, it was the advice and companionship of his library, which still languished inside the three packing cases that John Watson had recovered for him. He was looking forward to seeing his old friends again, for it was nearly four years since he had packed them away before leaving Lipscombe for the last time.

On Tuesday morning he had dressed, shaved and bounded into Anne's kitchen ready for work soon after half past seven. Anne was grilling bacon on the Aga.

"Full of beans this morning, aren't we?"

"I want to get going. It's so great having a place of my own again. Not that I've anything against this place" he added hurriedly, "but I've lived out of suitcases or in er, other rooms, for three years. I'm looking forward to being my own boss again."

Anne gave a wistful smile "I think I understand. You must feel disorientated."

She took a jug of fresh coffee that was bubbling on one hob plate and put it on the mat beside him.

"Be an angel, and pour it out would you. I want to get the breakfasts before Jane gets here, so she can get on and change the sheets for me."

"How many in last night?" asked Andrew, pouring the coffee.

"Three, apart from you. All businessmen."

"Can't be bad business."

"No, but I shall be shutting down in four weeks' time for Christmas. Tom's got two week's leave and Sally'll be coming home, so I shall take a break until the end of February."

"Going away?"

"I might go skiing in Austria with a friend. It's not fixed yet."

"Oh, whereabouts in Austria?"

"Near Innsbruck, Hall im Tyrol."

"I know it, lovely little town."

Yes, it had been a lovely little town, back in the early 'sixties, when there were over sixty schillings to the pound, and he and Pamela were on the way up. He sipped his coffee, remembering crusty rolls and *Kaffee mit schlag*, and *gluhwein* after a day on the mountains, and great log fires and glowing stoves and tinkling music. "The Hills are alive", he muttered bitterly to himself, "all *schmaltz* and *gemuethlichkeit*." But they'd been young then. Somehow the magic had worked and they had been happy. He suddenly found himself wishing that he were in Austria with Anne, and guiltily snatched himself back to the present as a car pulled up outside.

Jane, the help, came bustling into the kitchen. She saw Andrew and smiled,

"All right? Me ole doock?"

"Yes thank you, and you?"

"I ain't too bad considerin'."

"Considering what?" asked Anne. Jane sat down on a kitchen stool, offered Andrew a cigarette, which he refused, found herself one and lit up. She drew hard and gratefully blew out a long cloud of smoke, then, looking in Anne's direction said:

"Our Kelly's at it again."

"What is it this time?"

"Movin' in wi' that Gary. She wants to go to town an' live in 'is flat. I says she's got to wait till she finishes school. She says she's old enough to do what she likes. Well, she is sixteen I grant you, but she ain't goin' into town till the summer, an' then she's gettin' a proper place."

"What's wrong with the place she wants to go to?" asked Andrew.

"What's right wi' it?" retorted Jane. "That Gary's got it. It's in one o' them big ole' 'ouses up the Barrack Road. Accordin' to what she says, it's got one room up in the attic, no 'eatin' beyond a paraffin 'eater, an' share a loo an' bath on the next floor. Right death trap I reckon. 'E's payin' over all 'is 'ousin' benefit for it an' all!"

"What does Gary do?"

"Well, that's it ain't it? 'E don't do nothin'. Works on the Social."

"The what?"

"'E's on Social Security. 'E don't get no dole, but 'e does a bit o' bar work, that's 'ow Our Kelly met 'im, an' the Social pays 'is 'ousin' benefit an' electric an' that. What 'e earns is 'is beer money. Well, what sort o' set up is that?" Jane took out a handkerchief and blew her nose loudly. "She were doin' ever so well wi' 'er GCSEs till she met this Gary. Now she's moonin' about 'ome, 'er school work's gone to pot, an' all she can think about is gettin' out an' livin' wi' 'im."

"Short of persuasion, there's not a lot you can do" said Andrew, "She's over sixteen, and that's it."

"I knows that, but it don't make it no easier" said Jane, sweeping out of the kitchen.

Andrew picked up a copy of "*The Daily Telegraph*" which was lying folded on the table.

"Do you mind, Anne?"

"No, go ahead, help yourself. I've had a quick glance, but I usually have a good read after Jane's gone home."

He shook the paper open. It was a day when nothing much seemed to be happening in the world. The Government was being attacked by the Opposition for being soft on law and order. Hmm, he thought, I might disagree there, at least so far as lawyers are concerned. There was yet another scandal involving the Royal family; according to a spokesman for the Estate Agents the housing market was about to rise, according to a spokesman for the building industry it was going to be sluggish. Andrew yawned. Not a lot of change there in three years! He idly turned the pages and scanned the home news section. He suddenly sat up.

"Hullo! What's this?"

"What's what?" replied Anne, straightening up as she closed the dishwasher.

Andrew read: *"DOG RUSTLERS HIT BOTTOM. Two would-be rustlers of pedigree dogs were foiled when their get-away barge was stuck in the Grand Union Canal near Northampton. Police were called when thieves smuggling stolen pedigree dogs aboard their barge ran out of water at Stoke Bruerne locks...."* He glanced at the bottom of the article, there was no name, he read on, *"A police spokesperson said that the dogs were in a dreadful state, and that the RSPCA had been informed."*

"That's Sally," said Anne, "I should have known she was after a story when she asked you all those questions."

"I never knew she was in journalism."

"Only freelance, but she makes enough to support herself."

"Uh huh!" Andrew read on: *"A man and woman have been charged with stealing dogs and will appear before Towcester magistrates on Wednesday* - that's tomorrow." He grimaced. Sally certainly doesn't let grass grow under her feet. I hope British Waterways management don't take the *"Telegraph"*, for Stu's sake."

"They won't know he had anything to do with it, will they?"

"Only if he gets called as a witness."

"Will he?"

"That depends. If the thieves elect to be dealt with by the magistrates he is not likely to be needed, nor if they plead guilty, but if they elect to go for a jury trial at Crown Court, he'll be needed then."

"Why?"

"Well, you see he and Jim, the RSPCA Inspector, found the dogs on the boat on Saturday night, and gave the alarm Sunday morning, so he'll have to tell the Court all about that."

"But what's emptying the canal got to do with it?"

"Nothing really, but the press will make something of it. It's just the sort of silly story, with apologies to Sally, that sells papers.

"Um! Yes, you could be right. It would be an awful shame if he got into trouble."

"I don't really think he need worry, but it's better if he doesn't have to mention his part in the capture."

The varnish that Andrew had put on yesterday had gone quite hard. By the time he had finished in the farmhouse, raked the cabin fire and riddled out the ashes, it was after ten o'clock. He put on Radio 4 as he bustled about unloading the crates of books. In one of Anne's barns he had found an old sack trolley and was able to put this to good use, wheeling the tea chests from the barn where he had left them, to the end of the gangplank. The weather was cloudy, but not threatening rain, so he took each chest as far as the plank, then unloaded them piecemeal. Had Stu or someone been about he would have carried the chest aboard, but he dared not risk it on his own, so he contented himself with an armful of books at a time. He had emptied one case, and was well into the second when he heard his name being called. He blew the dust off the volume that he had just taken out, Palgrave's "*Golden Treasury of English Verse*", placed it in a temporary position on a shelf, and stooped out of the door onto the foredeck.

"You're busy" said Detective Sergeant Hollis from the bank.

Andrew gazed up at her. Today she was wearing a tweed skirt under a waxed jacket, and a headscarf. She looked more than ever like a country lady at a gymkhana.

"Hullo" said Andrew, "what can I do for you? Would you like to come aboard?"

He stepped up and offered her his hand as she came along the plank. She marched along it with great confidence, but took his hand all the same as she stepped down. Andrew observed that Emma had been quite correct; Sergeant Hollis did not wear a wedding ring. She looked with interest at the books on the shelves and at the pile on the floor.

"I'm still sorting things out" said Andrew, "I only bought the boat on Friday."

"Really? So who are the other two, Stu and Emma? I thought they were with you."

"They were. I bought the boat from Stu and he gave me a hand with my first voyage. He and Emma live on a boat, at Braunston."

"I'm afraid I need to talk to Stu, or at least, DC Roberts does. Have you an address for him?"

"I was afraid that might be so. Yes, I can find him for you. Would you like his mobile number?"

Hollis smiled, "I certainly would. I was afraid that I'd lost him."

Andrew put the kettle on and searched out his notebook with Stu's number in it. "Do you mind if I ask you a favour?" he said.

"It depends what it is."

"Can you just concentrate on his part in the identification of the woman and the dogs at Banbury Lane?"

"Come on," the Sergeant grinned, "what's he been up to?"

"Nothing that really concerns the police, but it's just a little awkward."

"You'd better tell me."

"How long can you spare?"

"As long as it takes."

"You'd better sit down then."

He took her jacket and scarf. She wore a sweater underneath and Andrew noted that she had a good figure. He hung the clothes up, noting a faint scent of *muguets des bois* that clung to them, and went back to the galley. Sergeant Hollis smoothed her skirt as she sat down, and crossed one neat leg over the other. Absently she pushed a wisp of auburn hair back from her face. She had grey green eyes, Andrew noticed.

Andrew told her the whole story, from when they had heard of the missing Jack Russell at Braunston, to the *denouement* of Sunday morning. When he had finished, she said,

"So *that's* how they were caught! You boaters are a crafty lot!"

"I wouldn't like British Waterways to find out, in case it makes life difficult for Stu."

"I see, well, he sounds a pretty resourceful chap. If they'd got past Cosgrove, we'd have lost them, and the dogs'd be in France or Germany or even further away by now. By the way, you were quite right about Luton Airport. We found a telephone number on the boat of a dealer who's well known to us, plus a shopping list of dogs and their prices. Roberts did some checking and found that the dealer has been regularly shipping so-called pedigree dogs out through Luton in crates, once a month."

"Have the accused said anything?"

"Nothing much. We can't nail the dealer. They say they've never heard of him. The number was given to the man by someone he met in a pub - you know the old malarkey they come up with. No, my guess is that they'll take what's coming, plead guilty to ill-treatment and take a chance that there won't be enough evidence on the stealing charge. They'll go straight back to dog rustling once the fuss dies down. They certainly won't shop the dealer and spoil the market. We can only do them on cruelty. The woman's got form there; two convictions, one in Essex, the other in Hertfordshire, both for ill-treating dogs. Last time she was banned from keeping dogs for two years, but the time's up now."

"What about the man?"

"Nothing significant. He's a van driver part time. He's got a few motoring convictions, parking on yellow lines, speeding, that's all."

"It certainly looks as if your best bet is cruelty, though surely you can make a theft charge stick."

"Not really. Mrs. Higgins identified her dog, so did the man from Braunston, but we can't identify the other six. Their story is that they found the dogs straying. Unless they come clean and confess, we haven't enough to get a conviction."

Andrew rubbed his chin. "Can they explain why the dogs have no collars, yet their owners presumably fitted them?"

"They just deny that the dogs had them on when they were found."

"A bit of a coincidence!"

"Exactly, but there we are."

"Well, sergeant, you will need some way of making the villains change their minds."

Hollis' eyebrows arched and she gave a lopsided smile,

"I hope you won't mind giving me a statement, with your side of the story, for what it's worth."

"Not at all. Ask me what you like."

Andrew's statement merely confirmed that Mrs. Higgins was looking for her dog on Saturday afternoon, that he had seen the boat tied up on Saturday night, that he had seen it pass Gayton in the early hours of Sunday, and that he had seen the conditions in the boat's hold when the dogs were found. Sergeant Hollis scribbled away on a notepad, then asked Andrew to sign it.

Andrew watched her drive away. He had felt attracted to her, just as he had felt an attraction for Anne. He supposed that it was enforced celibacy that was to blame, for his sex life with Pamela had been normal but unremarkable, until she had begun to compare him with Colin. The comparison was not sexual to start with, it had been about his earning ability and about his success in business. Then it had been about his dress sense, and about his riding and shooting ability. When Colin had gone to that conference at Princeton, he had overheard her talking on the telephone to him at 3 am. That was when he began to suspect that she was having an affair, and the very next day he drew that cheque in a desperate attempt to put things right and to win her back. That was the day, over four years ago now, that the sky began to fall, and since then any sex drive seemed to have left him. His fellow prisoners had made no secret of the fact that they found relief in masturbation, yet although he had no hang-ups on that score, unlike some of his contemporaries from public schools, he had not felt the need or desire for it. His libido seemed to have died with his marriage, such physical relief as nature seemed to require had come in the form of occasional nocturnal emissions, unaccompanied by the benefit of erotic dreams. He had mentioned this to the prison doctor, who told him that the condition was not unusual and was part and parcel of the trauma of being convicted and imprisoned. He had been free now, how long? Nearly three weeks. Well, he was grateful for the company of personable, attractive women. Sally was twenty-three, Emma was twenty-nine, Sergeant Hollis about forty or so, and Anne was in her fifties. At least the apparent lack of sex drive meant that he could be friends with them all, on equal terms. Or could it? What was it that Emma had said on Sunday about Hollis? That she fancied him? Nonsense, how could Emma know this? Womens' intuition? Phooey! There's no such thing, they are just more observant of some things than men. That's why Sergeant Hollis was a detective. She was probably a very good one. He smiled ruefully to himself and turned again to his books. Now then, where were those Penguin paperbacks that he'd bought when he was at Law School? Shelley? Byron? Keats? Ah yes, there they were. He fished them out of the case and blew dust off their spines. They could go with Palgrave and the rest of the poetry section.

Kate Hollis parked her car in the CID section at County Police Headquarters. She made her way through the Information Room to her office. Detective Inspector Marriott looked up from a screen as she passed.

"Ah! Kate. Can we get any further with these dog rustlers?"

"I'm not very confident, Sir. I think we'll have to go for cruelty."

"The RSPCA will do that."

"Yes Sir, I've got a few more ends to tie up though. I should like to nail Burson."

"What, Mr. Big at Milton Keynes?" Well. OK, but don't spend too much time on it. We've got bigger fish to land than him, Dooney for instance."

"Yes Sir." She went into her office. There was a note for her to ring Daventry police station. She picked up the telephone and punched the digits. She was greeted by the engaged tone, so she turned to the screen and keyboard on her desk while she waited. She logged on to records and called up the list of solicitors. She keyed in "Ellison, Andrew." The screen flickered, then spelled out "struck off roll as from 1: 1: 92." She flicked her fingers over the keyboard to reveal more information. She became so engrossed that she quite forgot her call.

That evening Andrew sat watching his television. There was a good film on Channel 4 and an interesting exposé earlier on. He made himself some supper, drew up the fire, washed up, opened a bottle of Fitou and by nine o'clock had settled snugly in a chair with his glass beside him. About twenty minutes into the film, he felt the boat rock. The sensation was followed by a bang on the roof, and a shout "Are y' on?"

He cursed under his breath, then went to the doors. Stu and Emma were standing on the gangplank. Andrew invited them in out of the cold. He offered them a drink, but they both declined.

"I could manage a cuppa, though" said Stu. Andrew looked enquiringly at Emma, who nodded. They both looked the picture of misery, thought Andrew.

He went into the galley, lit the gas, then filled the kettle and put it on. For the first time Stu smiled:

"When you've humped as many gas bottles as me, you'll light the gas after you've put the kettle on."

Andrew looked rueful. "I've still got a lot to learn. So, what brings you here?"

Stu and Emma looked at each other. She said:

"You'd better tell him, it's really your problem."

Stu shifted uneasily, then said, "It's a bit embarrassing mate, but, well, er... it's this." He fished in his pocket and brought out a creased bit of paper that he passed to Andrew. It was a letter from the solicitors in Coventry. Andrew noted absently that it had been folded in four quarters, presumably by Stu, and previously in three. Whoever folded it first was not an old time lawyer or secretary, used to folding foolscap. Andrew still folded A4 paper in foolscap fashion. He read:

"We have received your letter of 11th November, and note the contents. We must inform you that the matters raised are, in our view, quite irrelevant. We must insist on settlement by return of post, failing which our client reserves the right to commence proceedings with no further notice to you."

A slow grin spread over Andrew's face as he read the letter.

"Fee, fi, fo, fum" he said, "or, Promises! Promises!"

The other two looked expectantly at him.

"I told Stu the other day, you are probably dealing with an articled clerk, or fairly lowly minion. Look here, there's the list of partners that all solicitors must put on their writing paper. Now, look at the reference at the top of the letter. JCT, that's the writer's initials, 27, that'll be the file number, and that suggests to me that he or she is either new or doesn't deal with many cases. PWW is the typist, or secretary's initials. I don't see a partner with the initials JCT, and as there are only three partners anyway, it's not a big firm which will have qualified assistant solicitors to handle matters, so most probably your man is an articled clerk, who is learning the job."

"Quite so, Holmes!" said Emma, smiling in spite of herself, "but where do we go from here? Stu's still going to be taken to the cleaners," her smile faded. "Can't you write to them for us. We'll gladly pay you."

She looked imploringly at Andrew, who felt ashamed of himself for being so glib with them. He remembered old George Robinson, his Principal when he had been articled nearly four decades ago: "Always remember, Andrew, your clients may be clients, but they're also people. Legal niceties are fine for lawyers, but people have feelings and worries. Don't assume that people can have *your* lofty detachment." The old boy (Gosh, he would then have been at least forty!) had delivered this gentle rebuke and had cut Andrew down to size; now he was treating his new friends with the same sort of professional arrogance of which George Robinson had warned him. He suddenly thought, I must have been a right shit when I was young, and by God, I'm not much better now.

"I'm sorry, Stu" he said, gently, "but even if I was paid, I couldn't act as your solicitor. It's just not possible."

"Why not?" asked Stu, his honest face showing bafflement. Andrew sighed,

"Because I am no longer a solicitor."

"But you're only retired" put in Emma.

Andrew sighed again. "I've been a bit economical with the truth." He saw both their eyes harden. "I used to be a solicitor. I was convicted of mishandling money and sent to prison. I was struck off the roll for that."

Stu gulped. "I'm sorry mate. I'm really sorry. I just didn't know."

"You had no reason to. I've been trying to put all that behind me." Emma's eyes were brimming with tears "Oh, Andrew. I'm sorry too. I didn't want to pry into your life."

Andrew smiled "Forget it, both of you. You'd both have to know sometime. I was trying to work out how to tell you."

Stu said "So far as I'm concerned mate, I've only knowed you a few days, but you've always played straight. What's your business is your business, ain't it Emma?"

"You've put me all in a spot" she said, smiling in spite of herself, "of course, it's none of my business to know your past, and I agree with Stu. But I'm glad you told us."

"Well, that's settled" said Andrew, "Now, how do we deal with your wife's solicitors? For a start, you need to send off a holding letter to them. They won't be able to do anything for seven days, which gives you time to go and see about Legal Aid. The Citizens Advice Bureau will set you right there. As soon as they learn that you are after Legal Aid, they'll know that they can't bluff any longer. It'll also save your wife money in the long run, because they won't want her to run up too big a bill, since they won't have much chance of squeezing it out of you. They'll probably advise her to settle quickly. So, let's have a piece of paper. Thank you Emma. Right. Let me see...." He took a pen and scribbled away. When he'd finished he read the draft through, scratched out a couple of words and wrote in others. Then he read it through, moving his lips slightly as he read.

"That'll do for the present. Look. I'm more than happy to help you and give you advice. You two have more than earned it too. So there's no need to feel beholden. If anyone should, it's me. If you'd rather not have any more dealings with an ex-convict though, I shall quite understand. Really I shall" he added, seeing Emma's face.

"I can speak for both of us" she said, "we both take people as we find them, and until you prove otherwise, what you've told us makes no difference."

"That's right, mate" said Stu. "It don't make no difference to the number of locks twixt Cowley and Cowroast what you done." He smiled and put out his hand. "My word on it."

Andrew took and shook it. He felt a sudden sense of warmth for these new friends, such as he had not known since his army days.

After they had gone, Andrew poured himself another glass of Fitou and sat in front of the cabin fire. He'd missed the beginning of the film, and could not get into it, so he switched the television off. Now he had revealed his secret to three new friends, Anne, Stu and Emma. None of them showed the revulsion that he thought they would. But what about Sergeant Hollis? He shook his head. She was bound to find out sooner or later, why he even had to report to one of her colleagues for parole, but so what? Why did he care what she thought? Such thoughts continued to trouble him long after he had gone to bed.

Although *Romford* was fitted with a washing machine, Andrew had not so far used it. The normal electricity supply was 24 volts DC from batteries charged by the engine, but there was an alternative 240 volt AC circuit, which could be plugged into a land based socket via a long extension cable, or else run from a portable generator. Andrew had discovered an outlet socket in one of Anne's barns and she had agreed to let him use it, which saved the noise and inconvenience of running the generator when the boat was tied up. He now had over a week's supply of unwashed shirts, underwear, handkerchiefs and tea towels, so next morning, after washing up the breakfast things, he filled the machine and plugged in. While it gurgled and bubbled he rigged up a line fore and aft along the cabin top, then set about mopping down the outside of the boat, getting rid of splash and boot marks with cleaning liquid. The task was absorbing. He started at the front of the boat, coiling lines and tidying generally as he advanced. A thin sun broke through after an hour. He found himself humming and singing odd snatches in the morning light as the cleaning water glistened on the cabin sides. He was nearing the stern; having cleaned both sets of engine room doors, and was contemplating polishing the brasswork, when he heard the scrunch of car wheels behind the barn. At that moment he heard the washing machine give its final whirring. He was about to go into the cabin to switch it off, when he heard Kate Hollis's voice,

"Well, what a domestic scene!"

Kate, wearing a wax jacket over tweed skirt and boots, was standing on the bank, smiling down at him.

Andrew stuck his head round the door "Come aboard. I can't stop, I've got to check the washing machine." He ran to the kitchen, where the machine was bucking and heaving in the last throes of its cycle. The whirring died down as he got there, leaving the machine subsiding gently.

"It'll switch itself off won't it?" came Kate's voice from the door.

"I dare say, but I've never used it before. Stu told me to watch it in case it got stuck on its cycle. Make yourself at home, I want to get things pegged out while there's some sun."

He filled a plastic basket from the machine and clambered out on to the gunwale. Placing the basket on the roof, he arranged his washing from fore to stern and thrust a short shaft under the line so that it would catch the breeze. Kate watched him quizzically, standing on the foredeck gunwale, resting her chin on her arms on the cabin top.

"You've done that before" she said, as he smartly shook out a pair of underpants before pegging them. Andrew laughed,

"A sign of a good upbringing" he said, "school, army, university, bachelor flats, prison. Yes, I'm used to looking after myself."

Kate stood aside as he climbed back inboard. He really was a most attractive looking man, she thought. A full head of hair, albeit grey, a trim figure, alert eyes and an easy charm which younger men no longer seemed to have. Still, business was business. She said,

"I know you can look after yourself. I can read computer data."

Andrew grimaced "Truth will out, I suppose."

"Look," said Sergeant Hollis, "I'm not on duty today. Would you like to tell me about it?"

"You seem to know all about it."

"Only the official record. Not your side of it."

"I'll put the kettle on" said Andrew.

She let him talk for nearly an hour, merely interjecting the odd, brief, question. He once again felt an odd sense of relief as he told her, just as he had Anne, the whole unvarnished story. When he had done, she was silent for a while, then said:

"You know I'm in a position to check virtually every word."

"Of course I do, but somehow I think you believe me."

She smiled for the first time since he had begun his story. "Oh yes, I believe you all right. You see, I don't need to know much of what you've said, and you know it. I saw you were a top flight City solicitor before your trouble, and I also know that you don't get there by being stupid. I don't believe you deliberately set out to defraud. What percentage was there for you in that? No. I think you may have been persuaded to do something foolish, which because you were a solicitor, was criminal. I don't see you in the same league as most of my customers."

"If that's the case, would your conscience allow you to have dinner with a convict on parole?"

She was silent for a moment, then said:

"All right, but we'll go halves. I know a nice little place. I'm sure you'll like it. I'll pick you up here if you like. Eight o'clock, OK?"

Kate's chosen rendezvous was a discreet restaurant in a nearby village. The place had once been a pub and had been slightly, but not very artfully, altered to cope with its changed role. The Italian proprietor evidently knew Kate, and they were ushered to what had once been the snug. The Victorian wainscoting was still in place, painted sombre black, but the table was quite large, its napery crisp and spotless, the chairs were comfortable, and the wine glasses of a good size. Andrew glanced at the menu. It was the first time in over three years that he had entered a restaurant other than one attached to a pub, the last time he had been in Langans. The food on offer was not exactly *haute cuisine*, but very well worth eating. He chose a minestrone soup, followed by a lasagne; Kate chose Parma ham followed by a cutlet of lamb. They washed it down with the house wines, which Andrew found most palatable. Over the meal Andrew gently led her to talk about herself. Her father had been a doctor, with a rural practice on the Northamptonshire side of Banbury. She had worshipped him, but he had died suddenly when she was thirteen. Her mother had sent her away to a strict Anglican convent school soon after. She left when she was 18, and to her mother's dismay, instead of going to university, joined the police as a cadet soon after. At 20 she had married a fellow constable, again much to her mother's disgust.

Her mother remarried in her mid-forties and Kate saw little of her. She was an only child, her step-father was a company director, who was affable but never close to her. Mark, her husband, and her led a somewhat chaotic life, complicated by the police shift system. They had no children, and had drifted apart after five years. They had divorced amicably. He had since remarried, to a teacher and was now a uniformed inspector. They met regularly for professional reasons and had remained on good terms. She had found an aptitude for detective work and so transferred to CID; she had been a sergeant for six years now, and had all the qualifications to be an inspector, but promotion in small County forces was slow.

Andrew asked if she had ever thought about the Metropolitan Police,

"Oh yes. I've often thought of the Met, but I'd rather be in a small pool. You see, I was born in the County and my roots go deep. I love my job, but I also love the area. I was seconded to the Met for six months once, when the miners' strike was on. It was interesting and lively work, but I'm still a country mouse. I know virtually every farmer, poacher, gamekeeper, shepherd, canal man, railway linesman, road worker, electricity overhead gang and pub landlord in the south of the County, plus quite a few in the surrounding counties. They all know me, most of the older ones knew Dad, and they trust me. When anything's seriously amiss I can find things out that the Met would never know in twenty years. You see, most of the villages are still self-policing; the real problems are in the towns and the big estates on the edges of them. There are a few skid rows in some of the bigger villages too, but the edge of town estates are the worst. They're like transit camps, where most people have no roots, often no work and no hope. There are bad lads and social problems in the villages, don't get me wrong, but everyone knows the local baddies and they're quickly fingered. In the bigger communities they fade into the background and get away with it. In the country there are always eyes. Somebody's around feeding pheasants, lambing, hedging, looking after stock, up poles, all hours of the day or night. If you use the countryside right, you have an enormous ready-made information network. You get a keen town copper in, who starts leaning on people because their tax disc's out of date, or because the pub's a bit late closing, and that network dries up."

"But you have to admit that people must obey the law, even if it doesn't suit them. Cars must be taxed, pubs must keep hours."

"Sure, but you don't have to be heavy handed. A country copper will say 'by the way Fred, I'm round again next Friday, best get that car taxed by then', and if Fred hasn't taken the hint, he gets done."

Andrew sipped his wine and looked at her over his glasses. She had thin lips and high, arched eyebrows. She had put on a dark, high-necked blouse under a mid-calf dress. She looked more like the head mistress of a successful primary school than a detective. He said, "May I ask you a very impertinent question?"

"Go ahead."

"How old are you?"

She smiled. "I know how old you are, so I suppose it's only fair. Thirty nine in March."

"You are wise beyond your years. When I was forty or so, I thought I knew it all, but I would never have seen your job like that. I'm sorry. I must sound very patronising, but I don't mean to be. I've learned a lot this last fortnight."

"Not at all patronising. It's good to have someone to bounce ideas off."

Andrew sighed. He patted her hand across the table.

"Me too." She took his hand and held it for an instant. Andrew suddenly felt a desire for this bright, intelligent woman; such as he had not known for years. Gosh, he thought, when she was born he was in Cyprus! Yet she had a maturity of judgment allied with a sort of natural laid-backness, which negated any such age difference.

After a sweet and coffee with, for Andrew, a Drambuie and, for Kate, a cigarette, Andrew signalled for the bill.

"No you don't!" Kate exclaimed, "The agreement was, halves."

In the car park, Kate said "I've drunk enough of your coffee, let me make you one at home."
Andrew raised his eyebrows.
"Far away is it?"
"No, only the next village."
"Why not then?"

Kate's home was a modern brick house in a back lane off the High Street of the next village, but the garden, though small, gave it a cottagey air. In the glare of the security light, which her car triggered, Andrew noticed a winding path from the street to the front door, low stone borders and a small lawn. The house crouched under the lee of an old stone barn.

Inside, the house was tastefully modern, veering, Andrew noted, towards but not becoming, rustic kitsch. True there were Laura Ashley type curtains and furnishings, but there were some fine coloured prints on the walls with, he noted with a start, what appeared to be an original Vernon Ward painting, of the sort that Pamela had always coveted. There was an open fireplace with an electric fire in front of it, and along one wall, well filled bookshelves. While Kate bustled about in the kitchen, he glanced along the shelves. There was Archbold's *Criminal Pleading*, Stone's *Justices' Manual* and bound copies of case reports, but there were also books about wild life, art, religion, numerous Penguin Classics and similar paperbacks. Andrew noted Homer, Cicero, the *Anglo Saxon Chronicle*, Chaucer, Shakespeare and Jane Austen, neatly arranged in chronological order, among Kate's chosen companions. He was looking at the labels on her CD collection when she came in with the cups and coffee.
"Do you read much?" he asked.
"Not as much as I would like, but I still get through a fair bit. I think that something to do with books may have made me split

up with Mark. He was only interested in facts. Typical copper really."

Later Kate dropped Andrew at the farmyard. Before getting out he took her hand.

"Thanks for a lovely evening, Kate, I've really enjoyed it. Perhaps we could do it again soon."

"Why not? I don't think there's a law against criminals kissing police."

He leaned across and kissed her on the cheek, then, almost as an afterthought, kissed her fully on the lips, putting his arm round her as he did so. Her arm went round his neck and pulled him to her, and for a full two minutes they kissed passionately. He felt himself grow erect as she pressed to him, it was the first time he had consciously felt such a thing happen for years. She breathed heavily, and then broke away. As she did so, Andrew felt himself climax. They both got their breath back.

"I'm sorry," said Andrew, "it just happened."

"Nothing to be sorry for. The end of a perfect day. I'd best be going though, I'm on duty early tomorrow."

Andrew delicately adjusted his dress as he climbed out of the car. The front of his underpants felt wet, he smiled to himself. Just like a teenager again! It must be forty years since that had happened to him.

"Keep in touch", said Kate, settling back in her seat. Andrew leaned in once more and gave her a chaste peck on the cheek.

"I'll keep in touch" he said. He watched her drive away before crossing the yard. He noticed Anne's curtains twitch as he did so, and felt a pang of guilt. There was nothing between them, but perhaps it was somewhat cheeky to meet another woman on her property. In spite of that, he felt a sense of elation as he climbed aboard his boat. For the first time since his trial he had felt real, physical desire for a woman, even though she was so much younger - or perhaps because of it. He also liked her. This could be dangerous, he thought.

After he had undressed and washed, he lay on his bunk trying to read. Sleep, deep and satisfying, came to him almost immediately. He had enough consciousness to switch off his bedside lamp to save his batteries, before blackness enveloped him.

Before Kate Hollis reached the main road she pulled out a mobile telephone and punched in a number. Almost immediately it was answered.

She said "Bait taken."

There was a brief acknowledgment before the telephone went dead.

Although over the next few days Andrew thought constantly about Kate, the two did not meet. She was working until late, and Andrew did not wish to upset Anne by inviting her to the boat. Nonetheless he found himself fantasising conversations and situations that involved her. In his more lucid moments he recognised these as symptoms of infatuation, but even so looked eagerly forward to their next meeting.

With Anne he remained on friendly terms, although she was somewhat more distant than she had been. She still produced the odd cup of tea or coffee, but he was not invited indoors to the extent that he had been.

Winter was perceptibly replacing autumn. Two nights after Andrew's dinner with Kate there was a thin film of ice on the surface of the canal. December came in with gales and pouring rain, for several days the rain thrummed on the cabin top and the boat lurched at its moorings as the wind tore at the sides. The canvas over the fore deck had to be permanently buttoned down and still ballooned outwards and attempted to break loose. Andrew was obliged to come and go via the stern cabin and engine room, only opening the front doors to get at fuel and other supplies in the fore lockers. Only one day in the first week offered respite from the elements. On the advice of Stu, given by telephone, Andrew took the boat the short distance to the nearest sanitary station in order to pump out the cess tank. He managed this on his own, and on the return voyage succeeded in stopping for a lunchtime drink and sandwich at a convenient waterside pub.

Consequently it had gone three o'clock before he got back to the farm. He had arranged a midships line, which rested on the cabin top in a position here he could slip ashore holding it. This was also on Stu's advice, and very useful it was too. It saved dashing forward along the catwalk or over the cabin top when he came in to the side. Like everything Stu had shown him, it was neat, tidy and eminently commonsensical.

As he came through the bridge in the last of the daylight, Andrew saw Anne standing on the copings of the old wharf. She waved to him as he caught sight of her. He brought the boat as near to the side as he could, left the engine in neutral and jumped ashore with the midships line. He caught the line round a convenient stump to check the way of the boat.

Anne said "You're getting quite expert."

"There's still a lot to learn."

"If you've got a minute, do you think you could pop up to the house for a cup of tea?"

"Of course, I'd love to. Give me ten minutes to tie up and get things straight."

Anne had made tea and cut slices of home-made cake. She set these out on plates on the kitchen table. The low beamed room, with the dried flowers hanging from the beams, the fitted oak units, the hanging plates on the walls, the lovingly polished copper and brass, the large, green Aga simmering gently, epitomised an English country kitchen to Andrew as he came into its brightness from the darkening world outside. He found himself thinking back to those early years at Lipscombe, when he would come in from the City, or from a hard day at Court, to such a kitchen, with his supper set out for him, perhaps a welcoming gin and soda, and a couple of glasses of wine with the meal. Without realising it, he sighed.

"Penny for your thoughts" said Anne. Andrew shook his head.

"No deal, not even for a tenner!" He sat down at the table; Anne sat opposite and poured the tea. "Well," he said, "what's the problem?"

"It's not really my problem, but do you remember Jane, my help, talking about her daughter the other day?"

"Oh yes, her boyfriend and the tip where he lives."

"That's right. Well, she - Jane that is, was in a right state this morning. Her stupid daughter's left and gone to live with the boyfriend in town, instead of taking her mock GCSEs at school."

"If she's over 16, there's not a lot one can do."

"I thought so, and Jane knows this, but if she could be persuaded to come home it might be all right."

"Of course, but who is to do the persuading? Me?"

"No, but you do know how the law works. Is there any way?"

"Not really. Strictly speaking she must still attend school until Easter, but that might be hard to enforce. She doesn't have to live at home."

"Jane is worried sick. She thinks she's throwing her chances away by getting out of school without her exams, and she also thinks she could end up on the game, that part of town is notorious for it, and also she thinks the flat is a death trap."

"Hmm. These are sensible arguments. But are Romeo and Juliet sensible? I suspect that if they are teenagers in love they think nobody else has ever experienced such feelings in the whole story of creation and nothing we old fogeys can do will alter things."

Anne was silent for a moment, then said "Jane helped me through a very bad time after Jim died. I feel I owe it to her to try to help. You see, I er,.. I sort of wondered if you could ask that policewoman to help. I mean, I don't want to pry, but you seem to see her quite often, I er..." She trailed off lamely.

Andrew shifted uneasily. "Look, Anne, there's nothing between us. We've met for a meal, and I like her, but she's not my girlfriend if that's what you mean. I've no influence over her, and she knows my murky past. She found it out from records."

Anne thought, *if she found out all about you, yet still went out for a meal with you, she must be interested in you*, but said nothing.

After a moment Andrew said, "She might be interested in the 'scam' aspect. I could mention it to her and see if she can put pressure on the landlord, but it's a very long shot."

"I'd be really grateful if you could do that; Jane's left me a photocopy of the boyfriend's rental agreement for you to look through."

Andrew smiled to himself; the two women had obviously decided to put him in the frame as a troubleshooter. He took the photocopy that Anne passed over to him and glanced through it. It was not a tenancy but a licence to rent furnished accommodation. The couple had no security of tenure, and could be put on the street any time the landlord wanted. He glanced at the landlord's name, and his eyes widened. There was something here that he was very sure Kate would be interested in.

"Leave it with me" he said.

Later that evening, Andrew rang Kate, she was not in but there was an answerphone so he left a message on it. He decided to take Anne for a drink at the pub where they had gone the first evening that he had stayed at the farm. Apart from a few rudimentary Christmas decorations it looked much the same. As they entered, the landlord rose from a hand of dominoes that he was playing beside the fire with the same two customers as before.

"Evenin' Anne, evenin' Sir." He lifted the bar flap and stood expectantly.

"Good evening Joe" said Anne; she lifted her handbag. "My round, I think. A pint for Andrew and a Cinzano and lemonade for me please."

As the landlord attended to the order, the little ferret-like man, whom Andrew remembered as Sid, said:

"You got yourself a boat, I 'ears."

"Yes, certainly. I'm most grateful for your advice. I went to Braunston as you suggested and ended up buying just what I needed."

"Oh ah! I 'eard you 'ad a bit o' sport the other Sunday mornin' down the locks."

"We sure did."

"'Ad the coppers down there an' all, didn' yer?"

Andrew nodded and Sid chuckled.

"I'll wager a sovereign they wasn't lookin' fer them as emptied the pound. More like them wi' the dugs."

"You're probably right."

"I knows I'm right, me ole doock. I reckon young Stoo Roberts knood a thing or two about them rum customers. 'Ow did the coppers know them dug pinchers was under the main road at that time o' the mornin'? And 'ow was it that young Stoo turns up just as they was bein' nicked? An' if that pound was emptied by someone in the night, 'ow come it didn't flood over at Bottom Lock?" He winked and laid a finger along his nose. "Some boogger knoo what 'e was at, I know."

Andrew supped his beer, "I'm sure I haven't the faintest idea what you mean", and gave Sid a sly wink. There was a roar of laughter from the other men. Sid, grinning, said,

"You'll do, mate. You'll do."

Anne looked at Andrew, who raised his eyebrows in reply.

"I think you're accepted," she said.

Kate found the message on her answerphone at eleven thirty that night, when she came in. Andrew's voice said: "Kate. Andrew. I'd like to have a chat sometime about something that's come up. It's Wednesday evening, 6.25. Cheers."

She rang the number that she'd rung the night she went out with Andrew. After a few words she hung up. Looking thoughtful she thumbed through her organiser file. Tomorrow morning she had an hour or so free.

Chapter 6
Further and Better Particulars

Andrew had arranged for his post to be delivered to Anne's address, from where he could always pick it up. One advantage of his disappearance from electoral rolls, solicitors' lists and telephone directories was that he received no junk mail, but sometimes he felt almost regretful that the computers knew him no longer. The lack of postal rubbish had tended to increase his sense of alienation from his previous life, so it came as a surprise when, on Thursday morning, he heard Anne's voice calling him from the wharf and saw her brandishing two letters. She refused Andrew's offer of a coffee, excusing herself by saying that she had much to do in the house. Andrew looked at the envelopes. One was typewritten and postmarked Guildford, Surrey and bore the name of John Watson's firm on the back. Doubtless a statement from John, the other was hand written, with an indecipherable postmark. He vaguely recognised the writing. He slit the envelope with a vegetable knife. It contained an early Christmas card, with a jocular message on it and a folded piece of paper inside. Andrew unfolded the paper and read:

42, Wilmot Street, Islington, NE1 5th December.

Dear Dad

John Watson told me that you were out on parole and gave me your address. I wish you'd told me, but I suppose I don't deserve to be taken into your confidence. I'm bitterly sorry that I didn't come to see you when you were inside, but I was so angry with you for, as I thought, ruining all our lives. I realise now that I was wrong, and that I was being extremely selfish in taking that attitude. I think we were all influenced by Mother, and she was influenced by Colin. John has since told me that he believes you were set up, and the more I see of Colin, the more I think that John is right.

You see, Dad, he's a real shit. Mother won't hear a word against him, and says we owe everything to him and nothing to you, but I have reason to believe he's two timing her. He is always very pleasant to Simon, Jane and me, but he has made sure that any money that Mother has is under his control. Since he became an MP he has become even more insufferably pompous than he was. There is nothing that I can put my finger on, but I believe that he's up to something fishy.

Still, enough of my moaning. How are you? I can't believe that you are living on a barge. Is it very cold? Are there lots of rats? I'd love to see you some time. All us kids have been worried about you, but out of loyalty to Mother I suppose, we've not been in contact. However it's nearly Christmas and that brings memories of happier times.

So, Dad, all the very best, and I hope you can forgive my absence.

Your loving son,

Joe.

Ps I am still in journalism, working as a book reviewer.

Andrew sighed deeply and felt hot tears prick behind his eyes. He felt ashamed that he had not attempted to meet his children since his release. In fact he had done his best to put them out of his mind, along with Pamela, after they had appeared to have turned their backs on him. He had deliberately refused to be hurt, but now the wound stung. For a few minutes he sat, motionless in his chair, his mind whirling. As it gradually cleared, he felt a faint gratification that at least Joe wanted to be in touch again with him. He also felt a grim satisfaction in the news that Colin Shorland was not so bloody wonderful after all. His bitter feelings for Pamela were shot through with a sudden sympathy. Perhaps he still loved her after all. He shook his head, as if to clear it. No going back. No 'U' turns. No more the past.

He vigorously set about washing up the breakfast things, after which he polished all the internal brass in the boat. Since Stu had left him a considerable collection of this, it took him all morning. He rubbed and polished in the way he had learned in the School CCF, and which had stood him in such good stead, if good stead were possible, with CSM Dunton. He concentrated his entire mental process on the elimination of tarnish and the obtaining of a good shine. When he had done, he made himself a cup of coffee and sat thinking over it for a while. As so often, in the past, when faced with a difficult problem, he found that an hour or so concentrating on some mundane but absorbing task had cleared his brain. He got up, hunted out some writing paper and a pen and then sat by the breakfast bar in thought. Then he began to write, slowly at first, then rapidly and confidently:

NB Romford. Grand Union Canal. 7th December.

My dear Joe,

I was really delighted to get your letter this morning. It was wrong of me not to tell the family of my release, all I can do is to ask you all to think of my state of mind at the time. As you said, you didn't come to see me, so I, wrongly, assumed that the family had unanimously rejected me. You can therefore imagine how happy your letter has made me.

I am sorry to disappoint you, but my living conditions are extremely tolerable. I am living on a boat, not a barge. Although the hull is very old, my friend Stewart, or "Stu" as he's known up and down the canal, tells me it is over 100 years old, the accommodation is very comfortable and warm. I have a solid fuel stove which heats the whole living area at the cost of £2.00 per day, and rats are conspicuously absent!

I am in remarkably good health, physically the late regime was quite healthy. Mentally I am happier and more relaxed now than I have been for years. I have made a good number of friends, and they are people who are friends because they get on with me, not because I can do them a favour, or because I'm richer, or because I've got an attractive wife. Colin is a good example of the latter sort of friend. I'm gratified to know how you feel about him, and I can well understand your protective feelings for your Mother. All I can say is, at this stage, that it is difficult for me to be clear about any of my feelings. I would be a most unnatural parent if I did not feel joy at the prospect of reconciliation with my children, but reconciliation with your Mother is another thing.

Anyway, Joe, I'm really glad to hear from you again, and I hope your affairs prosper. I may well have to come up to town before Christmas and, if it's possible we could meet. I'd really love that.

Thanks for the card and your address. Give my love to Simon and Jane when you see them, and tell them I'd love to hear from them.

Your loving father,

Andrew.

He read the letter through several times, addressed an envelope, folded the letter to fit it, inserted it with a final glance, then sighed and licked the gummed flap. As he sealed it he realised with a start that he had not even opened, let alone looked at, the letter from John Watson.

When Kate Hollis drove into the farmyard ten minutes later, she found Andrew preparing lunch somewhat absently.
"Oh, hello Kate" he called through the kitchen porthole, "come aboard."
Kate stepped over the gunwale and opened the cabin doors.
"I got your message. What's the problem?"
"Oh, right! It's just that I had something else on my mind. Yes. I think that there's a scam going on in town. Anne's help, Jane, has had her daughter clear off to shack up with a lad in a bedsit. She - Jane that is, thinks the flat is a death-trap and that the landlord

is a crook."

"So what? There's lots of places like that. Life's too short to investigate every one. What about the Social Services?"

"She's over 16, but that's by the by. I thought you might be interested in the landlord."

"Why should I be?"

"The landlord's name on the letting agreement is JD Properties Ltd."

Kate frowned "And so..?"

"If you were to search the Companies Register at Bush House, I'll wager any money you like that JD stands for John, AKA Jack, Dooney."

"Ah!" Kate's eyes lit up.

"This photocopy" said Andrew, taking out a piece of paper from a drawer, "gives the Registered Office as somewhere in Wellingborough Road, Northampton. If I am not mistaken, that was where I went the other day to clear up some outstanding business on Anne's behalf. I think the signature is that of a man called Willis. Mr. Willis, I am more than certain, was one of the charmers who called round here the other night to threaten Anne."

Kate's mouth was firmly set, but there was laughter in her eyes as she said "don't tell me, you settled the matter on Anne's behalf."

"Well, er, yes, I did, saved you the job. Nothing illegal, of course."

"Of course. May I see the paper?"

Kate took it and looked at the signature for and on behalf of JD Properties Ltd. It was a squiggle, but had some resemblance to the name Willis.

"That's useful. Thanks Andrew. I think I owe you."

"How about dinner?"

"My place or yours?"

"I'm easy really."

"Then come round to mine. You know where it is now. How about tonight?"

"Fine, when?"

"Oh, I'll be ready for about eight. Do you like watching videos?"

"It depends what."

"I've got some film classics if you like."

"That sounds great to me. Oh, just one thing, a favour if you like. Could you or somebody lean ever so slightly on Jane's daughter, just a little bit, so that she gets to finish her school course?"

"Leave it to me, Andrew. What's the address? And the girl's name? Kelly? OK. It'll give me a good excuse to pop round and see what I can find on the ground."

Andrew parked in the Back Lane by Kate's house. There was a persistent drizzle falling, but it was not cold enough for a coat. He locked the car and, shielding himself with an umbrella, walked up the winding path to the front door. He glanced at his watch, just five past eight. He rang the bell.

Kate opened the door, wearing a plastic apron over her clothes. She smiled, put the umbrella in a stand in the porch and showed Andrew into the sitting room.

She had uncorked two bottles of red wine and poured out a glass for each of them. Andrew proferred two bottles of Fitou, which she placed in the hearth beside a crackling log fire.

"I shan't be two minutes, just bringing some sauce to the boil. Make yourself comfortable."

Andrew sat back in a chintzy armchair, sipping his wine. Medoc, by the taste and not at all bad. A CD was playing softly; he strained his ears to catch it. Mahler, he thought. He preferred Bach.

Kate removed her apron and came to sit down. She was wearing a belted denim dress with a white blouse, which accentuated the full curves of her bust. Her trim ankles were set off by neat, natural court shoes. Andrew felt a rush of attraction as she moved gracefully across the room, a faint scent of *muguets des bois* about her.

"Well, we struck pay dirt this afternoon" she said. "The Registered Office is the same as the Loan Company's office. I went round to the address you gave me for the flat and it sure is a dump. It's an old Victorian terrace divided into about ten apartments; next door one way is a Care in the Community hostel run by an Asian, the other way seems to be a flourishing brothel. I saw two fellows whom I know to be drug dealers and pimps hanging about outside. I've got an old school friend who works for Social Services, so I rang her. She wouldn't say anything over the 'phone, but we met for lunch and she told me that they had suspicions that some of their Giro cheques were not being cashed by the beneficiaries, and that the place was under their own surveillance. I don't wonder that Jane is worried about her daughter. Some of the inmates next door have histories of violence and sexual assault, and nearly every night there's a beating up or worse in the brothel. I had a look in the apartments, including our Kelly's, and they are firetraps. Hardboard partitions, people using paraffin heaters, overloaded electrical circuits. Somebody ought to tell the silly little bitch to get real."

"How do you do that?" asked Andrew. "In my experience, when an adult tries to tell a teenager what to do, they just dig their heels in. The only way to get my youngest son to straighten himself out was to get his friends to lean on him."

Kate laughed. "It's refreshing to hear someone who doesn't talk like a Social Sciences lecturer. 'Peer pressure' is the accepted term."

"Peer, schmeer, it's still the only certain way. I think Jane ought to work on her daughter's friends."

"You're right of course, Andrew. I didn't mean to upset you."

"No upset at all, my dear. I need to come to terms with the world I find myself in."

"Understood. Well, sit down. Supper's ready."

Kate was no mean cook, and her dinner table was as well organised and efficient as everything else she undertook. The starter was a mackerel *paté* with a dry Chardonnay to go with it; then a rack of lamb with *ratatouille* and parsley potatoes, accompanied by a Medoc. As they ate, they talked and exchanged ideas. Andrew felt a meeting of minds as the conversation ranged over so many topics. Several times their eyes met, by the end of the main course their hands touched across the table. By the sweet course, which was a light sorbet with a sweet Chablis, Andrew felt her leg brush his under the table, he responded, feeling himself becoming aroused once more.

They finished the meal and sipped a cup of coffee. Andrew leant back in his chair with a sigh,

"Something I had forgotten existed, Kate. Thank you."

"For what?"

"For a good dinner in company with an attractive woman."

She smiled. "Thank you, but I owe you, you know."

"You owe me?"

I owe you. You've been more than helpful in a big one that I'm working on."

"Not the dogs, surely?"

"No, but you've given me a useful lead, and it could be a winner."

"On Dooney I suppose."

Her eyes flashed and she gave her lopsided smile. "No comment."

"I could give you some more on him."

"Not tonight, Andrew. Pleasure comes before business." She got up and began clearing away the remains of the meal. Andrew rose to help.

"Sit still. It's all going in the dishwasher. Have a drink and relax."

"Thanks, but I'll be over the limit."

"Well then, have a rummage through the video classics then. I don't mind what you put on. I shall be done before the credits are over."

Andrew went to the video cabinet. She certainly had a fine collection of classics. He ranged along the titles. Hollywood greats, French Classics, pre-war and wartime British, Ealing Studios, Boulting Brothers. After some thought he selected "Brief Encounter", feeling that there might be a certain aptness in the title. He remembered seeing it twice before. Once, when he was about eight and his mother had taken him to see it in spite of its "A" Certificate. He had liked the railway sequences, but had become bored with the rest. The second time was in a little cinema in Walton Street, Oxford, back in the late 'fifties. What was its name? *The Electra*? No, that was the one next to Elliston and Cavell's. *The Scala*, that was it. The scout on his landing used to call it *The Scayla*, and he'd gone with who..? Damn, he'd forgotten. Up at St. Margaret's and reading History she was, but her name had gone. He remembered the year though, 1959. His first year after National Service. He slotted the cassette into the player and set it to play. He sat back on the settee to watch the credits.

Kate came in just as David Lean's name came up on the screen. "How's that for timing?" she said, sitting beside him. He took her hand. By the time that Trevor Howard had introduced himself to Celia Johnson, their lips had met. His arm went round her waist and he drew her to him. She responded by hooking her arm about his neck and drawing him in turn. Andrew caressed her side as she kissed him with passion, forcing her lips hard against his.

A train shrieked through Carnforth Station as his questing hand undid her dress and began to feel the firm roundness of her breasts under her blouse. She began to breathe deeply and, thus encouraged, he undid more buttons and unhooked her lacy satin bra. Her free hand explored downwards into his trousers. He could feel himself fully aroused and straining now. He wondered for a split second whether he would let himself down by being premature. *Ejaculatio praecox* came dinning into his head, a phrase he had once heard used by a doctor who was an expert witness in a rape case, but the thought was swiftly forgotten as her fingers undid the waistband and unzipped him.

Cups of tea rested under steam from the tea urn in the refreshment room as he shifted his hand from her waist to her thighs, which were encased in sheer material. By Gad, he thought, she was wearing stockings too, not tights. That should make things easier! His hand slid on to naked flesh. Kate's fingers were working into the top of his underpants and she groaned with pleasure as she slid her fingers along him. Andrew's hand moved upwards to stroke her silk knickers. She moaned again, and Andrew panted, "Oh, Kate! Kate!" as they plunged into an even more passionate kiss.

"Give it to me" she whispered, "give it to me hard."

"I didn't come prepared" muttered Andrew, suddenly feeling a pang of guilt.

"It doesn't matter. I'm on the pill, and you've got to be clean."

"What? Er, I've had a shower today."

"No, silly, you're not HIV positive."

He laughed. "Not much chance of that. I don't dig with the other foot either."

It was her turn to laugh. "I've never heard that expression before, at least not in that context." She lay back, unbuttoning the rest of her dress as she did so. Andrew paused for a moment, regarding appreciatively her well-shaped legs and stocking tops spread wide, and her white French knickers, then took her there and then, on the chintzy sofa. She gasped and began to writhe. He thrust and she gasped again. "More! Andrew, darling! More!" He plunged again and again in delirious frenzy.

Her shrieking climax was drowned in a locomotive whistle and thunder of coaches as Andrew simultaneously felt himself explode within her.

Later, they lay, side by side, their clothes still dishevelled, holding hands and gently caressing. Kate smoked a cigarette, which Andrew lit for her. "The three best things in the world" she said, "a drink before and a smoke after."

"Wanton hussy" said Andrew, kissing her.

"You don't have to go" she said. "Stay here and have a drink."

"You're on" he said. He rose, stepped out of his trousers, which were now in a heap on the floor, went to the fireplace and poured out two glasses of wine. Kate looked at his lower body approvingly. He was still remarkably slim and with a trim bottom. His pants, still bulging at the front, displayed a manly figure and curved enticingly over his rump. Although older, he was still desirable. She felt an almost motherly concern for this elderly, bruised, yet still cheerful man, who was old enough to be her father, just, yet had no apparent embarrassment at being half naked in her presence.

Andrew handed her a glass of Medoc and looked admiringly at her. Those slim legs, glistening in their stockings, her jutting breasts still partly inside the lacy satin bra, and her firm torso would be sufficient, he thought, to ruin the contemplation of a Trappist monk, and God knows, the last four years had been monastic enough. Although his testes ached pleasurably with their unaccustomed exercise, he felt a great contentment sweeping through him, as the frustrations and bitterness of the years began to seep away.

"Kate, oh Kate, my dear. The albatross has fallen from my shoulders."

"I'm so glad. Really I am. But you don't know how much I need it. To cap Coleridge with modified Kipling, 'Single women in police stations don't grow into plaster saints'."

She smoothed her rumpled knickers. Andrew was pleased to see that she was not prudish about displaying herself to a lover.

"It was better than I'd ever remembered it" he said.

"Let's go to bed" said Kate, "you can stay the night."

Andrew woke from a deep sleep to see morning light glowing behind bedroom curtains. For a split second he was disorientated, then remembered where he was. Apart from his blue underpants he was naked. Beside him lay Kate Hollis, sleeping soundly under part of a duvet, her auburn hair spread across the pillow. Memories of last night came flooding back, the passionate and urgent lovemaking on the settee and the deliberate, slow, but equally passionate acts that had followed in the bedroom. Time and again he had satisfied Kate, using all the tricks that he remembered, until, long before his normal bedtime, they had collapsed, exhausted, happy, and locked in one another's arms.

For Andrew the experience had been the deepest balm. For so long he had been cut off from physical relationships that he had forgotten the deep satisfaction that came from them. It must have been fifteen years since he had enjoyed such a sensuous experience. He remembered it well. He had had to spend a week in Manchester on a Crown Court case, working with Counsel every night until after nine thirty, then, after the verdict he had returned to his office in the City on Saturday morning to catch up on a week's correspondence. In the evening he had gone home by train to Lipscombe. Pamela had met him at East Grinstead and had been everything a tired but successful man could have wanted from a wife. After dinner, when the children had gone to bed, for they were still very young then, he had taken her with a passion that he was not to know again until last evening. This vigorous and attractive woman had given him back his essential maleness, and he was content.

He drew the curtains and looked out into a clear, frosty December morning. Over a cluster of thatched roofs he could see, framed in the lacy branches of winter trees, the brown stone of a church tower with the gilt figures of its clock face catching the rising sun. Eight twenty three, he noted, turning to his watch which lay on the bedside table to check. As he did so, Kate stirred. Andrew padded downstairs barefoot and made two cups of tea. When he returned, she was still lying under the duvet, but it had slipped from her shoulder, exposing her full, round right breast. Putting the tray down, Andrew gently covered her up. She stirred again and opened her eyes. Andrew bent down and softly kissed her cheek. She smiled lazily, yawned, sat up and stretched.

"Hello, Andrew. What a lovely wakening!" She put her arms round him and they kissed. Suddenly she went rigid, "Jesus! What the Hell's the time? I've got a conference at Daventry at ten."

She leaped out of bed, wearing only the silk French knickers of the night before, and ran to the bathroom.

"Bring my tea in, there's a dear" she called. Andrew took it in to find her seated on the lavatory.

"I'll have it here" she said. Andrew set the mug down on the laundry box beside her and backed out rapidly. There were some aspects of liberated womanhood that he still found hard to cope with.

Andrew, dressed in his shirt and trousers, went back to the kitchen to hunt up some plates. He made toast and coffee while Kate bumped and banged overhead. After a few minutes he heard her coming downstairs. She had showered and tidied her hair, drawing it severely back into a neat bun. She was wearing a formal dark trouser suit over a white jumper. She looked the very model of a decorous professional woman, with no outward trace of last night's sensual voluptuary. Andrew self-consciously ran a hand over a bristly chin.

"Do you want a bath or a shower? There's an electric shaver in the bathroom."

"Thanks all the same, but I'll change when I get home."

She noticed the breakfast things laid and smiled at him, "Oh, great! You really are housetrained. I forgot the alarm."

"I wonder why."

They both laughed. Kate said, "It was wonderful, Andrew, it really was."

"And for me, too."

Kate sipped her coffee, finished a mouthful of toast and marmalade, and then asked "What were you going to tell me about Jack Dooney last night? And why does he mean anything to you?"

He began to tell her about Anne's problem and what he had learned from Joey Caroni; after a few sentences she cut him short. "We're going to have to go through this in detail, but I'll try and catch you later on. Meanwhile I've got to fly, it's nearly nine and I must pop into the office first. Can you let yourself out?"

"Just let me put the rest of my clothes on, and I'm ready to go now."

"OK. Put everything in the dishwasher."

Three minutes later Kate was pulling the front door to behind her. Andrew went to his car and scraped the frost off his windscreen. Kate opened her garage door and drove her car out. Andrew pulled the door shut behind her.

"I'll come to the boat this evening, and we'll go through everything."

"Right. I'm going to leave the farm for the moment, and I'll take the boat to the bottom of Stoke locks. I should be there from about three. My turn to feed you. Say about seven?"

"Fine."

When Andrew drove down the lane to the farm, his mind was still on Kate. He parked, waved to Anne and unlocked the boat. The fire had gone out, for he had not made it up before going out, and the saloon felt chilly. He busied himself lighting the fire and coaxing the gas fired hot water boiler into doing its duty. After ten minutes, the water had warmed nicely and the fire was crackling cheerily in the stove. He went through to the back cabin to light the range, for if he was going to steer the boat today he would need some warmth by his feet. He glanced out of the stern hatch, to be greeted by the sight of two chimneys smoking well. Satisfied, he showered, shaved and changed his clothes. He made and drank a coffee, then went to the farmhouse to collect any post. Anne had gone shopping, but Jane was there, unloading the washing machine.

She nodded to Andrew, "All right then, me old doock?"

"I'm all right," replied Andrew, accustomed now to Northamptonshire social niceties, "and you?"

"I en't so bad. What're y'after? The post?"

"I just called in for it. What's the news of your daughter?"

"Our Kelly?" Jane's cheery face took on a tight-lipped look.

"She's still wi' that Gary up the Barrack Road, in that bloody 'orrible place."

"Oh dear. I'm sorry to hear that."

"She 'ad someone round yesterday. A woman inspector or summat, told 'er it were a fire 'azard an' that. Scared 'er it did, 'cos she were tellin' me on the phone that some o' the dossers what lives there smokes in bed. She said there's a flasher lives next door an' all. Gary says if 'e does it at 'er e'll give 'im a bloody good 'idin'."

Andrew thought, if the daughter were that rebellious, she'd hardly be on the telephone to mum every day, but said nothing beyond "Do any of her friends visit her?"

"I dunno. She's got a best friend in our village, Tracy, but they en't seen much o' one another since she cleared out last wik."

"I'll bet if Tracy were to go and see her, she'd soon come home. You see, I think she's dug herself into a hole from which she can't escape without losing face as far as you're concerned. If her friend thinks she's living in a dump, she'll probably tell her, and that might be just enough to tip the balance. From what you tell me, I don't think she'll take a lot of persuading."

"I 'ope you're right. I'll tell Tracy to tell 'er...."

"No! No!" Andrew interrupted "Don't tell Tracy to say anything. Just give her the address and let Kelly make her own mind up. If she thinks Tracy has been sent by you, she'll most likely dig her heels in."

"Well, if you says so" said Jane doubtfully.

"I'm sure so" said Andrew. "Anyway, would you mind telling Anne that I'm going away with the boat for a few days? I shan't be far away, probably Stoke, if she wants me for anything. I'll leave my car here 'till I get back, perhaps on Monday."

Jane squinted at Andrew. "She en't too 'appy bein' 'ere on 'er own you know."

"I know that, but Sally will be back tonight."

"It en't like 'avin' a man about the place."

Andrew laughed. "Well, it's nice to know I'm wanted, even if it's only as a watchdog."

Jane looked arch. "I know it en't my place to say so, but I think she thinks more o' you than that. But still, you got your own life to lead."

"Quite so, Jane" said Andrew, making for the door, "but don't forget to tell her. I'll give her a call this evening to make sure she's OK."

Romford's engine started at the first touch of the starter button. Andrew slipped the tiller bar in place, untied the fore end and pushed it out, then let go the stern rope as Stu had shown him. Remembering the advice of his mentor, he kept his feet on the bank and leant against the cabin to force the boat gently out into deeper water before engaging gear. When the gap between boat and bank had widened sufficiently, he stepped aboard and stood in the steering position, closing the cabin doors round his lower body. A comforting warm draught of air from the range by his feet rolled up round him as he pushed the gear rod forward. The engine note changed and a lazy bubbling came from under the counter as the propeller began to bite. *Romford* started to move forward.

Although it was now mid-December, it was not particularly cold, but the day was overcast and slightly misty. Compared with when he had first arrived a month ago, the winter had advanced considerably. Then there had still been vestiges of greenery and the rags of autumn colour in the hedges, now the countryside was completely bare. A deep quiet, broken only by the muted throbbing of the engine, the bubbling of the wash and the occasional distant roar of a train, had settled over the countryside. A few birds wheeled in the sky above him, the odd magpie swooped about its nefarious business in the hedge, otherwise he was alone in the wide landscape of a gentle valley, his way being punctuated at intervals by graceful brick bridges.

It had gone half past two, and already signs of evening were showing as he came past the long arched overflow weirs that mark the approach to Stoke Bruerne locks. There were no boats tied on the crumbling brickwork of the old wharf on the right, so he headed in and was soon snugly tied up to mooring rings. Andrew made a cup of tea and stood for some time in the doorway of the back cabin watching the December dusk swallow up the countryside. The little range by his feet glowed cheerfully with the teakettle simmering on its hobplate. He sighed contentedly, it really did seem as if the bitterness and stress of the last five years or more was at last behind him; these last few days both his family and his new friends had reached out to him, and he had rediscovered his sexuality. For so long he had preserved a carapace of nonchalance, but as the darkness set across the valley, counter-pointed by the moving necklace of head and tail lights on the distant main road, he felt that shell was weakening and a new concern for others and for their wellbeing was growing within him. At the very core and centre of this he kept seeing Kate Hollis. He shook his head, striving to regain his mental armour. Whatever happens he must not fall in love. He pulled the slide shut over his head and went through the engine room to the stateroom. He placed the television aerial on the roof, switched the set on, pulled the curtains and drew up the fire. Presently it began to rain, by five thirty it had settled down to a continuous drumming on the cabin top. He bustled about in the galley preparing a meal, alone in a warm, lighted island amid the hissing, driving rods of rain lashing the dark landscape.

Kate arrived soon after seven, dashing across from her car with a coat over her head. Andrew had heard her car pull up on the wharf and had the front canvas cover of the foredeck open for her. She dropped down from the wharf into Andrew's arms. She was carrying a briefcase, which she put down on the deck before putting her arms round his neck, Andrew briefly jerked the canvas cover closed with his free hand, then their lips met.

Breaking free, Kate followed Andrew into the stateroom. He took her coat, noting that she was still dressed as she had been when they had parted that morning. She sat down, shook her head free of raindrops, crossed her legs and took out a cigarette packet, "Do you mind?"

"Not at all," said Andrew, taking a box of matches from the galley. He lit her cigarette and gave her an ashtray. She inhaled deeply, then blew out a cloud of smoke.

"Gosh! That's better. What a day!"

Andrew poured her a glass of wine. She took it and sipped appreciatively.

"I've had three case conferences today, sent two more to the DPP, interviewed two suspects and organised an identity parade. What a thrilling life! While I'm still psyched up, I might as well talk to you about Mrs. Clarke and her run in with Jack Dooney."

"I was going to serve supper, but it'll wait."

"OK. Business before pleasure." She took a lap top computer out of her case, set it up and tapped some keys. "I've already put down some of what you've told me. Let's just see if I've got it straight." She read over her notes aloud, Andrew nodded when she had finished.

"OK so far."

"Good. Now, what was it your friend Caroni had to say about Dooney?"

Andrew searched his mind for details of the conversation with Joey that afternoon in the East End. Before replying he said, "Look Kate. I don't want Joey brought into this. He trusts me, and he's one of my oldest and best friends."

"I'll just log it as 'information received'. No names."

"Good." Andrew told her as much as he could remember, then of his visit to the Finance Company's office and his discovery of Willis' name. Kate chuckled.

"Disgraceful! A professional man stooping to such tricks! Do you think you're a member of the CID or something?"

Andrew grinned ruefully, "I'm not a professional man any longer."

"Sorry Andrew, I didn't think..."

"That's all right. Anyway that's about all that I can tell you."

"It's very useful. You see, I've got a hunch that Dooney is somehow mixed up with a man called Burson..."
Andrew started so violently that he spilled some of his wine.
"Not Roland Burson?" *Et in arcadia ego* he thought again, as black memories came flooding into his mind.
Kate's eyes were impassive. "You know him?" she asked.
"If it's the Roland Burson, aged in his early fifties now I suppose, who runs property companies and has interests in money lending concerns, I most certainly do."

He was silent for a while. Bitterness welled up within him again as he forced himself to confront the past. Burson had been one of Colin Shorland's clients, he recalled grimly. Joey had once warned Andrew about him, but he seemed on the face of things to be above board. Some of his property deals, though, had seemed a little dubious. There had been talk of pay offs to planning officials and councillors, but nothing concrete. Burson had put pressure on Colin for the firm to drop Joey Caroni as a client after he had been sent to prison. This had caused an open rift between the partners even before Andrew had discovered Pamela's infidelity.
"He was associated with my ex-partner, Colin Shorland" Andrew said at last.
Kate nodded. "I know" she said, gently.
"You know?" Andrew almost shouted, "You *know*?"
"It's all on the computer, that he is associated with Shorland, and I know you were in partnership with him, because I've looked you up. I told you so."
"Yes, you did. But it's all something I want to put behind me."
"We think he's got a finger in Dooney's rackets, which probably include the dog stealing scam."
"Well, well. The plot thickens. To think I escaped to the countryside only to find the shadow of the past over everything, including you." He glanced sadly at Kate, who was tapping at her laptop.
"Andrew, it was a complete chance that threw you beside me over

the dog stealing business. Now it turns out I may be on to a bigger thing than I thought. With your help I could perhaps put Burson and a few other like villains away, and perhaps give you something back."

"Like what?"

"Like your good name. You see, from where I'm sitting, it looks very much as if you've been stitched up."

"Me? Stitched up? What are you talking about?" A harshness had crept into Andrew's voice.

"Well," said Kate in the same level tone that she had used all along, "I haven't just been doing normal police work. I've had a fair number of faxes today from my pal in the DPP's office involving the case of Regina versus Ellison."

Andrew grimaced. "So you know everything there is to know about me."

"No I don't" said Kate quietly, "but I know enough to see that the case against you was full of holes, and that you could have cleared yourself, but didn't. Also that some of the evidence may have been manufactured."

"Look, Kate. It's all behind me now. I borrowed money from Trust Funds without proper authorisation, I was caught, I was sentenced, I did time, I was struck off. End of story. New Story. I start again; I recover something from the wreck and set off in a new direction. I meet an attractive woman who makes me feel great. Now don't start trying to mix the plots. There may be a buried can of worms, but I just don't want to reopen it."

Kate sighed. "It's your choice of course. You can help me put Burson away and show up one Colin Shorland for the greasy creep that he is, or you can carry on turning your back. But somehow I don't think the latter course is you."

"I'm sorry to disappoint you my dear, but much as I despise and detest Shorland, I want no revenge. It's against the few principles that I still have."

Kate smiled. "All right, but what can you tell me about Shorland. Just info, not revenge. Where did you first meet him?"

Andrew slowly poured two glasses of Fitou, gave one to Kate who placed it beside her laptop, and took a hefty sip from his as he sat down. While he did this he was collecting his thoughts. This was an old courtroom trick that he'd learned from a venerable barrister that his Principal used to brief back in the fifties. Do something that requires no thought, and do it deliberately. It takes the other person's eyes off you and gives you time to think.

"It must have been '72 or '73," he said eventually. "The Viet Nam war was going on, and there'd been a big demonstration in the West End, with lots of arrests and shouting about police brutality. I had been in Court all morning, and dropped into the Law Society's Hall, in Chancery Lane you know, for lunch with another solicitor. There was a young, newly qualified man in the bar and he was arguing with an older man about the demonstration....."

The older man was a West End solicitor with a practice famed for representing clients who had run up against the accepted public morality of the time. He had defended a Labour MP accused of fraud, and a Conservative MP accused of importuning young men. At the time he had achieved considerable notoriety for defending IRA suspects and attempting to have them released on bail. The older man had said:

"No matter. They have a right to pass and repass over the highway, and they have a right to express opinions aloud, so long as they are not obscene or defamatory."

"But they don't have a right to assault policemen" the younger one had said.

"Nor do policemen have a right to assault them. They may merely use reasonable force to restrain a person committing a criminal act."

"And if such a criminal act means hitting a policeman with a steel scaffold pole used to carry a banner, the police are entitled to respond. Especially so when the end of the pole has been ground off to a point."

The older man had picked up two glasses of beer and was looking towards a vacant seat by a colleague. He said, softly: "When I was your age, exactly the same things were being said about Mosley and the Blackshirt marches. Police brutality on the one hand, organised hooliganism on the other. I dare say lawyers in Berlin and Munich argued about marches and protests before 1933. Just think on this. If the powers that be feel that police brutality is necessary, they will make it so. Good afternoon." He had walked away leaving the younger man talking to no one. Andrew, finding himself beside him, smiled and remarked "Match abandoned?"

The younger man laughed, "Some you win, some you lose. My name's Shorland, Colin Shorland." He held out his hand, Andrew took it, "Andrew Ellison" he said.

Shorland then must have been about thirty or so. He was fair-haired, balding slightly; somewhat round-shouldered and spoke with a clipped, military accent that Andrew suspected was not his original one. Andrew came back to the present. "That was our first meeting. Later I met him professionally, and at official functions. We became quite friendly, especially after I hit the headlines when I defended Joey Caroni in '78."

"Tell me about it" said Kate.

"Well, Joey came to me in March of that year." He laughed. "That's not quite right. He rang me up at home in fact, we were old friends. He was in the nick and I went to see him that night."

"How come you were so friendly?"

"From our army days. We went through basic training and the Cyprus emergency together. I was commissioned, he was a corporal, but we always got on."

Kate thought, *I can believe that. You'd get on with anyone you liked, irrespective of class, background or gender.*

Andrew continued, "Joey was accused of murder, an East End gangland killing, and I took the case on. He'd been set up by two bent detectives, and counsel eventually broke their evidence down. Joey got off and the CID men were later charged with perjury and attempting to pervert the course of justice, and went to prison themselves. Shorland was very interested in the case, and approached me about a partnership. At that time my previous partner wanted to move over to the Bar. He was a Company Law specialist, and now he's a QC. Perhaps I should have tried Company instead of Criminal Law. Much safer!" He took another sip of wine. "We had a good Company practice going, and

Shorland was beginning to get known as a Company lawyer. It seemed a good idea at the time. I would not say he was a friend, but he was certainly an acquaintance that I found reasonably congenial. So he came into partnership with me in the autumn of 1978. He certainly ran the Company Law side of things well, and expanded it."

"What was his background? What did you know about him?"

"Not much, I suppose. One went more on his legal capabilities than his social graces, even in the 'seventies. All I know is that he was a grammar school boy, like myself, I think somewhere in the North. He did his National Service around 1960, one of the last to go through it, and got a commission in the Pay Corps. Went up to Cambridge afterwards and read law, did three years' articles with a firm in the City, and had been qualified about six or seven years when I met him. He'd been something in the Young Conservatives in the 'sixties and was adopted as a Tory candidate in the '74 election. That's about it really. Oh, he didn't get in, but that was probably more to do with politics than personality."

"Did he strike you as someone with money?"

"Oh yes, he was well off when we met. But you know, I don't think he'd always had money. You can often tell with people if they've always been used to it, or if they've come into it later in life. He always said that his father owned a clothing factory which he sold out in the 'fifties. Apparently he lived quite well at Cambridge, and supported himself well while he was in articles. He had a flat in Maida Vale when I met him. He bought himself into the partnership with cash - no bank loans or anything."

"What about his political career?"

"He eventually got in at a by-election. I suspect he gave the right handouts and the party found him a safe seat. I hear he's become quite a backbench guru on financial affairs, but that's been since our association ended. Just another of the things thrown at me was that my indiscretion had caused his career to be blighted!"

"Would you say he was ambitious?"

"Ruthless rather than ambitious. If he wants something he'll get it, like Pamela, my.., my ex-wife. Whatever his ambitions may be, they are well served by his ruthlessness."

"So why don't you think he may have set you up?"

"I didn't say that. I just want to forget."

"Deep down you know, don't you?"

"Know what?"

"That you were fitted up."

"Come on, Kate, we're going round in circles."

"All right then. Tell me about Shorland and your financial problems."

"It must have been in early 1979, after Shorland became my partner, that we bought an old farmhouse in Sussex. It was the aftermath of the Joey Caroni business. The business boomed, there were all sorts of consultancies, articles to be written, I was in demand as a guest speaker all over the place and could name my price, and property prices were depressed; it was what they called 'the Winter of discontent', so, on Shorland's advice we sold our place in Wimbledon to an American who was prepared to pay what we asked, and bought Lipscombe at a bargain price from a tax account farmer who wanted out of the UK. In the summer, when we'd got straight, I invited Shorland down for the weekend. That's when he met Pamela. Soon after she began getting expensive ideas. We weren't too badly off, but she wanted more. It mightn't have been so bad if she'd been working, she was an architect, but once we moved into the country she gave up work. Got ideas of playing the Lady of the Manor, I suppose, so we had to have horses in the stable, a Range Rover and all the other trimmings, right down to the designer green wellies. It wasn't long before I was in dire need of extra capital and Shorland knew how to get it. Remember the inflation of those days? Running at over 20% at one time. Well, I'd been able to pay cash for Lipscombe, no mortgage, so Shorland said to mortgage it for every penny I could, and watch the capital value of the house increase. Everybody did it in those days, so I did as well. Of course, with interest rates sky high it cost a lot, but then in the 'eighties the property boom began and our Conveyancing Department took off with it." Andrew exhaled slowly. "Those were the good years. Property values in London and the South East went through the roof, just as Shorland prophesied, and so did the firm's profits. All the other gurus in the City and Fleet Street said it would keep on going." He gave a short, bitter, laugh. "They never learn. We had had a property boom and bust in 1973 and no end of people burned their fingers, but no, it was buy, buy, buy, and finance it all with the equity. When it all started going pear shaped for me was when the investment folio that I'd largely financed with mortgage capital went ping in the '87 crash. I had two youngsters up at University and another in the Sixth Form, my wife wanted to enlarge the stables to cope with a new riding school that she'd started, and we had a huge bank loan to finance. All of a sudden the investments that supported all this were gone."

"So what did you do?"

"Took what seemed to be the only course and borrowed more. We had massive Trust Funds in our Clients' Account, the trustees were only getting seven per cent when interest rates were over twelve and a half, so Shorland put it to me that if I borrowed enough at ten per cent, secured, from the Trust Funds, we would all be better off. The trustees would get more, and I would pay less. Well, to be brief, that's what I did, only Shorland meanwhile had buggered off to a conference in the US. It was about then that I found that he and Pamela were having an affair."

"So far," said Kate "I can't see that you had done anything criminal."

"If you had done what I did you wouldn't have acted criminally, but the Solicitors Act forbids principals to borrow from their own Trust Funds, even if the trustees do well out of it. When the Law Society's auditors picked it up, Shorland denied all knowledge of it. There was no paperwork connecting him with it, and he had the perfect alibi. He was in Philadelphia when the transfer took place."

"How much was the loan?"

"Half a million."

"Jesus! The interest alone would be fifty thousand a year."

"Quite so, but at the time I could well support it out of earnings. I was clearing more than double that before tax. However the auditors had a severe sense of humour failure over the matter. Shorland managed to get me out of the partnership and to put himself in the clear. He got my wife as well. My share in the deal was three years."

"And you still don't think you were stitched up?"

"It doesn't matter what I think. The record is there. Oh yes, Mr. Justice Cocklecarrot, or whatever his name is, said examples must be made. People in positions of trust who abuse it must pay the price."

"But three years - well, it seems horrendous. I mean, by comparison, some violent criminals get less, and, if you didn't harm anyone and nobody lost by it, it all seems most unjust to me."

Andrew gave a sardonic smile. "Surely you've been in the police long enough to know that justice is a somewhat debased currency? The judge in my case was notorious for his dislike of solicitors. There's very little love lost between the Bar and the Law Society, and I was the one who got in the crossfire."

He got up and opened the glass-fronted door to the stateroom stove. The embers of the fire were still glowing, but the fire was choking itself on ash. Kate watched him silently as he riddled the grate before throwing a few pieces of fuel from the hod on to the fire and closing the door. When he had finished, she said:

"You have got it badly."

"Got what?" He straightened and looked directly at her.

"The downs."

"Meaning?"

"You've got a downer. I suppose I would too if I'd been treated the way you have been. Thank God I've never been used to money. I would be terrified shitless if I had the sort of debts you seem to have had."

"Ah, but it's all relative to income. Remember Mr. Micawber's maxim. As long as what goes out is less than what comes in, you can manage. When times were good we were living high on the hog as the Americans say, the problem is, how do you live through bad times? I thought I'd found the answer, but I was wrong. It's all a matter of luck really, and I just was unlucky in that the Stock Market crash in '87 caught me bending. I was a darn sight more lucky with the property crash in '91 and after. My pal John Watson was looking after things for me by then, and he sold Lipscombe just before it happened. He paid off all the debts and left me with enough over to buy this boat and to live modestly when I came out. If I'd not gone inside when I did, I would have been forced to sell at the wrong time, and would have lost everything. Sometimes fate is less of a bastard than it seems at the time. At least, that's my philosophy." He moved across to the galley. "Dinner'll be ready in five minutes. Nothing very special I'm afraid. Spaghetti Bolognaise."

"I wondered what I could smell cooking. It smells delicious too. May I use your bathroom first?" Kate closed her laptop and put it away in its case.

"Of course, I'll show you."

Andrew had prepared rather more than a simple spaghetti Bolognaise. There was a special piquant cheese sauce to go with it, and another bottle of Fitou, which had been opened before Kate arrived and had been adjusting itself to room temperature while they had been talking. While Kate was elsewhere, he arranged the dining table in the stateroom, laying two places and setting out glasses. When she came back in, he was lighting a candle in a holder to place on the table. She had taken off her suit jacket, the well cut skirt and white jumper emphasised her figure. She had put on a little make up and had arranged her hair. Andrew thought she looked ravishing and gave her an appreciative smile. "Gosh, what a super little bathroom" she said, smiling back. "I thought it would be a bowl of canal water and an Elsan, but there's running hot and cold and a real loo. What happens there? It doesn't empty into the canal surely?"

Andrew laughed. "No, it's got a holding tank, which has to be pumped out."

"Well I never, that's clever. Mind you, I'm not as squeamish about such things as some women. My Dad brought me up to rough it, took me camping and pony trekking from when I could walk, but even so, it's a bit of a relief to find all the amenities aboard. I thought it might be like some of those French country restaurants, where you get beautiful food and a pleasant atmosphere, but the loos are diabolical!"

"Stu has some horrendous tales to tell about such matters, but I think I would prefer to eat first. Some more wine?"

"If I have another, I shall be unfit to drive home."

"And so?

"I'll have another, please."

Chapter 7
Claim and Counterclaim

It was still dark next morning when Kate left. At her suggestion, she drove Andrew back to the farm to pick his car up, and he was back at the boat before dawn. For the next few days he stayed at the mooring below the locks, being unable to journey further northward because the flight was temporarily closed for repairs. He spent the time exploring the area, including visiting the Canal Museum and buying himself books and guides to add to his library. He saw Kate several times, meeting her for lunch twice and visiting her house in the evenings. Although they made passionate love on these occasions, they did not spend a night together again. He called in to the farm every other day to pick up any post and it was during his fourth visit that Anne asked him about Christmas.

"Only a week to go," she said, "I just don't know where the time goes!" And then, as if it were *à propos* of nothing. "What are you doing this year?"

"I really haven't made any plans. Kate tells me she is on duty Christmas Day, and will be going to her mother's on Boxing Day. I thought that I might go up to the top of Stoke locks and spend Christmas there. The locks are reopening tomorrow."

"If you like, you will be very welcome here. My son, Tom, is coming home on leave, Sally's going to be here, and we usually have a full programme when the family's together. You can ask Kate as well" she added, almost as an afterthought.

"That's very kind of you, Anne. And it's very good of you to mention Kate, but we're good friends, not what people these days call 'an item'."

Oh yes, thought Anne, *pull the other one*, but said "Well, if she's at a loose end, we always keep open house at Christmas. There's nobody staying, so guest rooms are free."

"I'll come down with the boat" said Andrew, "you can have too much of a good thing with guests in the house." In spite of himself, he thought back to the Christmas when Colin Shorland had been their guest at Lipscombe, and hurriedly put it out of his mind once more. To change the subject, Andrew asked after Kelly, Jane's daughter.

Anne smiled. "I don't know what your lady friend has been up to there, but apparently young Kelly's friend, Tracy, went to see her last Saturday and she was in floods of tears when she left. She told Tracy that she was scared to death of some of the neighbours, and the upshot was that Jane was watching TV on Sunday night when in walked Kelly. She'd got a taxi home and had left Jane to pay for it! So, she's come home now, Jane has made her promise to swot up all her missing school work in the holidays, and her headmistress has agreed to let her sit her mock exams as soon as they start in January."

"What about the boyfriend?"

"Apparently they had a great row and bust up, and he threw her out. I think he'd probably got someone else lined up, but Jane tells me that he was angry about the police snooping about. If you ask me, he's a wrong 'un and Kelly's well rid of him, but you can't tell her as much. However, I think perhaps she was glad of the excuse to come home, deep down, because Jane says she doesn't seem to be moping at all, which if it had been all genuine on her side, she would have been. I think Jane would like to thank both of you."

"There's nothing to thank either of us for, but it's good to know that some stories have a happy ending."

When he met Kate at her house later that day, he told her the news. "I think she's well out of it" Kate said, "the town Division has been having a look round there. You remember Sergeant Jeffries?"

"Who?"

"The sergeant who took your parole details when you first came."

"Oh, him. He seemed a decent enough chap."

Kate hung his coat up and went into the kitchen to make a pot of tea.

"He is." She called as she lit the gas. She came back into the sitting room and sat down beside Andrew on the settee. "He's an old-school copper, and none the worse for it. Well he's lived in the town all his life, and knows it inside out. I popped in to see him the other day and sounded him out about JD Properties Ltd. and other things. He said that the local beat bobbies have been suspicious of goings on in that area for some time. There's been a number of teenage kids turning up there and taking rooms. They think that the girls get recruited for prostitution and some of the lads become rent boys. It makes it all the more easy to get them involved in drugs. There's another scam too. We think that JD Properties gets its tenants to declare that the flat is furnished, but it isn't in fact. The landlord then claims Housing Benefit payments from the DSS. Jack Jeffries is the Community Officer for the area and keeps in touch with all the schools round about, so he soon hears about playground drug dealing. Recently it's become much more blatant, even in the lower schools, and they have good reason to think that a good deal of it is centred on this particular area. I asked him to keep me informed about things, but not to bust it wide just yet because I thought I might be on to the people behind it. My Chief Superintendent has got his own plans and he'd be a bit peeved if dear old Jack buggered them up through being a bit too keen."

"Ought you to be telling an ex-gaol bird all this?"

"Not really, but you see Andrew, I feel I can talk to you about things like this without it going further, and you do know what I'm talking about too. That makes a difference."

"Kate, darling, I know only too well what you mean, but you mustn't become too dependent on me. Don't get me wrong, we've got a great relationship, but I'm not ready to settle down yet."

She turned her face to his and gazed straight into his eyes. "That goes for me too, Andrew. You know I think we both need each other, but we both need room to manoeuvre."

"What does that mean, exactly?"

"Look, I'll not beat about the bush. We're both adults and neither of us is inexperienced. I don't mind admitting to you that I'm a very sensual person. I need sex regularly, but I'm choosy. I can look after myself if I have to, and if there isn't a man that I am attracted to, that is what I do. I'm not ashamed of it, but I would rather bring myself off than have a relationship with a man who bored or disgusted me. With you sex is great. It's everything I would ever want in a relationship. I also like you very much. I see you as an honest person and a good friend, a confidant even, but I don't ever want to belong to anyone again. I had enough of that when I was married to Mark. Perhaps if we'd have had children it might have been different, but much as I need your company and your loving, I'm a bachelor girl at heart. Are you very hurt?"

Andrew smiled back at her. "I think I know exactly what you mean. Until the other day I thought that sexuality was a thing of the past for me. I still feel that way about a committed relationship, and frankly, I was getting worried about us. If you are happy with things as they are, then I most certainly am. In fact I can hardly believe my good fortune. It's the sort of thing that young men dream of, but rarely attain. I certainly never did in my youth."

She took his hand and placed it on her bust, with his free hand he caressed her thigh, noting that again she was wearing hold-ups. With any luck he thought, she might also be wearing French knickers again.

Two days later Andrew took the boat back to the farm. There was a letter waiting for him with handwriting that he recognised as being Joe's. He took it from Anne, noticing that his hand was trembling slightly as he did so. He tore open the envelope and read:

Islington,
17th December

My Dear Dad,

It was really good to hear from you again. I am sorry that I haven't replied before, but I have been involved with deadlines in the run up to Christmas. I have been in touch with both Simon and Jane in the mean time, and we all want to see you soon. I have given both of them your address and they will be in touch.

If you are up in town in the near future I would very much like to see you. Things that I mentioned before, about CS, seem to be coming to a head. I know that you probably don't care what happens to Mother, and that she deserves all that she gets, but she is our mother after all. I don't really want to put things in writing, or even talk about them over the telephone, but would very much appreciate talking things over with you fairly soon.

Your loving son,

Joe.

Andrew bit his lip. Anne stood by the Aga, a kettle in her hand, looking at him.

"Bad news?"

"No, not really. It's just a bit mystifying. It's my eldest son, and he thinks something odd is going on with my ex-wife and her fancy man, and wants me to know. He won't say anything in writing.... I suppose I trained him well there! But I gather the rest of my children are concerned too. I'll try and get up to see him immediately after Christmas."

"I think you ought to. After all, it is the time for families to get together."

With Anne's help, Andrew had brought his car back to the farm, so next day he drove into Milton Keynes to do some belated Christmas shopping. He had already bought and sent off numerous cards, but he felt that he really ought to spend some time and money on his newfound friends as well as on his neglected family. On Anne's advice he left early, after breakfast, and even so found difficulty in parking outside the huge shopping complex. Once inside, the commercial Christmas *bonhomie* was overwhelming. Giant plastic Santas grinned down at him amid festoons of plastic greenery. Syrupy carols were being piped out of loudspeakers that normally oozed muzak. With every minute that passed, the crowd was becoming denser as cars and buses unloaded their cargoes of determined shoppers. He decided to start at John Lewis's and work his way through to Marks and Spencers. He had written a list of names, and his method was to go round all the relevant shops once, then once he had assessed the goods on offer, to start buying. He bought a piece of Wedgwood pottery for Jane and a pair of earrings for Emma in John Lewis's; a set of sockets and Allen keys for Stu in Halfords; he found a good quality pen for Joe in W.H.Smith's; some crystal jewellery for his daughter Jane and some boxed spices for Jill Watson in a little shop off the main precinct. John Watson was easily catered for, he was an avid reader of historical novels, so Waterstone's came up with the latest Flashman story for him and a travel book for his other son, Simon. That left both Anne and Kate and here he found himself in difficulties. For the first time he realised that Anne meant more to him than just a quick visit to a chain store. He realised that he ought to buy her something more special, for she it was who had really set him straight this Autumn, and as for Kate, well he had already seen something in the lingerie line that he knew she would like, but again, he wanted to give her something more than that.

Frustrated, Andrew staggered out of the shopping centre weighed down by parcels, which he carefully put in the boot of the car, then decided to try and get something to eat away from the noise and crowds. Just by chance he found himself heading towards the old A5, so followed that road into Stony Stratford. Here he found himself more at home. It was much quieter, and with the sort of old fashioned shops that he remembered from his boyhood. He found a parking place in a tree-lined square, and walked into the main street. Old coaching inns thrust signs across the fairway, there was a fascinating mixture of building styles, from late Mediaeval, through Georgian and Victorian to the present day. In a small antique shop he found an early nineteenth century engraving of Northampton Market Square for Anne, and a Georgian pewter fruit bowl for Kate. Happy with his purchases, he had them wrapped in a parcel and decided to treat himself to lunch at a Chinese restaurant that he had heard several people speak well of. The young man in the antique shop held the door open for him, and was giving him directions to the Restaurant, when someone drove by in a large Mercedes. There was a traffic chicane just beyond the shop, which caused the car to slow down. As it did so, Andrew caught sight of the driver, his window being momentarily lowered as he flicked a cigarette butt into the roadway. Andrew was just thinking what an oaf the driver must be to do that rather than use his ashtray, when something about him caused him to look more closely. He was certain he had seen him before, then recognised him as Mark, the shaven headed employee of JD Properties Ltd. There was a passenger in the back of the car, which had smoked glass windows, but there was something about him that Andrew recognised as familiar too. He was bulky, dressed in what looked like a camel hair coat, and was smoking a cigar. As the car moved forward, the passenger leaned forward to speak to the driver, and Andrew caught his profile. Instinctively he stepped back into the shop doorway. The last time he had seen those features had been over four years previously in the office of his partner, Colin Shorland. Unless he was very much mistaken, the passenger was Roland Burson.

"So, let me get this straight," said Kate. "You are certain that you saw Roland Burson in the back of a car driven by someone employed by Jack Dooney?"

"Absolutely" said Andrew.

They were sitting in the bar of an old coaching inn a few miles north along the A5. Andrew had rung Kate from a call box within minutes of sighting Burson, and he had decided to forego his Chinese lunch in favour of a pub one with her, but as she was still nominally on duty, it had to be within her own county. Kate was in a hurry, being half way between two appointments, but had nevertheless set up her laptop and tapped away while they chatted. Christmas cards from the landlord's customers were festooned above them, merging with paper decorations and tinselly wreaths, the bar menu advertised turkey with all the trimmings, but Kate had opted for a lasagne and Andrew for cod and chips. They had found an empty table in a bay window looking out along the road.

"There must be some local reason for Burson to be in Stony Stratford" said Kate, "nobody drives through it any more, it's been bypassed three times."

"How do you mean, three times? Isn't once enough?"

"Not really. When I was little, the main road ran through it and it was really busy, then the M1 opened and took most of the long distance traffic, then there was a local bypass, then the new A5 through Milton Keynes, so nowadays people only go there to shop or work, or else they live there. I suppose there are a few tourists, but I'd hardly put Burson down for one of them."

"Hmm. That's an interesting point. Does he live locally?"

"Our information gives an address in North London, Hornsey, I think, and a place in Jersey. Of course, he doesn't have to tell the police every time he buys or rents somewhere else, only criminals like you have to do that." She grinned at Andrew.

"What do you suspect him of, or is it classified?"

Kate looked round the bar. They were alone in the window seat; nobody else was taking any notice of them whatsoever. She said in a low voice, "It is really, but I don't mind telling you. There's drugs of course, and prostitution, what you may call 'run of the mill' stuff, but there's a whole lot more, including stealing pedigree animals, large scale organised poaching, social security scams, VAT scams, protection rackets, you name it. We know he has friends in high places, and suspect there's corruption. Generally he's bad news, and we know it but can't prove it."

Andrew was silent. He was well aware that the police did not investigate someone unless there was very good reason to, nor did they deal in unfounded rumour. He had always suspected that Burson was a dubious character, but, apart from the business over Joey, had had no reason to connect him with wrongdoing. He sipped his shandy and sat back looking at Kate. On the face of it she was just an attractive younger woman whose company he enjoyed and who made him feel good by her presence. She sat opposite him, wearing what Andrew took to be her normal working dress of jeans and a body warmer jacket over a high-necked jumper. She looked every inch a healthy, red-cheeked country woman, yet he already knew the unsuspected physical depths of her passion, he was certain that there was far more to this person than he had yet discovered. Two things puzzled him about the whole affair, and they were: why were the local police concerned with Burson if he did not live on their patch? and was it just a coincidence that he was connected with him? He put the first question to Kate. She looked hard at him for a second, then replied.

"You really ought to ask my boss, Detective Chief Superintendent Baskerville, and I'm sure he wouldn't tell you."

"In other words, he's been briefed at a very high level."

"Something like that. I can tell you that when we started this investigation a few months ago, we were only interested in Jack Dooney. Since then Burson has come into the frame. I can claim some responsibility for that. Jim Marriott, my DI, was unwilling at first to believe that he had anything to do with Dooney, but, thanks to some of the information you gave me, we've established a connection. I happen to believe that he gives Dooney orders rather than the other way about."

"OK. I'm with you so far, but why are *you* interested? Surely

Burson is the Met's pigeon?"

"On the face of it, yes. But there are reasons that I can only hint at, and even then, not in a pub." She smiled sweetly and rose from her seat, "I must fly, and I must go and powder my nose first."

She walked towards the ladies room leaving Andrew musing. There was obviously something political going on and he was being used, but what was it? He realised with a start just how much he liked Kate, and how he hated to see her being used as well, then pulled himself together. It was no good becoming emotionally involved. Let the affair between them take its course, no doubt they would eventually tire of one another, but don't let emotion come into it.

When Kate drove into County Police Headquarters at Wootton Park she noticed that there was a large, black Daimler saloon in the place marked as being reserved for Chief Constable and that his car was missing. When she went into the CID office there was a buzz of gossip going on. No sooner had she reached her desk than the telephone on it chirped. Inspector Jim Marriott's voice said, "When you've got a minute, Kate, pop into my office."

Two minutes later, Kate knocked at Marriott's door. There was a pause, and then the Inspector opened the door himself, looked swiftly both ways along the passage and invited her in. He indicated a chair, sat down himself and then said, "Well, what did lover boy come up with?"

Kate grimaced at him "You're only jealous. Anyway, he told me that he saw Burson in Stony Stratford this morning, being driven by one of Dooney's men that he recognised. From what he said it was one of the two who were involved in that business at Mrs. Clarke's place about a month or more back."

"Good. Well the latest is that we have a mandarin from the Home Office with us today. He's come to see the Chief Constable and the Chairman of the Police Committee, who are meeting him at a private house, well away from here. Chief Superintendent Baskerville is in his office, and I am to take you there right now. Something big is up, and the place is buzzing with rumours. All I can tell you is that Burson means big trouble."

Detective Chief Superintendent Baskerville was in his late fifties, approaching Andrew's age, Kate thought, but fatter, shorter and balder. He was wearing grey trousers and a double-breasted blazer with brass buttons. He rose when Kate entered, which she ascribed to a residual politeness from the days before the police force was accustomed to dealing with ambitious women officers. "Come in, Jim. Sit down both of you." He closed the door carefully, like Marriott he looked both ways along the corridor before doing so.

"Right, I'll waste no time beating about the bush" he said, "cigarette?" He proferred a packet of Silk Cut, both the others refused. "Just as well," he said, "It's only a matter of time before the Thought Police make even thinking about a fag a sackable offence." The others laughed politely. He took out a pipe, charged it with tobacco, lit up and exhaled.

"Jim," he began, "You've been in this force how long?"

"Fifteen years, and seven years before that with the Thames Valley"

"Yes, and you, Kate?

"Over twenty, starting as a cadet."

"I've done nearly forty, and my father did forty seven years. We are all what could be called old sweats. I know your service records, commendations and all that, and there's nothing that can be thrown at any of us that'll hurt. I'm telling you this because we are likely to be involved in the sort of thing that I hate. I've known a few instances of it before, and unless one is very careful it can bring about the end of one's career and a whole lot of nastiness. Very briefly, the Chief is talking to the Home Office in a secure place. When a Chief Constable is afraid of being bugged you can tell that there is something wrong."

He took a pull at his pipe and blew the smoke down his nostrils.

"I'm not going to say any more in here about the matter. What I've said is common gossip, but I want to warn you both that you are likely to be put on something where you will answer only to me and the Chief, you will be assigned a special office to deal with it, and you will be relieved from normal duties until further notice. To be fair to you both, I'm giving you twenty-four hours to think things over before going any further. I'm not bothered about my career, mine's nearly over, but you two have a long way to go yet, and it could be either good or bad for you. Let me know tomorrow afternoon. I shall be in the clubhouse at the golf course. If it's fine we'll go for a walk."

The two junior officers looked at each other, their eyes met.

"One o'clock then?" said Baskerville. Marriott agreed for the pair of them.

"What's all this about?" asked Kate, when they were back in Marriott's office. " Is the Burson/Dooney case getting too much for him?"

"Walls have ears, Kate, even here. Just leave it that we've been asked to do a special investigation."

Andrew bumped down the lane in his car in the last of the afternoon. As he rounded the barn towards where he usually parked he saw there was a rather ancient and battered Land Rover standing nearby. He lurched to a stand to be greeted by Stu.

"Hullo, Stu, what can I do for you?" he asked.

"Just dropped in to give you summat" Stu replied, rummaging in the back of the Land Rover. "Here you are." He held up a bulky parcel and an envelope. "All the best fer Christmas, my old mate."

"Hang on, I've something for you two as well" said Andrew. He opened his boot and drew out two packages, thinking what a good job it was that he had had them gift wrapped that morning. "The card's on its way, I posted it in Towcester the other day."

"I know, we've had it already."

"How's the divorce matter going?"

Stu smiled broadly. "You was about right, mate, in what you said. Her lot's changed their tune a bit now. I think we're going to get it all settled in the New Year. Good job and all. I didn't want to fall out with Wendy, but it looked as if I was going to until you squared them up for me."

"That's good to hear."

"What's happened about them dog stealers?"

"Tell you the truth, I don't rightly know. I did hear that they had been charged, but I don't think the case'll come up till after the New Year."

"It's a funny thing about their boat" said Stu, "It ain't from round this part of the cut. My mate Jack Turvey reckons she were built a few years back round the Wyrley."

"Where?"

"Round the Wyrley. The Wyrley Cut, the other side of Birnigum."

"Oh, the Wyrley and Essington Canal" said Andrew, more to himself than to Stu.

"That's the one. Some bloke down the North, near Chester had her built, then she were sold last year. Jack says she loaded a few ton of coal or summat at Suttons last week, but he don't know who it were for, or where it were going. He reckons the bloke on her was the same as we caught the other morning, so he ain't been frit off the cut. Jack tries to be sociable like with him, but he don't want to know. Jack says 'Bollocks, let 'im get on with it!'"

Andrew, thinking of some of his City acquaintances to whom this philosophy might have been profitably applied, smiled internally, but managed to keep a straight face. Stu, unaware of the effect of his last utterance, then said that he had to be gone, for he had only dropped in while passing. The two wished each other the compliments of the season, Andrew asked to be remembered to Emma, and Stu jumped in the Land Rover to bounce away up the lane into the dusk.

Monday had officially been the shortest day, but Tuesday seemed even shorter because it was overcast. Kate and Jim Marriott made their way to the golf club house just before one o'clock, to find all the lights ablaze and Chief Superintendent Baskerville sitting in a club chair lit by the glow of fairy lights from a bushy Christmas tree. Kate thought he looked like a shaven Father Christmas and almost expected him to advance on her calling Ho! Ho! Ho! He wasted no time over pleasantries however, and bustled them outside, picking up a windcheater from the cloakroom on the way. "We'll go over by the pond" he said, "I know it seems paranoid, but these days you never know what surveillance devices are being used."

They walked over to where a small fountain trickled and bubbled. Baskerville turned and faced them. "Well?"

"I'm in it with you, boss" said Marriott.

"And me" said Kate.

"Good. I'm glad to hear it, though I would have understood if you'd wanted out. Now, what's it about?"

He glanced behind him, and over their shoulders, before continuing in a low voice, "I can't tell you too much, because I don't know too much myself, but the gist of it is that it is believed there are people high up in the Met who are in Burson's pay, that MPs are also involved, and that it is more than just good dishonest criminal business involved. We have reason to believe that a VAT racket is being used to finance operations of terrorists in this country, and that Dooney is one of their men. There has got to be absolute security, hence the cloak and dagger nature of today's meeting. The whole thing is being coordinated by the East Midlands Regional Crime Squad, to which you are hereby seconded as from now. Our job is to ferret out who and what is involved by uncovering as much of the Burson/Dooney business as we can, but we don't want any gossip getting back to the Met so that people can cover their tracks. I've got roles for both of you, so listen carefully. As the lady on the telly says, 'I will say zis only once'." He began talking rapidly in a low undertone. The other two listened intently.

Kate rang Andrew at the farm later that evening. Anne answered the call and promised to get Andrew to call back. A few minutes later he was talking to her.

"Look, darling, something's come up, and I'm going to be on duty all over Christmas. Yes, I know it's a bore, but that's how my job goes."

"You know Anne's invited you here."

"That's sweet of her, but I just don't know when I shall be free."

"Is it the business we talked about on Monday?"

"Something to do with it. Look, I'll catch you tomorrow. Can I come to the boat?

"Of course, come for supper."

"I'll tell you what, I'll bring a Balti. My treat"

"I'll provide some booze then."

"Not too much, I may have to drive after."

Anne had set a deadline for Wednesday night for all to be ready. The next day was Christmas Eve, and that was when Tom and Sally would both be home. Tom's plane landed at Heathrow at one and Sally was going to pick him up on her way home, so the house was a whirl of activity as the countdown to Christmas ticked away. Jane had hoovered every room in the building, and Anne had then charged in behind her arranging Christmas flowers and decorations, a foray had been made to the cash and carry from which Anne's car had returned deep freighted with bottles of wine, cases of beer and a wide selection of spirits, Andrew had found himself drawn into this activity, at first against his will because it was too reminiscent of days when his own family was with him, and when he was more than just a spectator. He was pleasantly surprised to find himself selecting a suitable Christmas tree from a nearby farmer's plantation, to find himself setting it up in Anne's sitting room, and to be fussing with fairy lights. He also found himself charged with setting up a cask of draught Hook Norton bitter in the still room which led off the farmhouse kitchen. He had not drunk much beer himself for years, not since his rugby playing days in fact, but Anne said that her son Tom as very partial to Hook Norton and so had laid in a supply. He even went so far as to put his own small Christmas tree on the cabin roof and to run a twelve volt circuit of lights from his boat battery. As he arranged holly garlands and Christmas cards he suddenly made the amazing discovery that he was enjoying it. Anne, secretly glad to have a man about the house to look after those technical chores like testing lights and lugging sacks of potatoes and casks of beer which she was quite capable of doing, but detested, found herself happier than she had been for weeks. By Wednesday evening she was as satisfied as she ever would be that the preparations were complete, so she allowed herself the luxury of accepting Andrew's invitation to a glass of wine aboard the boat.

She stepped down onto the foredeck, ducking under the canvas awning that Andrew had been unable to dispense with, and came into the stateroom where Andrew was pouring out two glasses.

"Bordeaux this time, not Fitou" he said, "I've found a case in Tesco's that's really quite worth drinking, and only just over £3 a bottle."

Anne took the glass and subsided onto the settle. "Phew! That's what I need. Why do we do it at Christmas? It's not as if the children were little."

"I suppose it's because deep down we need to do it. Please, Anne, smoke if you like. I've got plenty of ash trays"

"Oh, Andrew, you're an angel." She took a packet of cigarettes and a lighter from the pocket of her stonewashed jeans, selected one, lit it and blew an appreciative cloud of smoke. "At last! I feel I can relax now." She lay back puffing her cigarette with evident enjoyment. Andrew, rather guiltily realised that some of the wrapping paper for his Christmas presents was on the floor in front of her and bent to pick it up.

"Don't bother to tidy up for me" said Anne, "I'm more than happy just to be relaxing."

Andrew looked at her over the top of his glass and grinned. He sat opposite her on the armchair. She really was not a bad looker, he thought, if it hadn't been for Kate, he might even have been tempted to..... But no, that was a foolish thought, and one that he would never have considered until Kate had reawoken the old urges within him. She was a very pleasant person, and a good friend. He had no right to presume such things.

Anne was sitting completely relaxed, as if they were an old husband and wife team instead of two people who had only known one another for less than two months. Suddenly she said "Andrew."

"Yes, Anne."

There was a silence for a moment, then, "Look, I know I've got no right, but...Oh, what the Hell? Do you care very much about Kate?" Andrew's eyes widened somewhat. He fell back on his legal training.

"Now that is a leading question" he said, smoothly.

"Oh, don't be offended. I should never have asked you."

"I'm not offended, just taken by surprise. I wasn't expecting it." His eyes were not giving anything away, Anne noticed. He would make an excellent poker player, she thought.

"Sorry, I should not have asked. It's none of my business."

Suddenly Andrew's face broke into a radiant smile. "If you think it's your business, I'm very flattered. Yes, if you really want to know, I do care very much about her. Yes, we are lovers, and yes, she makes me very happy." He paused a minute to let the words sink in, then went on: "And you must also know that I value your friendship very much, that I think you are a very nice and attractive person, and your friendship also makes me very happy. I think our relationship is somewhat different though, and if you find that is too much to live with, I'll gladly disappear out of your life. You must remember that I met you at a very difficult time for me, and your friendship helped me a great deal. I may be a gaolbird, but I don't renege on things like that."

Anne smiled. "I had no right to ask you that question. No right at all, and you had no need to answer it. You enjoy your happiness with Kate. But I would be very sorry to see you go. You know, you've been just as good a friend to me." She stubbed out her cigarette, drained the glass and rose to go. Andrew rose too, she held out her hand to him, he took it and their eyes met.

"Thanks for everything" she stood on tiptoe and kissed his cheek, "now I must get back, the mince pies will be done." As she ducked under the canvas on the way out she said "I am always here if you need me" and skipped off into the dark leaving Andrew rubbing his chin in a thoughtful manner."

Kate's car drew up in the farmyard, setting off the security light. Andrew had been keeping an ear cocked for it, and had the canvas thrown back ready as she came along the wharf carrying a plastic carrier bag marked *"The Maharajah Balti House"*. She ducked down on to the boat and spread out the food on the breakfast bar. Andrew kissed her proprietarily.

"Good Lord, Kate! We'll never get through all that, surely."

There was a great pile of Peshwari Naan, cartons of prawn, mushroom, beef and chicken biryani, spicy scents rose from it, like fog.

"I could eat a dead horse between two mattresses, let alone my share of the naan" said Kate, "I've been at it all day without a let up." She sat opposite Andrew, her eyes sparkling. "Come on, get stuck in. I've got some news for you."

Andrew brought two plates out of the oven where they had been warming, and placed them by the waiting cutlery on the breakfast bar.

"What's that?"

"More on our Mr. Burson for a start. You see, he does live on our patch after all. He's got a house in Milton Keynes, one of those very swish ones with its own waterside frontage. At least, he doesn't own it, our friends in the rating department tell me it belongs to something called 'Tactile Systems Ltd.' They faxed me a copy of the company notepaper and, lo and behold! At the bottom, the registered office address, somewhere in the City, and 'Chairman and Managing Director, R.H. Burson.' I got the Thames Valley to pop round for a check up, and it's one of those house that have their own basin leading out of the canal."

"I wouldn't know, I've not been down that way yet."

"Ah. Well, my guess is the place has got to be worth about quarter of a million. But don't you see? It would be just the place for those lovelies we picked up the other morning to land the stolen dogs." She saw Andrew's eyebrows uplift in silent query, but went on, "I remember you yourself saying that they might need a depot handy to an airport, well, Luton is only twenty minutes or so away from there down the Motorway."

"As a lawyer, I was paid to deal in facts and proof of facts rather than suppositions. I suppose your theory could be correct, but how could you prove it?"

"As a detective I have to deal in suppositions based on the few facts at my disposal, but I think there is a way to connect Burson with the dog stealers. Doesn't your pal Stu know what's going on along the canal?"

"Well, yes, I suppose he does in a way. He calls it 'the towpath telegraph'." Andrew stopped suddenly, "now that's a funny thing!"

"What is?"

"He was here the day before yesterday, when I got back from lunch with you in fact. He was asking if I knew what had happened about the dog stealing case, and then he mentioned something about that couple."

"What? What did he say?" There was an edge to Kate's tone that Andrew had not heard before. She's a jack through and through flashed momentarily across his mind. He wrinkled his brow and searched his brain cells.

"He said something about them loading the boat recently, since the dog business, at somewhere called Sutton, and that his mate, Jack Turvey, found the man a surly so and so."

"Have you got a map of the canals handy?"

"Yes, sure." Andrew went to his bookcase and spread out Stanford's large folding map of the system on the floor. The two crouched over it, Kate moved so that she was not in her own light. "Sutton. Well there's Sutton in Surrey, that can't be it, hang on, I've got a police gazetteer in the car." She scrambled to her feet and went outside, while Andrew searched all along the midland canals and rivers for a place of that name. Kate was back in seconds, flicking the book open to the letter S.

"Sutton Scotney, that's in Hampshire, miles away. Sutton Bridge, now that's nearer, but it's still sixty or seventy miles away, down on the Wash." Andrew nodded.

"How about Sutton Courtenay, near Oxford?"

"Is it by a canal or river?"

"It's on the Thames."

"Could that be the place?"

"I really don't know. Anyway, Stu never said *what* cargo he was supposed to be loading. It can't have been illegal if everyone on the canal seems to know about it, and come to that, somewhere down in the Thames Valley is a bit far away. I don't know an awful lot yet about how the system works, but I would say that Sutton Courtenay is a bit too far to travel in a short time with a boat. Ah! Look!" He reached behind the bookcase and drew out a small baize board with papers pinned to it. "One of Emma's ideas" he explained, "a sort of waterway traffic control board. This has got a list of all the current winter closures for repairs, look, there's the one at Stoke Bruerne that finished last week. 'Stoppages' Stu calls them. Here we are! Oxford Canal." He scanned down the list "the way I see it, it hasn't been possible to get through since the day after our little fracas at the locks. He could only have gone to the Thames two ways, this way, which has been closed for repairs for three weeks, and I certainly haven't seen or heard of him going past, or down the Oxford Canal. So he can't have been at Sutton Courtenay."

"Then where? And what was he loading? And why? Would Stu

know?"

"We could always ask him, but finding him might be difficult over Christmas. He's got a mobile, but it's not always switched on."

"Try him. Use mine." She held out her mobile telephone to Andrew, who took it and punched in Stu's number. The instrument gave a few buzzes then a mechanical sounding female voice told him that the number was not available.

"Damn!" said Kate; "anyway, I'd like to check that as soon as possible. I suppose he and his mates might be able to tell me the whereabouts of that boat. I'm as sure as I can be without a signed witness statement that it's got some connection with Burson."

"The dogs, I'll grant you, it's a reasonable supposition, but what else? Is he an illegal coal merchant?"

Kate smiled in spite of herself. "Look at this map, Andrew, and think of your history books. Didn't the canals help get the industrial revolution off the ground? Isn't virtually every large industrial conurbation centred on the canals or rivers? Look at it, Liverpool and Manchester, Birmingham and the Black Country, the West Riding, Bristol, London, all of them connected by a highway that the world has forgotten, except for holidaymakers and the likes of you. Tell me, have you ever heard of the police pulling over a barge?"

"Boat, please Kate, Stu gets very shirty..."

"All right, boat if you must, but don't you see? There's a direct route into the heart of nearly every great town or city in Central England. If you wanted to shift quantities of stuff about the countryside secretly, wouldn't that be a way? I'll bet there is hardly a copper in the country could tell you what places this canal goes through, let alone the rest of the system."

Andrew looked at Kate with respect, "I must say, as an ex-criminal, that thought had never occurred to me. But what do you think is being shifted as well as dogs? Drugs?"

"Could be, or it could be even more serious."

"How so?"

"Look, Andrew, I know we have a 'special relationship', like

Britain and the USA, but this really is for your ears only."

He saw that she was suddenly solemn and his tone changed from the semi-amused to the serious. "Don't tell me if you think I'm a security hazard, but solicitors, even ex ones are like Catholic priests, client confidentiality is like the confessional you know."

"I'm not your client."

"I think you've come to me for advice though, or is it complete carnal lust?"

"Now there's a question! Seriously though, we have reason to believe that quantities of Semtex are being moved into city centres by the IRA or a similar lot. Since the Baltic Exchange bomb it's been getting harder than ever for them to move lorries or vans into the centre of cities, but a boat outside the Convention Centre in Birmingham say, or by the Granada studios in Manchester, or even Canary Wharf, would hardly be noticed until it exploded. Special Branch have even uncovered a plan to leave a barge full of explosive outside the Houses of Parliament."

"My God! You're not serious are you?"

"I am. My bosses aren't, because they don't realise how easy it would be, but they do know that Burson is somehow mixed up in it, along with Dooney and, we are almost certain, your friend and respectable Tory MP, Mr. Colin Shorland."

Andrew whistled. "Shorland's a shit, but even he couldn't be involved in something like that."

"I don't happen to think he knows what he is involved in. I think he believes he is merely involved in a bit of money laundering and has his tracks well covered. But, just suppose a big one went off somewhere and he was publicly implicated, in other words, his dabs were found on it, wouldn't there be a big political stink?"

"Well, yes, but how could they find that he was involved?"

"I don't know yet, but Burson and his like are dead clever. You can bet your socks and underpants that he's got some way of linking him to the business without it hurting Burson."

"All right, supposing your thesis is true? Why link Shorland with it?"

"Oh, Andrew, surely you can do better than that. What is the government's majority? Shorland would be forced to resign. There would have to be a by-election, which the Government could well lose, and in the meantime, what are the Ulster Unionists going to say? Can't you hear Ian Paisley and his like banging on about 'Tory complicity in the betrayal of Ulster'? It could well bring down the Government and play right into the hands of the terrorists."

"Why should anyone think that a pompous ass of a solicitor would want to blow up Birmingham or anywhere else? Look I know Shorland. He's a snirp, but he's never given me the slightest inclination that he's a traitor. Not to his country at least."

"And who would have ever believed that of Sir Roger Casement, a respected civil servant? Or of Erskine Childers or Sir Anthony Blunt even. If evidence needs to be manufactured, there are ways of doing it. Every DC knows that."

"And what does Burson get out of it?"

"Who knows, maybe a payoff, maybe a knock for knock arrangement about distributing drugs in Ireland, maybe just kicks, knowing that he was the *eminence gris* who brought it all down."

"I don't believe that I'm hearing this, it's some Christmas joke. You don't mean to say your bosses believe this nonsense!"

Kate looked hard at Andrew, her lips set in a tight line.

"It's not a matter of believing, Andrew, it's a matter of knowing. All right, we don't yet know the motive, perhaps we never shall, but we have very good inside sources. You see, it's connected with something else."

"Something else, for God's sake! What else?"

"Somewhere, in the Met, there's someone who isn't kosher. You know what these big set-ups are like, jealousies, backstabbing, empire building and all the rest. Nobody knows who can be trusted when the chips are down. We have had a big noise down from Whitehall this week, ensconced with the Chief Constable in conditions of great secrecy, and my boss has pulled me out of ordinary duty, along with Jim Marriott, my inspector, to investigate allegations made by other police officers about members of the drug squad. All I can tell you right now is that the trail leads to the top and to outside public figures. There's blackmail, of course, and paedophilia involved, so it could blow into an almighty scandal, unless it is covered up, and then of course it becomes political."

"Did you let yourself into this voluntarily?"

Kate nodded. Andrew took a long sip of his wine. She obviously meant what she said. It was not an elaborate piece of make believe if a Home Office boffin and the Chief Constable were involved; he had come across this sort of thing before, although not on such a large scale as this appeared to be. But there was, at the very back of his mind, some nagging doubt. Something was not quite as it seemed, although Kate appeared to be completely sold on the idea. He was not convinced about Shorland yet either.

"How is Shorland supposed to be involved?"

"What, in the corruption business? It goes a long way back. Before he knew you, in fact, but in those days it was small scale, now it's big. I can't really say any more, but I'm asking you for help, again. We badly want to get them Andrew, rotten coppers make it all smell bad, and you don't owe Shorland any favours."

On Christmas Eve, Andrew woke feeling vaguely depressed. He and Kate had not parted on bad terms, but he had just the notion of a feeling that all was not right with their relationship. They had not made love, apart from kissing one another tenderly, and perhaps that was the problem he thought. Perhaps he was missing his oats now that he had got back into the practice. He badly wanted to see her again and to possess her as he had done, but she was not at all sure when they would be able to meet again. Blast it! Just as one was becoming fully alive again, her job interfered. He was not at all sure whether or not he wanted to know about her present task either. An evil mischance seemed to have brought him to where these unwanted spectres from the past, like Shorland and Burson, rose gibbering from where they had been consigned to haunt his new life. Kate wanted him to plunge back into a past that he wanted to forget. For the first time he began seriously wondering whether his feelings for her were love, or the infatuation of an older man for an attractive younger woman, who had the power to revive his vanished youthfulness. Amid such gloomy thoughts, he made himself breakfast and carried out the normal morning chores of boat dwelling.

He took his presents round to the farmhouse. He had given Kate hers when they had parted the night before, and she had given him a small parcel with strict instructions that it was not to be opened until Christmas morning. Anne took them and put them under the tree, made him sit down in the living room and brought him a coffee. He was tempted to ask her opinion on the matter, and then thought better of it. After all, much of what he had been told was confidential, and it was unfair anyway to burden Anne with his own problems. He turned his attention to her cheerful chatter about the imminent arrival of her family. In spite of himself, he was soon borne along with Anne's enthusiasm and found himself as excited as any child. It was four Christmases since he had experienced what might be regarded as normal. First he had been on remand, on bail certainly, but an outcast from his home, living in digs in South London and desperately trying to salvage something from the wreck. John and Jill Watson had invited him to their place, but he could not face the cheerfulness of it all, and had made his excuses. The next Christmas he had been in Pentonville, waiting for his transfer to an open prison, the less he thought of that the better; and then there had been two years in Ford. That had been grim, but bearable. Now, suddenly, he had been pitch forked into an old fashioned family Christmas among people whom he had not known until six short weeks beforehand, and something of his old love of the season was beginning to return. His mind came, inevitably, round to those Christmasses at Lipscombe, which Pamela liked to call "Dingley Dell Christmasses." In spite of the hokum, there really was something Pickwickian about them, the house guests (Colin Shorland among them, he thought, with a shudder), arriving on Christmas Eve, the buffet supper, the marshalling of the excited children to their beds, the Midnight Mass in the hushed, dark church with the glowing tree in the side aisle, and quiet drinks after by the log fire afterwards; then there would be the noise of excited children on Christmas morning, the long preparations for lunch, the drive to church for Matins and the red-faced vicar sipping his sherry by the fire in Lipscombe's big drawing room when they came home. There was the ritual of the present unwrapping, then lunch with a monster turkey from Leadenhall Market to be carved; the walk in the countryside afterwards, and then the Christmas night games and jollity. He found himself with an almost childlike expectation for what was to come.

Sally's car came bouncing down the lane in the wan sunlight of the winter afternoon. Anne ran to the door as soon as she heard the engine breasting the rise which overlooked the farmhouse. The car shot into the yard and pulled up with a jerk near the door. Anne ran out to the passenger door, which was thrown open. A tall young man with fair hair, wearing a Barbour jacket and a ratting cap bounded out of the car and took her in a bear hug. Sally, wriggling herself from the driving seat called "Steady, Tom. Don't break her!"

Andrew, somewhat sheepishly, came to the back of the car to help with the cases. Sally smiled at him. "Don't be put off, he's quite capable of carrying his own cases."

The tall young man turned round, setting Anne back on her feet. "I'm so sorry, let me do that." He put out his hand, "you must be Andrew, I've heard a lot about you. I'm Tom."

"I guessed as much" said Andrew, "I've been looking forward to meeting you."

Anne said, "Well, now the introductions are over, let's get Christmas under way. Tom, you're in your old bedroom. Oh, thank you Andrew, his cases can go straight up."

"Are you sure?" asked Tom. "Tell you what Sally, old girl, give us a hand with the prezzies."

When Andrew came downstairs from depositing Tom's cases, everyone had gone into the sitting room. Tom was standing with his back to a roaring log fire with a glass of beer in his hand, Sally was sitting on the floor beside him holding a glass of gin and tonic, and Anne was fussing with a tray of snacks. She offered one to Andrew, who declined. "I'll have a beer though, if I may."

"Of course." She was about to dart into the kitchen, but Andrew said "leave it to me. You talk to Tom. I know where it all is." He went to the stillroom and drew himself a pint of Hook Norton bitter. Tom grinned at him on his return.

"I hope you like it. This is the first proper pint I've had for yonks." Andrew sipped his beer. It had a pleasant, malty taste and seemed in excellent condition. He was glad that he had set it up the day before so that it could settle. He glanced at Tom.

"I would have thought you would have had plenty of beer in Germany."

"Oh yes, but it's all lager and the like. Some of it's pretty good, and we get English beers in the mess, but they are all gassed up. This is the first one drawn from the cask, without a generous helping of CO_2 in it."

"Ah, that makes the difference. I'm not a great beer drinker, but this is very tasty."

"The trouble is, it goes down too quickly. My CO calls it 'driving beer', but even so, I wouldn't want too much of it if I was going to drive anywhere." Tom took another sip, then said "And how do you like it here, Andrew. I take it you're not a native?"

Here we go, thought Andrew, the social chitchat's over, now for the cross-examination. He looked across the room at Anne and Sally. They were oblivious to the two men, deep in conversation. He lowered himself into an armchair, Tom sat by him, and the two looked at one another, almost Andrew thought, like two boxers entering the ring. I'd better start, he thought and said "How much has your mother told you about me?"

"Quite a bit, but you tell me what you want to."

Andrew talked for a long time. Tom listened intently, chuckling occasionally at the odd dry comment. Andrew found him a good listener. He would make a good solicitor, he thought, should his army career fail him. He began to tell him the unvarnished circumstances of his conviction and Tom asked him if he really wanted to talk about it.

"Mother told me you were trying to make a new start, but you don't need to go into details."

"I would rather be up front with it. Confession is good for the soul, as I told your mother once."

Tom was silent and heard the older man out. When he had finished he said "You know, I guessed you had something like you've told me in your past, but Mother has never said. She always implied that you were on the receiving end of a divorce, but there were a few things that didn't quite stack up." He smiled. "Thank you for being so frank. I appreciate it very much. Mum's a tough old thing, but I would hate to see her hurt. You know, the world is full of bastards and con artists. Please forgive me if I may have seemed suspicious at first."

Andrew smiled in return. "I would have felt exactly the same if I had been in your shoes. Anyway, that's enough about me. Tell me all about yourself. I was a subaltern once, although only National Service."

"Were you now? What branch?"

"Infantry. Nothing intellectual like the Sappers."

Tom laughed and launched into a long account of his current posting. Andrew felt the years slip away as he rattled on about his Company, the Brigade and the Division and a scandal involving a smuggling scam amongst the officers of an infantry battalion in the same brigade as his troop. "Oh, yes, apparently it's been going on for donkeys' years" said Tom "but some of them got too blatant even for the army to turn a blind eye. The

Redcaps picked up a few last year and a few resigned their commissions. Nobody was Court-martialled, but the frighteners were put on. Apparently quite a few short service people made enough to set themselves up in Civvy Street in the past, and, if you ask me there are too many people in high places who were involved for the matter ever to come out in open court. I think the army has had to bite the bullet and accept a cover up."

"What was it about?"

"Mainly duty free booze, but there were rumours of drugs as well. There's always a certain amount of military hardware going back and forth to the UK. Well, a case full of, we'll say, electronic components, or time expired ammunition, or motor vehicle salvage, can be fairly easily doctored to carry a few dozen cases of wine or beer. If you've got an outlet this side, and a partner who can keep his or her mouth shut, you can have a nice little earner. If it's drugs, then you can be into big time money. Excuse me, yes Sally, I'll have another pint of Hooky please. How about you Andrew?"

Andrew's mind went back to the days when he and John Watson were junior battalion dogsbodies. He told Tom about the time when Corporal Caroni J. had fixed up his unofficial taxi service for them to shoot off into Salisbury to meet a couple of girls one night. The taxi was an Austin Champ that was supposed to be engaged in the transport of their respectably married Commanding Officer to the station, only the two subalterns encountered the very same officer, with a simpering blonde from Tidworth on his arm, in the Red Lion Hotel later that same evening. The tale still made him chuckle after nearly forty years.

After supper, and a pleasant evening chatting, they all decided to go to midnight mass at the nearby village church. The church was cold, with missing glass in the windows. It was the first conscious act of worship that Andrew had undertaken since before his conviction. In prison he had attended chapel, but only bodily. His faith, never very strong, had been deeply shaken by events and his mind could not accept what his eyes and ears told him. His contempt for the clergy and their preaching had been carefully concealed, but he had felt no desire to enter a place of worship since his release. Now, as they stepped up the path through the yews to the old stone church with its glowing windows, he felt more at peace with himself. He did not however take the sacrament, being merely content to hear and join in the old, loved carols and lessons.

Anne knew the rector and several of the congregation; they exchanged greetings as they left, walking under dark, bare hedges to Anne's car. Tom drove home saying that he needed practice in driving on the proper side of the road, and early Christmas morning seemed as good a time as any to get some. They bumped down the lane to the farmhouse in a cheerful mood. Anne was secretly very pleased that Andrew and Tom were getting on so well, Sally was glad to be home and to relax from the pressures of journalism, Tom was pleased that this new stranger in his mother's life seemed to be a pretty decent egg in spite of his fears, and Andrew was still allowing himself to be carried along by the mood of the season.

"Let's all have a drink, and open a present each" Anne suggested as they pulled up in the farmyard. She led the way into the house. The familiar scent of burning logs rolled out to met them. The old clock ticked quietly in the hall, its case reflecting the lights of the Christmas tree. Brightly wrapped presents were stacked high round the tree. Anne took Andrew's hand as they came in and glanced meaningfully upwards. He drew her face towards him and kissed her fully on the lips under the mistletoe, causing her to sigh. He released her and held her at arm's length.
"Why the sigh?"
"Oh, nothing. Just memories that's all."
"What are you two oldies up to out there?" came Sally's voice from the sitting room. "Come on in. I'm dying of thirst and

curiosity about the prezzies."

The two walked into the sitting room to be met with a shout of laughter. "Mummy, you old thing! It's no time at all since you told me off for snogging under the mistletoe!"

Tom was pouring drinks. "Come on, let's have a toast to us all." He passed glasses of whisky to the others. "To us all and absent friends"

"Absent friends!"

The trilling of the telephone broke in on the party with a crashing suddenness.

"Who on earth can that be at this time of night?" muttered Anne, as she slipped out to the extension in the kitchen. The trilling stopped. They heard Anne speaking.

"Yes, this is the right number.... yes, he's here..... No, we hadn't gone to bed. I'll put him on."

She put her head round the door, "Andrew, it's for you. Take it in the hall. Someone called Joey."

Andrew's head spun. Who on earth could want him at this hour? He went to the hall and lifted the receiver.

"Andrew Ellison."

"Andy, boy" said Joey Caroni's voice "Fank gawd I fahnd yer. Listen pal, we're in big trouble 'ere. Some bastard's tried ter kill Fiona."

Chapter 8
Christmas Day

Andrew found a space in the hospital car park, locked the car and strode off across the wet tarmac towards the main entrance. There was a long glassed-in foyer, and through the windows he could see Joey pacing backwards and forwards like a caged lion. A small girl sat solemnly in a chair at one end of the foyer clutching a teddy bear. As Andrew dodged through the automatic sliding doors, he noticed that the wall clock above the reception desk was pointing to 10.27. Inside a loop of tape oozed a mixture of carols and seasonal songs; opposite the reception desk a lit Christmas tree was piled round with packages wrapped in Christmas paper. A bored looking woman was swabbing the floor underneath a banner decked with gold holly leaves and bearing in big, red, snow-capped letters the politically correct legend, "Season's Greetings."

Joey came towards him, arms outstretched. The little girl also got up and trotted over to him
"Andy, pal, good o' yer to come. This is Chloe, our daughter"
He hugged Andrew to him. Andrew noticed that his eyes were red rimmed. Chloe, a serious looking, dark haired seven year old looked up at this tall stranger that her father seemed so fond of. Andrew stooped down and took her hand,
"Hullo Chloe, I'm Andrew, one of your Dad's old friends."
Chloe smiled at him. "Happy Christmas, Mr. Andrew. This is Teddy." Andrew gravely shook hands with the teddy bear. Chloe went on. "Have you had any presents today?"
"No, not yet, Chloe, Father Christmas was still doing his rounds when I left home."
"I've still got to open mine. He's already been to our house, but

I've left them till I've seen Mummy. Teddy's got some presents too." Andrew glanced up at Joey to see tears in his eyes.

He straightened up and turned to Joey, "I came as soon as I could. I was well over the limit when you called. I had to get some sleep and then plenty of black coffee!"

"Yer didn' 'ave ter come, but I ain't 'alf glad ter see yer."

"How is she?"

"I dunno. Pretty rough I reckon, but you knows what they're like in 'ospitals. Won't tell me nuffink, except she's in intensive care. No bastard's bin near me fer an hour. Christ! What a bloody 'ole. Can't even 'ave a bleedin' fag."

Chloe, having inspected Andrew from a distance, and deciding that she liked him, trotted back to her chair and sat cuddling Teddy.

"What happened to her?"

Joey sighed. "She were comin' aht o' my club at Woodford. Jus' crossin' the car park. She'd kep' on abaht checkin' the tills Christmas Eve, an' that's what she done. She 'ad Gary, the manager wiv 'er, walks back towards 'er car wiv 'alf the night's takin's in 'er bag. Some bastard comes up side of 'er in anuvver motor, smacks 'er wiv the driver's door, jumps aht and coshes 'er an' cuts the bag chain wiv bolt croppers afore Gary realises what's goin' on. There's anuvver guy grabs Gary an' belts 'im one, they must 'a nicked the bag and drove orf, but afore they does, one of 'em kicks in Fiona's 'ead while she's laid on the ground." He turned away, clenching and unclenching his fists.

"Why did 'e 'ave ter kick an' cosh 'er? I can lose the money, it wouldn't be the first time, but I can't lose 'er. Why did the bastard kick 'er?" He walked away and gazed out of the window at the empty car park. After a while he turned round to Andrew, his eyes glittering. He spoke softly, with a slight catch in his voice.

"I wants them bastards, Andy. I wants them, an' them as put 'em up to it. If it costs me every penny, I wants to see 'em nicked, an' I don't want some smart arsed brief gettin' 'em orf."

"Joey, you know I'd do what I possibly could for you, but I'm not in any position now to do so. Anyway, why don't you leave it to the police?"

"Leave it aht, Andy. The bloody ole Bill's still just as bent as when they fitted me up last time, an' you knows all abaht that."

Andrew digested this. From what Kate had told him he had strong doubts about whether the police would even bother to pursue the matter. There were apparently only two witnesses, Fiona and Gary, the manager. If the police really were bent and this was some sort of warning from a gang to Joey, or some sort of revenge for something that Joey had done in his murky twilit world of clubs and promotions, then it was doubtful whether they would progress the matter very far before running out of leads. He'd come across it before, and he knew that there was no love lost between some officers of the Metropolitan Police and Joey. He sighed.

"So, what do you want me to do?"

"Look, you ain't got nuffink to lose. Nuffink ter stop yer bein' my agent, is there? You don't 'ave ter be a brief ter be a private dick does yer?"

Andrew looked hard at him. It was true enough what he said, and damn it all, he'd employed enough enquiry agents in the old days to know how they went about things. He was about to reply when he heard a woman's voice:

"Mr. Caroni?"

A blue uniformed staff nurse had come through a pair of double doors leading into the foyer. She was followed by a man in his forties and a somewhat younger woman, both wearing surgical coats. Joey rushed towards them.

"What is it? Is she gonna be all right?"

The man said "Mr. Caroni. My name's James Blackham, I'm the surgeon who has been treating your wife; this is Angela O'Brien, my assistant. Mrs. Caroni is out of danger."

Joey took the surgeon's hand. "Thank Gawd fer that, an' thank you too Mister, an' you too, Miss. Can I see 'er nah?"

Blackham shook his head.

"She's out of danger, but she's not conscious. We've had to remove a clot. Luckily the ambulance people got her to us in time. Another five minutes and we could have lost her."

"Oh, my Gawd. When can I see 'er then?"

"You can't go in now, she's unconscious." The surgeon glanced doubtfully at Andrew. "Perhaps if we could have a word in private, Mr. Caroni?"

Joey drew himself up. "Yer can say anyfink yer likes in front of my mate 'ere. 'E's my best friend. Mr. Andrew Ellison."

Both surgeons shook hands in turn with Andrew. Blackham said "Well in that case, shall we sit down?"

The nurse found four tubular steel chairs and set them out. Joey nodded his gratitude and lowered himself down slowly. The two surgeons sat opposite him.

"You see, Mr. Caroni," began Blackham "we've still got to carry out scans to see whether or not there will be permanent damage to...."

"Damage?" Joey interrupted, leaping to his feet, "damage to what?"

"Look, Mr. Caroni. Please sit down. You must try to let me explain. I don't want to worry you unduly, but the human brain is a very complex piece of equipment, and like all such pieces of equipment it can be easily knocked out of order. Sometimes things can be put right reasonably easily, sometimes it's more complicated. The brain is, fortunately remarkably resilient considering how complex it is, but at this stage we have to assume the worst." He paused, looking keenly at Joey, who stared blankly back.

Angela O'Brien had a slightly husky voice, with a trace of Irish. She said "It's a rotten thing to have to think of, especially at this time of year, but Mr. Blackham and I would not be doing our duty to you or our patient if we were to give you false hopes."

"That's right" said Blackham. Joey put his head in his hands and nodded it dumbly in response to the two surgeons. Blackham put his hand on his shoulder "I promise you, we will do everything in our power. I want to put her under observation now, we'll let you know as soon as it's OK to see her, but that may be some little time yet. Don't give up hope."

The two surgeons went back through the double doors, the nurse asked if she could get the two men anything, but Andrew shook his head. "We'll be all right, thanks." She pattered away. Joey remained sitting, silent and immobile for several minutes. Andrew pulled up his chair beside him. Chloe left her chair and climbed on to her father's knee.

"Where's Mummy?" she asked.

"She's 'ere, but she's very poorly, my darlin'. We may not be able to see 'er just yet."

"I want to see Mummy."

"So do I darlin', but we 'as ter do what the Doctor says." Joey hugged his daughter and then said, "You make sure that that Teddy don't get into no trouble."

The little girl scurried back to the chair where Teddy had been left sitting. After a while Joey said, "Andy, pal. I can't get my 'ead rahnd it. Wot's 'appened ter Fiona? Why won't they give me a straight answer?"

"They're trying to let you down gently, Joey. From what they say, I think that they think she's suffered brain damage. Look Joey, you're an old friend, so I'll not mince words. You know I never have done with you." Joey nodded. "The fact seems to me that they're worried that she may be a cabbage."

"That's wot I fought they was tryin' to tell me. D'you fink there's any 'ope?"

"Joey, I'm an ex-lawyer, not a surgeon. We've just got to hope."

"And pray."

"Yes, pray, Joey."

Although Andrew had always thought that Joey's Catholicism sat lightly upon him, he was not really surprised to hear him suggest prayer. The barrenness of his own religious feeling suddenly struck him. How could he, Andrew Ellison, master of his own fate, pray in such circumstances? Less than twelve hours ago he had been in church, but where was his religion? In all his troubles he had proudly borne his head up, and had carried his griefs and disappointments within himself, without recourse to prayer. In fact he had always looked upon religion as a sort of child's comfort blanket which a grown person could manage without. Yet he could scarcely despise Joey in his present misery for running back to the comforting arms of Mother Church. Perhaps a bit more humility on his own part might not have dug the wells of bitterness so deep as to be beyond the reach of religion. He moved towards the coffee machine that stood near the reception desk.

"Coffee, Joey?"

"Yeah, all right pal," Joey replied absently, still sitting, staring at without seeing a wall notice board filled with fraying paper notices. When Andrew came back with a black coffee for Joey he followed his gaze. Joey appeared to be studying intently an advertisement for a New Year's Eve dance at the local nurses' home.

"Memories, Joey?" he asked.

"What?" Joey started, took his coffee and refocused his eyes.

"Memories. The nurses' home at Aldershot."

For a moment Joey looked blank, then as comprehension dawned he smiled, for the first time since Andrew had met him that day.

"You ole bastard! 'Oo was it wangled the invite?"

"And who was it brought in the surgical spirit?"

In spite of himself, Joey grinned as the memories came back to him. It was during basic training, when they were all squaddies together, Andrew had met a student nurse at a NAAFI dance and had dated her. She in turn had invited Andrew, Joey, John Watson and two other members of their Section to the Nurses' Home Halloween party. This was to be a most decorous affair, in the manner of the times. The comrades had learned beforehand that there was to be no smoking, no alcohol, no close contact between the sexes, finish at 11.00 pm sharp, and all under the eye of the Matron, a severe but not uncomely unmarried lady in her forties. Refreshments were of the sandwich and sausage roll variety, and Matron herself had prepared a non-alcoholic orange punch. It was this that had been the undoing of the occasion, for Joey had done a deal with an East End mate of his who was serving nearby in the RAMC. This involved the swapping of some extra boots and cap comforters that Joey had "acquired" for a pint jar of surgical spirit. This last of course had found its way into the punch. By nine thirty it could be said that the joint was jumping. Several nurses had become somewhat *dishabillé*, Elvis Presley and Bill Haley's Comets had replaced the records with tangos, quicksteps and waltzes, two medical students had been carried out insensible and Matron was giggling and trying to undo a Houseman's shirt. By ten, Matron had gone to bed with a headache, leeringly escorted by the Houseman, and the party developed into what Andrew supposed modern teenagers would have termed "a rave." Fortunately perhaps, for the sake of the nurses' reputations, the perpetrators of the outrage were too drunk themselves to do more than fumble at uniforms and undo a few buttons. Andrew recalled attempting to navigate the party past the Guardroom at the barracks, having attempted to sober up Private Caroni J.G. in the Nurses' Home lavatories. It was fortunate that the fearsome CSM Dunton was absent from the barracks that night, for the progress of the greater part of No.3 Section across the Square was erratic in the extreme.

The two sat silent for a while as the memories played back.
Joey said softly "it's bin a long time ole pal, but I suppose that's why we're still mates."
"That's why" said Andrew. "It's well over forty years ago. We've been through a good deal, and I hope we'll have some more distance to go yet."
"I 'ope so pal, I really 'ope so."

Suddenly the double doors opened again and the two surgeons reappeared. Andrew looked at the clock and realised with a start that he had been with Joey for over two hours. Blackham was smiling this time. Joey sprang towards him.

"Yes, Mr. Caroni, I think she's going to be all right after all. She recovered consciousness and spoke five minutes ago, but I've put her back under sedation."

"Can we see 'er doc?"

"You must remember that she's not properly conscious yet, so no trying to wake her, or to ask questions. Mr. Ellison, will you make sure Mr. Caroni obeys?" The surgeons were both smiling now.

"Yes, of course" said Andrew, "may we go in?"

"The nurse will show you. Follow her", said Blackham. Joey and Chloe trotted behind the staff nurse like two terriers following a dignified retriever. Andrew walked behind talking with Blackham and his assistant in low tones. The older surgeon said "there's a woman police officer waiting to interview her, but I've managed to keep her at bay for the present. It looks as if some sort of criminal assault was involved."

"From what Joey - Mr. Caroni - tells me, that seems very likely."

"Umm. I'm afraid this hospital sees too much of that sort of thing these days. We're almost like a frontline casualty clearing station sometimes."

"You sound as if you're ex-services."

"Yes, that's right. I was with the RAMC for ten years. Just about to leave and take my bowler hat, when the Falklands business blew up. Found myself treating our lads and Argies alike on a hospital ship. Not a great difference between that and this place on a Saturday night if you ask me. Here we are, she's in a ward on her own."

They followed Joey, Chloe and the nurse into a small room at one end of a general ward. Fiona was barely recognisable under bandages and tubes. She lay breathing gently as Joey leaned over her.

"Just describe 'im to me my darling" he was whispering as Andrew came beside him.

"Now then, steady on Joey. You heard what Mr. Blackham said." Joey sighed. He bent over her and whispered, "Just remember, I loves yer. Keep finkin' o' that." He softly kissed her cheeks and brushed away a tear from his own as he rose. "I'll sit wiv 'er if that's all right."

"Of course" said the woman surgeon.

"I don't want 'er to be short of anyfink. She's to 'ave wotever's goin' ter do 'er the most good."

"Would you like me to fix that for you, Joey?" asked Andrew.

"That'd be real good of yer. Oh, and Andrew."

"Yes, Joey."

"I've ruined yer Christmas for yer. I shan't ferget that. But fanks fer comin' when yer did. I don't know 'oo I'd 'a bin able ter call on. If you wants ter clear orf nah I'm wiv 'er, an' she's goin' ter be OK, I understands pal."

"As long as you need me, Joey, I'm at your disposal."

Joey smiled at him. "You're a good 'un Andy boy, but we shall be OK nah. Shan't we Chloe?"

The girl's solemn dark eyes looked at Andrew. She stood quietly beside the bed, still clutching Teddy.

"Well, I'll go and talk to the Almoner, and leave you two in peace, but promise me that you won't disobey Mr. Blackham's orders."

"Course I shan't." He stood up and straightened his back, "very good Mr. Ellison, sah!"

Andrew grinned back. "Carry on Sergeant Caroni."

There was a tall, well built man of about thirty-five and a younger woman waiting outside the Almoner's office when Andrew got there. The man had a collar and tie but his top button was undone and the tie knotted about half an inch below. Andrew recognised the hallmark of the Metropolitan CID. The Almoner nodded in Andrew's direction as he came in, the man walked over to Andrew and said, somewhat condescendingly,

"You a mate of Mr. Caroni's then?"

"Who wants to know?"

The man produced a warrant card. Andrew managed to read the name Detective Sergeant Flower and compare the face with the photograph before it was snatched back. He said politely, "What can I do for you?"

"You can tell me who you are, for a start."

"My name's Andrew Ellison. I'm an old friend of Mr. Caroni's"

"How old a friend?"

"Forty years. We were in the forces together."

"Forces? 'Im? I don't believe it! What was it, the Salvation Army?" Flower's lip curled. Andrew felt his hackles rising and curbed his tongue with difficulty. Steadying his voice he replied, "No, and he got something more than the Police Medal too."

Flower looked sharply at him. "Bloody smart pensioner aren't you?"

"No, I don't draw a pension, but I will admit to being smart."

The woman spoke. "What exactly do you do, Mr. Elliston?"

"Ellison. I'm self employed."

"Self employed what?"

"We haven't been introduced. I don't give such details to strange women."

The woman sighed and produced a warrant card, Andrew scrutinised it, but the woman said,

"Detective Constable James, Metropolitan CID."

"So, now we all know one another. Isn't that cosy."

"You still haven't told me what you do."

"Oh, this and that. I suppose I'm a writer and philosopher."

"You're certainly not a comedian" commented Flower, "where do you live?"

"No fixed abode, really" replied Andrew, "I'm a sort of Bird of Passage."

"Got any ID?" asked DC James. Andrew found his driving licence in his wallet and passed it to her. It still gave his address as Lipscombe House, Sussex. She passed it to Flower, who raised his eyebrows. There was a subtle change in his demeanour when he spoke next: "Would you mind telling me why you are here?" a miniscule pause, "Sir."

"Not at all. Mr. Caroni rang me to tell me of his wife's accident, so I came straight away."

"I see, sir. Are you involved in some sort of professional way with Mr. Caroni?"

"I might be, but I should like to know what business it is of yours whether I am or not."

There was an awkward pause, then Flower said "I'll be quite frank with you. Are you being engaged by Mr. Caroni as an Inquiry Agent? If you are, then I must advise you that we have matters in hand, and will deal with them as appropriate. We do not wish to see Mr. Caroni take matters into his own hands, so far as the law is concerned, know what I mean? Sir?"

"What you are saying, if I get the message right, is that you are putting the frighteners on Mr. Caroni, just in case he decides to take revenge his own way, right?"

"Right."

"Well, let me tell you something. I would give Mr. Caroni exactly the same advice, were he to ask me for it, but I am in no way Mr. Caroni's agent, merely an old friend. Now, if you will excuse me officer, I need to talk to the Almoner."

When he had made the arrangements for the future care of Fiona, Andrew returned to the small ward where she had been placed. Joey and the girl were still sitting there, Joey silently stroking her hand and gazing down at her face. Her head was swathed with dressings and there were tubes taped to her, but her expression seemed peaceful, and she was breathing normally. Andrew told him what arrangements had been made, and Joey promised to be in touch as soon as Fiona regained consciousness. Andrew touched his old friend on the shoulder, kissed Chloe, nodded shortly at the two detectives, who were sitting uncomfortably on chairs in the corridor outside, and made his way to the car. Once inside he sat in the driving seat trying to collect his thoughts. It was obvious that the police suspected that the matter involved some sort of gangland feud, rather than it being a straightforward matter of robbery with violence. So much was patently obvious from the way in which the two detectives had tried to put the frighteners on him. It was obvious too that they did not know who he was, nor of his connection with Joey, but it would only be a matter of time before they started digging. His prison record would then come out and who knew what cans of worms might be dug up, particularly if the police were as rotten with corruption as Joey thought. "Damn!" he said to himself, "Damn! Damn! Damn!" First there was Detective Sergeant ruddy Kate Hollis using her female wiles to entrap him into some sort of sordid business involving Colin Shorland and Roland Burson and who-knew-who else, now there was poor old Joey entreating him to get involved in some sort of gangland feud. In both instances his past had come back to haunt him; his wish to fade into the background and begin a new life, which had started so promisingly with the boat and Stu, was rapidly being denied him, and he could see no way out. In a grim mood he backed out of the car park and set off towards Central London. There was something else he might as well do while he was in town.

He found Wilmot Street without much trouble. It was one of a grid of mid-nineteenth century streets, which had been intended by its developer as a place for clerks and respectable artisans to live. As the Underground and bus networks spread it had gone down in the world, until by the time of the Second World War most of its three storey houses had been subdivided into cheap tenements. The Blitz had made a few gaps in the rows, but then had come the gentrification years when up and coming young things rediscovered the inner suburbs. Now there were neither respectable clerks and artisans nor rootless proletarians living there, but advertising executives, PR experts, fashion designers, along with rising politicians, barristers, accountants, merchant bankers and the like. No.42 differed little from the rest, except that it retained its Victorian panelled front door and large-paned sash windows. There was a parking space a few doors along, Andrew parked, took a package from the boot, carefully locked the car, then walked back and rang the doorbell of No.42. There was a pocket-handkerchief sized front garden, paved with concrete slabs on which an ancient Skoda was parked. A bay window protruded into this and Andrew could see the glow of Christmas tree lights through a gap in the curtains. He looked at his watch. It was only just one o'clock; he hoped they would not be sitting down to lunch just yet. Anne had promised to keep lunch until two thirty, so he had just enough time to do what he needed to do. Footsteps sounded in the passageway, a light appeared in the fanlight over the door, there was a sound of chains being withdrawn and the door opened to reveal a pleasant faced young woman wearing a Mothercare maternity dress. She looked blankly at Andrew and smiled hesitantly.

"Yes?"

"Does Joe Ellison live here?"

"Er, yes, he does."

"Are you nearly ready for your Christmas lunch?"

"No, not yet, who shall I say wants to see him?"

As Andrew was about to reply a male voice called out from the back of the hallway. "What's the problem, Jenny?" A tall, fair young man in his twenties came into the hall. He was wearing a white apron and wiping his hands. As Jenny turned to speak to him he caught sight of Andrew standing in the doorway and stopped, rooted, his mouth agape.

"My God! DAD!"

"Happy Christmas, Joe" said Andrew, taking his hand and shaking it warmly.

"Come in" said Joe, "Jenny, this is my father, Andrew Ellison."

The girl smiled, somewhat doubtfully, at Andrew.

"Pleased to meet you" she said. She had a slight London accent.

Andrew smiled and nodded at her. He was unable to speak for the moment and was conscious of the fact that his mouth was still gaping. Joe waved him inside, he followed him along the hall passage before turning off into a large room running the full depth of the house. It had presumably been made by knocking down the former dividing wall between the front parlour and the back sitting room. A dining table, laid for two stood in the rear part, there were chairs and a sofa in the front part along with the television, video and music centre. Christmas decorations hung from the walls, Andrew noted approvingly that they were floral arrangements in the main, and that someone had mounted the Christmas cards on strips of red and green crepe paper and hung them from the picture rails rather than stringing them across the room like drying washing. At last he found his voice.

"I do like your decorations, they are really good."

"Jenny made them. She's pretty clever at that sort of thing. Sit down, Dad, please."

Andrew took the proferred chair and smiled at his son's girl friend, who beamed back. "I'm a graphic designer," she said.

"Well, I'm not surprised. You must be a pretty good one." Jenny smiled and blushed.

"Well, Dad, this is a surprise" said Joe, "would you like to stay for lunch? We've got plenty, haven't we Jenny?"

Jenny nodded, a little doubtfully Andrew thought. He replied, "Well, Joe, that's very good of you, but I won't impose. I've no right to turn up on your doorstep on Christmas Day unannounced and expecting to be fed, besides, I'm expected in Northamptonshire at three. But thanks all the same. I just wanted to see how you were, and as I've been to see Joey and Fiona Caroni this morning, she's in hospital in Woodford, I thought I'd call in on my way back."

"Gosh! What's the matter with her? Something serious? She's not all that old."

"Not like Joey and I you mean. No, she isn't. She was involved in an accident last night, but I think she's going to be OK. I also wanted to give you this" he added, taking a small packet from his jacket pocket and giving it him. "I'm sorry Jenny, I didn't know about you."

Jenny smiled again. Joe looked uncomfortable as he took the packet. "I'm sorry, Dad. I've got nothing for you, and I ought to have told you about Jenny, but I wasn't expecting you to drop in out of the blue. I was going to write."

"No problem, Joe. I understand, really I do."

"Shall I go and make some coffee?" asked Jenny, tactfully edging towards the door. She sensed that the two men needed to be alone for a while.

"That will be lovely" said Andrew.

After she had gone out, Joe undid the package and found the gold nibbed fountain pen that Andrew had bought in Milton Keynes. He exclaimed gratefully.

"Just the job, Dad. I still do a hell of a lot of writing longhand. Jenny does all the typing and word processing in this house.

Andrew leaned back in the chair and raised his eyes quizzically at his eldest son. "Well?"

"Well, what?"

"What about her?"

"Oh yes, Dad, you're going to be a grandfather."

"I'm glad that my powers of observation are still holding up at my advanced age."

"I'm sorry, I er, I didn't want you to have any more worry."

"Worry, my boy," laughed Andrew, "I've got nothing now to worry about. I do perhaps need just a little time to take everything in. I'm the last person who should be lecturing you."

"You're still my father."

"I'm glad you see it like that" said Andrew softly, "Anyway, I hope you're pleased about it."

"Yes, very. I'd like to marry her, but she doesn't want to commit herself."

"I should have thought she'd already done that! Still it's your affair, I'm here if I can be of any help. When is it due?"

"April"

"Well, keep in touch. How are your brother and sister?"

By the time that Jenny returned the two were animatedly exchanging news. Andrew learned that Simon had finished at university and was working as a surveyor in the West Country.

"I'm glad he's found some use for his bump of geography", and Jane was in her last year of articles to a West End solicitor and living in Ealing. She had been in her second year at university when he had gone to prison. He had often thought of them during his sentence, and how much he would have liked to see them receive their degrees. It seemed that Jenny was well known to and accepted by all of the family except Pamela. Neither of the young ones mentioned the fact, but Andrew had not been an advocate for nothing, and knew instinctively when someone was on their guard when talking of another person.

Andrew said "You mentioned something about your mother in your last letter. What's going on?"

Joe and Jenny looked at one another. After a pause Joe said "I don't really know, but I do know that Colin has been seen in various restaurants and clubs with one of his young female graduate researchers. I think though that there's something more than him having a bit on the side. Sometimes Mother seems worried stiff over something, but she won't say anything to any of us."

"Hmm. I don't suppose that she'd say anything to me either."

"No, I suppose not, but I'm certain something fishy's going on. We went over to Reigate the other weekend - that's where they live now, handy for Colin's constituency- we took over Mum's present and a card for Colin. I can't really bring myself to give the bastard a present. Mother wasn't expecting us, and when we arrived it was obvious that she'd been crying. She tried to gloss over it and said that she'd been watching a weepie video, but she was all pale and nervous, not like her usual self."

"That's right" said Jenny, "she's usually cheerful and pleased to see Joe, but that day we could hardly get a word out of her."

"Anyway" continued Joe, "Colin wasn't there. He was away on constituency business, or so Mum said, so I popped up to his study to leave his card on his desk. While I was in there, his office 'phone rang. He's got his own line into the study for official business. I wondered if I should answer it, but he had his Answerphone set and after two rings it cut in. I wasn't taking a lot of notice, because I was looking at some press cuttings about him which were lying on the desk, they were from an article by a friend of mine, when I heard this man's voice on the Answerphone giving a message. It sounded Irish, but I couldn't be sure, you know how those things distort. It sounded something like 'I've told your wife time's running out. Don't fail to deliver', then it said 'Carrickfergus, repeat, Carrickfergus'. I played it back to make sure, and wrote it down. In fact I played all the tape back, but all the rest was typical MP's stuff, you know, about meetings, questions etc. I tried dialling 1471, but whoever made that call had blocked it so that it couldn't be traced. It was just a coincidence that I was there when the message came in, but the caller certainly didn't sound as if he was ringing Colin to enquire about his health."

"And after that you wrote to me?"

"Yes, that's right. I mean, I've never liked Colin. I've always thought him a shit, but I'm sure he's got himself involved in something nasty and poor old Mum is having the frighteners put on her by someone. Not a very pleasant Christmas thought."

"It certainly isn't. Mind you, there could always be another explanation."

"Such as?"

"Lord knows. But there always could be. Anyway, what do you expect me to do about it?"

"Nothing really, but I think it's right that you should know. I suppose you think it serves her bloody well right."

Andrew smiled. "I might have thought so once, but I don't now. However, it's not for me, nor you, to interfere unless she asks. You can tell her when you next see her, that if she needs help she can look to me, but I'll not interfere."

Andrew glanced at the dashboard clock as he came down the slope to the M1. It was just 2.15. He had spent longer with Joe than he intended, but was glad that he had done so. People from the past were reaching out to him, first Joey, now his ex-wife even if it were only at second hand. The numbing isolation that he had felt when he was first released, when the Watsons were the only people that had seemed in any way close to him, had given way to this strange new life style where perfect strangers had become his intimates and his family were the strangers who wished to be friendly. Even if the Law Society had no need of him, at least his family did. That was as good a Christmas present as any. He glanced at his rear view mirror. The fast lane was clear, the motorway was nearly empty, no heavy lorries or vans, just a few cars. He accelerated away from Junction 2, his spirits lifting as he sped northwards.

With an empty motorway Andrew made good time. As he bumped down the lane towards the farmhouse he noted that he was just over five minutes late. He parked in his usual place and walked across to the front door. Anne had seen him arrive and opened the door for him.

"Come in, come in! We're nearly ready."

Andrew had left the farmhouse when it was still dark, before eight, and had merely grabbed a quick cup of tea and a biscuit before going. It had taken him much longer than he expected to find the hospital; even though the M25 had been almost empty, he had got mixed up in Epping Forest somehow. He had had another coffee at the hospital, and another and a mince pie at Joe's. Now that he had stopped driving and working against the clock, he suddenly realised how hungry he was when he caught the aroma of roasting turkey and other things wafting in from the kitchen. Anne seemed a little flushed, he thought, as he hung his coat up in the hall. He felt he ought to apologise.

"I'm sorry I'm late. I called in to see my son."

"Not to worry, we're not quite ready ourselves yet. Have a drink."

Anne led him into the sitting room. Sally and Tom were sitting on cushions on the floor and chorused Christmas greetings. They were in front of a huge fire piled with logs which gave forth a pleasing scent; they also seemed a little flushed.

Tom got up. "Let me get you a drink, Andrew. What is it to be?"

"Oh, just a small beer please."

Tom lumbered, somewhat unsteadily, out to the kitchen. Anne asked after Fiona and Andrew explained. He took a glass of Hook Norton bitter from Tom and took a sip. It tasted superb.

"If the rest of the day is as good as this, it should be perfect", he pronounced.

Much later, he found himself, just as on that very first day that he came to the farmhouse, sitting facing Anne across the fire. The logs had burned to white skeletons above glowing embers. Tom and Sally had both gone to bed. All four had washed up the plates and dishes after dinner, they had played games and drunk several bottles of wine until they found that nobody was making any sense whatsoever of *Trivial Pursuits*. They had watched a video of *Love Story* after which the two younger ones had gone to bed, declaring that they were tired out with relaxation and that they needed some rest before going to a motor bike scramble on Boxing Day morning. Andrew went out to check the fires aboard the boat and had stood for some time on the wharf in the mild December night. The countryside was deathly still, an owl hooted somewhere and a vixen barked shortly, but there were no trains rattling on the railway a mile across the field, no blue flashes from the catenary wire, and no throbbing boom from the motorway two miles beyond the ridge with the tall spire. A slight south westerly breeze sent clouds scudding across the starlit sky and kept a frost at bay. Even the ever-present glow from the nearby towns and the motorway seemed muted in the strong silvery moonlight that came and went with the clouds. Then Andrew had sighed and returned to the house, where Anne had made hot drinks for them both.

"It's only two months since I first sat here" he said, sipping his hot chocolate, "yet it seems much longer. You know, Anne, my life really began again that day. Everything good that's happened since - getting the boat, meeting Stu and Emma..."

"And Kate Hollis" put in Anne with a wry smile.

"And Kate Hollis, all started that day I first came here."

"So what happens now?"

"What happens now? I really have to think. Joey Caroni wants me to work for him for loads of money. Kate Hollis wants me to get involved in one of her investigations which she thinks could clear my name, yet I don't want either of these. Now my son wants me to find out who or what is worrying my ex-wife. Yet I'm like Garbo. I just want to be alone. It's a great temptation to get aboard *Romford*, start the engine and just vanish."

Anne bit her lip. "But isn't that just a little bit selfish, not to mention cowardly? So many people need you, and you are the last person I would expect to run away from anything."

"Perhaps you don't know me as well as I do" he said, with a wry smile. "It's quite true though, I'm afraid. I'm afraid of what I might uncover, afraid of the consequences of making waves, afraid that innocent people or that people I love and respect will be drawn in and hurt. You see, Joey wants me to collect evidence against whoever put Fiona in hospital, Kate wants me to clear my name because she believes that I was framed by certain people that she is gunning for, and that will help her get her inspector's pips, I have no doubt. Oh yes! " He saw Anne's eyebrows raise in unspoken query. "Much as I like her, I have no illusions about Sergeant Hollis' ambition. My son, Joe, meanwhile is, I strongly suspect, trying to effect reconciliation between his mother and I. All these folk know that I've got the skills and ability to do what is needed, but I just don't want to get involved, and do you know why? Because I think it is all part of one huge great, corrupt, rotten business and once you start poking about in things like that, Lord knows where it will end and who will be hurt, and I don't even exclude you."

Anne shifted in her chair. "Well my dear, only you can make that decision. All I can say is that Kate Hollis won't be the only one to miss you if you decide to move on."

Andrew stood up, carefully placing his empty cup on an occasional table.

"I ought to go. Thanks for your vote of confidence though."

He bent over her, took her hand and squeezed it. Anne rose from the chair, she did not try to disengage her hand.

"Bless you Andrew, it's been a lovely Christmas, even though you had such a nasty surprise last night." She turned her face towards him, he stooped slightly and their lips met. This time it was no party kiss under the mistletoe, they suddenly found they were kissing passionately. Andrew drew her to him, feeling her firm body pressing against him. He was aroused and sensed that she was as well as they clung together. He tenderly caressed her and she responded with more urgent, gasping kisses on his mouth. Anne knew that she passionately wanted this vigorous, handsome man who had so recently burst into her life. She had been alone for so long, now that she knew that the children liked him, she wanted him more than anything else.

"Stay the night" she murmured.

It was well into Boxing Day when Andrew drifted off to sleep beside Anne. They lay, naked, on her bed, their clothes still strewn across the floor. He had quite forgotten to open Kate's present.

Chapter 9
A process of elimination

On the morning of Boxing Day, Andrew decided to move. Nobody was stirring in the farm when he dressed, tiptoed downstairs and let himself out soon after nine o'clock. He opened up the front doors of the boat and went in his cabin to see Kate's present sitting unopened on the sofa in dumb reproach. An unpleasant feeling of guilt came over him. The cabin was cold because the fire had gone out, ash and dust blew from under the stove as the draught from the doors caught it, and the brass was dull, all of which were somewhat lowering to his spirits. He set about putting things to rights with visions of Kate and Anne interchanging with the song from *Cabaret* about *Two Ladies* running on a mental loop of tape. He had never been promiscuous and found himself somewhat out of depth in this situation. Some men might have gloried in the idea of having two concurrent affairs, but not him. True to his lawyer's training, he analysed the position as he did his chores. One thing became clear, for the time being he must get away from this mooring. If he was going to do as Anne suggested, and deep down he knew that was what he had to do, then he must detach himself from emotional entanglements. He was fairly sure that his real feelings were for Anne no matter that he liked and was attracted to Kate. On the one hand he was going to have to work with Kate, but whilst she was fun and good company, somehow he could not see himself sharing a life with her. On the other hand he could, he believed, easily settle with Anne, but one tumble in bed did not necessarily mean permanence. It would be fairer to both women were he to move to neutral ground temporarily.

He cleared the grate, emptied the ash and cinders, then kindled a new fire. It crackled and spat encouragingly in the stove and a thin stream of wood smoke rose from the cabin chimney as he swept and dusted. Once he had finished he made himself some toast and coffee and opened Kate's present. It was a bright brass safety chain for the range chimney, with its links formed of heart shaped pieces. He had several times seen such things on passing boats and had admired them, noting how well they set of the sombre black chimney pipes and brightened up the stern end of a boat. It was the sort of thing that one would never give to anyone who lived in a house, it was too bright and flashy for a cottage, but it looked just right on a boat. There was a note from Kate inside the box:

Dearest Andrew. I hope you'll like this. Happy Christmas. Give me a ring Boxing Day. See you soon. Kate.

As he was finishing his coffee he heard footsteps outside, followed by a knock. Anne's voice called "Are you there?"

He opened the doors and helped her down, kissing her lightly on the cheek. She was wearing jeans and a jumper and no make up. Andrew looked at her covertly, a few lines, a few grey hairs, slightly plump, but nevertheless a most presentable woman, even without make up.

"Oh, yes. You can look at me like that" she said in mock severe tones "now you have had your wicked way with me."

"I'm sorry, Anne. It just happened. I feel awful about it. Oh, please sit down. Coffee?"

"Yes please, but don't apologise."

"I suppose it was the drink, or it may have been the stress of seeing Joey and my son... or being overtired, or the romantic video... Oh damn! One excuse after another." He lit the gas under the kettle. "It was inexcusable."

"Andrew, listen. I seduced you; you didn't seduce me. You behaved entirely properly until we kissed goodnight. I encouraged you. For goodness sake, stop being a lawyer and thinking that I'm going to take action for sexual harassment or something. I'm not a fifteen year old virgin straight out of a convent, I'm a fifty four year old widow and I know what I'm doing."

Andrew smiled at her across the breakfast bar. "The attraction was mutual. But honestly Anne, you talked some good sense last night, and I have to tell you that if I'm going to do what everyone seems to want me to do, I shall have to get away from here for a few days. It's hard for me to say this, but I'm going to have to work with Kate. I can't just break off relations, and it would be most unfair to both of you to keep bringing her here. I still feel rotten about last night", he added.

Anne sighed. "You don't have to feel rotten about anything. I'm the one who should feel rotten, and I don't."

Andrew had made the coffee. He brought it round to her. She took it and looked into his eyes. He smiled his lopsided smile.

"You're a very good person, Anne. Too good. I don't want to hurt you, that's why I feel rotten."

"You haven't hurt me. Last night was the happiest night I've known since... since before Jim died. I used to think that I would be a traitor to him if I had anyone else loving me, but since you turned up it's almost as if he's been there telling me to let go and be myself again. Even if it never happens again I shall always remember this Christmas. Now, off you go to your lovely policewoman and don't give me another thought."

"That" said Andrew quietly "is the very point, Anne. I can't exclude you from my thoughts. I've thought about you all morning. Maybe it seems that I'm running away. Well, I'm not. I'll be back, but don't think you'll be forgotten in the meantime. I just don't want to get emotionally involved with anyone until this job's finished, so I'm going to cut loose for a time. We can still be friends, and I'll keep in touch regularly, but let's keep all deeper relationships on hold until I've sorted the business out, and Lord knows how long it will take."

"If we're still going to be friends, what are you doing for New Year?"

"I haven't decided yet. It depends how I get on with Joey Caroni's job."

"Well, if you can make it, we usually go to the pub at Stoke Bruerne for New Year's Eve, carry on the party wherever it takes us, and end up having breakfast at the "Greasy Spoon" on the A5 or somewhere like that, go to bed for a while, then go out somewhere for lunch. After that I'm usually shattered."

"How will you get home? You can't drive, surely."

"Oh, Good Lord no. I leave the car at home and get a taxi."

"You could always stay aboard with me, and you can take that invitation however you want to, but it's offered in a genuine sense. You could have my cabin."

"What about Tom and Sally?"

"Plenty of room for them as well, so long as they've got sleeping bags."

"I won't hear of you turning out for me."

"If you are that worried, either share with me or sleep in the back cabin."

"Ooh! You are awful!" The two laughed together.

"Is it a deal then?" Andrew asked.

"I think so."

"I'll make sure that the boat is at Stoke, even if I'm not. You can always use it, I'll let you have a spare key."

"Good. I'll look forward to it."

By midday Andrew was ready to leave. The low winter sun struck a long shadow from the farmhouse and barns and beyond it the water sparkled in cold brilliance. He untied the fore end and was about to push it out into the channel when his ears caught a curious drumming sound, which grew steadily louder. Anne had come out onto the wharf to say goodbye, and listened too.

"It's one of those very old engines that the boats used to have", she said, "Jim used to get very excited about them. Single cylinder engines, I think he called them."

Andrew listened. The drumming tempo slowed, to become interspersed with an occasional hiccup. A boat's fore end, riding high in the water, showed in the bridge, so he waited, his fore end swinging gently outwards. An empty working boat, its brasses shining bravely in the low sunlight and with a butty boat hitched up tight behind, swam steadily across in front of him, its engine beating with a slow, irregular, hiccupping sound. It was steered by a youngish looking man in overalls, donkey jacket and trilby hat from beneath which dark hair protruded. A lad in his late teens, also dark haired, stood beside him on the far gunwale; both had steaming mugs on the cabin top in front of them. The butty was steered by a fair-haired woman, well wrapped in an overcoat and scarf. All three looked at Andrew, smiled and nodded in his direction. The motor boat steerer called across to him "Going up Stoke?"

"Yes, I hope to."

"We'll turn 'em round for you."

"Thanks very much."

The man waved and wound his throttle wheel. The hiccupping stopped, the steady drumming sound resumed, and the boats seemed to leap forward. As the stern of the butty passed him the woman called "On your own, are you?"

"For today, yes."

"Ah, hah!"

The two boats swung off towards Stoke, brasses twinkling, smoke rolling from the cabin chimneys. Andrew followed, but long before he had reached his old mooring place at Stoke Bottom lock, he saw the water bubbling from below the gates of the lock which indicated that the boats had already passed through and were indeed "turning 'em round" for him. By the time he reached the lock, it was empty and ready for him. He scrambled ashore with a midships line, pushed open a gate and pulled *Romford* in with the line. He could see the working boats just leaving the next lock, below the main road bridge.

It was the first time that Andrew had worked through locks on his own, but he tried to remember as much of what Stu had told and shown him as possible. Thanks to the boats in front, he had each lock ready for him, so all he needed to do was to push a gate open, pull his boat in, close the gate behind him and then let the water in from above. After the main road lock, where the dog stealers had been trapped, he was able to walk up to the next lock to open the gate while the lock he was in filled up. By now the working boats were out of sight, but when he reached the fifth lock, called by Stu "top o' the Thick", he was cheered to see a boat approaching, for the next lock was out of sight. The crew, an elderly couple, wished him a Merry Christmas and told him that the working boats had mentioned to them that he was following, so they had left the next two locks ready for him. Andrew thought how this travel, where everybody helped one another, differed from the mad *sauve qui peut* of the roads.

The sun was dipping behind the tower of Stoke Bruerne church as Andrew came to the last lock. The air was still and already a chill was setting in, although it was not yet three thirty. He had last seen the place before dawn on a dark, wet morning. Now, in the fading light, he saw what he had only vaguely glimpsed before - the stone and brick buildings lining the banks and giving the impression of a flooded village street, the Museum, the Boat Inn, the Wharf, the hills closing in as the canal approached Blisworth tunnel, looking for all the world like a stage set. There were a few visitors about and several boats moored above the lock, including the working pair that had passed him, from whose brass-ringed chimneys grey smoke rolled vertically upwards. It was as if Andrew had moved into a time warp taking him back a half-century or more. Apart from the 'seventies restaurant building on his left and a few notices, nothing much seemed to have altered since the end of the Hitler War. Some boats lay against a wharf loaded with bags of fuel, other working boats were clustered outside the Canal Museum; some of the boats were decorated with holly garlands or Christmas trees, a few more modern ones had coloured lights.

Andrew found a telephone box near the pub when the lock had filled. He rang Kate at home, but she was not in, so he left a message on her answerphone to say that he would be in *The Boat Inn* from seven o'clock onwards. Returning to the boat, he carefully closed the lockgates behind him with the aid of a bystander, then let the boat slowly trickle past the moored boats, getting a friendly wave from the people on the pair of working boats as he did so. He tied up near where they had stopped on his last visit with Stu. After he had cooked himself some supper and washed up, Andrew shaved, changed and walked back to the pub. He had to cross the lockgates to do this, and wondered idly whether they ever took their toll of over enthusiastic drinkers.

A door led into a cosy little bar with wooden settles round the walls and a roaring fire in the grate. There was a scattering of four legged wooden stools round wooden tables. A couple of men in shooting clothes and Wellington boots stood at the bar with a golden retriever and a black Labrador bitch at their heels. They nodded to him as he entered. He ordered a pint of bitter and had sipped perhaps half of it when Kate came in.

"Happy Christmas, Andrew" she said, kissing him on the cheek.

"Evening, Kate said one of the men at the bar, "Merry Christmas."

"Good evening, Jack, and the same to you" she said, smiling at him. The other man nodded at her, and she nodded back.

"Who are you after this time?" asked Jack, "He ain't done nothin' while 'e's bin sittin' there." He indicated Andrew.

"You watch it" replied Kate. "I'm boning up on the Game Laws especially for you."

The two men laughed. She continued "I'll bet you two have been on the big shoot today. Did you do any good?"

"Bloody Sherlock 'Olmes wi'out 'is trousies" said the other man, and Andrew joined in the general laughter as he ordered a mineral water for Kate. When the laughter had died down, Jack said "It weren't too bad today, I got three brace, 'e got two. I'd 'a done better if me bloody dog 'adn't let me down." He then went on into a lengthy explanation of how his Labrador had blotted her copybook by failing to pick up before his partner on his right at the shoot. While this was going, on the door opened to admit the two men and the woman from the working boats. Andrew, still standing by the bar, greeted them and offered to buy them a drink. "You saved me a good deal of hard work this afternoon."

"Ah, we know all about that" said the man, "it's not easy when you're on your tod."

The three sat down in a vacant window seat, Andrew brought their drinks over and introduced himself and Kate. The couple were called John and Margaret Jones; the younger man, Peter, was their son. In the course of conversation, Andrew discovered that John had been the fleet manager of a road haulage firm until he had been made redundant some two years ago. He and Margaret had first come to the canals as holidaymakers twenty-two years before. They had bought their own cruising boat and had paid off the mortgage on their house before John's redundancy, so they had let the house, sold the cruiser and putting that with the redundancy money, had had enough to buy the pair of boats. Peter, by good fortune, was just leaving school when the redundancy came. Margaret, who was a teacher, had managed to find supply work in several areas, but, she explained, they had managed latterly to find sufficient work for the boats to allow her to largely give this up. The had heard about Andrew from Stu and Emma, with whom they were friendly, and had in any case recognised Stu's old boat. Stu had apparently spoken highly to them of Andrew, so it was only natural to help the friend of a friend.

Kate asked them where they were going.

"We're going to load solid fuel after the New Year, for London", said John, "our house is down that way, and there's a stoppage coming off lower down, near Rickmansworth, so we'll stay there until March. I've got a job to do in a boatyard for two months after mid-January, and so has Peter."

"So where are you picking up this load?" asked Kate.

"Suttons" replied John. Kate and Andrew's eyes met.

"Where?" asked Andrew.

"Suttons. Suttons Stop. That's what we call Hawkesbury Junction, near Coventry. It's where the Oxford Canal joins the Coventry Canal. Stu and Emma's going to be there for New Year."

Kate sipped a coffee in *Romford's* stateroom and smiled at Andrew. They had made their excuses and left the pub soon after discovering where Suttons was, and had gone back to the boat to exchange news. Pleasant as the pub was, there were things that neither wanted to be overheard. Andrew had told Kate about Fiona, and how Joey wanted him to find the culprit. She found the idea amusing.

"Should you be telling me this?"

"Probably not, but I think you can help me, and I can help you."

Kate smiled. "You mean by me feeding you confidential info?"

"And by me getting you more dirt on Burson."

"I suppose it's a deal. By the way, what do you make of this Suttons place? Is it in the centre of Coventry?"

"I don't know, but it might well explain what our dog stealing friend is up to. I'll talk to Stu about it. Oh yes, another piece of news. Someone seems to be threatening Colin Shorland."

"Really? What's that all about?"

Andrew told her what Joe had told him. When he said "Carrickfergus" Kate's eyes widened.

"Well, well. That's interesting. Very interesting."

"Is it an IRA password?"

"No, it's not. That's what makes it interesting. I certainly owe you for that."

She would say no more, and Andrew, recognising a professional at work, did not attempt to draw her further.

Later that evening, Kate drove Andrew to the farmhouse to pick up his car. She drove away to her home, telling Andrew that she needed to go to bed early because she had a long day at work to face, but left him her special number so that he could get in touch with her at work. Before arriving home, she pulled off the road in a lay-by and had a short conversation on her mobile 'phone with Superintendent Baskerville.

Andrew was woken next morning by the clattering of John's single cylinder engine as the pair got under way at daybreak. He looked out of the porthole as the boats glided past in the bleary half-light. Looking at his watch, he saw that it was nearly half past seven. He rolled out of bed, showered, shaved and dressed, made a quick cup of tea and some toast, and was on his way to the car park by eight. There was comparatively light traffic on the M1 that morning, most people were still on holiday, and he made good time round the M25 to the Chingford turn off, and arrived at Joey's house before ten thirty. He had not been there before, for Joey had moved to his new place while Andrew had been in prison. It stood on ground that had been cleared from Epping Forest, and was surrounded by a wall with razor wire on top. Andrew pulled off the A104 onto a tarmaced drive that was almost immediately blocked by an ornamental iron gate overlooked by a security camera. He stopped and went to get out to speak to the entryphone, which he could see in the centre of the gate, by the latch, but before he was properly out of his car there was a click, the gates swung open and Joey's voice, disembodied and metallic sounding, said "Come on in, pal."

Once through the gates, the drive curled across an immaculately manicured lawn to a large Neo-Georgian house set amid flowerbeds. A swing and a slide on the lawn advertised that a small child lived in the house. Everything was well manicured, even for the depth of winter; the house walls sported bright yellow burglar alarms and a closed circuit TV camera nosed back and forth from the eaves. Joey certainly was not taking any chances, Andrew mused.

As Andrew pulled up and parked, Joey opened the front door.
Andrew locked the car and strolled to the door to be greeted with
a bear hug. Chloe ran to him calling "Hello, Mr. Andrew!"
Andrew bent down and lifted her up in the air "Hullo Miss Chloe,
how's Teddy today?"

"Very well, thank you. Mummy's getting better."

"I'm very glad to hear it."

A dark young woman in her twenties came out from a doorway
and took Chloe's hand. "This is Imelda, Mr. Andrew" said Chloe,
"She's my bestest friend."

Andrew bowed gravely to Imelda, "How do you do, Imelda."

"Very good, senor. Now, come wiz me Chloe, and let your Papa
alone wiz ze Gentleman."

"He's not a Gentleman. He's Mr. Andrew."

All the adults laughed. Chloe pouted and went off with Imelda.
Joey smiled after her.

"How's Fiona?" asked Andrew.

Joey led him into the hall and took his coat, "She's aht o' danger.
Come rahnd yesterday, but pretty poorly still."

"Thank God she's come round."

"That surgeon geezer was pretty good. They saved 'er life, that's
fer sure. This way, pal. Coffee? Tea? A drink o' summat?"

Joey ushered him into a spacious sitting room, furnished from
Harrods by the look of it, thought Andrew, glancing at the
watercolour landscapes on the walls.

"Coffee please."

Andrew sat down on a Laura Ashley fabric armchair and looked
about him. The influence of Fiona was obvious. Joey always used
to favour heavy, solid furniture set off by pictures of chubby
Madonnas or oil painted scenes from the New Testament. His old
house at Waltham had a tangible air of an Italian bourgeoise home
of the early twentieth century; now the atmosphere was much
more *Homes and Gardens* good taste. He noticed that the Christmas
roses in a thin, tall glass vase at the centre of the mantlepiece were

drooping. He doubted whether Joey had noticed that they needed water.

Joey came out with two mugs and handed one to Andrew. He sat down opposite, and took a sip of coffee.

"Well, Joey," said Andrew, "what's it all about?"

Joey grimaced. "I meant what I said the other day, pal. I wants the bastards what did it, an' I wants 'em put away, like what you an' me's been put froo. Nah! Nah! Andy boy, wait for it," he had seen the warning lift of Andrew's eyebrows, "surely I ain't got ter spell it all aht again for yer?"

"No, Joey, I'm sorry, just carry on and tell me what I need to know."

Joey leant back in his chair and began his story. It was a not unfamiliar tale to Andrew, and much as he had expected from Joey. Over the last few years since Joey's release from prison, and with the financial knowhow provided by Fiona, Joey had developed a substantial chain of clubs, pubs and restaurants in North and East London. Along with his interests in fight promotions and backing promising young pop stars, this had made him very wealthy. He was not one to seek publicity for himself, and always tried to keep as low a profile as possible so far as the public media were concerned. Yes, of course he had had to cut a few corners when he was starting out, Andy knew all about that from years back, but he'd always played as straight as he could, hadn't he? These days, with Fiona looking over his shoulder he couldn't be anything but straight could he? Anyway, over the last few months, he'd had a good few reports from his various managers that trouble seemed to be on the increase. There had been some nasty scraps on Saturday nights in some of the clubs, a lot of glass had been broken, and there had been more than one fire in the pubs and restaurants. Things seemed to have got worse since he had ordered his managers to clamp down on any drug pushing that was going on, and then he'd found that two managers were taking kick backs from pushers, so he'd sacked them. He'd got his own hard men, who kept an eye on the clubs and pubs for him, but it seemed to be getting beyond their control. In the run up to Christmas he'd had three restaurant windows smashed while customers were eating inside, four bad brawls in pubs, and a whole lot of damage done in all of his clubs. The Bill were getting fractious and telling him to put his house in order, or he'd have half his business shut down. Now there was this business with Fiona, and it was no accident, nor was it just an opportunist snatch. The job had been planned and you could bet it was a warning to him. Some bastard wanted his little empire.

Andrew got up, paced over to the window and looked out at the bare garden. Imelda was pushing Chloe on the swing. It all seemed so normal, so far divorced from the dark world of drug rings and protection rackets that Joey was hinting at.

"So far, Joey, I follow you. It wouldn't be the first time that this has happened, but who's behind it all?"

"I'll tell you summat fer nuffink" said Joey, "remember that time you got me off the 'ook on a murder rap? All them years ago? You didn't do yerself no favours by doin' that."

"I always thought it set the firm up, it wasn't long after that Colin Shorland joined us, and he'd heard about us through your case."

"Yeah pal, an' so did Roland Burson."

"Burson? What the Hell's he got to do with it?"

"A bleedin' lot I reckon. Look, you can see there's a lot wants me aht of the way, can't yer? Well, there's a few as wanted you aht of the way an' all. After you got busted, they gets me nicked an' all don't they. If it 'adn't been fer Fiona, I'd ha' lost it all when I was inside."

Andrew's eyes widened. Something of what Kate Hollis had told him came back to him, about his being set up. But how? And why? Shorland was a shit it was true, but would he really have gone to those lengths to set up his partner?

"Well, if there's so many who want you out of the way, let's make a start and see who we can eliminate."

"That's me old Andy, pal."

Joey offered Andrew a cheroot from a leather case. Andrew shook his head; Joey selected one, lit it with a plastic lighter, took a pull on it and expelled a cloud of blue smoke. There were, he said, three possibilities. One was a Jamaican based gang of Yardies. They had got a good deal of South London sewn up, and were well known in the drugs scene. Several of their hangers-on had been seen in Joey's clubs, and it was quite likely that they wanted to extend their influence north of the River. Then there was Alex McKinnon. He was based round Kings Cross, and into brothels and gambling. Joey knew that he would like a cut at some of his betting shops, whilst clubs and pubs would be a way into more respectable business. He came from Glasgow and had close connections with gangs there. Then there was Roland Burson. He had been seen in some of the better class clubs recently and there was a long-standing feud between him and Joey. "Nuffink I can pin on 'im, but 'e's twice as slippery as the Yardies an' McKinnon put togevver."

Andrew tugged at his chin. "So much for the theory, what have you got to back it all up with?"

"Not a lot, pal. That's where you come in. I wants you ter find aht 'oo's behind it all, and above all, 'oo give Fiona a beatin'." He got up and walked over to one of the watercolour landscapes, clicked something, and the picture slid aside to reveal a wall safe. He clicked the combination lock, opened the safe and took out a packet. "What I'll do is this. This is for starters, for settin' up expenses like. Anyfink more you need, just ask. When you've finished there'll be twenty grand how you wants it, notes, gold, dollars, euros, you name it."

"But Joey, I can't do it for that."

"Orl right, thirty grand. Forty?"

"No, Joey, you don't understand. I can't take money like that off a friend, and anyway, you can't be sure that I'll come up with the goods."

"Oh yes you will, Andy pal. You see, I knows yer fer a good 'un. And don't give me all this crap abaht not takin' money. I ain't short, an' if you don't take it the bleedin' Government will. 'Ere, catch!" He threw the packet to Andrew, who caught it, his face still registering wonderment. It felt both bulky and heavy.

"There's five grand there fer starters, an' don't bleedin' argue. If you don't want it, give it ter some charity, but I want some names."

"I'll do it on just one condition" said Andrew.

"What's that?"

"I'll find your man or men, and I'll nail them with evidence, but I want you to promise me that you won't take things into your own hands, that you'll leave it to the law. That's all."

Joey stood as upright as his stout frame would allow,

"Very good, Mr. Ellison, Sah!"

"Carry on, Sergeant Caroni."

Kate Hollis crossed her shapely legs in front of the fire in *Romford's* cabin and sipped from a glass of Tequila and coke. She had come direct to the boat from her office that afternoon once she had received a telephone call from Andrew, so she was wearing what she only half jokingly referred to as her female empowerment suit, a straight skirt and boxy jacket over a fine weave jumper and a gold necklace at her throat. Andrew found it difficult to keep his eyes off her, and she knew it. However, apart from the clothes, she was in a businesslike mood.

"So, pal Joey wants you to sort it all out, and you've agreed to do so" she commented when Andrew had finished his tale.

"That's about it."

"And do you think Burson is your man?"

"I don't know what to think, that's why I've told you about it. I need to bounce ideas around."

"Well, I'll do a deal with you. If you let me know anything you turn up on Burson, I'll let you know what I can dig up about the Jamaicans or McKinnon."

"OK. It's a deal."

"Good. What are you doing tomorrow tonight?"

"Nothing really."

"Then come to my place. I've got a few friends dropping in and I can show you off to them. You can stay the night if you want to have a drink or two. You have a choice of beds."

Andrew grinned at her, "Shameless hussy. You're on."

Kate's idea of having a few friends in was to virtually throw her house open to the entire village, the Constabulary, on and off duty, in and out of uniform, and any other people who happened to be passing. The local publican had set up a bar dispensing draught beer in the kitchen, and it was here that eventually the epicentre of the party located itself. Andrew found himself in a large and cheerful group of policemen, farmers, builders and similar rural characters and their wives and girlfriends. Some word of the dog rustling had got out locally and he was surprised to find that he had, quite unbeknown to himself, become something of a local hero. A bulky man of his own age put a tankard of draught beer into his hand and said "Cheers!" Andrew took a pull and sighed. The bulky man smiled.

"I think you needed that."

"I certainly did."

The big man put out his hand. "Jack Baskerville. Kate's boss."

"Andrew Ellison."

"I've heard of your exploits over the dog rustlers. Jolly well done. Can I have a quiet word?"

Andrew followed him into the hall, which was almost deserted as the party got going. Baskerville said "I'm glad Kate brought you here. You see, I know all about you and your spot of bother." He laughed. "Don't worry, Ellison. You've nothing to fear from us. But I do understand that you have certain knowledge that we could use, and that we may have information that would be useful to you in a certain type of investigation. I'm just telling you this off the record, so that you don't think Kate is being compromised."

"I'm an ex-criminal. Should you be saying this to me?"

"And I'm an old hand country copper. There are villains and villains, and I'm putting myself on the line to say that I don't think you're as bad as you'd expect me to think. I think we can help one another, but please, you know the law as well as I do, keep inside it. We can sometimes bend the rules, but I won't bend the law."

"Thank you, Baskerville. I appreciate that." Andrew raised his glass, "Cheers, again."

"Cheers" replied Baskerville.

Andrew's recollection of the rest of the evening was somewhat hazy. He remembered seeing Jack Baskerville and his wife leaving soon after his conversation in the hall. Baskerville had given him a friendly nod as he left. He had finished off his pint and then someone had put a glass of whisky and water in his hand. He remembered standing with a plate of *canapés* in the sitting room explaining the workings of a canal lock to a farmer's wife and the local primary school headmistress, he had a vague recollection of dancing in the kitchen with Kate, and he had a vivid memory of washing up piles of glasses at some small hour of the morning whilst Kate dried them.

It was not until Kate snatched away a curtain to let in daylight that he regained full consciousness. He was lying on a bed wearing just his pants. His shirt, trousers and jumper were hung over a nearby chair. Kate, dressed in a housecoat, smiled at him.

"Well, you certainly enjoyed yourself last night."

Andrew groaned. "Oh my God! What happened?"

Kate laughed. "You were the star of the party. I think it must have been the Scotch that got to you. You had everyone in fits."

"I did? What on earth did I do?"

"Just talked. Oh, you did sing a song once, something about elephants."

"Elephants?"

"Elephants. It was somewhat *risqué*, but none the worse for that."

Andrew groaned again and pulled the bedclothes over his head.

He just wanted to be left to die.

Kate however was relentless. "Honestly, you were absolutely brill. I never knew you had such talents. Old George Ashby nearly had a seizure, he laughed so much."

"Who the Hell's he?" he muttered from beneath the clothes.

"The old farmer whose wife you so successfully charmed."

"Oh Lord! What else have I done? Did you put me to bed?"

"No, you did. About half past two you had helped me wash up some glasses, then suddenly announced that you had had a long day and would everyone excuse you, and you went upstairs, rather like a judge leaving court. When I came up about an hour later, you were fast asleep here, in my bed."

Andrew leaped up as if he had been stung. "Oh, God Kate! I'm so sorry. You must think I'm a proper bastard."

"Lie down you silly man. Of course I don't. If I'd thought that, I would never have asked you here. Let me say, you behaved with perfect propriety all night, even if you did get into my bed. My honour is perfectly safe, I regret to say. Anyway, no harm's been done. Let me make up for the hurried breakfast you had last time. Just say when you feel like getting up and I'll cook something for you."

"Kate, you're an angel. I feel better already." He took her hand and kissed it.

"You naughty old thing. Do you know, I might just have the Kate Hollis special cure for a hangover."

"What's that?"

Kate opened her housecoat and showed him.

Kate's telephone rang just as they finished a late breakfast. Kate reached for a scribbling pad and muttered responses as she wrote. When she put the receiver down, she tore a piece from the pad and handed it to Andrew. Her script was clear and bold. It read *"Winston Crawford, Bat and Ball, Peckham"* and *"The Caledonian Commission Agency, York Road."*

"What's this?" he asked.

"Two starting points for you. Winston Crawford is a barman at the Bat and Ball. He's your first contact for the Yardies; the other one is where you can get in touch with McKinnon. You don't need to know where you can find Burson."

The M1 was getting too familiar, Andrew thought, as he drove south soon after midday. This was the third time that he'd travelled along it since Christmas Eve, and there were two more days of the old year to go yet. As it was still quiet, he decided to head for the very end and cross Central London. He followed the Edgware Road to Marble Arch, then went via Hyde Park Corner and Victoria Station to Vauxhall Bridge, past the Oval Cricket Ground and so to Peckham. He found the Bat and Ball in a side street not far from the station. He parked in a respectable looking residential street, and walked back to the pub. It was a typical London street corner pub, but the one time Victorian decor had been painted over with bright pinks and yellows. A remorseless beat filled the quiet afternoon as he walked up to the door. Pushing the brass handle, he stepped in and peered through a haze of smoke. There was a faint smell of incense, rather like a Catholic church, he thought, and a sea of black faces looking at him with puzzled expressions. Many of the customers had their hair in dreadlocks and wore bright knitted caps. He observed that he was the only white person on the premises, but the looks he received were more curious than hostile. He made his way to the bar. A well built young man wearing a baseball cap came up to him.
"Can I help you?" He spoke with a South London accent. His manner was neutral rather than hostile.
"I'll have a pint of shandy, please" said Andrew.
"This ain't a whitey pub, guvnor."
"I don't mind, if you don't."
A ghost of a smile crossed the barman's face. He said no more, but went and made Andrew his drink. Andrew paid him, and then asked if he knew Winston Crawford.
"What if I do?"

"I'd like to talk to him."

"What about?"

"Business. I'm not a policeman, and I'm quite alone."

"You must be mad, cock."

"Probably I am. But I'm not here to make trouble. I just want to see him."

The barman turned on his heel and went through a door behind the bar. He reappeared a few seconds later and said "You just wait there. Someone'll see you in a minute."

Andrew had taken a few sips when he felt a touch on his shoulder. He turned to face a very tall coloured man of about thirty-five with a livid scar down one cheek. The man's dark brown eyes bored into Andrew's. His face was expressionless. When he spoke he had a West Indian tone, but his English was perfect.

"Are you looking for Winston Crawford?"

"I am."

"Who are you?"

"My name's Ellison, Andrew Ellison. I need to see him on business."

"Any ID?"

Andrew took out his driving licence and showed him.

"How do I know you're not going to try anything?"

"You don't. You just have my word."

"Come with me." The big man nodded to the door. When they were outside in the street, the man looked up and down it then produced a mobile telephone. "I'll put you on to him" he said, punching in numbers. The ringing tone was quickly answered. The man spoke into it in an undertone, and then handed it to Andrew. The voice at the other end sounded wary. "Who are you?"

"A friend of Joey Caroni."

"And what do you want?"

"I want to talk some business for him."

"Stay there." The line went dead. Andrew handed the telephone back to the scarred faced man, who pocketed it, nodded and vanished into the pub.

Andrew paced up and down outside the pub for several minutes. It was beginning to get dark and the air was chilly. Suddenly a Volvo estate car swung across the road. It was driven by a young coloured man wearing a knitted hat. It pulled up beside him and the rear door opened. A well-dressed coloured man, also in his thirties, was sitting on the back seat. "Get in, please, Mr. Ellison" Andrew climbed in, to be met by a snub barrelled revolver pointing at him. "You must excuse the informality" said the well dressed man, "but I shall have to blindfold you." So saying he handed the revolver to the driver, who kept Andrew covered, and produced a silk handkerchief, which he tied over Andrew's eyes. Andrew made no resistance, and the car soon sped off. He tried to engage the well-dressed man in conversation, but was abruptly told to keep quiet. The car threw him several ways as it twisted and turned through the streets, and then it drew up in a dark place. Andrew was hustled out and led through a passageway that smelt of urine, guided up some steps, and then through some doors into a lift, which also stank. He felt himself rising, and then stop, then he was urged forwards along another passage. They stopped by a door, he heard a bell ring, and almost immediately was pushed through the doorway. His blindfold was removed, and he found himself in a well-furnished room with picture windows looking down on what he took to be a panorama of South London at night. There was a soft, rhythmic sound of reggae music and again the faint scent of incense. A huge coloured man wearing a bandana over his dreadlocks was sitting in an easy chair with a glass of white rum in his massive paws. His face was impassive as he motioned Andrew to sit down.

"What's your business whitey?" he rumbled.

"I'm looking for Winston Crawford."

"So I heard. Well, I might be him, or again I might not be. Who you and what do you want with him?"

"I want to ask something on behalf of Joey Caroni, and to give him a message. It doesn't matter who I am."

"Go on. Have a drink?"

Andrew shook his head. "He wants to know if you are interested in things north of the river?"

The huge man's eyes widened. "And why might he want to know that?"

"So that he can do a deal."

The man smiled, splitting his ebony face with snowy white teeth. He was dangerous, Andrew thought, but probably a straightforward villain.

"Now listen here whitey. You got a big nerve bustin' in here, an' I thinks you might need a spankin', but, Hell! It's Christmas, an' I'm in the mood for peace. Now you jus' go back to yo' Mr. Caroni an' tell him that there ain't no such man as Winston Crawford. Winston Crawford, he in the boneyard a long, long time, but I knows who he wants to talk to. You can tell him that no one here gives a fuck for his business north of the river. If we wants it, we'll let him know, but, shit man! There's enough trouble this side of the water from the Babylon and them others without we stick our heads up someone else's asshole. What was the message you had?"

"In view of what you've said, there's no message. Thank you for your time."

"Don' mention it whitey. Say, I admire your bottle, comin' here. You's too old for these games."

Andrew laughed. "Maybe I am, I'm not as young as I was."

"Take care, now. This part of town's a dangerous place for your sort. Best I send you back to Peckham in the motor." He nodded to the well-dressed man, who stepped forward and replaced Andrew's blindfold. As Andrew was led through the door, the big man said "Jus' one moment." The little procession stopped. There was silence for a moment, and Andrew tensed himself for an attack of some sort. The deep voice rumbled "Thank your stars you done good to one of my boys when you was inside, *Mistuh* Ellison."

All the way back to Peckham Andrew puzzled about the last remark. How on earth did the big man know his name? It was not until he had been dumped, rather unceremoniously, on the pavement by the *Bat and Ball*, that it came back to him. Before he had been transferred to the open prison, while he was in Pentonville, there had been a young black prisoner on his floor, sent down for some sort of drug offences, but a pleasant enough lad. He had fallen foul of some of the shaven headed scum who called themselves National Fronters. Apparently he had not shown them enough "respect", and Andrew had come upon three of them laying into the boy on a staircase. He had waded in and held them off until a warder arrived. The three had been put on Governor's report and had lost privileges. That was why they had set about him on the stairs some days later, and he had recalled sufficient of his unarmed combat training to put all three in hospital. Well, well. It was a small world.

By the time Andrew arrived in the Kings Cross area, it was nearly eight. He found a place to park off York Road by a respectable looking pub near the canal. He wondered whether he would ever bring himself to take his boat along those dark waters between the warehouses and modern flats. As soon as he could get shot of this business of Joey's, he would take himself off into the greenest depths of the country. There was nothing that attracted him to the city, especially the dark, seedy parts that he seemed to have to visit today. He walked over York Road Bridge into a land of decaying industrial buildings and boarded up shops. A couple of mini-skirted prostitutes watched him with bored indifference from a doorway. Soon after he found the Caledonian Commissions Agency.

Once upon a time the building had housed a perfectly respectable shop, greengrocers or ironmongers perhaps, but now the plate glass windows had been partly boarded up and the remainder whitewashed over. The door was ajar, and within he could see the white glare of fluorescent tubes and the blue flicker of TV screens. He pushed the door and entered. Inside was a bare, dusty room with a few flyblown chairs occupied by punters watching what appeared to be an American trotting race. He crossed the room to a counter divided up at one end into booths, like a pawnshop. A bored looking girl behind the desk looked up from her magazine at him.

"Yes please!"

"I'd like to see Mr. McKinnon please."

"'E ain't 'ere."

"Then someone who can speak for him."

"'Ang on." She wriggled backwards off her stool and disappeared. A few moments later she came back with a sharp-featured young man in a tight fitting suit.

"Yes?" he inquired. He had a tattoo on each hand, by the base of his thumb. That on his right hand said "love", the one on the left said "hate."

"I need to see Mr. McKinnon, on business."

"And 'oo are you?"

"My name is Ellison, Andrew Ellison. I represent Joey Caroni." The young man disappeared and reappeared a few moments later beckoning Andrew towards a lifting flap in the counter. Andrew scrambled through, into a room behind the shop, through a doorway and up an uncarpeted staircase. At the top was a glass-panelled door, on which the young man knocked. A voice called "Come in!". Andrew opened the door and walked through into a sparsely furnished office, lit with yet another fluorescent tube. Facing the door was a desk behind which sat a somewhat unprepossessing little man in a check suit. His head was almost bald apart from two sandy tufts on each side above his ears; his face had the marks of many encounters with razor blades, boots, fists and knuckledusters, his eyes were concealed behind a pair of opaque shades. Andrew placed him as about the same age as himself. He waved Andrew to be seated, and almost immediately a chair was placed behind him by a large man in an ill-fitting tuxedo, who materialised out of the shadows behind the door and remained standing behind him. The little man took a cigarette from a packet on the desk and lit it. He did not offer Andrew one. Suddenly he rasped, "Ye're business?"

"Am I speaking to Mr. Alex McKinnon?"

"Aye."

"I'm here on behalf of Joey Caroni, of whom you will have heard."

"Aye."

"He wants to know whether you are interested in any of his concerns."

"Aye."

Andrew thought, *this is going to be hard work. Still, two could play at being taciturn.* He said nothing for what seemed like an age. Then McKinnon spoke:

"Ha' ye nothin' to say mannie?"

"I'm waiting to hear from you."

"Well noo, what are ye' offerin'?"

"I'm offering nothing. I want to know what you're interested in."

"Is that a fact?"

The time for pussyfooting was over, Andrew decided.

"I'm here to tell you this McKinnon. If you want to do business, then out with it, and we'll discuss a fair price. If not, and if it's you who is giving Mr. Caroni grief just now, then remember that two can play at that game!"

McKinnon suddenly sat bolt upright. He whipped aside his shades and two hard, black eyes glared at Andrew.

"Naebody threatens Alex McKinnon like you just have, ma mannie, see you!"

"Then I'll tell you straight. If it's not you who is giving the grief, then there's no threat. Take it or leave it." Andrew could feel the tension at that moment, and was uncomfortably aware of the big, silent man behind him. It almost felt as if he was touching the back of Andrew's neck. The tension was suddenly broken by a great shout of laughter from McKinnon,

"Well said ma mannie! There's nae threat tae Joey frae Alex McKinnon. Nae threat at all. Mind, if he's in the market tae sell, I might be interested in some o' his properties. But ye can tell Joey frae me that I've enough grief of ma ain wi'oot causin' him ony. Now, forbye ye'll take a dram on it."

It was not until he got back to the car and took off his coat that Andrew realised how near he had steered to danger. As he went to hang it on the hook beside him, he noticed the unmistakable mark of a cutthroat razor on the back of his collar. Suddenly he was glad that McKinnon had only offered him one glass of whisky. He was very glad that he was out of that seedy emporium of his. He just hoped he would not meet a police car on his way home.

Chapter 10
New Year

On New Year's Eve, the weather, which until then had been mild, suddenly became frosty. The wind dropped in the small hours, and by the time that the sun rose there was a perceptible iciness in the air. Puddles froze, and although the day was cloudless and the sun shone from a sky of almost unearthly blue, there were several places out of the sun where hoar lay white all day. Andrew rose late that morning; he had got home at nine thirty and gone straight to bed, feeling the effects of Kate's party of the night before. He had found his fire out, and had not even bothered to relight it before going to bed. Now he had cause to regret this omission, the boat was icy cold inside, despite the sun that poured through the portholes after he drew back the curtains. Shuffling along in his slippers and dressing gown he cursed his stupidity, raked out the ashes and relit the stove with a firelighter and some chopped sticks that he had kept behind the stove on Stu's advice. He put the kettle on, yawned and stretched then settled on a stool by the breakfast bar to wait for the kettle to boil. By the time that he had made himself a coffee, it was time to put more coal on the fire, and by the time he had drunk it, heat was beginning to radiate through the stateroom and the central heating pipes were warming. Feeling in a somewhat better humour, he shaved, dressed and went to the telephone box. He rang the special number that Kate had given him and found gratification in hearing her voice at the other end of the line. He told her that he was certain that McKinnon and the Yardies could be eliminated from involvement with the attack on Fiona, and that he had to visit his old friends John and Jill Watson in Surrey for lunch, and then go to a party that night near where he was moored.

"What a social round!" exclaimed Kate, "still, you'd best make the most of it. Once everyone gets back to work on Monday, you'll be doing plenty of leg work."

"I know" replied Andrew ruefully, "I've no great wish to keep going to and from London, but the sooner I get this job sorted, the better. If the weather holds, I might move the boat a few miles nearer London after the holiday."

"Gosh, that sounds fun. I could give you a hand if you wanted. I am due a few days leave, provided I remain on call, I can go any time after tomorrow."

"You could be on then. Are you free tonight?"

"No, 'fraid not. I shall be slaving over a hot computer monitor until God knows what time."

Before leaving for the Watson's, Andrew made up the stove fully and closed it down so that it would just tick over and keep the chill out of the boat. He was away by midday and at the Watson's just in time for lunch. Fortunately, John being a creature of habit, sat down to lunch at one thirty sharp. Andrew, knowing this, was able to slip into their drive with two minutes to spare. He was careful to drink water only at lunch, following his narrow escape last night from being over the limit, but secretly reasoned that at least he had a good excuse for not drinking John's Liebfraumilch. After lunch they both went into John's conservatory sitting room. The view over the downs was much clearer today, and Andrew sat for several minutes wrapt in the scene while John fumbled about with the coffee and poured drinks for himself and Jill. Jill had told them both to go and chat while she put the things in the dishwasher, and then get herself ready for going out that evening, but she'd love a drink.

At length, John finished and sat opposite Andrew, who stirred his coffee absently. Eventually Andrew said, "Do you think I might have been set up over the Trust money business?"

John blew a cloud of cigarette smoke down his nostrils and squinted at him.

"Now's a fine time to ask that question. Four years ago would have made more sense."

"Maybe, but I didn't know then what I know now. Do you think Shorland might have had a hand in it?"

"Look, Andrew, anything's possible. I can see he'd every reason to do so, but why would he need to do it? He wanted you out of the way? Well, he could have got you shifted much easier that framing you. I'm not saying that he didn't frame you, but from where I'm sitting it looks doubtful. Why do you ask anyway?"

"Joey Caroni thinks he and Roland Burson may have been behind it."

"Joey! Well, he's a downy enough old bird, and he's got enough fingers in pies. You've seen him lately I take it?"

"Yes, Christmas Day in fact. Fiona was attacked and beaten up Christmas Eve."

John whistled "Good Lord! I remember now seeing something on the TV about an attack on a woman in North London on Christmas Eve; I never thought it was poor old Fiona. How is she?"

"Recovering. She was pretty badly hurt, but she's pulling through."

"What happened?"

Andrew explained what he knew about the attack on Fiona and how Joey was taking it. He did not inform John of the job that Joey had given him. After he'd finished, John said:

"Why don't you go and work for Joey? He could do with a good brain now that Fiona's out of action."

"Sure, but I don't really fancy his milieu."

"Beggars can't be choosers. You'll be lucky to get as decent a return on your money next quarter as you will do this one. Interest rates dropping, property values still depressed, I can't guarantee you a never-changing income."

"Oh, come on, you'll expect me to work for Colin Shorland next."

"Well you could do worse. Trust a Pay Corps man to get his feet in the trough."

"I never knew he was a Pay Corps man."

"Oh yes, at least according to himself. I was only looking at his old CV the other day. It's still with your file."

"What!" exclaimed Andrew. "You've still got it?"

"Well, yes. When your partnership broke up, remember I went to Lipscombe and bagged a whole lot of your stuff? There were several files relating to the partnership that I removed for safekeeping. Very handy too while you were living the life of Riley in nick, I was able to clear up a lot of problems on your behalf without keep having to come to visit you."

"Where are they?"

"In my study. I don't keep things like that in the office. Would you like to see Shorland's documents?"

"Is the Pope a Catholic? You bet I would."

"Hang on a minute then. I'll get them."

John got up, and went outside. Andrew could barely contain his excitement. Until yesterday he had been inclined to regard the suspicions about Shorland and Burson as somewhat fanciful and circumstantial, but his interviews with the other most likely suspects in the Fiona case had led him to believe that there might be something in it. He had already come to the conclusion that he needed to acquire every scintilla of fact about Shorland and Burson that he could. John returned a few minutes later with a box file.

"Here we are. There's not an awful lot, merely his letter of application to you, and his CV. The rest of the file is all partnership documents and accounts, oh, and minutes of partnership meetings. Nothing very earth shaking, I'm afraid."

Andrew opened the file. On the top, held down by a wire spring clip was a photo copy of Shorland's application to join the firm, and attached was his *curriculum vitae*. Andrew released the clip and carefully drew out the document. It was dated 1978. Andrew pursed his lips and read aloud:

"Educated, Lincoln Grammar School for boys... Yes, I remember that. He told me his parents could not afford to send him away to school. 'A' levels... school prefect... National Service, basic training with Sherwood Foresters 1961, then OCTU, Mons Barracks, Aldershot 1962, commissioned into Royal Army Pay Corps. Well

I never. Fancy my forgetting that! I suppose it hardly mattered back in the 'seventies when he came to us. Served in Germany with BAOR, left army in 1964, went to Cambridge and read law. Now there's a funny thing. How come he could do that when his parents couldn't afford to send him to boarding school?"

"Maybe he or his father had made good."

"Possibly. Good Honours degree, 1967. Articled to James Hawtry of Higgins and Higgins... yes, I remember all that. Final Exam 1970, then all the firms he'd worked with. All good firms for high flyers, all good references as I recall. Hmm! Very interesting. Mind if I take a copy?"

"Keep it. It's yours. I've got no use for it."

At the back of Andrew's mind, something was stirring. Something in the CV rang a bell. He cudgelled his brain to try to recall what it was. It was something that he had talked about very recently with someone, but it was not with Kate, it was somebody who had no connection with the matter in hand. Who the Devil was it? Maybe he was getting senile. Like the other morning when he had no recollection of what he had got up to the night before. There was something else there too; Kate had said he had sung a song about an elephant.

" I say, John," he said suddenly, "There was something I've been meaning to ask you. Did we ever sing a song about an elephant in the army?"

"Elephant? I can't think of one. Oh, hang on a minute, do you remember that actor chap in B. Company, used to bring the house down with a song, I can just remember the tune. *Tra, la, lalala la, tra, la, lalala la. I was the hole in the elephant's bottom.* I'm happy to say I don't recall any more."

"That's it! That's the one! Apparently I sang it the other night at a party. It must be forty years since I last heard it."

"Did you get the words right?"

"Damned if I know. It went down a storm apparently."

"What on earth made you bring that up just now?"

"Something in that CV rang a bell. I've had a conversation recently with somebody that connects with something in that CV, and there's some connection with the elephant song too. Buggered if I can work it out though."

All the way back to Northamptonshire, Andrew's subconscious mind was turning over this conundrum, it was not however until later that evening, when he met Anne and her family in the *Boat Inn*, that part of the riddle resolved itself. He had paid a brief visit to the boat to check that his fire was still burning and had washed and changed. Since he had snatched a quick supper in a Service Station on the way home, there was nothing to keep him aboard. By the time he had gone across the lock gates to the pub it was getting on for nine, and the place was jumping. The tiny bar was packed, he forced his way through the crowd to the adjoining bar, which was slightly less full, to find Anne, Sally and Tom sitting round a table with some other friends. Anne introduced Andrew, while Tom went to get him a drink. Andrew took his glass and said "Cheers", and almost instantly recalled his conversation with Tom on Christmas Eve, before the summons from Joey had driven it out of his head. Tom had been talking about some smuggling scam that certain officers had been involved in. He managed to find a place next to Tom and asked him about it.

If possible, the celebrations that evening outdid those organised by Kate. The pub continued to fill with people until by midnight it seemed that it would be impossible to squeeze so much as a matchstick into the building. Andrew lost count of the drinks that he had, but at least his recollection was not quite so hazy as the other night. In fact his head remained remarkably clear. He put it down to the fact that he stuck to beer, along with Tom, and refused even a single whisky at midnight. When the hour eventually struck, it seemed that the entire clientele of the place went mad. A huge chain of interlinked hands was formed as the strains of Auld Lang Syne rang out. He found himself in between Anne and Sally, when it was all over he received a passionate kiss on the lips from the first and an affectionate peck from the other. He and Tom shook hands, as did virtually every other man in the pub, whilst it was noticeable how many women were being kissed or were taking a leading part in the action. Afterwards, all three walked back along the canal bank to Andrew's boat, where he brewed some strong coffees. Everyone was a little merry, but not outrageously so. They all sat in the stateroom round the little stove, which had been persuaded to burst into full life. Sally sat on the carpet, her knees drawn up under her chin, Anne sat beside Andrew on the settee, Tom lay back in an armchair, his long legs towards the fire. The wall clock indicated that it was two thirty am.

Tom swallowed some coffee, and then asked "Why did you ask me about that smuggling business tonight, Andrew?"

"Just a conversation I had with someone earlier today. A coincidence really?"

"I see, it's just that Sally keeps on to me about it as well."

"Well it's a good story" said Sally "I've been doing some investigation into middle class crime, you know the sort of thing..."

"Only too well" said Andrew ruefully.

"Oh, Gosh! I'm sorry! There I go again, putting my big foot in it."

"Not to worry" said Andrew smiling, "I can take it."

"Well, to be quite frank" said Sally, "most people regard financial offences as middle class crime, because most crimes that we hear about in the papers are committed by the less advantaged. Stealing cars, beatings up, burglaries, ram raiding, they're all underclass crimes, most gang leaders get where they are because they have organisational ability beyond that of their immediate peers. But when you do get a middle class professional mixed up in racketeering, you have a potentially dangerous situation."

"I take your point" said Andrew, "but surely the reason that most middle class people do not get involved in organised crime is simply that they don't need to. Their whole life style ensures that the fat of the land drops into their laps quite legally."

"Yes, quite so, but there are some people who still use their talents and managerial abilities, their education and their contacts for illicit purposes rather than socially accepted ones. Those are the ones I'm interested in. Like those chaps that Tom was talking about who were smuggling drugs. What makes them do it? Shortage of money? Desire for recognition? Sheer devilment?"

"And you're doing a story on this?" Andrew asked.

"Yes. Tom told me about the army scam, and I thought straight away that there was a good story there, so I cleared it with my editor after Christmas, and I shall be starting in earnest next week."

"I do hope you'll be careful" Anne put in, "for goodness sake don't start stirring up any more crooks. That episode last month was quite enough for me, and I wouldn't want you to go through anything like that."

"Don't worry, Mummy, I'm a big girl now. I've covered much riskier assignments."

"Maybe, but mums always worry."

"If what Tom said is true, and some people in high places have been involved in a cover up, it could also run you into other problems" said Andrew. "I know I'm a good one to talk, but once you start turning over stones, you can find things which don't always pay to bring to the light of day."

After a while the subject was dropped. Andrew had made up a bed for Sally in the back cabin, one for Anne in the spare cabin, and, at Tom's insistence, he had kept his own, with Tom shaking down on the stateroom settee, which could be pulled out to make a bed any way. All of them had brought sleeping bags. The two women made their way to their beds soon after, Andrew and Tom sat over a nightcap in the stateroom.

"Do you think there's any mileage in this idea of Sal's?" asked Tom, "I think she could be opening a mega can of worms."

"Had you asked me that question twenty four hours ago, I would have said she was wasting her time. Now I'm not so sure. I think I may know somebody who got himself up the ladder by the very same way that your luckless junior officers made such a cock up of. She will have to be very careful, that's all I would say. Another dram?"

Andrew had made arrangements with a nearby cafe for a full English breakfast to be served at 10 am on New Year's Day. The party was not quite as bleary eyed as it might have been, and consequently did justice to the meal. The cafe was in a converted chapel nearby, and the atmosphere was both welcoming and spacious. The proprietor supplied newspapers in the manner of a Parisian or Viennese cafe; so all four buried themselves in the Bank Holiday editions over a large steaming jug of coffee. By unspoken mutual consent nobody spoke, until suddenly Andrew said "Good Lord!"

The others looked up curiously.

"I'm sorry, I've just been looking at the New Year Honours lists, and I've found someone I know."

"Really?" said Sally, "what sort of honour? A gong?"

"No, a knighthood." He read aloud. "Knights Bachelor. Shorland, Colin Leslie MP, for services to the Conservative Party." Well, if there's one thing that will persuade me not to vote Tory next time, that's it."

Anne said "You don't sound exactly thrilled."

"I should think not. The man's an absolute... oh! Words fail me. He used to be my business partner and is now married to my ex-wife." He stopped for a moment. The thought of Pamela being a Lady had just come to him. "I'll tell you what, Sally, if you want to dig some dirt, you could do a lot worse than start there." The others gazed open mouthed. This was the first time that any of them had seen Andrew angry. It was also the first time that he had mentioned his previous life other than in confidence. Andrew put down the paper and drank some coffee. "I'm sorry, people, I didn't mean to spoil your breakfasts." He recovered his composure and breakfast continued otherwise undisturbed.

After they had finished, Andrew proposed taking them all back to the farm by boat. "I need to run the engine, and I've stayed here rather too long. It'll save you getting a taxi anyway." He had said, so, after a quick check over in the engine room and a swill with the mop over the paintwork, they started. Both Tom and Sally understood the basic principles of working locks, so they were dispatched ahead to prepare the road while Andrew and Anne worked the boat through. The frost was still holding, although the sun was bright, so there was a thin skimming of ice across the canal once they were clear of the Top Lock. They worked steadily down, Andrew now really enjoying the sensation of being the head of a team rather than a junior partner, as he had been with Stu, or general dogsbody, as when he was on his own. By the time they had passed Yardley Wharf, the sun was going down behind the hills and the air was getting icy. Andrew only intended to spend the night at the farm before pushing on somewhere towards Leighton Buzzard or Tring next day, he still felt that he should distance himself from Anne until his investigations were over.

Once tied up though, Anne insisted that he come indoors and treat himself to a bath or shower after they had collected his car from Stoke Bruerne. He felt that it would be churlish to refuse, besides, Tom and Sally were both leaving tomorrow, and he enjoyed their company. Meanwhile Sally announced that she was going to make supper for everyone, and Tom busied himself about laying and relighting the sitting room fire. He thought wistfully of his own children, and how they might get on with Anne's, but sternly forced his mind back to the present.

Taking a complete change of clothes with him, he unashamedly enjoyed the luxury of a lengthy shower without the worry of running out of water. Tomorrow he too would get back to work unravelling the tangled skein of Joey's affairs, but for the time being he wallowed in the sybaritic comfort of Anne's bathroom.

In spite of the efficient central heating system with which *Romford* was fitted, Andrew felt a distinct chill next morning when he woke. He noticed that the condensation on the inside of the cabin porthole was frozen. He padded into the stateroom, raked the fire, put more fuel on it and opened the draught. He lit the gas in the galley to make himself a drink and found that the place warmed up very quickly. Drawing aside the curtains, he peered out into a chilly half-light. The trees and grass outside were rimed with frost, and when he moved across the boat, causing it to roll slightly, he heard the creak of ice. Looking out onto the canal, he saw that it was frozen right across, with perhaps an inch of ice. He pursed his lips. This could prevent him moving on for the time being, and could be embarrassing too. Much as he liked Anne's company, he still felt that he should keep himself distant. In any case he would have to be meeting and talking with Kate on business, and it was hardly fair to Anne to carry on such business from her home. Blast the damned weather! He shaved, dressed, made breakfast and washed up in a foul mood. By the time he was ready to go ashore, it was nearly half past eight, which meant that the roads would be packed with commuters on the first day back to work after the holidays, and he fumed yet more. It was with the greatest difficulty that he forced a smile for Jane, sitting in Anne's kitchen with her starter cup of coffee.

"Woy oop! A right misery goots we got 'ere, me ole doock" said Jane, catching sight of Andrew's face. In spite of himself, Andrew laughed. "That's better, you 'as ter 'ave a good laaf, mate! What's oop? Lost a tenner an' found a quid are you?"

"No, Jane, I'm sorry to be a misery. It's just the damned weather getting up my nose, it's stopping me from moving on, and I really need to do so. Anyway, what news of your daughter over Christmas?"

Jane smiled at him. "She come 'ome Christmas Day. 'Er Gary got beat up Christmas Eve an' 'ad ter goo t'ospital, they kep' 'im in over the 'oliday. Boxin' Day 'e gooed ter 'is mum an' dads' in Semilong."

"Where?"

"Semilong, it's part o' Northampton."

"I see."

Jane went on. "First thing Christmas mornin', I 'ears the door knocker a'gooin', I looks out, there's a taxi outside an' our Kelly on the doorstep. Course, I 'as ter pay the man off, she en't got no bloody money, are she? Poor little boogger's bin up 'alf the night in Casualty. She found Gary layin' in the street outside wi' 'is 'ead kicked in. Ambulance takes 'in to 'ospital and 'e comes round about two in the mornin', once she knows 'e's OK, she walks back to their place an' sticks everythin' in two rubbish sacks an' clears out. Gets to my place about 'ar pas' six, so I puts 'er straight ter bed. She don't wake up till bloody dinnertime! Still, it turns out all right 'cause I'd got 'er presents an' cards an' that at 'ome."

"So, you had a reasonable Christmas then."

"Yeah, it were a bloody good 'un. Your idea ter send 'er mate Tracy round 'elped. I doubt she'd 'a took a lot o' notice o' me."

"Who beat the boyfriend up?"

"'E won't say. Nor will our Kelly. But Tracy reckons though that 'e got done over for not payin' 'is benefit over. See, where they was is supposed to be furnished and the tenants gets 'ousin' benefit, but the flats ain't furnished and they 'as to pay the benefit giros over to the landlord. Either that she says, or someone wanted 'im to pimp for our Kelly. Between you an' me, Tracy says it were a right dump where they lived. Kelly told 'er she got flashed at by the bloke on the next floor, an' there was like a knockin' shop in the next 'ouse. She told Tracy she could 'ear 'em at it in the bedrooms. Course, she won't say nothin' to me about it. Any way, I'm glad she's 'ome. I rung 'er 'eadmaster first thing 's'mornin'. 'E says she can goo back an' do 'er exams, so I told 'er she ought ter 'ang on till May, then we'll see if we can't find somewhere a bit better for both of 'em. She'll be over sixteen then."

"Does she want to marry?"

"Between us both, I don't think she's quite so keen on it as she were. She knoo it weren't allowed, you know, to go off an' 'ave sex at 'er age, like, but Doctor Robinson gi'ed 'er a prescription fer the pill, so she en't got 'erself up the duff, I'm glad to say. Now she's 'ad ter live wi' all them no 'opers, she knows she's got ter get 'er act together like, else she's goin' t'end up the same way. Mind, I shan't stop 'er if she wants ter get married to Gary, but I think she's 'ad 'er little taste o' freedom an' it en't quite as good as what she thought it would be. She 'ad a good long talk wi' 'er mum Christmas night, an' she's bin as good as gold since."

"How about the boyfriend?"

"She went ter see 'im. 'Is dad were goin' ter throw 'im out on the street when the 'ospital sent 'im 'ome. 'Is mum made 'im see sense, but poor kid en't in no condition to be put on the street. 'Is dad says 'e's got ter goo this wik. Bloody shame en't it? I en't surprised the poor boogger took up where e' did. It's bloody 'ard fer kids o' that age ter get decent lodgins. I'd 'ave 'im, but I en't got the room really, an' anyway where we lives, 'e's too far away from 'is work."

"Where's that?"

"Pub in the middle o' town. 'E was promised a flat ter goo wi' the job, but that fell through."

"The lad seems a proper loser."

Jane looked hard at him, "'E en't no different from a lot o' kids 'is age, me doock. If you en't got the right GCSEs, or if you en't got a family to 'elp you, you don't 'ave much of a chance of a decent job or 'ome these days."

Andrew said nothing. He knew, from the men he had rubbed shoulders with in prison, just how truly Jane had spoken. There were sometimes, it seemed to him, unbridgeable gulfs between the educated middle class and the likes of Gary. Still, there might be some way that he could help.

"Look, Jane, I don't want to interfere, but I think there might be something that we could do for Gary in the short term, you know, until he gets a Council flat or something."

Jane looked doubtful. "I likes the lad, but I don't want 'im marryin' my Kelly, or livin' wi' 'er, unless both on 'em realise what they're lettin' 'emselves in for. She's 'ad a narrer escape, an' I don't want 'er gettin' involved until she've finished 'er schoolin'. She can go ter Tech or summat an' learn a job and do what she likes then."

"I'm just thinking of something to keep Gary off the streets and out of the clutches of the sort of people who beat you up if you don't pay over what's rightly yours, or expect you to put your girlfriend on the streets."

"I'm wi' you there. It'd make our Kelly 'appy an' all. She's a soft 'earted boogger."

"Excuse me a minute, I must make a 'phone call."

Andrew managed to get through to Stu on his mobile.

"Andy, mate! 'Appy Noo Year to yer! 'Ad a good Christmas?"

"Very good thanks. And the same to you. Where are you now?"

"Froze in at Suttons. There's three pair on us goin' ter try ter break the road ter Braunston termorrer."

"And the best of luck. Look, Stu. Do you know anyone who has got a boat on the River or cut at Northampton who'd like a live in caretaker for a few weeks? I know of a young lad who could do with somewhere handy to the town for the rest of the winter."

There was a pause while Stu considered. "Not off 'and I don't, but leave it wi' me till termorrer. I'll arst around. Gi' us a bell this time termorrer mornin' an' I'll let you know."

"How's Emma?"

"All right mate. We 'ad a bit of an 'eavy few days an' she en't woke up yet!"

"Tell her I'm ashamed of her!"

"I will mate! Good to 'ear from you again. We 'eard you was at Stoke Boxin' Day. Our mates John an' Maggie seed you in the pub there. They're startin' wi' us in the mornin'. They loads today, arter us an' Jack Turvey."

"Hear from you tomorrow then."

"Yes, mate. Shall 'a' to go, wagon's just showed up from the plant."

Stu rang off. Andrew went back to the kitchen. He thought it would be as well not to raise any hopes, so said nothing of his conversation to Jane. Anne had come downstairs, the two youngsters had departed early that morning, and she had gone back to bed once she had seen them off with a cooked breakfast. Now she had bathed and was ready for what else the day might bring. She smiled at Andrew. "It looks as if you may be stuck here for a while."

"I'm afraid it does. It's a bit of a nuisance because I wanted to move closer to London while I do a job."

"Well, stay here and commute. You're always welcome."

"Thanks. I called in to see whether you wanted anything from Northampton. I'm going there today."

"Oh, well, if you wouldn't mind being an angel and popping into Tesco's for me, there's a few things I'm short of until I get in there for my next big shop."

Andrew parked his car in a multi storey park near the town centre and made his way to the reference library. He spent a long time consulting telephone and street directories, *Who's Who*, and the current *Statesmans Year Book*. He also looked at the Electoral Roll for several parts of Northampton and wrote down several names. By the time he had finished it was early afternoon. He found a fish and chip saloon nearby which had been recommended by Stu, and found that it was well worth the visit. After he had eaten, he telephoned Kate. She agreed to meet him after she had finished that day, and suggested that he came to her house for tea. Once he had done Anne's shopping and restocked his own larder, it was time to make his way to Kate's. She had not long been in herself, and was still in the dark trouser suit that she wore when on official business.

"Make yourself a cuppa if you like", she said, "I must get into something a bit less formal, and I'm dying for a shower. When you're stuck in an office full of smoke and other people, you get real stale. Shan't be long."

Andrew made a pot of tea and carried it into the sitting room. Lustful memories came flooding back, and he forced his mind to the present. After a few minutes Kate, in clean pressed jeans and a sweater, came downstairs. He poured a cup of tea and passed it to her.

"Mmm! Thanks. Just what I wanted. Well, how was your day?"

"Slow. I found out some interesting facts which I think you might like to know, and there are a few ideas that I would like to bounce off you."

"Right then, let me get my lap top and we'll get started."

Kate said very little, but tapped away at the keys of her laptop while Andrew talked. Once or twice her eyebrows raised, but she remained silent. Once he had finished, she struck 'save' with a flourish. "So", she said, "you want to sort out Burson and Shorland at last. I'll check out those lists of companies in which Sir Colin, as we must now call him, has an interest tomorrow first thing. What do you want to bounce off me?"

"Now that is a leading question" leered Andrew.

"I asked for that, you dirty old man" she laughed, "but business before pleasure, please."

"I have a hunch that Shorland was involved in some sort of smuggling, years ago, when he was doing his National Service in Germany, and that is how he set himself up when he came out of the army and went to Cambridge. Now, of course, all that is old hat, but I just wonder whether Burson was somehow also involved and used that to blackmail him. I'm also pretty certain that Burson is trying to gain control of Joey Caroni's clubs and things, probably to launder money. Now, I've given you Shorland's other business interests, which as an MP he has to declare. I'd very much like to know how often Burson's name crops up as a co-director, or a debenture holder or some such connection."

"Have you any ideas about your own conviction?"

"How on earth do you mean?"

"Well, you told me once, you defended Joey Caroni on a murder charge and got him off. Who was he supposed to have murdered?"

"A small time protection merchant. Moses Levin was his name. Joey had a grievance against him, but he certainly didn't kill him, or have him killed. In the end we proved that two Metropolitan plain-clothes men had fitted Joey up. Mind you, although they were later disciplined and made to resign, and they went down for attempting to pervert the course of justice, I always felt they were the sacrificial lambs."

"What were their names?" asked Kate, tapping away once more at the laptop.

"Detective Sergeant Casey and Detective Inspector Robertson. It was in 1978. Old Bailey case. *Regina versus Caroni.* If you can find the transcript, you will see the dirt we managed to dish. Old George Ingham led for the defence, a first class QC and an honest man. Rare for a lawyer! I think it was George's reputation as much as the evidence that swayed the jury, but I never had any doubt about the matter myself."

"Right. Didn't you once tell me that Shorland wanted you to drop the case?"

"Yes, I did. " Andrew stopped and his jaw dropped. "Good God! No... It couldn't be... By God it could have been!" He got up and paced across the room. If I understand what you're getting at, it certainly fits in. You think, don't you, that Burson tried to fit up Joey in 1978 and that Shorland was his man in our camp? God! How could I have been so dense as not to see it? Somebody wanted Joey's businesses and tried to fit him up. I got him off and exposed the whole set up, so I was eventually disposed of. And meanwhile somebody is still trying to unseat Joey."

Kate looked up at him as he paced backwards and forwards. "That's what it looks like from where I am. I've been trying to convince you for weeks, but now you seem to have convinced yourself."

"It fits, the more I look at it," said Andrew, "Joey was vulnerable through the VAT irregularities. I couldn't do much to help there, but Fiona saved his Empire for him when he was put away. That's why somebody tried to kill her. Get rid of Fiona, and that's Joey's Achilles heel. He's no good at the everyday bookkeeping side. He's a brilliant fixer, organiser, moneymaker, but his weakness is in the bookkeeping. His first wife, Maria, used to do it all. When she was ill and died of cancer, it all went to pot, that's when he got done for VAT offences. I knew all along he had not been on the fiddle so much as got himself in a muddle, but the authorities wanted to make an example, so he went inside."

"So, where do we go from here?"

"You tell me."

"To be quite frank, Andrew, there's not much more that I can tell you at this stage. We think that there's a Mr. Big in there somewhere, who's mixed up somehow with Burson, or maybe Burson is Mr. Big. We are pretty certain that Burson has Shorland on his payroll. Like you, we are convinced that Burson wants control of Joey's business, but we also know that there are other similar organisations under threat. They seem to be getting desperate for cash outlets for laundering money. The main sources of their funds are drugs and a big scale VAT scam, but there is some sort of political twist to it. The IRA seems to be the main suspect at the moment, presumably because they need to pay cash for Semtex and Kalashnikovs and they aren't getting the money in from the US like they used to. Of course, it may not be the IRA at the back of it. It may be a splinter group, but Dooney is certainly involved with Burson, and he's definitely got an IRA pedigree. It's a murky business, and getting hard evidence is almost impossible. Still there is some, but it's all circumstantial at the moment."

"And that's it?"

"That's about it. Is there Any Other Business?"

"Not that I can think of."

"Then pleasure it is." Kate lowered the lid of her laptop, put it carefully down on an occasional table, and, turning to Andrew kissed him on the lips. "Let's go to bed."

Chapter 11
Twelfth Night

When Andrew got back to his boat later that evening, there was a message for him waiting at the farm to ring Stu. He did so and almost immediately it was answered.

"Andy, mate! Thanks for ringin' back. You must be bloody psychic or summat. There's this bloke what's got a boat down at Billin', on the River below Northampton, 'e's got ter get it off its moorin' next week, an' wants ter get it ter Braunston ter sell it. Trouble is, 'e's left it too late, the Arm's shut until March fer repairs, an' 'e don't want to leave it in the town wi'out anyone on it."

"Is he happy to rent it out for a few weeks?"

"E'd like someone ter look arter it for 'im 'till May or June. Reckons 'e'll get a better price then, but 'e's got ter leave 'is moorin' at Billin' 'cause it's bin promised ter someone else. 'E were goin' ter shift the boat at Christmas, but summat got in the road."

"Is there somewhere reasonably decent in Northampton for the boat to stay?"

"Oh ah! Round the back o' the lock island in the park's pretty safe. All 'e's got ter do is ask the ol' boy at the boathouse."

"Right, thanks Stu. What sort of day have you had?"

"A bit bloody rough, mate. We got to 'Illmorton seven o' clock tonight. Took us ten hours from Suttons in the ice. It en't freezing too much tonight, so we're goin' to 'ave a go fer Braunston termorrer, an' our mates John an' Maggie's goin' ter try fer the Top o' Buckby."

"It's frozen right across here, but you could probably break it."

"Ah. They got forty tonnes on the pair, so they'll bust it all right, it's gettin' 'em round the turns that's the 'ard bit. Wi' a bit o' luck, they may get ter Stoke the day arter."

"Anyway, Stu, what's the name of this friend of yours?"

"Roberts, Graham Roberts. I'll gi' yer 'is number. 'Ang on while I find it."

There came the sound of muttering from the other end, then Stu announced that he had found it, and dictated it to Andrew. "Just mention my name when you speaks ter 'im."

Andrew rang the number and was answered by a pleasantly modulated voice. Graham Roberts, it seemed, was a music teacher at a large school just outside Northampton, who was moving at Easter to take up a post in the North of England. If Stu had recommended anyone to him, that was good enough for him. Andrew explained what he had in mind.

"I live on a boat myself, and I am quite happy to take responsibility, but, from what I know of this lad, he's a decent enough boy who deserves a chance. I'll keep an eye on him to start with, and he'll look after your boat for you, and pay you a bit of rent."

"Tell you what", said Roberts, "If he'll keep it clean and aired, run the central heating and so forth, I won't charge him. But he will have to pay for any damage. I've got an inventory for the boatyard, so we'll make that the basis of the agreement."

Next morning, Andrew put the idea to Jane. She was somewhat taken aback, but soon warmed to the idea. "I bin worryin' about the poor boogger. At least 'e'll be somewhere until Kelly finishes 'er exams. I'll tell Kelly ter bring 'im over ter see yer as soon as she can."

"You needn't bother. I'll pop in to see him in the pub this morning. I've got to go to town again, them I'm going to London this afternoon. I'll see what he thinks."

Andrew found the *Fox and Trumpet* with little difficulty. It nestled on the corner of what had once been two streets of shoemakers' cottages just outside the town centre, and which were now gentrified in a similar fashion to his son's place in Islington. A chalked board on the pavement announced the culinary delights available at lunchtimes and evenings. The place looked rather seedy but respectable. He went in to the bar, which was empty save for an ear ringed youth with the remains of bruises on his face and a cropped head who was vacuum cleaning the carpet. He straightened when he saw Andrew.

"Yes Sir, can I help you?"

"Is your name Gary?"

The boy looked suspiciously at him. "It might be" he said sullenly, "'Oo are you?"

Andrew smiled and held out his hand, "Ellison, Andrew Ellison. Kelly's mother works for my landlady."

A great relieved smile broke out on the boy's battered face as he took the proferred hand. "You're the bloke 'er mum keeps on about. The lawyer what lives on a barge."

"That sounds like me. Look, have you got a minute to spare?"

Gary's face immediately took on its suspicious look again. "I ain't done nothin' wrong Mister. Honest I ain't"

Andrew spoke gently. "I'm not here to make trouble. I'm here to help. If you want it, that is."

"How can you 'elp me? I ain't got no money to pay yer."

"I'm not after money. I'm not after anything, but I do know something of how you got those marks on your face, and I would like to help you not get any more."

The boy switched off the vacuum cleaner, straightened himself up and walked behind the bar. "Did you want a drink Mr. Ellison?"

"Only a shandy please. I've got to drive to London. Will you have one with me?"

"A coke please."

"Fine." Andrew put a five pound note on the bar and Gary gave him change. He took a pull of his shandy and said "How would you like to live rent free within ten minutes walk of here for the next five months?"

Gary's eyes widened. "Not 'alf I would. But what's the catch?"

"None beyond the fact that you would be living on a boat. It's all furnished, bathroom, central heating, colour TV, the lot. I know someone who wants a boat sitter until the spring, and Kelly's mum suggested you. She seems to be quite fond of you."

"Ah, she ain't a bad ol' gal. Me an' Kelly wants to get married."

"So I understand. Well, Gary, it's not for me to act as matchmaker or otherwise, but I think Mrs. Dawson would make one condition."

"What's that?"

"That you let Kelly take her exams next summer so that she can get a decent job."

"Is that all? I tell you Mr. Ellison, when she come to live in the flat wi' me, I kep' on to 'er about 'er schoolin', but she wouldn't listen. I suppose we done wrong really, but I tried to do the best for 'er. I told 'er to goo 'ome fer Christmas even. She tells 'er mum I chucked 'er out, though."

"I'm hardly the person to make any moral judgement on the rights and wrongs, but you seem to me to be a decent enough chap. I suggest you put all that behind you. If you like, I'll run you over to look at the boat. It's at a place called Billing at the moment, but I believe there might be somewhere down in the Park where you could keep it. I can't do anything today, but what about tomorrow?"

"The boss'll let me 'ave some time in the day. 'E ain't a bad 'un neither. 'E's promised me to let me kip on 'is settee if me ol' man chucks me out again."

Andrew finished his shandy and got up from the bar stool. "Right then, how about this time tomorrow?"

"That'll be great. Thanks ever so much."

"You're welcome. See you tomorrow then."

In spite of traffic on the M25, Andrew reached Joey's house in less than two hours. Chloe and Imelda let him in, Chloe was very excited.

"Hullo, Mr. Andrew. Mummy's getting better, she's woken up and talked to me."

Andrew glanced at Imelda. "Is that so? Perhaps she'll come home soon."

"I seenk so, Meester Andrew. Meester Caroni ees 'aving a showair, so please to come into ze seetting room. I make you some coffee, yes? Or you like a dreenk?"

"Coffee would be fine."

Chloe took Andrew's hand and led him into the big sitting room. Teddy was sitting in a chair by himself; Chloe lifted him up and brought him over to Andrew. "He's looking forward to when Mummy comes home," she said.

"I'm sure he is."

"He cries because he misses her" explained Chloe, "and I have to tell him to be a brave Teddy, but he won't cry any more when she's home."

"It's good to know that he's not letting it get him down" said Andrew solemnly. The little girl pulled Teddy to her and cuddled him, regarding Andrew with a steady stare from her dark eyes. She's going to be a real beauty when she's grown up, he thought. Then the door opened and Joey came rolling in, arms outstretched into which his daughter flung herself. He picked her up and kissed her, then set her down and looked at her from arms' length.

"Well, Mr. Andrew, wot do you fink o' this young lady, then?"

"I think she is a very well brought up young lady."

Chloe smiled at him, took Teddy and ran back into the hall to join Imelda.

"So!" said Joey, I take it you've 'eard that Fiona's on the mend?"

"Yes, and I'm very pleased to hear it."

"Any luck so far?" He waved Andrew to a seat and sat down himself.

Andrew told him that in his opinion the Yardies and Alex McKinnon could be eliminated. Joey listened, nodding in agreement from time to time. Andrew then expanded on his ideas about Burson and Shorland. When he finished, Joey laughed bitterly.

"An' I fought you was the smartest brief in tahn. Yer silly bugger, did you fink I didn't know them two bastards fitted you up? O' course I did, an' I fought you knoo it an' all. Question is, 'ow do yer prove it?"

"That's going to take a little time, but I just might have an idea."

"That's my ole' Andy. Well you jus' keep at it pal. Any money yer needs, let me know."

"I think what I need more than money is a bit of practical assistance."

"Yeah? 'Ow?"

As Andrew explained, Joey's face began to form itself into a wide grin. "No problem at all, Andy pal, no problem at all" he said when Andrew had finished.

After Joey's house, Andrew's next call was to the Land Registry. He got there just before the doors closed. At first the clerk at the desk was unwilling to be helpful, but when Andrew opened his wallet to pay the Search Fee and he saw a quantity of banknotes inside it, he became rather less difficult. Andrew surreptitiously pinned an additional fifty-pound note to the Search Request Form and winked at the clerk. Within a surprisingly short time the information that he required was forthcoming, and Andrew set forth towards the M25 and home with a light heart. At Toddington Service Station, he stopped and telephoned Kate.

"Would you like another address in Milton Keynes to watch?" he asked.

"Whose?"

"Colin Shorland's, or at least one of his properties. His main residence is in Surrey."

"Andrew, you're a star."

He dictated an address to Kate, arranged to meet her later at her house, and put the telephone down. He got back in the car and drove out of the Service Area onto the M1. He felt at ease with himself, just like he used to when a case was going well, and began to hum to himself. A tune came into his head, and he subconsciously began to sing the words. First the chorus, then the verses, that comic song they used to sing in his army days,

"Tra la lalala la, tra la lalala la,

We've got pockets inside of the skin,
For bottles of Bass, when we've got 'em,
But the audience, they always bloody well boo
When there's froth round the Elephant's bottom!"

He swerved suddenly, and narrowly avoided hitting a lorry sideways on. By God! That was it! That was what had been at the back of his mind since Kate's party! The Elephant song! That was what connected Shorland and the smuggling back in the late 'fifties. He riffled through his mental databank and it began to come back to him. Until Junction 15 appeared he kept it to the back of his mind, but as soon as he had left the Motorway he pulled into the first layby and thought hard. Very slowly at first, then faster, it came back to him. The office Christmas party in 1973, it would have been. Colin Shorland had been there, of course, as a partner. Andrew had been reminiscing about a Christmas party in Cyprus, in the Troodos Mountains seventeen years before, then Shorland had told him an army tale of how certain dutiable goods had been transported between the base in Germany and the UK inside the Battalion band's bass drum. Unfortunately the wretched soldier whose task it was to carry the drum had emerged from the plane at Northolt and overbalanced, pitching head first down the steps to the accompaniment of loud clinking. Andrew had laughed at the tale, and asked Shorland what the end result had been. The matter had been hushed up by the Military Police, he said, and then somewhat abruptly changed the subject. He had never again mentioned his military career to Andrew. That was the one and only time. It was his conversation the other night with Tom Clark that must have jogged his memory. Still pondering, he restarted the engine and headed for Kate's house.

Kate had several files of photographs on the floor of her sitting room; when she let Andrew in, she had been sorting through them.

"You're not supposed to know anything about this, but they're ID photos of members of a certain police force. I'll put the kettle on."

"Mind if I have a look?"

"Go ahead. I'm supposed to compare them with photos taken in clubs and pubs and by surveillance cameras. It's bloody difficult to make positive identifications." She went into the kitchen and busied herself with tea things. Andrew knelt on the floor and opened several files. As Kate had said, they were all fairly boring ID shots, hardly Lord Snowdon quality. He turned over a photo of a youngish policewoman in uniform blouse. There was something familiar about her, he thought, and looked at the details underneath. "James, Sharon Lesley, Constable. d.o.b. 7/6/68." There then followed details of constable James' career and of her posting to CID. Now where had he seen her? Somewhere recently, ah! Yes! Christmas Day.

"Are these suspects, Kate?"

"Not yet. I'm checking them all out. Most of them, if they've been naughty boys or girls, will be at a fairly low level. There may be a few though, who will go in the frame for greater things."

"This one, DC James, she was at the hospital when I went to see Fiona, on Christmas Day. She was supposed to be one of the coppers by her bedside. Her boss was a nasty piece of work. We did not hit it off."

Kate came in with a tray and placed it on an occasional table.

"What was his name?"

"Flower, I think. Detective Sergeant Flower."

"Let's have a look." She knelt down and thumbed through a file. "This is the one for the higher ranks. Ah! Here he is!" She took out a file and opened it. "Flower, Kenneth George, Detective Sergeant. D.o.b. 31/7/58, Hmm, about my age. Is that how you remember him?" She pushed the file over to Andrew, who squinted at it.

"Yes, that's him."

Kate read down the file. "This is one that there's been a query on" she said in a strange tone which made Andrew look at her sharply.

"What sort of query?"

"Suspicious associates. Mind you, that doesn't necessarily mean anything. We all have suspicious associates, you for one. I'll have to look up the photofile at the office. Still, thanks Andrew. It could be a lead, you never know."

"I'd like you to find something on him. He struck me as a rotten guy."

Kate said nothing as she poured out a cup of tea then asked, "How much milk?"

Andrew smiled his lopsided smile at her. He knew her well enough now to know when not to push too far.

"Just a dash, please."

The next day was Saturday, and Andrew found the traffic fairly brisk as he drove into Northampton to pick up Gary after his weekly shop at Tescos. He was glad of a break from what was getting to be a somewhat tiring enquiry. Too much legwork and too much driving. In the old days this sort of thing was done by articled clerks, and he found himself increasingly being reminded of his own younger days when George Robinson was wont to send him out on similar enquiries.

Gary was waiting outside the pub and hopped straight into the car when Andrew stopped. He was able to give Andrew good directions to the eastern part of the town, but even so he had several tries before he found the side road that led across a bridge over a busy trunk road and down to the moorings where he had agreed to meet Graham Roberts. Eventually the side road led across flat meadows to a pair of steel gates set in a barbed wire fence, which reminded Andrew of a top-security prison. A notice asked visitors to ring and wait, and after a short space a slight, bearded man in his mid-forties and wearing jeans and a Barbour jacket appeared. He introduced himself as Graham Roberts, and he unlocked the heavy gates from within. As soon as the car had passed through, he relocked them. Andrew got out of the car and shook hands with him.

"Sorry about the heavy security" he said, "but we're really under siege down here."

"How come?" asked Andrew. Roberts nodded in the direction from which they had come.

"The estates up there" he said. "It's the car stealing and ram raid capital of the area. I think the kids must be potential SAS. Until we put up the gates and fences, we were continually getting break-ins, fires, vandalism, you name it. Even now, at weekends even in winter, you daren't leave the gate unlocked for a minute. I'm not sorry that the boat's going somewhere safer. It's a pity really, because it's quite pleasant down here in summer."

He led Andrew and Gary across an island to a long row of moorings on a backwater. There were all sorts of boats, most of them looking more like river cruisers than canal boats, and mostly sheeted up and under wraps for the winter. They stopped by a dark blue, steel cabined narrow boat, about forty feet long. On the cabin were the names "*G. & .S. Roberts, Northampton*" and ahead of that, by the engine room doors, "*Behemoth*." Roberts saw Andrew lift an inquisitive eyebrow as he read the name.

"The S is for Susie, my ex.," he explained. Andrew nodded sympathetically.

"I know, I've been there myself."

"These things happen. She went off with one of my colleagues a year ago."

"I've been there too."

Roberts grinned sympathetically. "And you're just getting started on the business, I take it?" he said to Gary. The lad had been silent so far, but smiled sheepishly. "Well, I'd better show you over everything, and how it all works." Roberts pulled aside the tarpaulin that covered the front deck, unlocked the front door and motioned the pair of them inside.

To Andrew the boat was nowhere near as well fitted or laid out as *Romford*, and it had a modern, welded hull which did not have the same character, but he could see at first glance that it was nonetheless comfortable and an enormous improvement on a spare settee or a cardboard box on a bit of waste ground so far as Gary was concerned. They spent a full hour going over the boat and its machinery. Gary showed an intelligent interest in things mechanical, and it was obvious to Andrew that he had a feeling for such things. Finally, as they came ashore again, Roberts said, "Look here, I don't want any rent for it, as long as it's looked after. Just to make things simpler though, I shall ask a deposit of £500.00, which you'll get back in June, provided it's in the same state as it is now."

Gary's face fell.

"It's a fair enough deal, sir, but I ain't got that much wi' me. I can't go to the bank for nothin' 'cos I ain't got no fixed abode. They won't even let me open an account."

"I shouldn't let that worry you, Gary. If you want to move onto the boat, that can be arranged," said Andrew. He thought, privately, that envelope of Joey's should more than take care of a little matter like that, and the lad could be a useful ally, especially if the money put him outside Dooney's clutches. "Once you're aboard, I'm sure you could use Kelly's mum's address to open an account."

The youngster's eyes lit up. "I could start saving summat, you mean?"

"You certainly could. Look, don't let the money worry you. There's lots of ways round that which won't hurt the pocket very much. The main thing is to get yourself somewhere decent, and I don't think you'll get a better chance."

Roberts smiled agreement. "Were you at school in town Gary?"

"Yes, sir." He told him the name of a big local Comprehensive.

"Ah then, you'll know Mr. Williams."

"Not 'alf; 'e were my English teacher."

Not a very successful one, thought Andrew, but let it pass.

"Well, I know him very well. Would he speak for you if I asked him?"

"'E might. I always got on wi' 'im. 'E were a good ole' boy."

"If Mr. Williams says OK, I'll only charge you for any damage at the end of June. How about that?"

"Cor, thanks Mr. Roberts. I appreciate that."

Andrew and Gary both shook hands with Graham Roberts. Roberts said he would telephone Mr. Williams later that morning and let Gary know the answer, provided things were all right, he could take the boat over tomorrow, Sunday. The three walked back to the gate. Roberts regarded Gary thoughtfully as he got in the car beside Andrew. There were so many decent lads like him caught in the joint trap of unemployment and under-education. He sighed as he unlocked the fortress like security gates. Why did so many feel they had to be toe rags? Maybe he was a fool, but perhaps he could stop one lad from going to the bad. Jim Williams was a decent sort; he'd know whether or not Gary was to be trusted.

After dropping Gary at the pub, Andrew drove back to the farmhouse. He pulled up in the grassy yard just ahead of Sally, who had driven down from London. She leapt out of her car calling, "Andrew! Just the person I want to see. Have I got some news for you!"

Andrew, paused in the act of unloading shopping from his boot, straightened up,

"Hello Sally, good to see you. Had a good week?"

"Not half! Gosh! I really must thank you for that tip you gave me about Sir Colin Shorland."

"Shorland?"

"Yes, surely you remember, or were you too drunk? You naughty thing! New Year's Day, when you threw a wobbly about him getting a Knighthood."

"What did I do? Remind me."

He walked across to the farmhouse door with her. He opened it for her as she struggled with two large bags. "Thanks Andrew. Mum'll probably have a fit when she sees this week's washing.

You know, when you said he'd be worth checking up on."

Andrew's brain was whirling. "Who? Shorland?"

"Yes, of course Shorland. I've had a wonderful week chasing him, and he's a Class One rotter. Oh! Hello Mummy. Mmmwah!" She planted a smacking kiss on Anne's cheek as her mother appeared in the hall.

"Who's a Class One rotter, darling?" asked Anne.

"Oh! This stinker who got Andrew in trouble. Anyway, lots to tell you, but I'm starving just now. What's in the nosebag Mum?" She whirlwinded into the kitchen, leaving Andrew somewhat breathlessly watching her. Anne's eyes met his, she winked at him. "I think we'll have to talk later" she said. "I think food therapy is required right now."

Andrew unloaded his shopping from the car and carried it across the wharf to his boat. The wind had gone round to the north east and was bitter when he came out of the shelter of the buildings. The warmth of the stateroom hit him with a cheerful blast. He put his stores away and began cutting himself some sandwiches. He would make a cup of coffee and settled down with them to watch the Rugby on his television, he thought. He switched on, opened the front of the stove and stoked it well, piled a plate high, and settled down. It was a good match and had just started.

The match had gone twenty minutes or more beyond half-time when he felt the boat lurch suddenly. It was not like when someone climbed aboard, more as if it had been brought up sharp by a rope. Andrew sat up and peered out. It was getting dark outside, and he could see little beyond the skeletal form of the towpath hedge and the horizon, some two miles away. A string of lighted beads indicated the progress of a train in the distance, and some orange lights were already picking out the village across the valley. He could see nothing untoward and was about to sit down, when the boat lurched again. This time he opened his front door to look out, getting himself nearly winded by an icy gust as he did so. There was a distant crackling and whistling sound, and as he strained his ears, he caught the rapid beating of a distant diesel engine. It had the staccato beat to it, which he already had come to recognise as that of a single cylinder engine. A reflected light glared off the water round the bend in the Stoke direction. Shutting his door, he ran to the other end of the boat, grabbing a coat as he did so. He skirted round the engine, through the boatman's cabin, pulled the slide open from inside and, with his coat round his shoulders, stood on the coal box looking up the canal. The headlight was well in sight now, and the engine note much louder. Dimly behind the headlight he could see the triangular shape of a working boat's tarpaulin cloths, but low down in the water. Behind it he could dimly make out the shape of another. The boats were forcing their way through the cat ice that covered the canal, which accounted for the crackling and whistling, and pushing a substantial displacement wave before them, which accounted for the lurching of his boat. The beat of the engine slowed as it approached the small basin where Andrew was moored. It was the family that he had met at Stoke Bruerne just after Christmas, the Joneses. Peter Jones was steering the motor boat and called out cheerily as he passed, his father was steering the butty boat, which, now it was loaded, was strung out on a long rope behind the motor so as to keep clear of its wash. Margaret, his wife, was presumably in the cabin, from whose chimney a comforting reek of smoke was whipped in Andrew's direction by the icy wind. John Jones caught sight of Andrew hunched up in the door hole.

"Hullo there, how are you doing? Happy New Year to you, if it's not too late!" he called.

"Fine thanks, and the same to you. How's Stu and Emma?"

"Not bad thanks. They've gone to Stockton. We're going to try to get to Fenny Stratford tonight. Just got to hope that it doesn't get any colder."

"Forecast says it will freeze hard next week."

"Tell me about it! That's why we're pressing on."

"Best of luck then!"

"Thanks." The boat glided towards the arch of the bridge. There was the sound of conversation to and from the butty's cabin, then John Jones called, "I nearly forgot. Stu said we were to tell you. We met your pals the dog stealers just north of Braunston. Heading for Suttons. 'Bye now!"

The boat was swallowed up in the arch of the bridge. There was a slight creak as the helm was put over, then she vanished. The beat of the single Bolinder engine increased in noise and tempo as Peter wound on the speed wheel and pushed in the oil rod to pull his butty out of the bridgehole, then slowly faded. Andrew felt a sense both of exhilaration and of sadness. It was wonderful to have glimpsed that sudden pageant of painted boats and polished brass, and to have suddenly slipped back nearly a century. He was glad that he was a part of that scene and was able to savour it, yet deep down he wondered if it could last, and more to the point, if his new found contentment could last much longer. Since Christmas it had had more than a little knocking. He desperately wished to be part of a world where his associates were the Joneses, and Stu and Emma, but increasingly it was one that impinged upon the likes of Alex McKinnon, Colin Shorland and Roland Burson. He somewhat moodily went back to the Rugby to find that the final whistle had blown and he had missed a spectacular try and conversion.

He made himself some tea and banked up the fire. The wind seemed keener than ever as night fell, and he wondered how long the Jones family would have to keep battling through it until they tied up. He was going up to the telephone box in the village to ring Kate when Sally spotted him crossing the yard to his car.

"Hi! Andrew. Don't you want to hear my story?"

To tell the truth, Andrew had completely forgotten, what with the Rugby match and the boats passing. Perhaps Sally might have more to add to what he had to tell Kate, so he called back, I'm awfully sorry, Sally, I was so carried away with the Rugby I never noticed the time."

She held the front door open. "Come in. Mummy's gone up to the village for something. Now's as good a time as any to talk, you know what an old fusspot she is."

Andrew didn't know, but let Sally rattle on as she led him into the sitting room. He refused another cup of tea and the offer of a whisky, on account of his having to drive, and settled down in a chair while Sally was talking. Almost without pause for breath, she launched into her tale.

"Well, you know I was going to do a story on Middle Class crime, and Mummy was a bit dubious, and you said why not look at Sir Colin Shorland? Oh, well you didn't exactly, but you did say I could do worse than look at him. Well. What do you think? The Editor of the paper that I've been sending in stuff for, he's a stuffy old Tory, but quite sweet in his way. When I mentioned Shorland he hummed and hawed and said give him twenty four hours, this was on Monday morning. He rang me on Monday afternoon and said *'go ahead'*. I thought this was a bit funny, because Shorland's one of his side, but still, I'd got the green light, so I thought *'perhaps he knows something and wants it brought out in the open'*. Anyway, I got a photographer and off we went that very afternoon. I'd found out from his Parliamentary secretary that he was in town, but not at the House, 'cos they're still on holiday, so we went to his office in the City..."

"Mincing Lane?" interrupted Andrew.

"That's it. Quite a posh place. Was that where you worked?" Andrew nodded. "I had a few photo's which I got from his Parliamentary secretary. I'd told her that I was interested in doing a profile on him as a new Knight" she interjected seeing Andrew's eyebrows rise inquiringly. A crooked half smile formed on his face at this revelation, *she certainly could get the bit between her teeth* he thought. "So, I went in as if I was a new client to make an appointment, and the receptionist told me that he was busy all afternoon, but might see me next day. We hung around outside and sure enough, about five thirty out he came and got into a taxi. I had my car on a parking meter just round the corner and we followed him. The taxi took him to Pimlico, down by the river, just off the Embankment, and dropped him. We followed him to a house, in Lupus Street it was. A big old house divided into flats. He went in, unlocking the door with his own key. Afterwards I sneaked up and looked at the doorbells. The door he went into had the name Thomas by its bell. When I checked it next day at Westminster City Hall there was only one occupant registered for voting, a Janet Thomas." Sally's eyes were sparkling at the recollection, "I think he's being a naughty boy."

"Well, so he may be, but a spot of adultery is not a crime, although it may sell newspapers."

"All right, but how about this then. Janet Thomas is a Researcher on the records of Central Office..."

"So what? He may have just popped in to check on the current unemployment figures for Dorking or wherever."

"True, but you see, we waited in the car for about an hour, then another taxi turned up, the driver went to the door and Shorland reappeared with a female. They were both well wrapped up, but you could see they were wearing evening dress. Now is it common for an MP to keep his evening dress in the flat of one of his researchers?"

"My studies in anthropology have never progressed that far."

"Right. Off they go, and so do we, and the taxi takes them to Langans. In they went, and we followed. Of course that was where we came a little unstuck. They had a table booked, but, since it was Monday, and since I had a twenty note for the head waiter, he found us a table where we could keep obbo. It was a little dinner party, and the photographer, Joe, he's brill, managed to get them, saying that he was doing a piece for *Tatler*. We nearly got bounced on our ears, but it worked, and the management accepted the story in the end. Anyway" she bent down to a brief case by her feet, "we got the pikkies, and here they are."

She held out a file. Andrew took it and opened the wallet. The quality was good, Joe certainly knew his stuff. There was a picture of the Office in Mincing Lane, which brought a pang of recognition even after four years, there was a picture, taken in daylight of the flat in Lupus Street, and then there were a series of pictures taken inside the restaurant. Shorland was at a well-laden table with a very attractive dark or brown haired girl of about twenty-eight, there were two other men in dinner jackets dining. One had his back to the camera, the other was a stoutish man of the same age roughly as Shorland who looked vaguely familiar to Andrew, and two other women, one elegant and in her forties, the other rather brassy looking and aged about mid-fifties. There was another photograph showing the same group, but this time the face of the third man. He was a slight, wolfish looking man, Andrew estimated his age to be perhaps mid to late fifties.

"And so?"

"And so," went on Sally, "we find another solicitor..."

"Jack Reeves!" Andrew interrupted, "Jack Reeves. Used to be a partner in Harrison, Beckley and Anstruther in Greys Inn Road. I used to drink with him years ago in the *Cheshire Cheese*."

"The very same" said Sally, "and we have reason to believe that you are not the only naughty solicitor. Mr. Reeves is believed to be a drugs courier."

"What!!" exploded Andrew, "Jack smuggling drugs? I don't believe it!"

"You may not, but the paper had a tip off before Christmas from someone in Customs and Excise that he might be worth watching. I only found this out when I showed the photos round on Tuesday."

Andrew sat in silence. The whole thing was getting too deep for him. Shorland he could believe was mixed up in something scoundrelly, but surely not Jack Reeves. A pillar of respectability, although he was fond of a little flutter at times, and he liked a drink or two... Sally was rattling on regardless. *Like Nancy Blackett on speed* he thought ruefully.

"The elegant lady is Mrs. Reeves, his second wife, then we have Barbara Moss, once a night club hostess, now the director of several companies in the entertainment business, according to Companies House. Next is her boyfriend, George Mandel, a hustler, calls himself a 'Commission Agent', an associate of several known criminals, served five years for armed robbery in the early 'sixties and a director of several of the same companies."

"I must say, Shorland picks some elegant company when dining at Langans' Brasserie, but that doesn't prove anything."

"Not on its own, but you might like to know Mandel picked up the tab for all of them with a credit card. The waiter on their table told me afterwards. Anyway, they left the place about ten, Shorland went back to Lupus Street, changed back into his city suit, got another taxi to Victoria, and then got a train going to Portsmouth about eleven fifteen."

"That would take him home. He lives down that way. I'll bet he told poor old Pam that he'd been late at the office."

"I was busy all next day checking out the facts, but the crime editor recognised Mandel right away, and gave me the tip about your friend Reeves. It seems he got himself into deep water at some West End gaming club, and only recently got himself off the hook. Harry - that's the crime editor, thinks he may be being blackmailed. We watched Shorland all week, but Parliament sat on Wednesday after the recess, and he's either been at his office, or in the House. He has visited Lupus Street though, on Wednesday and Thursday evenings and on Friday afternoon."

"Must have missed Prime Minister's Question Time. Miss Thomas must be doing a lot of research for him. Well, you have had a busy week!" He smiled. Sally thought she understood why her mother liked him so much. Although he was so old, he was still quite dishy in a funny sort of way.

"Well, of course I've got no proof that Reeves is a smuggler, or that Shorland is involved in anything underhand, but I think there is cause for suspicion, don't you?" she asked.

He nodded. "There's cause, but for heaven's sake be careful. Defamation is a dangerous card to play unless you've got ample proof."

From outside there came a noise of a car, headlights flashed through a gap in the curtains momentarily.

"Here's Mummy," said Sally. "Best not say too much to her, she gets terribly worried and protective."

"All right, but you must promise to drop the whole thing if it starts getting nasty in any way. Let the police do your raking for you if you have to. Meanwhile, may I keep the photos, just to get them copied for my own purposes?"

"What? Trust the Met? Ho! Ho!"

"Well, even so, drop it if it starts getting heavy. Otherwise I shall never forgive myself, and I want to stay friends with your mother. Promise now."

"Promise. You can keep the photos, but what are these *'other purposes'*?"

"Just say, I'm interested in writing a life of Sir Colin."

It was waiting outside the semi vandalised telephone box in a freezing wind that made Andrew decide to get himself a mobile telephone next Monday. A couple of giggling teenaged girls seemed to take for ever before their money finally rang out. Andrew gave them a glare as they ran laughing and tittering past him. He heard one of them call "Dirty old perve." as she ran. He pursed his lips. Some of what was said about the lack of manners of the young was true, a pity they weren't all like Emma or Gary, or even Sally. He supposed there were some lewd men of his age who would have made a pass at the baggages, but at least he was not one of them. When he got through to Kate she suggested that they met that evening, and she would bring her laptop.

"I think we need to exchange a certain amount of info" she said, "your place or mine?"

"It might be better to chose yours, if you don't mind that is."

"No problem. Bring your shaving kit and you can stay, that way you can have a drink without one of my colleagues breathalysing you."

Now that's an invitation you can't refuse he thought. He agreed to meet her at home after he had helped Gary and Roberts move the boat tomorrow morning. "Why don't I come?" asked Kate. I could do with some fresh air."

Chapter 12
Back to work

Andrew locked his car door and stared warily round. The park seemed reasonably vandal free, but it was after all a particularly raw Sunday morning in January. Kate, who had already got out, shivered and flapped her arms inside her Barbour. Gary, whom Andrew had not long before picked up outside the pub, did likewise. A Volkswagen Golf came crunching along the park driveway; Graham Roberts drew up beside them and wound down his window.

"The chap we want is over there" he waved towards a green metal footbridge that rose from the edge of a tarmaced space behind the upperworks of a pair of lockgates. He got out and the party walked across to the bridge. They crossed over the lower entrance of a lock on to an island on which a small boathouse stood. Roberts led the way to the boathouse, from inside of which came the noise of a radio turned up fortissimo and some desultory hammering. He put his head round the door.

"Stan!"

"Ullo! 'Oo is it? Oh, what 'o Graham me ol' doock!"

A stoutish, bespectacled, middle-aged man wearing overalls came blinking into the light. Roberts introduced the others. Stan shook hands, "Stan Hobson" he said. He looked hard at Kate. "I knows you, me doock. Where've we met?"

"I used to be Community Officer for this part of town, what? Ten years ago."

"Ah, yes, I remember, when we 'ad all that trouble with the glue sniffers."

"That's right. I've moved on since then."

"Well, what can I do for you?"

Roberts explained that he needed to keep his boat safe until the spring, but could not take it up the canal until the repair work on the locks was complete.

"So you wants a moorin' on the island, eh?" grinned Stan.

"And I'd like Gary here to live aboard as a caretaker."

"Well, provided 'e ain't a tea leaf, I don't see no problem. There's a place 'e can 'ave under them willers." He pointed to a spot on the other side of the island. "Nobody'll bother you there. I'll let you 'ave a key to the gate, an' if anyone wants to get on the boat when I ain't 'ere, or you ain't, they'll 'ave to swim."

"How much will it cost?" asked Gary anxiously.

"As long as you 'elps keep an eye on things, nuffink. An' if you're a bloody noosance, you can boogger off."

The party laughed. "Well, that's settled then" said Roberts. "We'll go and get the boat now and get it up here this afternoon."

"Where is it?"

"Oh, only down at Weston Lock. All right if we leave one of the cars here?"

"Quite OK. Have a good trip. See you in about two hours then."

Stan went back into the boathouse and the hammering resumed. The others crossed back to the cars and got into Roberts' Golf. Kate got into the front seat, Andrew and Gary squeezed into the back.

There was very little traffic, and soon they found themselves outside the security fence. Once the car was safely locked inside Roberts led them to the boat. He put Gary through a minute test of all he had told him before and found that he had not forgotten anything.

"Good, so much for the theory, now for the practical. I'll come up to the park with you, but you show me how you can handle it."

Andrew found himself remembering his own introduction to boating. It seemed so long ago, yet it was barely three months since he had been Stu's pupil, now he was helping to train another novice.

The mooring was in a backwater, so the first thing they had to do was to get the boat away from the mooring and into the main navigation channel. It was facing upstream and they had to go downstream.

"You're on a river here, remember," said Roberts "there's not a lot of current running at present, but there's always some. It's not still, like the canal."

He started the engine, Andrew went to the front end to cast off the mooring line, Roberts took the tiller and Kate and Gary stood either side. "I'll take her out and into the lock" said Roberts "then she's all yours."

He bent down and untied the stern rope; Andrew cast off the head and pushed out into the backwater. Slowly the boat began to move backwards with the current. Roberts engaged forward gear and pushed the tiller to the right. The boat straightened its course and hovered in midstream until Roberts went into neutral, then it began to move slowly backwards again. With a few bursts of ahead gear, they were soon at a point where the lock cut joined the back stream; Roberts allowed the boat to drift past the junction, then engaged ahead and drove round the corner into the artificial channel. "That's all there is to working downstream astern, now we're going to go upstream. Andrew, you know how a lock works; please will you take the key and shut the bottom gate while I show Gary what to do."

To Andrew's eyes it was an unusual lock. In place of the bottom gates which he was used to seeing on the Grand Union Canal there was a towering green steel structure straddling the entrance. A huge steel gate was suspended in the centre. Graham Roberts caught his curious expression.

"First time on the river is it? It's what we call a guillotine gate, you lower it behind us and raise it up once we've left the lock. They're there so that floodwater can be run through the lock if necessary. They can open both ends if they need to."

"How do you get through then, if both ends of the lock are open?"

"You don't. You tie up and wait for the floods to go down. One reason why I want to get above the last lock. Once the canal is reopened, you can get up to the main line at Gayton any time, but get prolonged spring floods down here and you could wait for weeks before you could move. Take the key with you!" he called as Andrew began making his way towards a steel ladder that led up to the lockside. He gave Andrew a small silver key. "Whatever you do, don't lose it. All the guillotines on the river are locked, and you have to release the winder with the key. They're a real pain to work too, a hundred turns up and a hundred turns down, but this one's worked by electricity. You stay here, Gary, watch what I do. You'll be doing it at the next lock."

Andrew climbed the ladder and made his way to the foot of the guillotine. There was a control box which he unlocked to find some push buttons inside. He duly pressed the one marked 'lower', a motor began to whine and the massive steel gate started to slide down, its counterweight rising to meet it. Eventually it seated itself on its sill with a thud and the motor stopped. After this the lock worked conventionally, except that as there was a fair amount of water already weiring over the top gates it was not necessary to draw any top paddles, the lock filled itself in a couple of minutes. Gary was given the controls and steered out of the lock, stopping at the landing stage just above it while Kate and Roberts closed the top gates. As soon as they had done this, Andrew pressed the 'raise' button. The gate began to rise and the lock emptied with a whoosh!

"That was fun," he said to Roberts as he stepped back on the boat. Roberts chuckled, "Say that when you've been to Peterborough and back. Apart from a handful, they're all manual. Go on, Gary, take her away."

With Gary gingerly steering they headed under a bridge in a large embankment. Once through it, the river broadened out. They had been protected from the worst of the wind until now, but, once clear of the embankment, they felt it across their faces like a whiplash.

"Carry on, Gary" said Roberts, "I'll get a fire going. I'll show you how the heating works when we tie up." He disappeared below, and soon a stream of smoke appeared from the chimney forward.

Behemoth differed from *Romford* in that it had an open stern deck rather than a cabin coming right aft. The idea was that a family or friends could all congregate on the stern deck and socialise while they were going along, rather than perch precariously on the gunwales, holding on to the cabin hand rails. This was doubtless fine for summer cruising, but on a chilly January day it was not so good. Andrew found himself longing for the warmth which came up from his cabin range when steering, also he found the noise of the engine, which on this boat was under the stern deck rather than in its own engine room, somewhat intrusive. Instead of the comforting chug! chug! of his Ruston-Hornsby there was a tinny rattle beneath his feet, whilst instead of the controls being immediately to hand inside the cabin door, here they were mounted on a column which the steerer had to reach for, moreover, they were of the teleflex variety, whereby one lever served as throttle and gear change. Not for the first time he felt very grateful that fate had steered him in the direction of Stu when he was a complete novice.

After about half a mile, Roberts directed Gary towards a channel which opened up on the left. It led through another bridge in an embankment and he explained that it was part of a flood relief scheme dating from the 'seventies. He pointed out where the old course of the river had gone, then they were back on a narrow cut leading to a lock. Gary managed to bring the boat into the lock remarkably well for a first time, and Andrew was surprised to see that it had more conventional gates than the last one. However they were very heavy and slow to operate, Kate having particular difficulty with hers. Another lock followed within a few hundred yards, then they once more emerged onto a broad stretch of water beneath a road viaduct. The centre of Northampton was ranged before them and Kate entered into an animated discussion with Roberts and Gary about the provenance of the various tower blocks and spires that they could see. The day grew colder; whiffs of coal smoke came from the chimney and whirled back to the group shivering at the stern. Nobody was sorry to see the park appear. They slipped under the green footbridge, went up through the lock, turned downstream past the spot which Stan had indicated, turned round in a wide part, and finally slipped under a tall overhanging willow into the bank. Stan had come out of his boathouse to take the upstream mooring line and Gary was at last brought to rest at what was hopefully to be his home mooring for the foreseeable future.

Andrew ran Roberts back to where his car had been left. As they drove through the suburban purlieus of the town Roberts said "You know, I spoke to Gareth Williams last night, Gary's old English teacher. He said that young man only needed encouragement to make something of himself. It seems his father is a decent enough sort, but over strict, Gareth always found the boy pleasant and helpful and I've been quite impressed with the way he handled the boat and things today. He left school last summer and hasn't been able to find a job I gather." He sighed, "The trouble is, you know, we always say we want a technical society, but we don't provide the education for it. It's not as if the likes of Gary are failures, I think the system fails them. It gives them a sort of nursery until they are sixteen, with all the nice things like art and drama and music and games, then bungs them out into a world that only wants technical qualifications which they haven't got, and haven't a hope in hell of getting, then wonders why they go wrong. I'll tell you what; the wonder is that so many of them end up all right, like Gary. And I speak as a musician myself!"
"You are probably right," said Kate, "but what's to be done about it? I think he's a nice enough lad, but I'll bet he didn't know I was a copper, or he'd have been off like greased lightning."
"There speaks experience" said Andrew, "but I think you underestimate our Gary. Anyway, we'll see. Isn't this the turn off for the moorings?"

As soon as they arrived back at Kate's, she went to the kitchen and put the kettle on.

"We've got a lot of ground to make up" she said, "I blame you entirely for what happened last night."

"Just listen to the hussy" laughed Andrew. "You virtually debagged me as soon as we finished supper."

"It must have been the Fitou then. Anyway, it was a great night, but we really should get on with the other business now, I shall need to have everything straight by tomorrow morning. I've got a meeting with Baskerville at eleven, and shall need to update him."

"And I shall need to see Joey, so I suppose we'd better get on with it. No naughty business then?"

"No naughty business. Yet. Be an angel, Andrew, and make the tea while I get my laptop started, would you?" She went to the sitting room, drew the curtains and took the little machine out of its case.

Andrew was reasonably familiar by now with the geography of Kate's house, so he soon had the tea things assembled on a tray, with a plateful of biscuits. He bore them into the sitting room. Kate tapped a few keys and sat back. "Good. It's up and running. I say, you'd make a wonderful butler. Had you ever thought of it as a career?"

"Can't say I had, but it's nice to know I've got potential elsewhere."

"Now" said Kate, "If I remember rightly, before we were so rudely interrupted by matters passionate, you had got some dirt on Colin Shorland."

"Yes. My sources tell me that he has a mistress, Janet Thomas, in Lupus Street, SW1."

"Good sources?"

"Very reliable."

"Address?"

Andrew told her and she tapped the information in.

"He also associates with a solicitor who is suspected of drug smuggling by the Customs and Excise..."

"You lawyers are a lot aren't you? What's his name?"

"John Reeves. I knew him myself years ago. I must say, he was the last person I'd suspect of being involved in that sort of thing, but there we are. Jack Reeves had gambling debts until recently; he's apparently paid them off. Another mate of Sir Colin's is..."

"Hang on. Let me get the info down about Reeves. Where does he live?"

"I don't know, but he used to be a partner in a firm in Grays Inn Road"

Tap! tap! tap! went the keys, as Kate noted down the address of Harrison, Beckley and Anstruther. "Right, Go on."

"Another associate is George Mandel, a well known hustler, served five years for armed robbery, and Barbara Moss, described as a nightclub owner, but also, I believe, a retired prostitute and an active brothel keeper."

"You've done your homework" said Kate admiringly when she had finished tapping.

"Not I," said Andrew modestly, "my sources did the work. Anyway, last Monday they all had a table at Langan's Brasserie, and a little bird got a photo of the lot."

Kate almost leapt out of her chair. "Really? Where is it?"

Andrew reached into his briefcase, which was lying in exactly the same place as it had been the night before when he had come through the front door to be overwhelmed by passionate kisses, and had collapsed onto the sofa. "Here." He held out the file that Sally had given him.

Kate's eyes were like saucers as she opened the file and glanced through them. "You darling! You super fellow! I'll never doubt your word again! This is going to be very handy indeed. Oh yes! I know they don't prove any shady dealing, but we've had a suspicion that Mandel was involved with the Burson lot for some time, and Barbara Moss is certainly not in the same league as Mother Theresa, although she's damned near as old."

"Miaow!"

"Well, give or take thirty years. She's mixed up with Burson too, she was his mistress, but not any longer. I think she finds younger ones for him nowadays. Maybe she runs George Mandel. Still, Shorland keeps choice company even for a Tory MP. What we don't know though, is what they're all up to. Any ideas? Drugs is a possibility."

"I think something is being moved in or out of the country, maybe from the continent, possibly Germany. Smuggling seems to be Burson's specialty."

"Yes, we ought to be looking at that side of things I know, but at the moment I'm more concerned with proving beyond a reasonable doubt that Sir Colin and Burson have a relationship that goes beyond a passing friendship."

"I know drugs may seem the most obvious thing to deal in, but there may be something else" said Andrew, "look at that dog rustling business. Oh yes, that reminds me, a pal of Stu's came past me last night and told me that the rustlers were on their way to Suttons."

"That's the place near Coventry where the working boats go to load cargo, isn't it? Well, there's something I've not told you yet. The man we picked up that Sunday morning is called Dean Black and he's got form. Two convictions for possessing cannabis resin, one for dealing. He got six months for that last year. The word is that he got onto heroin inside and that he owes money for it. The dog stealing may well have been to feed the habit."

Andrew rubbed his chin thoughtfully. "Hmm. He won't be the first to have got into the habit inside. I used to think it was easier to get the stuff inside than out, especially in Pentonville."

"Did you indulge?" A hardness in Kate's eyes belied the innocent expression on her face.

"Good God, no. My generation knew all about it in the fifties. You know, Huxley's Mescalin experiments and all that, but there was never the pressure on us to take anything, always assuming you could get it. No, I think we were more into sex, smoking and alcohol. I was too old for pot by the time the 'sixties began swinging! Since I've never been a great smoker myself, I had no cravings when I was inside, except for the odd drink now and then. Your party was the first time I've been anything like drunk for years."

Kate's eyes softened. "You must have come across the barons though."

"Oh yes, one of them was in the next room to me in the Open Prison. Charming chap, but then I didn't need anything from him. He'd been a car salesman, but his VAT and Income Tax returns were all wrong. He had a whole lot of chaps on the outside obligated to him for their smokes and fixes when they were in. Told me where to go to get a good deal, and I took his advice when I bought my car." A thought suddenly struck him. "By the way, has Burson got form?"

"I'd already thought of that. We can't find anything whatsoever on him, not even a parking ticket. And that's one of the things that makes me suspicious of him. If he really is Mr. Big, how come he got such influence over the other villains? Usually you find that they've done time, and that they become bigger time villains when they're inside, like your friend the car salesman. So many lesser baddies owe them that they have got ongoing enterprises set up for them when they come out. You know the film, 'The Italian Job'? Well, it may have been a comedy, but there's more than a grain of truth in it."

"You don't have to tell me." They both laughed.

Kate tapped some more at her laptop, then put it aside. "How about a film at the new Cinema complex? It's my last evening off for the rest of the week."

"Do you know, I haven't been to the cinema for years. I'm told it's all very different now."

"Not half. And it's not the place for snogging that it was in your youth I'll bet."

"Is that an invitation?"

After the cinema, Andrew drove Kate back home, declined a further invitation to stay on the grounds that the pair of them ought to be up and doing next morning early, and that he needed to make sure that the boat was all right. Frost had set in before they left for the pictures, when they came out the car was rimed with frost and all the windows frozen up. It took Andrew several minutes defrosting before they could leave the cinema car park. Kate opened the passenger door as soon as he stopped the car outside her house. "No, don't get out. We'll say goodnight here."

She kissed him quickly on the lips and slipped out into the freezing air, her breath smoked slightly as she said goodnight, then she turned away and walked quickly up the garden path to her front door. She did not look back as she opened the front door.

Andrew pressed the starter and drove off reflectively. There had been little real intimacy between them that evening. They had held hands desultorily during the film, but cinemas had certainly changed since he had last visited one. The old smoky gloom of the Regals and Odeons with their rows of smooching couples had gone. Now it was a glitzy foyer with dozens of stalls selling popcorn, sweets, and such, more like an airline terminal. In fact the impression had been heightened by the electronic board advertising the different screen performances and their times. The film had been a most forgettable American action movie, and there was no Newsreel or 'B' picture. He frowned slightly as he recalled Kate's somewhat distant mood and the hardness in her eyes when the subject of drugs came up.

It did not take long to get to the farm. The roads were virtually deserted and scattered with rock salt that was slowly turning the frosty surface to water. He reached the farm turning and bumped down the lane towards the farmhouse. Sally's car was still outside; evidently she had put off going back to London until the morning. As he pulled up in the yard, Anne opened the front door and called him. Once more he had a guilty feeling that he had been betraying her, then quickly told himself that she was just a friend, no more. Anne invited him in out of the cold and offered him a drink, which he refused. The sooner he got aboard the boat and got the heating going, the better. The little stove was a good one, but although he had made it up yesterday afternoon before leaving for Kate's, the chances were that it had gone out. He didn't want a repeat of last time.

"All right then, I just wanted to tell you that your friend Joey rang. He said he'll speak to you in the morning and wants a fax number where he can reach you. He's going to ring about nine, so I told him that I'd have you waiting by the 'phone. You can use my fax if you want."

"Thanks a lot, please don't think me rude, but I must get some heating going in the boat before it all freezes solid."

Anne shivered. "Yes it's certainly what the locals call 'a starved old night'. Sally's waiting until daylight tomorrow before starting for London."

Andrew crunched the frozen grass on the mooring, folded back the icily stiff canvas cover and gingerly let himself down into the frost-rimed well deck. The steelwork of the cabin was iced and nearly took the skin off his gloveless fingers as he did so. The cabin lock was stiff, but he managed to turn it and was pleasantly surprised to find the cabin both warm and dry. He put on the light and bent down by the stove, which still felt warm to the touch. Opening the front he saw there were still a few glowing embers, so remembering another piece of Stu's advice, he took some dry kindling from a plastic bag which was hidden behind the coal bucket, and thrust some sticks and a firelighter into the firebox. The firelighter began to smoke, then suddenly burst into flames. The sticks began to crackle cheerily, and he put a small shovelful of coal on them and closed the front. At least he was not going to have to spend all night unblocking a frozen heating system, as had a friend of Stu's. He noticed that the boat did not give under his weight in the normal way, and concluded that he must be frozen in. Taking his coat off he turned on the television. There would be a forecast soon. He found a half finished bottle of Fitou and a glass, and settled down in front of the revitalised fire.

The forecast had spoken of a hard frost setting in, and it did not prove wrong. Andrew woke next morning to ice on the inside of the cabin porthole, in spite of the warmth in the central heating pipe and radiator. His alarm went off at half past seven, and as he shuffled about in his dressing gown, he heard the sound of a car, Sally's doubtless, leaving. He yawned and looked out of a porthole. It was still dark, but the lights of the farmhouse showed a hard rime of frost everywhere. When he eventually dressed and opened the cabin door, the cold went searing into his lungs. The freezing air seeped into the warm stateroom where the little stove roared valiantly. He quickly shut the door and noticed that the canal was now frozen right across. Even where some heat had escaped from the hull of the boat, it was at least an inch thick. He wondered how the boats that had come past on Saturday evening had fared. In the pale early light, the bare trees and hedges looked bleak indeed, locked in an iron hard grip. A stick which yesterday had been floating freely now was fixed firmly in the ice as if it had always been so. A stingingly chill wind was blowing from the North East across the bare fields and shaking the branches of the taller trees. Looking up at the sky, he saw that although it was clear to the South East, where the sun was rising in a fiery ball, there was a line of grey cloud upwind, while smaller clouds were racing overhead, driven by the polar winds above. *Now*, he thought, *comes the real test of living aboard, we're in for some hard weather by all the signs*. He shivered and went back in the cabin. The warmth hit him and made his face glow.

After breakfast he made his way to the farmhouse. Level sunlight was gleaming on the frozen puddles, but there was no heat in the sunshine. Jane was washing up in the kitchen when he came in. She smiled at him.

"Whoy oop, 'ere's Mr. Matchmaker 'isself" she called as Andrew wiped his shoes at the door. Anne's voice answered from somewhere in the house.

"Matchmaker?" said Andrew, "What on earth do you mean?"

"Our Kelly thinks the sun shines out o' your arse. She's that 'appy wi' what you done fer Gary. She go down to the Park yesterday afternoon to 'elp 'im get straight, an' she comes 'ome over the moon. It's a lovely boat what 'e's got, an' 'e's that 'appy 'isself. The landlord where 'e works 'as told 'im /e can stay on workin' there till the end o' the month at least, and 'e's give 'im more hours to work."

"I'm glad to hear it, Jane. I hope it all works out for them. The trouble is, Mr Roberts'll have to sell it in the spring, then what?"

"'e'd better get 'isself sorted by then" said Jane, rather grimly, "but I reckon 'e'll be all right. I tells Kelly 'you make sure you takes the Pill my girl', 'cos if 'e gets 'er up the duff that'll put the tin 'at on everything. She's a sensible girl though, our Kelly."

"I'm sure she is, like mother, like daughter."

"Get away with you, yer naughty man!" Jane said in a mock angry tone as Anne came into the kitchen.

"I hope you're not trying to seduce Jane" she said, "I need her here."

All three laughed and were interrupted by the telephone.

"That's probably your friend" said Anne picking up the phone from the table.

"Hullo. Yes, Mrs Clarke speaking" pause, "he's right here. I'll put him on." She held the instrument to Andrew. "Go on, take it in the sitting room, you'll be quite private there."

Andrew took it, smiling his acknowledgment at her. He put the instrument to his ear as he left the kitchen. Joey's voice came from the other end.

"Andy, ole pal. Got some noos for yer."

"Go ahead Joey."

"I just wants ter fax yer summat. Ring me back when yer gets it. I'm not at 'ome, so yer'll need the number."

"You can fax me on this number" said Andrew scribbling furiously as Joey dictated the digits.

"Ta, pal" said Joey. The line went dead.

Andrew replaced the receiver and connected the fax machine. He went into the kitchen to tell Anne what he was doing, and while he was there, the telephone rang. After four rings the fax machine began to whirr and tap. A series of pictures began to emerge, and Andrew unrolled the first one. It was a little indistinct, but Burson could be made out along with three other men and four women. One of the other men looked like Colin Shorland, but Andrew could not be certain. He rang Kate at the office and told her. She sounded somewhat harassed.

"Get some faxed to me, will you. I'm in it right up to the eyes this morning. Tell you all about it later. Yes, I'd like to see the photos as soon as you can get hold of them. Bye."

Andrew rang Joey back and gave him Kate's fax number. Joey snorted down the telephone.

"'Oo's this then? Some bleedin' copper?"

"Of a sort. But she's all right. Not like some."

"I bleedin' 'ope not, pal. Listen. I'd like to see yer as soon as yer make it. There's a few fings I don't wanna say over the 'phone."

"I could slip up to see you today."

"That'll do well. Come an' 'ave lunch. I'm dahn the *Princess Caroline* from 'ar parst twelve. I'll 'ave the photos ready for yer."

"Good idea! I'll see you then, Joey."

After he rang off, Andrew went back into the kitchen. Anne was there alone loading clothes into the washing machine.

"I've got to go up to London again today, do you fancy a run up to the West End, while I'm busy elsewhere? I could drop you in Oxford Street, or by Harrods if you wanted."

She thought for a moment. There always was so much to do about the house, but she hadn't been to the January sales for years, and perhaps she could surprise Sally for lunch. She straightened up from the washing machine. "That would be lovely. When will you be going?"

"Oh, about eleven o'clock."

"Great. I'll be ready then."

Why? Thought Andrew, as he walked back to the boat, *why did I ask her, just off the cuff like that?* Was it, he asked himself, off-the-cuff politeness, or was it because he wanted her company? Whatever the reason was, he knew that he was glad that she could come, and that he would be in her company for some time that day.

After dropping Anne in Regents Street, Andrew drove eastwards. It was a long time since he had driven through the West End; all his recent visits to London seemed to take him to the seedier parts. He quite enjoyed the leisurely progress round Trafalgar Square, along the Strand past his old stamping grounds of the Royal Courts of Justice and Chancery Lane. He noted that *The Cheshire Cheese* was still there, although the great newspaper offices in Fleet Street were empty nowadays. Up Ludgate Hill and round St. Paul's, past the Mansion House and then, quite suddenly he was out of the opulence of business London and into the East End. Boarded up shop fronts, tacky advertisements greeted him and the pavements became less thronged as he drove deeper in, along the Whitechapel Road. Soon he came to the turning that led to the *Princess Caroline*. He found a space to park and went in. It was just one o'clock.

The same bored looking barman showed him upstairs to Joey's office suite. Joey looked up from behind a desk piled with papers as he walked in. It was the one where Fiona usually sat; Andrew wondered how he was managing with the paperwork now. A radio blared a continuous burble of pop music and inane comment. "Come in, pal, come in" Joey called. "Bit bloody cold today ain't it?"

"It sure is. How's Fiona keeping?"

"She's well on the mend. She's beginnin' to talk, an' she' s gettin' aht o' bed every day."

"That's grand. Is she going to be all right?"

Joey looked up at Andrew. His dark brown eyes glistened. "She's goin' ter be all right, but it was a bloody near fing. That surgeon knoo 'is bloody job. They told me arterwards she'd 'ad a clot which would 'a killed 'er if 'e 'adn't fahnd it." He bent over the desk and scribbled his signature on a letter then pushed the paperwork to one side. "That's it for nah. Let's get some grub. What d'yer fancy? Steak?"

"That'll do fine."

Joey picked up the intercom and spoke into it. Then he turned and said "well, your idea come up trumps."

"My idea?"

"Burson was in the club at Epping last Saturday wiv some ovver geezers. Your idea paid orf. We got some crackin' photos, an' the best fing is 'e's paid us for 'em."

Andrew then remembered that at their last meeting he had asked Joey to allow some freelance photographers into his clubs every weekend to see if they could pick up any visits made by Burson or his associates. Since the Christmas Eve affair, Joey was having all his premises fitted with closed circuit TV scanners, but the system was not working yet, so this would be a relatively easy means of surveillance. However Andrew had not expected such quick results.

"That's where those fax pictures came from, I take it."

"Right first time. But I got ter be very careful 'ow I lets yer know. Whatever yer do don't say nuffink on the dog an' bone abaht Burson or anyfink ter do wiv Fiona. The Bill's got it bugged."

"It's what?"

"Bugged, pal. I rang you this mornin' from me next door neighbour's, and used 'is fax. You remember them two coppers 'oo come ter 'ospital? They're tryin' ter stitch me up. Oh yes, pal" he had caught Andrew's momentary look of disbelief. "They're tryin', but not gettin' far. Like to see the actual photos."

He pulled an A4 envelope out of his desk drawer and passed them to Andrew. They were much clearer than the fax had been. Colin Shorland was most definitely there with Roland Burson. "Tell yer what, ole Roland didn't like 'avin' 'is picture took. Cut up a bit rough 'e did an' freatened ter smash up the camera. My lads persuaded 'im ter leave the photographer alone, an' 'e bought all the negatives. Or so 'e fought. Yer see the photographer lad ain't so stoopid, an' 'e'd got anovver camera 'adn't 'e? 'E used to be one o' them paparazzi blokes see, an' 'e must 'a knowed summat was up, so 'e'd rigged 'isself up wiv a miniature camera in 'is shirt pocket what's linked to 'is main camera. Burson gets the film orf 'im fer fifty notes, an' 'e's 'appy. I gets a set o' pictures from the ovver camera, an' I'm 'appy. Every bugger ends up 'appy. That's 'ow I likes to do business."

"One of these days Joey, you'll get your comeuppance."

"Not while I got you as my brief I won't." The two men laughed, but Andrew felt rather like he did the day that a grenade accidentally landed by him on a course and failed to go off. If Joey's line really was being bugged, they would have intercepted the fax both for him and for Kate. Burson and Shorland would almost certainly have been alerted, and he would have had to be constantly looking over his shoulder, not to mention Anne. If Sally were also to be connected by some slip, the fat would have been truly in the fire. He said, slowly, "Thanks for thinking two jumps ahead of me. It never occurred to me that the police would be bugging you. How do you know?"

"It ain't too difficult, pal. You gets noises, know what I mean? That Detective Sergeant Flower's aht to pin summat on me, I knoo that day I saw 'im in 'ospital. Day arter Boxin' Day I gets this sort of buzzin' on the ole dog an' bone before the diallin' tone. I've 'ad it ever since, so I ain't takin' no risks. Wouldn't be surprised even if this place ain't bugged, or at least they've 'ad a go. My lot's pretty loyal, but you never know."

"Would it be better to talk somewhere else then?"

"Yeah, maybe. I don't want 'em showin' up at 'ome now Fiona's gettin' better. Where's best?"

"How about my car. We could take a drive down to the river or somewhere."

"An' if anyone sees me get in your motor, they'll be on to you. Nah, we'll take a chance an' keep the radio on."

"If you say so."

"Right, nah, if you looks at them photos you ought ter see two o' Burson's minders. I 'eard that one on 'em as seen lookin' rahnd the Chingford Club the day before Fiona got done over."

A thought struck Andrew.

"D'you think they'll come into one of your clubs again?"

"No reason why not. We didn't chase 'em aht. Why?"

"None of 'em are wearing gloves in this picture, if they come in again, make sure you whip their glasses away and keep them safe. I can get them fingerprinted, and if any of the crowd have got form, it'll show up. Then we can find who they are. You see Burson probably thinks he's pretty safe since he's undoubtedly got some of the Met stitched up in his pocket, so he's not likely to suspect anything. Have you got a digital mobile 'phone?"

"I can get one."

"Good, so will I, we'll keep in touch with them, they'll not bug us that way."

"That's my ole Andy, pal!" said Joey with approval.

After leaving Joey, Andrew drove the short distance to Islington. He rang his son's doorbell and was greeted by Jenny. She smiled and invited him in.

"Joe's only just popped out to the post-box. He's got a deadline to meet for a magazine review and the fax has packed up."

Andrew smiled, taking the proferred seat. "And how's my prospective grandchild?"

Jenny grimaced. "I'm sure it's going to be a boy, and he's going to be a footballer. The kicking that I keep getting! There's every chance that it'll be born taking a penalty. Other than that, I'm fine."

"Well, you must take care of yourself. Don't go lifting heavy things and all that."

"Joe said you'd probably make a fuss."

"Well, I can't help it. It's my first grandchild you've got there."

"I promise you I'll deliver it safe and sound. Tea or coffee?"

"Tea would be lovely."

"I'll go and get some." She went into the kitchen leaving the door open so that she could continue the conversation. Andrew got up and paced round the room looking at the pictures, most of which seemed to be modern and quite beyond his comprehension. The books in the several cases that lined the walls were of more interest to him. There were works of topography, travel, social history, poetry and a wide selection of somewhat battered cheap classics, ancient and modern. Waugh and Amis were there and several new writers whose names Andrew did not recognise, reclining beside Thackeray and Dickens. George MacBeth and Mackay Brown nestled beside Arthur Miller and Shakespeare and Marlowe. Lady Thatcher's *Memoirs*, somewhat ironically, rested beside a translation of Suetonius' *Lives of the Twelve Caesars*. Not exactly his taste, but nevertheless a library that he would find interesting; presumably some of the books were Jenny's.

"I'm glad you called" came Jenny's voice from the kitchen, "because Joe's very worried about his mother. He said he was going to ring you this evening to talk about it."

"Oh. What seems to be the trouble?"

"Well, he's very cagey about it, and won't talk much. I don't know why. We don't have any secrets from one another, but I just guess he gets all screwed up when he talks about her. Your divorce hit him very hard you know." Jenny came back carrying a tray. Andrew instantly sprang towards her.

"Here, let me carry that."

"Nonsense. I'm not an invalid." She set the tray down on an occasional table and began pouring the tea. "Sugar?"

"No thanks. I've given it up. I think it spoils the taste."

"Yes, Joe's been pretty worried I think, but now you're here you might ask him. He had a 'phone call from his mother this morning while I was out. When I got in he seemed very upset, but it's hard work sometimes getting him to talk about things."

Somewhat ruefully, Andrew saw himself in this view of his eldest son. Jenny turned her head towards the hallway. "I think that's him now!"

There was the sound of a key grating in the front door lock followed by a rush of cold air as the door opened. Joe's voice called "Hullo, it's me!"

"Come in, darling!" called Jenny. "We've got a visitor!"

"Have we, who's that then? I only just caught the afternoon post by the skin of my... Oh, gosh! Hullo Dad! What brings you here?" The two men shook hands warmly.

"I was in this part of town on business and thought that I'd call and see how you were."

"Well, I must say, this is a pleasant surprise. I was going to try and ring you tonight, if I could find you, that is."

"What's the problem?"

"It's Mother, you know things weren't too good at Christmas with her?"

"Yes, I remember."

"Well, she rang me earlier today. She can't take any more. She's left Colin Shorland."

Chapter 13
Interim dividends

Andrew nearly dropped his teacup and saucer. His brain whirled. It was difficult to repress a feeling of grim satisfaction at the thought that Pam had had her comeuppance, and then somewhat more charitable feelings began to surface. He must have sat for several seconds with his jaw dropped, before he managed to ask, "so, what's she doing with herself? Where's she gone to live?"

"She went to Jane's flat last night, and, so far as I know, that's where she's going to be for the next few days."

"And that's at Ealing somewhere?"

"Yes. I'll give you the number if you want."

"Well, Joe, I told you at Christmas I wouldn't interfere, but do you really think she wants me sticking my oar in now?"

"I think she's desperate to talk to anyone; even you."

"It's going to be difficult today. I've got to meet someone at four to give them a lift home. I wanted to get away from town before the rush starts. I'll tell you what. You give your mother a ring and tell her that you've seen me and told me about it, and give her my number. No. On second thoughts, I'll ring you this evening and find out what she wants me to do." It would never do if she rang the farmhouse and Anne answered. That would put her off immediately. It would be better to let Joe be the intermediary for the time being.

Joe grinned. "Go on, Dad, don't be shy. You've got someone else in tow haven't you?"

"No, it's not that, at least there's no one specially involved, but I don't want to get your mother involved in my new lifestyle. She'd hate it, and she'd remind me of things that I want to forget. I'll do what I can to help her, I'll even let her cry on my shoulder, but I don't want her getting involved with things in Northamptonshire.

Does this sound terribly selfish?"

"No, Dad. Quite honestly I don't think you owe her any favours after the way she treated you. I love you both, but that doesn't make me blind. I think you're being a real good egg by even considering helping her."

"You make me sound a right prig, but there you are." Andrew drained off his cup and stood up. "Look, I must dash now. I'll ring this evening, I promise."

The two men shook hands again, Andrew kissed Jenny on the forehead and left. Joe watched him from the front step as he got into his car. He shivered; the cold was biting even in this London street, what it must be like up where Father was living now didn't bear thinking about. He closed the front door and went to the telephone. He dialled his sister's number in Ealing.

Andrew pulled up beside the kerb opposite Selfridges. Anne was waiting there with an armful of shopping bags and parcels. Defying the possibility of a traffic warden, Andrew helped her stow them in the boot, then drove off towards Edgware Road. He crawled steadily from traffic light to traffic light up to Marylebone Road, then began threading his way towards Lord's Cricket Ground and Swiss Cottage. Meanwhile, Anne chattered away about her day, how she had met Sally for lunch, where they had gone and what she had bought. Andrew found himself acknowledging most of the conversation with grunts and nods as he worked his way out of London. As they began to speed up along Hendon Way, he began to relax and say a few more words. By the time he had negotiated the flyover at Brent Cross and found himself on the first stretch of the M1, he had become more communicative. By the time they were beyond Scratchwood Services, he found himself telling Anne about his former wife's troubles.

Anne looked sideways at him when he had finished. They had passed the M25 junction and were approaching the A5 turnoff. "I think we could both do with a break" she said, "why don't you pull off the motorway here and we'll find somewhere in Dunstable? I can't be doing with Motorway Service Areas."

Andrew smiled his crooked smile at her. "All right then." He pulled over into the slow lane and down the slope to the A5. At once the pace of things altered, he glanced at the dashboard clock, it was nearly five o'clock. There was a fading reddish glow in the western sky as they came into the centre of Dunstable. They found a place to park and got out of the car. The freezing air struck them like a blow in the face, making them gasp. They hurried into a small precinct with a tearoom, found a table for two and sat down at a tiny table under which Andrew had difficulty in putting his knees. Anne took a cigarette and lighter from her bag. There did not seem to be anything to stop her smoking, she raised an eyebrow at Andrew, who nodded and smiled, so she lit up. A spotty faced teenaged girl hovered beside them with a menu. "Yes please."

Andrew took the card and began to fumble for his spectacles. "Come back in a minute, would you? I'm not sure what's on offer yet." He smiled and the girl retreated. Anne chuckled.

"This reminds me of that scene in 'Brief Encounter' where they meet for tea in the market town."

Andrew was not at all sure that he wanted to be reminded of that film, especially by Anne, but he nodded and smiled absently. Eventually they both decided to have tea and toasted teacakes. After the girl had clattered about serving them Anne said "well, what are you going to do?"

"Ring her and find out what the trouble is. I shall have to use the one in the village, I meant to get a mobile today and forgot. There's no way I could ask to use yours."

"You know, you're very welcome. But you won't need to."

Anne reached for her handbag, felt inside and drew out a small cardboard packet. "For you. It's the least I can do to say thanks." Andrew goggled, took the package and noted that it contained a mobile telephone. "I got it in London today" said Anne, "it's got all its batteries and things, and there's a number assigned to you."

"I-I-I don't know what to say. This is quite unexpected. You really shouldn't have..."

"Nonsense!" Anne interrupted, "If I want to buy you something I will, so let's have no more polite evasions. I'm fond of you, you've been a good friend to me, and that's an end of it." She leaned back in her chair and exhaled a long cloud of smoke. "Maybe I'm a wanton woman, but that's how I am."

Andrew leaned across the table towards her; taking her hands in his, he raised them to his mouth and kissed them. "I appreciate that very much. Now you must let me pay for tea."

As soon as he had gone back aboard *Romford* and attended to the fire, Andrew got his new telephone working. He was glad that Anne had remembered what he had forgotten, because he was already realising the benefits of being able to work from his sitting room as it were rather than the draughty confines of the local telephone box, with all its concomitant teenagers and their loathsome habits. The first call he made was to Joe. Joe told him that Pamela would like to hear from him, and gave him the number of Jane's flat. Andrew in turn gave him his new mobile number. He told him that he had acquired it on the way home, but thought it best not to elaborate upon how he had done so.

Andrew pressed the digits of Jane's number. His daughter's voice gave him a shock when he heard it. She had been a sixth former when he had last heard it, now it was slightly deeper and much more assured. He said "Hullo, Jane. It's Dad."

Was it his imagination, or was there an almost imperceptible hardening of the tone?

"Oh! " a pause, then " How are you? You really took me by surprise."

"I'm sorry, my dearest. How are you keeping? It's so long since I heard from you."

"Yes, I suppose it is. I'm fine. Mother's here, I gather she wants to speak to you."

So that was it. There was once a time when he and Jane had had a relationship that he would have described as ideal for father and daughter. Then there was real love and warmth, now she was cold and distant. Andrew sighed.

Pamela's voice came on the line. "Andrew?"

"Yes, Pam, it's me. I'm sorry to hear of your trouble."

Pamela's voice was sharp. "Don't waste your sympathy. I've made a mistake, and now I'm paying for it."

"We've both made mistakes, but that's all in the past now."

"Maybe it is for you, but it's not for me. Look, Andrew, I know I've no right to ask this of you, but I really could do with your advice."

"Why not see a solicitor?" Andrew instantly regretted the barb, but was unable to repress it.

"If you really want to know, it's because you are the only person that I can talk to and who would understand the whole story."

"I'm sorry, Pam, but I can't advise you on legal matters. You must know that. I'm not qualified any more."

"Yes, I know all about that. I don't want legal advice so much as good advice."

"All right then. When and where? I think we ought to choose neutral ground."

"Tomorrow if you can. I've got a car, what about 'The Bell'?"

"Aston Clinton?"

"That's the one. Early lunch, like old times?"

Like old times indeed! He used to be able to afford the prices then. They used occasionally to pop out there if he had business with one of his main clients in Hertfordshire. Although it was not so very far away from where he was now living in terms of distance, it was light years away in terms of experience. Well, perhaps it would do no harm, just this once.

"All right. Shall we say just after twelve?"

"That'll be fine. See you tomorrow then."

"Till tomorrow."

Pamela rang off. Andrew looked dazedly at the telephone. To

think that the very first call he would make on it would be to his son and the next to his ex-wife. Life was unfolding rather too fast for his liking. He cleared the instrument and rang Kate's home number, only to hear her answering machine, so he rang her office number. She answered almost immediately, sounding tired.

"Oh, hullo. I was hoping you'd ring. What's new?"

"Plenty. Did you like the faxes? I've got some better copies."

"They were great. Now then, Joey's going to get me a set of fingerprints of all the villains who come into his club so that we can identify them."

"How's he going to do that? Ask them to ink their fingers?"

"No. They all drink from glasses, don't they? He also thinks his 'phone line is being tapped by the Met, or somebody."

"Well, if they have got permission to do it, they must have gone pretty high up the ladder. Of course it may be an unofficial snoop. If it is, then it can't be used as evidence."

"Tell me about it. Also, my ex-wife's left Shorland."

"Has she now? That's a turn up for the book. Do you know why?"

"No, but I'm going to find out tomorrow. We're meeting for lunch."

"Oh, where?"

"'*The Bell*' at Aston Clinton."

"Crikey! A bit out of us flatfoot's league if you ask me."

"Not if you're bent."

"Very funny. The fingerprints are a good idea though; we might get some definite information as to who is who. Make certain that each glass is positively identified though, we may not have some prints on file, and anyway it's nice to put faces to prints."

"Trust Joey. He'll get it right."

The frost had hardened considerably overnight, and *Romford* hardly moved at all when Andrew got up next morning after a somewhat restless night. He knew that he had to see Pamela; at the same time he did not feel that he could do so, and still remain in control of his feelings. He had got up several times, poked the fire, which did not need it, and fiddled about generally. He had eventually drifted off in the small hours. Consequently he was not at his brightest when the alarm woke him to a dark morning. He made himself some breakfast still wearing his dressing gown, washed up, then shaved in leisurely fashion. He decided that he would not wear his business suit, but a blazer and slacks instead. That should be sufficiently formal for where he was going. Pamela was sure to be dressed to kill, but she was welcome to do so. He had had enough of playing her games, and didn't need to do so any longer. Even so, he found himself selecting a good aftershave and dabbing *Eau de Cologne* on his handkerchief, and was almost angry that he had done so without thinking.

He drove to Aston Clinton via Aylesbury. Looking at his road map, it seemed as if there was a route through Leighton Buzzard, which followed the canal, but he did not know it as yet. Another time he would explore it, but today was different. He wanted to get to the meeting, and get it over with. The ice bound country looked forlorn as he sped along the gritted main road. Slushy salt had been thrown over the verges giving them a dirty brown appearance. The traffic swished past, cars, vans, heavy lorries all unheeding what lay beyond the hedgerows and verges. It was to that, that he wished to return as soon as possible. He had not had this feeling when going to London to see Joey, although he was always glad to leave town on his way home, and had no desire to stay overnight anywhere than in the countryside.

Circling the gridlock of Aylesbury town centre, he worked round the ring road, noticing as he did so, that he crossed a frozen canal, and came out on the A41 London road. A few minutes later he had parked his car and was sitting at the familiar bar of '*The Bell*'. He glanced at his watch. It was only just twelve, he was somewhat early. Perhaps he should have kept her waiting, but no, he decided, he must stop this pettiness. Trying to score points off one another was futile. He ordered a mineral water, and had taken two small sips when Pamela entered.

She was every bit as elegant as she had been four years ago when he last saw her. Slim, medium height, hair perfectly coiffured, she was wearing a neat two piece lime green suit, a pearl necklace, expensive looking tights and shoes to match her suit. Andrew realised again, as he had done so many times in the last years when he had not seen her, why he was attracted to her. She was, even in middle age, still a beautiful woman. She caught sight of Andrew and walked towards him, he rose, took her hand and shook it formally. She bent her cheek towards him for a formal kiss of salutation. Andrew noticed that she had rather plastered make-up round her cheeks and mouth. She never used to do that.

"So, Andrew. We meet again!"

"We meet again. What will you drink?"

"Just a Perrier water please."

Andrew turned to the barman, caught his eye and ordered. "I've ordered a table for half past" he said, "shall we sit?"

He led the way towards the lounge, indicating to the barman where they were going to sit. Pamela lowered herself gracefully into a chair, displaying a modicum of silken clad thigh as she did so. Andrew noticed, but found that he was strangely unmoved. Perhaps Anne and Kate were more powerful antidotes than he realised. Once upon a time, such a gesture would have had him at her instant beck and call, wanting more. Perhaps she caught some nuance of his expression, for she quickly moved her skirt to cover herself. Obviously, thought Andrew, his eyes had not betrayed him by dilating their pupils.

The barman hovered with the Perrier water. "Would you like to see the menu here, Sir, or at the table?"

"Oh, at the table, I think" replied Andrew. Pamela smiled, showing white teeth beneath her thin lips.

"You haven't lost your *savoir faire.*"

"I suppose not. Tell me, how's Jane? Getting stuck in to Trust Accounts?"

"A pity you didn't pay more attention there, I'd say," (*she's lost none of her tartness*, Andrew thought) "she's certainly enjoying life.

I think she has inherited her Father's advocacy powers."

"She didn't seem to want to say much to me last night."

"No. I dare say she didn't" Pamela's lips were tight together.

"Anyway, hadn't you better tell me what you want to tell me? Joe told me you were worried about something."

Pamela glanced round the comfortable lounge. There was nobody anywhere near them. A party of businessmen had just come in and were clustering round the bar; apart from them they were alone.

"Look, Pam, if it's any consolation to you, it gives me no pleasure to know that you've left Colin." *You lie in your teeth*, he thought, *but I've got to get her started.* Pamela gave him a thin-lipped smile. "Thank you, Andrew. Yes. I've left him. I couldn't take any more." She fumbled in her handbag for a cigarette, her hand shook ever so slightly as she put it in her mouth and lit it with silver lighter.

"I'm sorry, I don't smoke at all these days" Andrew said, watching her. She sucked greedily and then expelled a long cloud of smoke. "It's all right. I suppose I shouldn't either." She paused and looked hard at Andrew. "How much do you know about Irish politics?"

"Not a lot. I know the difference between Sinn Fein and the Unionists, that's about it really."

She nodded. "About as much as us English know or care, and far more than the majority do. Well, Colin is on a backbench committee, which calls itself something like the Anglo Irish Parliamentary Accord. They have been trying to build bridges between all the major political parties here, in the Republic and in the North."

"Seems an excellent idea, but I can't see it ever getting very far. At least it keeps the politicians talking, as if anything would ever shut them up."

"Quite. I would not have thought that there was anything to worry about in such a movement. That is, until last summer, when we came back from visiting some of Colin's opposite numbers in Dublin. You know what an awful right winger he is, anti-Europe, anti-immigration, anti-Semitic, anti almost everything that makes life interesting and in favour of everything boring, like hard work, money and being a po-faced low churchman. We had been together for most of the time, but he went off on his own for a few hours on two or three days and said he was meeting privately with some Ulster Protestants. I didn't worry because I thought if that really was the case, then he's welcome to them. I was absolutely certain that there was no other woman involved. Then, when we got to Heathrow, we were going through Customs and he seemed to have a funny turn. We had to call an ambulance and there was a terrible fuss. I had one hell of a job reclaiming the baggage and getting it sent home."

"You say he *seemed* to have a turn."

"Yes. That's right. Because once we were in the ambulance and tearing down the road to hospital with me holding his hand he suddenly perked up. He stopped the ambulance, got up off the stretcher, and told them he was fine. He'd just had a dizzy spell, brought on by too much to drink in the aircraft. Well, this was rubbish, because he only had one double whisky all the time we were in flight. He told the crew that he didn't need their assistance, thanked them all very much and offered them a fifty pound note between them to set us down out outside Hounslow Underground Station. He said he would write to the Ambulance Trust, on Commons writing paper to put matters straight with their bosses. So, we pulled into Hounslow and caught the Piccadilly line to Victoria. All the time we were waiting for the train, he kept looking over his shoulder, and all the way up the escalator at Victoria it was the same. So when we got home to Dorking, I asked him straight out, what game he was playing."

"And?"

"He hummed and hawed, and beat about the bush, then said that he'd received threats from an terrorist agent. When we were coming through Customs, he spotted a well-known IRA terrorist coming through behind him. I asked why he didn't call the Airport Police, and he said it would only have resulted in a shoot-out and lots of others being hurt. He guessed that if the terrorist were going to take a pot shot at him, he would hardly dare do it if he were surrounded by Airport staff, photographers and general gawpers."

"Sounds reasonable. But why on earth should the IRA want to bump him off? Surely they've more important targets, with respect to Sir Colin."

"I really don't know. But I can assure you that he wasn't fooling. Two days after, I got a most peculiar message on the telephone from someone with a strong Irish accent."

"North or South?"

"Oh, I wouldn't know. He sounded like that vulgar little Irish comedian, you remember, the one that used to make you laugh so much."

"Frank Carson? Well, he's got a Northern Irish accent. Go on."

"This man told me to tell Colin that delivery time was getting near, and to tell him that somebody wanted to meet him at Ferguson's or something like that. I couldn't get it all, because he had confused me. Then he rang off."

"Did you try to trace the call?"

"I dialled the call-back number, and the line was blocked."

"This name you think was Ferguson. It wasn't Carrickfergus was it?"

Pamela's eyes opened wide in astonishment. "Yes, it was" she cried "how on earth did you know?"

"Merely an educated guess" said Andrew smoothly. "Ferguson's a Scottish name, but there's a place near Belfast called Carrickfergus. Northern Ireland you know."

A waiter, who had appeared beside Andrew, coughed discreetly to gain his attention. "Your table is ready for you, Sir."

"Oh, thank you. Allow me." He helped Pamela up from her seat and followed the waiter into the restaurant. They had a table for two in a quiet corner.

After they had ordered, and Andrew had chosen a light white wine to go with lunch, "after all," he said, "we've both got to drive home, so we'd better take it easy," he took the conversation up where they had left off. "What was he supposed to deliver?"

"I wish I knew. I passed the message on to him, and he went berserk. He swore at me, told me that I was interfering in his business affairs, that I should not listen to cranks and so on and on. Anyway, I've had several calls since, and I've always told the caller that he must phone his private line, or mobile number, but last Friday was the last straw. I've had my suspicions that he was having an affair (*Did you, now?* thought Andrew), you know the usual things" Andrew's eyebrows raised in mute question. "Oh, yes you do. You've handled enough divorces in your time. Excuses for staying in town overnight, late sittings in the House and so forth, mysterious drawings on our joint account, credit card billings to Interflora, Janet Reger, Chanel and the like, when I know damn well I've had no flowers, knickers or scent given to me. This time the Irishman said that if I didn't pass on to him that Ferguson, or whatever, was getting impatient, he was going to send pictures of someone called Janet Thomas and him to the press. Then he rang off."

Pamela fumbled in her bag for a handkerchief, dabbed her eyes, and took a gulp of wine. Andrew smiled sympathetically at her, he found himself feeling just the tiniest bit protective towards her. Perhaps time was healing the bitterness somewhat. He let her compose herself while the waiter set an *entrée* in front of them. After a moment, she took up her knife and fork and began dealing with the fish *paté*. She ate a little bit, then laid down the cutlery and continued.

"Of course, we had the most awful row when he came in that evening. He threw all sorts of things at me, that you were a loser from whom he'd saved me, that I was just a money-grubbing strumpet. Oh, it was awful. Then he hit me. I've seen him angry before, but never like that. He punched me in the face." (*Aha! That explains the plastered make-up*, thought Andrew) She sighed deeply. "I've never struck another adult, and very rarely the children when they were naughty, but I just lost my temper completely. I slapped his face back. Oh, Andrew, how awful. There we were fighting like gypsies at a fair. I felt so shamed. I turned away from him, ran upstairs and packed my bags. I left that night and went to Jane's. So, now you know. Yes. I've had everything I deserved for betraying you. I know now what a rotter he is, and all I can say is, I'm sorry."

Andrew was silent for a moment. There was no triumph in this, his ex-wife creeping back to him like a whipped puppy, yet he found it hard to repress a grin at the thought of Pamela smacking Colin Shorland's smug, bloated face. On the other hand, the ruin of his career, the destruction of his family, nearly four years taken out of his life, let alone the humiliations and hardships of prison and his public disgrace, could not really be forgotten just because an attractive woman wanted to say sorry.

He absently finished his *paté*, then said, "I'm sorry it's had to be like that. Look, I'll do what I can to help you sort things out, but I've got no money and no house now. Nor am I a solicitor."
Pamela's eyes were full of tears. "I don't really deserve anything, but I would be glad of your advice. I've no claim on you after the way you've been treated, but perhaps we could be friends again."
"I think I can go along with that, Pam, but you must know you've hurt me pretty hard."
She put out her hand and touched his forearm. "I know. I have to live with it. I'd like to be friends though."

The pair were silent for a while. The waiter cleared away the *entrée* and brought them the next course as they both sat silently, lost in their own thoughts. He served the vegetables, asked Andrew if he wanted another bottle of wine, to which he merely shook his head, and bustled off back to the kitchen. Eventually Pamela said, "At least the food hasn't got any worse in the last four years."
"I've certainly had to eat worse" said Andrew, "you should try the food in Pentonville."
"Don't rub it in. It hasn't been all roses for me, you know. Oh yes,

I'm sure you think the same as everyone else. Tory MP's wife, best of everything, plenty of blue hats for the Party Conference, such hardship! But I had to put up with his violence, his gambling and drinking, his mood changes, the awful greasy people he brought home to be entertained. That Roland Burson mentally stripping me every time he came to dinner and pawing me when he said goodnight."

"Burson!?"

"Oh, you remember him. He used to come to Lipscombe with Colin."

"Oh yes, I remember him. What was he doing with Colin?"

"Some business they had together. Colin used to meet other MPs and ministers, Burson was often there."

"Was he now." Kate would be interested in this little titbit. "I never knew Shorland was into gambling. The horses or roulette?"

"Both. Burson has interests in both bookmaking and gambling clubs. Colin owed him a lot of money at one time."

"But not now?"

"No. About a year ago he told me that he had squared everything up. I believe him too, because he had a betting limit at one time, but he hasn't got one now."

"Um, yes, that does seem likely. How did he pay Burson off?"

"I don't know. He says he made a killing on the stock market over one of those big privatisation things. I said he should be careful about dabbling in things like that, because the Press would murder him if it got out that he was insider trading. But he laughed it off."

The dessert was brought. Pamela toyed with hers, Andrew ate his with relish. He always had had a sweet tooth, and, if erotic dreams had been lacking in prison, there had been no lack of dreams in which sumptuous desserts featured. The conversation wandered into family matters, and here they found that they had so much of common interest over the doings of their offspring and other relatives, that coffee came and went and before they knew it the time was half past three. They sat before the fire in the lounge almost as if they were still married.

The shrilling of Andrew's mobile 'phone broke into the cosiness. Andrew had a momentary panic as he searched for the thing in his pockets. It was Joey.

"Andy, pal. The Eagle has bleedin' well landed. Can you call in today?"

"I can be with you in under the hour. Home or away?"

"'Ome, pal. See yer."

Andrew smiled at Pamela. The lunch had turned out better than he had hoped. Now it was time to consolidate gains. "I'm sorry. I shall have to go. That was someone that I'm doing a bit of work for. Something has come up, and I need to go and look at it."

"Who is it? Anyone I know?"

Andrew was just about to tell her that it was Joey Caroni, then thought better of it. Besides, Pamela had never liked him; she thought him vulgar.

"I very much doubt it. He's a good client."

"Client? I thought you were..."

"Ex-solicitors don't have to abandon everything. I can't act for clients in court or do conveyancing, or act as an executor or trustee, but there's a lot I can still do, if people trust me. And some still do."

"I think I know why" said Pamela.

Flurries of snow were falling over Epping Forest as Andrew drove into Joey's driveway. Joey came bounding to the door, his face beaming.

"Come in, pal. 'Ave a bleedin' drink. Let me take yer coat. Cor, fings ain't 'arf moved since yesterday dinner. Best fing, though, is Fiona's gettin' up an' abaht. She's goin' ter be orl right. I'm goin' ter take 'er to the Canaries next munf, if she's goin' ter go on as well as she 'as bin. 'Ow abaht you comin? Bit o' sunshine'd perk you up a treat. Bring a friend if yer like. Wot abaht that widder woman, eh?" He nudged Andrew playfully in the ribs. Andrew looked at him affectionately. This was the old Joey, generous to a fault in his elephantine way. He hated having to decline.

"Look, Joey. I must get this job done. If the trail goes cold, I'll never forgive myself. And I can't do it if I'm sitting on a terrace in the Canaries."

Joey's face lost its beam for an instant, and then perked up as quickly. "Yes, you're right, pal. Take a seat."

He ushered Andrew into the Laura Ashley sitting room. Andrew sat as Joey went to pour him a drink. "Only mineral water, please Joey. I've had wine at lunch, and I daren't have any more."

"Please yerself" said Joey, pouring himself a substantial gin and martini. "Anyway. The next good noos is, Burson, Shorland and three 'eavies wiv a crahd o' tarts, comes into the club at Finchley larst night. I'd put the word rahnd all my managers ter let me know as soon as they shows up in any o' my clubs or pubs. Abaht 'ar parst ten Abey at Finchley gets me on the ole' dog an' bone. 'Joey' 'e sez, 'them geezers wot you told me abaht, just walked in 'ere.' 'Keep yer eye on 'em' I sez. 'Serve 'em drinks an' make sure you 'andles their glasses wiv gloves.' Well, you see, it's a bit posh this club, an' I makes the bar staff wear tuxedos an' dickey bows, an' some on 'em wears gloves anyway, jus' ter take the piss. So I finks *'we can use this'*. 'I'm comin' straight over.' I sez, make sure you knows 'oos glass is what.' Well, ole' Abey's a bit puzzled I s'pose, but 'e does as I tells 'im. Good boy that one, pillar of 'is synagogue. I tells 'im 'is rabbi would be prahd. I'm straight over there, like a rat up a pump. Time I gets there, they'd 'ad one rahnd an' called fer anuvver. 'Abey serves 'em 'isself. 'I'll get you noo glasses' sez 'e', all posh like. Time I'm there, 'e's got all the glasses in 'is office, an' each one labelled. I decides ter play fer safety, so I collects all the glasses after the second rahnd an' all. Bofe times they 'ad the same drinks. Burson drinks G an' T. Shorland 'as scotch, the 'eavies 'as pints o' lager an' the five tarts all 'as Daiquiris an Malibus an' that sort o' stuff. No problem identifyin' 'oos drinks are 'oos. I 'as a squint myself froo the two way mirror be'ind the bar, 'an there they are. One o' the 'eavies, an older, sharp featured lookin' bastard, 'as got a little counter fing, an 'e's keepin' a tally on 'oo's drinkin' what. 'E seems ter be wiv the older tart.

The bastards. I knows what they're after."

"Yes, it does look a bit like they're openly sussing out your clubs for some reason. Where are the glasses now?"

"I got 'em 'ere. I tries ringin' yer this mornin' at the widder's, but no one ain't there. When I does get 'er this afternoon, she tells me you've got yerself a mobile, an' gives me the number. She's a good 'un I reckon. You wants ter keep on the right side of 'er!"

"Thank you Dr. Caroni! Let's have them now, Joey. I'll get them to forensic as soon as possible."

Joey pulled a large cardboard box from behind his chair. He opened it. In it, carefully wrapped in newspaper and tissue were twenty glasses, each carefully labelled, with each label having a number on it. Joey caught Andrew's look of inquiry. "Abey ain't no bleedin' fool. I reckon 'e's worked fer Mossad. Time I'd got there, 'e'd not only labelled the glasses, but 'e'd put a number one on 'em ter show what round it was!"

Andrew laughed. "He sounds as if he's done this sort of thing before." He looked again at the glasses. They were all stamped with the logo *Criterion Club*, even better. "Good for Abey. I take it your club's name is the *Criterion Club*? Right. I'd best waste no time. I'll get them up to Northamptonshire as soon as possible."

As Andrew drove out of Joey's, his headlights suddenly reflected off a car parked in the trees opposite the gate. His first thought was that it was a courting couple, then on reflection thought it perhaps rather early for such amusements. In the split second that his lights caught it though, he could have sworn that there was only one figure in it, a man in the driver's seat. The car pulled out behind him as he drove off, switching on its lights as it did so. Andrew's vision was blurred by snow, and blinded by the headlights now behind him. He thought it was a blue Mondeo but could not be sure. The lights came up close behind him, then dropped back and pulled off the road. *Taking my number*, flashed through his head, but then he was automatically slowing down for a junction and had to change his concentration. He would tell

Joey that someone was watching his house as soon as he had a secure line to do so. At the first petrol station that he came to, he stopped and rang Kate. She told him to bring the glasses straight to her house and that she would be there to take them from him.

As he drove north from the M25, the snow got heavier. By the time that he had reached the Northampton turn off it was falling in great flakes that continually obscured the windscreen. Kate's house was in a village close to the motorway, but to reach it he had to leave the well-lit and salted main road and venture down a narrow lane between hedges. Drifts were beginning to pile up by gaps in the hedge, he realised that he had to not only get the evidence to Kate, but she had to get it to Forensic, and if the roads were blocked this could take some time. He left the glasses in the back of the car and ran up the path to Kate's front door. Kate was wearing a housecoat and her hair was in a turban when she opened the front door. "Christ, what a night! Come in."

Snow whirled round Andrew's legs as he stood by the door. "Can we get the evidence somewhere safe?"

"In here. I'm going in at five tomorrow morning."

Without a word, Andrew turned and ran back through the snow. The box was still there on the back seat. He breathed a sigh of relief. Ever since he had seen that car follow him from Joey's he had been half afraid of being followed and even stopped. He was sure that Burson's henchmen would not scruple to use violence if necessary. Either they did not suspect what he was carrying, or the blizzard had helped him make good his escape. He set the box down in Kate's hallway, puffing somewhat.

Kate said "let's have a complete update. I'll go and get my laptop."

Andrew did not stay the night. It was still not eight o'clock, but Kate had to be at work early, so he struggled back to the farm along roads that, in spite of salting and gritting, were showing signs of blocking. The lane down to the farm was a nightmare of skidding and sliding. Eventually he ran into a drift almost in sight of the farm and was unable to move. Remembering his mobile he rang Anne's number. She told him to leave the car where it was, they would get it out with a tractor in the morning, and come down to the house for a warm drink. Ten minutes later he was sitting in what had become his usual chair in front of a roaring log fire, relaxing with a glass of hot whisky toddy. Anne insisted that he stay for supper and sleep in the house, rather than go to the boat. Andrew was too weary to do more than make a token resistance. He and Anne sat up until the small hours and he opened his heart to her as he had never been able to do so before. They sat side by side on the sofa holding each other in easy intimacy as the logs gradually subsided into a fiery glow. It seemed the most natural thing in the world to go to bed together.

The glaring reflection of a snow-filled world woke Andrew soon after seven. He found his pants at the bottom of the bed, slipped them on and padded to the window. He pulled back the curtains to be faced by a brilliant sunrise in a cloudless sky. Anne groaned and rolled over. She suddenly sat up in bed, blinking and holding the duvet modestly over her bosom. "Oh, Andrew, darling. I'm so glad that you're still here." Andrew glanced down at his semi naked torso. "Is that another invitation?"

"Now, now, don't be greedy." Anne's eyes sparkled. They both embraced and kissed. Anne suddenly called "my God! Jane! She'll be here any minute, and then everyone in the County will know what we've been up to!" She leapt out of bed, grabbing a pair of silk knickers and a bra from the radiator where they had been airing, and fled into the *en suite* bathroom.

"Very commendable" called Andrew, "but she's not going to be here just yet. Unless she's driving a snowplough, that is."

Anne, wearing a dressing gown, came to the window and stood beside him. The farm stood isolated in a wilderness of white. Trees and hedges were blanketed with snow, the lane and farmyard had disappeared, drifts even ran onto the ice of the frozen canal. It was a scene of breathtaking loveliness, but life had to go on. They kissed and began washing and dressing. It looked as if it was going to be a busy day.

How busy it was, Andrew could scarcely remember afterwards. One thing was certain; he had never enjoyed such hard physical exercise for years. The first thing to do was to clear the yard and make paths to the barns and to the wharf. Poor old *Romford* had apparently become part of the surrounding land. A drift ran from the wharf right up to the cabin sides, and Andrew found himself excavating a trench just to reach his stern deck. The foredeck was completely buried; thank heavens he had pulled the cloth covering tight. He managed to wriggle himself on to the stern deck, which was heaped high with snow. Shovelling and brushing this away and onto the ice of the canal, he blew onto the padlock and got his key inside. The stern doors were stiff, but eventually flew open and he stepped down into the back cabin. It was cold, but dry. The heating pipes that ran round it were lukewarm, but this had been sufficient to keep the worst of the frost out. He worked his way forward, through the engine room, past his sleeping cabin and the bathroom to the stateroom. The stove had just a trace of red embers in the bottom of it, so he found some kindling wood, remembering Stu's advice with gratitude, and a firelighter, and put them on top of the glowing coals. Before he had finished raking out the dust and ashes from beneath, a fire was spitting and crackling. He put some coal on and pushed the front doors open beneath the cloths. A shower of snow down his neck greeted him as he undid the buttons to fold them back, but he felt a sense of elation. His lifestyle was back in business! Smoke poured out of the cabin chimney to confirm it.

Later, he discovered how to start Anne's ancient blue Fordson tractor, which sat in a barn most of the year awaiting tasks such as this. His short apprenticeship with Stu had given him some idea of how to get heavy engines going, and an encouraging put! put! put! was his reward. Anne drove up the lane with him clinging on the back, and together they managed to drag his car out of the drift and into the shelter of the tractor barn. Then they charged back up the lane, clearing a path through the snow to the main road. By now it was lunchtime and the pair of them were working as a team and enjoying it to the full. They careered back to the farmhouse for some lunch. Anne went to prepare it while Andrew brought in more logs and coal from the barn across the yard. On his second journey his telephone rang. He blew on his hands and took it out to answer it. Kate was on the line.

"Look, Andrew. For God's sake keep this to yourself, but there's been a development. I got the glasses tested for fingerprints by forensic first thing, Baskerville organised a priority search on the National database and we've just had a preliminary result."

"Which is?"

"Everyone's glass except Burson's and Thorland's can be identified with a known criminal. Thorland of course we wouldn't expect to have done."

"What about Burson?"

"That's it. His glass shows no fingerprints matching any living criminal. They do however match those of a dead one! "

Chapter 14
A small domestic matter

For the second time in three days, Andrew found himself jolted out of complacency. Firstly there had been the news that Pamela had left Colin Shorland, now Burson was not Burson. He changed the telephone over to his other hand, and steadied himself against the barn doorpost. He did not speak for several seconds, causing Kate to ask if he was still there.

"Yes, I'm still here. Who the hell is Burson then?"

"According to records, the fingerprints belong to one Joseph Hannagan, who supposedly died in 1973. Hannagan had convictions for drug dealing and extortion going back to the late 'sixties, and a string of petty crimes before that. He served at least one long prison sentence. That's all I know at the moment. The Governor's getting Central Records to come up with more details as a matter of priority. It's a real stroke of luck, because we're supposed to destroy fingerprints of dead persons. Somehow these got overlooked."

"Well, that's a turn up for the book. What about the others in the party?"

"Ah, now. We've got names for all of them. Two, apart from Burson, or Hannagan, and Shorland, you know already. George Mandel and Barbara Moss."

"I had a feeling they might be involved."

"The others are small time villains and prostitutes. Mandel is known to have convictions for extortion and receiving, Moss has form for shoplifting, keeping a disorderly house and being an accessory to grievous bodily harm."

"Charming associates for Sir Colin, I'm sure. Whatever will his Chief Whip have to say?"

"I rather think Barbara Moss is his Chief Whip. She's supposedly into sado-masochism, according to her record. Seriously though, we've had some information via some mate of the Governor's that Shorland is a bit keen on the S & M."

"I'd believe anything I heard about the man now. So. Where does all this leave us now?"

"I'm not too sure yet. I'll call you back as soon as more develops."

"Did I tell you, the Met are watching Joey? He thinks they've tapped his lines, and there was a car outside his gate keeping obbo last night. I'm pretty sure they took my number."

"Well, they know you're a pal of Joey's all ready, don't they?"

"I'll bet they'll trace the number and find out who I am and where I live, though."

"Christ! Your address on the log book is care of the farm, isn't it?"

"That's just what I'm thinking. If word gets back to Burson, or Shorland at least, they may well start putting two and two together."

"You know what? As soon as the frost lifts, why don't you clear out somewhere on your boat? If you find somewhere in the County to stay until the heat is off, we can arrange for someone to keep an eye on you."

"Fine. But in the meantime what do I do? We've just opened up the lane to the main road. I should have left it blocked."

"Keep close to the farm for the time being, and make sure Mrs Clarke doesn't get hurt. I'll think of something, but make sure you can get your mobile in action quickly. It's quite possible they won't suspect that you are any more than a friend of Joey's who wants to wish him well."

"I don't trust that Detective Sergeant I met at Christmas. He's bad news."

"Andrew, I've got to go. Don't worry; I'm sure we can keep the farm protected. See you soon, shall I?"

"Not if I'm a bloody prisoner here. Still, we can keep in touch by 'phone now."

"Yes we can. Bye now!"

Andrew kicked moodily at the doorpost. The joy had suddenly evaporated from the day. He was not concerned about himself, that was his own affair, and he ought to be able to look after himself. What concerned him was the involvement of Anne in this. He had no right to bring her in, but by his stupidity in getting himself traced through his car, she could find her home once more invaded by the sort of people whom Andrew would not wish her to be concerned with. He had no doubt at all that DS Flower would check his particulars when his number was put through the computer, and find out that he no longer lived at Lipscombe, as he had told him, and that he would become suspicious enough to carry out further checks. If Kate had been able to get information about him from the police computer records, Flower would as well. There was only one thing for it. He would have to come clean about the whole matter with Anne. No good lying or pretending. She might as well be on her guard from the start. But damn it! He was just becoming fondly attached and thought that she might be doing the same, and this had to come between them. Anne came out of the kitchen door carrying two mugs of tea. He took one from her and said "look Anne. There's something I think you ought to know. Shall we go inside?"

Anne listened without interruption until he had finished his story. He told her as much as he dared about the Burson matter, how he had been watched leaving Joey's, and how it was suspected that DS Flower and doubtless some of his superiors were suspected of corruption, and how he was certain that Sally was onto the same story, but only in part. "And so you very rightly think I've dragged your whole family into this mess, and you've got every right to be angry."

"I'm not angry, Andrew. Look, if anyone dragged anyone else into this mess, it was me. You got mixed up with these things, including Kate Hollis, because I was mixed up with them first. Oh yes, I know you met her over the dog business as well, but you met her here first, because you played the knight-errant. And you only got in touch with your friend in the East End because you wanted to help me, so for goodness sake, stop feeling bad about it all. I'm not very happy about what Sally's up to, but she's a grown up now, and there's nothing I can do to stop her. Instead of feeling guilty, let's be positive. Let's face up to whatever we may have to. Don't think I'm not scared, because I am, but I'm behind you in all this. We should be able to face them out."

Andrew took her hands, drew her face towards him and kissed her.

"Why the hell didn't I meet you years ago? You don't know how good what you have just said makes me."

"Well, that's settled then" said Anne, laughing and tossing her hair, "what do we do now?"

"At the moment, I'm not sure that Flower knows of my connection with Shorland, but it must only be a matter of time before he finds out, then we shall need to be on our guard. It's a blasted nuisance that the canal's frozen, or we could move away for a few days. I think it's only a matter of time before the whole gang is arrested, but the police won't move until the evidence is absolutely cast iron, so that bail can be refused. When they do move, the political pooh will hit the windmill and no mistake, so we will have to be extremely circumspect."

For the umpteenth time since his conversation with Kate, Andrew glanced up the lane towards the main road. Nothing was stirring in the whole snowbound landscape, but it was only a short time to dark. What if they cut off the electricity? There would be no security lights, and if Dooney's men were involved, they knew of the existence of those.

"Have you any candles?" he asked.

"Yes, I always get them out at times like this. But we've also got a standby generator in the barn."

"You've what?"

"A standby generator. When we first came here there was no electricity, so Jim got a mains generator from somewhere. It's all still there, with some sort of contraption to make it cut in if the mains fail. I don't know if it would still work."

"Let's go and look. If I can't get it going, I know a man who can."

They crossed the yard into the barn adjoining that where the tractor lived. Andrew noted that the main supply to the farm came in to an insulator on the wall and then, via a hefty cable, disappeared inside. Another cable went along the wall of the barn and then across the yard to the house. He surmised that this was the main supply to the house. It had not occurred to him before that there might be a break inside the barn into which a standby generator might feed. Anne switched on a light in the barn, which she used as a coal and wood store. A sheeted machine was just visible under a pile of old vegetable crates which Anne kept for kindling wood. Andrew heaved several aside and pulled off the tarpaulin cover. It was a twin cylinder Lister engine coupled to a generator. He noticed an isolating switch in the 'off' position. He looked for the starter batteries and found them in a bank at the back of the engine. He asked Anne when she had last used it.

"I think Tom got it going last summer. Yes. It was then. We had a bad thunderstorm, and the electricity went off for several hours. He was on leave, and spent some time playing about with it, then got it going in time to save the contents of my freezer."

"The batteries should be all right then."

He found a button that looked like a starter button and was about to press it when he suddenly had a thought. What was it that Stu always said? *Turn it over by hand first to get the oil moving.* He took hold of the starting handle, moved the decompression levers and began slowly cranking. The engine was stiff. No doubt the lubricating oil was thick with the cold. After a few turns, it became easier and the injectors began to squeak as the diesel fuel began to atomise inside them. He turned the handle faster, and threw over a decompression lever as he did so. The engine spluttered, and then stopped. Next time. He whirled the handle faster before dropping the lever and was rewarded by a muffled cough, then another. He dropped the second lever and the engine began to cough louder and louder, puffing black smoke out of the exhaust manifold. The coughs came faster and faster, the smoke cleared and the engine was running. It settled down to a steady beat. Andrew turned and grinned at Anne.

"Bravo!" she called over the din.

"I'll check the fuel tank" called Andrew.

"It's over here. I think a pipe comes off the one we use for the tractor."

There was a square galvanised tank mounted on a stout wooden frame outside the barn. Andrew found a ladder and used it to clamber up to the tank top, brushing the snow away until he found the filler cap. Anne passed him up a dipstick. "It's nearly three parts full" he called.

"It should be. I had it filled up last summer and we've only used the tractor about twice since, until today. It holds two and a half thousand litres."

"What's that in gallons?" asked Andrew, whose mathematical prowess did not stretch to European calculations.

"About five hundred and fifty gallons."

"That should be plenty to see us through." He climbed down. The exhaust from the engine came out through a pipe in the barn roof. A series of little blue puffs showed that the engine was running normally. "Good. Now all we need do is check that the switchover gear works."

The ammeter showed that the batteries were well charged, so that all seemed to be well. Searching on the inside wall for the main cable inlet, Andrew found the Company fuses and a main switch and cut-out box. "Oh, yes" said Anne, "that's where I have to reset it if we trip out when we're using machines outside the house."

"And do you have another trip and fuse boxes in the house?"

"Yes, just inside the front door. But your electricity for the boat comes off this one. It's on a separate meter from the house."

"Excellent. Now we'll see if it works." He lifted up the fuel supply lever on the engine and its chugging died away to silence. "Right then. Are you ready?" He turned the main switch off, plunging the barn into darkness. Immediately there came a loud click as the starter solenoid engaged. The starter motor began to whine and the engine coughed back into life. The light suddenly came back on.

"I imagine there's only enough to run the lights, but that could be just what we want" said Andrew.

"That's right. Jim said I mustn't have both the TV on and the washing machine. It'll run one or the other, or the lights, but at least we'd be sure of some power if we needed it."

"We'll just have to be careful, that's all. Keep the candles ready, so if the power goes off we can make it look lie we're all in darkness. Then the security light should catch them."

The office shared by Kate Hollis and Jim Marriott was on the top floor of an old leather warehouse in the town centre. Arrangements had been made with the County Librarian, who used the building as a bookstore, for two desks, some filing space, telephones and a fax and computer terminal to be installed. Several piles of old books had to be moved aside, to the disgust of the librarian's staff and especially of the severe looking lady who was in charge of the building. She had sniffed loudly at the various requests made by the Chief Constable through the prominent person of Detective Chief Superintendent Baskerville. While Andrew and Anne were looking to the defences of the farm, a conference was being held in this dusty little office.

Baskerville had squeezed his bulky frame into a steel framed chair, such as the County Supplies Department thought suitable for employees of the Grade of Head of Department or above, Marriott had appropriated an ancient swivelling chair, and Kate was perched on what looked like an upholstered version of a laboratory stool. Outside the sun shone on a vista of Central Northampton, the chief focus of which was the tall Carlsberg Brewery building, from which gobbets of white steam swirled against the pale blue January sky. Snow had melted on the flat rooftops below where the sun had shone on it. Elsewhere it showed starkly white except where traffic had churned it into an icy, coffee coloured slush. The three police officers, though, had no time for such aesthetic considerations. Chief Superintendent Baskerville had just arrived and was distinctly conscious of the fact that he needed his pipe. The librarians however had posted on the walls stern injunctions against smoking. Baskerville took a pipe out of his jacket pocket and looked longingly at it.

"Go ahead, Sir" said Kate. "Jim and I don't mind."

Baskerville grunted. "I suppose someone will have to prosecute us, or else complain to the Chief Constable." He put the pipe in his mouth and blew down the stem, then tapped the dottle out into his hand. Kate moved a wastepaper bin towards him and he threw the ashes into it. Rummaging in his pocket for matches he found a box of Swan and his pouch. He took out a pinch of Tom Long, and began rubbing it between his palms.

"The Home Office are getting the wind up" he said. "Mind you, if they knew what we knew about Shorland's involvement, the Home Secretary would crap himself before he got to the Commons. Probably will too, when the fertiliser hits the fan. Carrickfergus could blow any moment." He charged his pipe with Tom Long and sucked it appreciatively. "The question is, do we let things ride for a while and consolidate the evidence, or do we pick them off one by one, or do we jump in with what we've got and go for the lot now?" He lit a match, held it to the pipe and drew in. Dense clouds of smoke began to fill the room as he got his personal conflagration under way. "That fingerprint job was well done, Kate. What else have you got so far on Burson,?"

"Thank you, Sir. I'm pretty sure we will be able to hang a murder charge on him, but it's only circumstantial just now."

"Right. Jim. Put me in the picture about him."

Marriott unrolled a crackling bundle of fax paper. "CRO sent me this just now, Sir. It's the last information they had about Joseph Hannagan, alias Burson."

"Let's have it, so we can all hear."

Marriott read from his papers. "Joseph Paul Hannagan, born 1941, Staffordshire Royal Infirmary, Wolverhampton. Mother: Bridget Hannagan, no profession, but a note on the file written in pen and ink says that she had convictions for prostitution and theft. Father: William Black: profession private soldier. The War was on, Sir."

Baskerville puffed his pipe. "I do remember something about it. Go on."

"Sorry, Sir. That was the Birth Certificate. CRO file says he was brought up in a children's home; first conviction, 1955. Theft of bicycle. Walsall Juvenile Court. Put on probation. Then there's a string of minor offences, ending up with Robbery with Violence in 1957. Sent to Home Office Approved School, absconded and recaptured. Sent for Borstal Training and released in 1959. Then called up for National Service. Served with South Staffordshire Regiment and RASC. Posted to Germany 1960, signed on as a regular and came out in 1965. Good service record, held rank of lance corporal, then corporal. That's all on his Service Record, Sir."

Baskerville nodded. "He seems to have stayed out of trouble with us until 1972, when he was convicted at the Old Bailey on charges of conspiring to commit criminal acts, receiving stolen property and demanding with menaces. Ten other charges taken into consideration. Sentenced to three years, of which he served two. Released in September 1973 and reported killed in a fatal motor accident in November 1973."

"Whereabouts?"

Marriott rustled his papers. "Somewhere near Guildford, Sir. Ah, here it is. On the A3, two miles east of the town. The inquest was adjourned twice, eventually the Coroner recorded 'death by misadventure'. He was the only person in the car, which was burned out after hitting a tree. The body contained traces of marijuana, but was so badly charred it could not be identified, except by a steel engraved cigarette case and the remains of the clothing. No dental records, no fingerprints and it was before DNA testing."

Kate asked "What happened to the body?"

"Apparently some friend paid for what was left of the body to be cremated after the inquest."

"Very handy" rumbled Baskerville.

"I've got an old mate in the Surrey Force" said Marriott. "Met him years ago on a course at Bramshill. I rang him today when I got the fax, and he can remember the incident. He was only a cadet at the time, but he was given the job of tidying up the papers and photos etcetera afterwards and he said that his old DI was never convinced that the accident was kosher, but they had a pub bombing by the IRA on their hands and one thing and another, it got forgotten. Nobody made any fuss, so that was it. It does look as if the Coroner may have had some doubts about it all, if he adjourned the inquest twice. Possibly that's why the dabs survived on file. Anyway Paul's digging the file out and he's going to send it up by courier as soon as he gets it."

"Well done, Jim. I wonder if someone put a little pressure on somewhere for it to be forgotten about."

"I wonder..." Kate began.

"What?" The Chief Superintendent fired a cannon-like burst of smoke as he spoke.

"I wonder whether there is any connection with Hannagan's being posted to Germany."

"What with?"

"Well, look at his record. All petty thieving and small time stuff. Then he appears to go straight while he's in the army and goes to Germany, then suddenly, ten years later he's up at the Old Bailey charged with big time stuff. Then he appears to be killed soon after coming out of prison. Andrew Ellison tells me that he first met Burson in the mid seventies, and he was in the money then, and involved with Colin Shorland. I'm pretty certain some other poor devil died in that car crash. Hey!" She suddenly shouted. "What a bloody fool! Of course! Has Burson got a passport?"

"He must have" said Marriott. "We know he was abroad only last month."

"Get it checked" said Baskerville. "I'll pull any strings. Wait. Let me have that 'phone." He dialled a number and the others heard the ringing tone. A voice crackled at the other end. "Charles? Harry Baskerville... Yes Harry... Good to speak to you again too. Look, I need a favour, matter of Home Office business, you know." A sustained crackling came through the telephone. "Well, I know how things are, but you can have a word with the Home Secretary himself if you like." Crackle, crackle. "We need some passport details urgently." Crackle, crackle. "All right. You can ring me back on this number" he spoke the digits. "Right you are! I'll expect you back in a few minutes." He put the telephone back on its rest. "Bloody Whitehall, they hate being asked to get off their arses. Especially the Foreign Office. Still, Sir Charles isn't a bad sort. It'll cost me a round of drinks at his club though."

"Sometimes, Sir, life can be a real bitch" commented Jim Marriott. Baskerville drew and puffed and grinned back at him. "We have to make sacrifices in the Force. Now then, Kate. What have you dug up so far about Sir Colin?"

"You've had a printout of everything up until this morning, but I haven't had a chance to put down what Ellison told me last night. Ellison's ex-wife has confirmed that Sir Colin has been threatened and the Carrickfergus connection. There was some sort of commotion involving him at Heathrow back in the summer. He apparently faked a funny turn as he was coming back from one of his meetings in Dublin with the Anglo Irish Peace Accord Committee. Went off in an ambulance, then gave the crew a fifty note to drop them at Hounslow Station."

"Have you checked this with Heathrow?"

"I've asked their Security Chief for any information he can raise, including whether or not any known terrorists were sighted in the airport that same day. It doesn't help that we've got no exact date beyond mid-July, it was soon after the big Orange march on the 12th apparently, but I suppose I could find out when the Dublin meeting took place."

"Better do that, but let Heathrow rummage about first. Give them the date after they've looked closely at all their records and CCTV stuff for the rough period. That way we might turn up something else. Jesus!" Baskerville jumped as the telephone on the desk shrilled. Kate picked it up. "Kate Hollis" she said, and then held it out to the Chief Superintendent. "Your friend at Whitehall" Baskerville put his pipe on the desk and took the receiver. "Yes, Charles."

After a brief conversation he replaced the receiver, turned to the other two and said "all lines clear to the Passport Office. We have to send faxes of my signature to Sir Charles and the head of records to set the ball rolling, but he's giving us as much help as his department can."

"We can do that right now, Sir" said Kate, pulling a sheet of fax headed paper from her drawer. Baskerville took it, scrawled his signature and Kate inserted the paper. While the machine whirred, Baskerville got up and paced about the dusty office. "We've got to get this right first time" he said at last. "For me, it'll be my swansong. Whatever happens I'm on track for my lump sum and pension, but if we goof, you two will pay for it. It'll be early retirement and no mistake."

"We knew that when we joined" said Marriott.

"Yes, I know. I'm just pointing it out again. We can't have anything going off at half cock. We've still got to get to the bottom of Carrickfergus, and from what I know about it, we could have a lot of blood on someone's hands if we don't watch it. So I vote 'softlee, softlee catchee monkey'."

Andrew telephoned Kate later that day and told her of his fears. She whistled. "I'll talk to the boss about it. You know what they're like about resources. I don't think we can mount a twenty four hour watch on the farm just on a suspicion."

"No, I don't expect that, but could you have some sort of response ready at short notice? If we're going to get walloped, we shall have some notice, and my 'phone is digital, so it won't be tracked. How about a five minute back up?"

"Leave it with me. I'll talk to the Boss."

Some more snow fell that night, but did not drift. It was deep enough in the lane to cause Jane to skid somewhat as she drove down to the farm next morning. She brought news that Kelly and Gary were back together as friends, but she had not shown any inclination to move in with him down in the Park. "If you asks me, me ole doock, she's better off at 'ome. That place's full o' flashers an' them."

"It would be a little cold for a flasher at the moment" said Andrew gravely. Jane laughed "snap it orf like a cold carrot, I reckon." Anne discreetly left the kitchen to hide her mirth.

The rest of the day passed quietly, but after Jane had gone Andrew found some sheets of shuttering ply in a barn and began cutting them and screwing them to the window frames. "I don't want anyone trying to smash their way in through a downstairs window like last time. And this will hold them up. Ever minute we can gain will give the police time to get here." He caught a glimpse of Anne's face and put his hand out to comfort her. She looked at him, her face a picture of misery.

"I'm afraid, Andrew, really afraid."

He put down the screwdriver and took her arm. "Yes, Anne, I know, and I'm the one to blame. But we've got to stick it out now. If we manage to make Burson's lot show their hand, we shall have done a good job. We'll come out all right. I promise. I've been in tighter holes. Trust me."

She gave a rueful smile. Andrew's mind flashed back to that ambush in the Troodos Mountains, and how he and Sergeant Caroni had rallied their shaken men and returned fire with rifle and Bren until the following motor column had come up and the terrorists had dispersed. At least this time the attack was not unexpected. He kissed Anne on the cheek. "Just don't worry. When the lights go out, that's when we start worrying. You get upstairs with a candle and my mobile 'phone and get Kate's number."

When he came in a few minutes later, Anne had gone to a locked cupboard in the kitchen and opened it. "I think we may need this" she said, "it was Jim's. I still keep up the licence for vermin control." She turned round and handed him a double-barrelled shotgun. "There's plenty of cartridges for it in this tin."

Andrew raised his eyebrows. "I jolly well hope we won't need it, but thanks all the same." Privately he had thought that the expected visitors might well be armed. It was comforting to know that he would at least be able to face them on equal terms.

After supper they put on a video, but neither of them could settle to watch it. They both found themselves getting up and pacing about, or going out to the kitchen on some pretext. It was almost a relief, when, at five minutes past nine the lights went out.

Andrew immediately came alive. "This is it! All switches off! He seized the torch which he had put ready by his chair and put the light switches in the 'off' position. As he did so, he heard the Lister generator across the yard start chugging into life. The television came back on. He turned the sound down. Anne was lighting a candle. "OK, I'm going across the yard. Don't open to anyone except me and bolt the door behind me, then upstairs with you and ring the police." Andrew turned the television off. The Lister died away. "We'll have to keep something on or the security lights won't activate."

"I'll put the light on in the upstairs loo" said Anne darting upstairs. *Good girl,* thought Andrew, *the light doesn't show outside the house.* The generator chugged back to life as she turned the switch. So long as the visitors did not realise that there was a standby supply, they might yet surprise them. He took the shotgun, quickly undid the front door and slipped across the yard to the opposite barn. Behind him he heard Anne slip the bolts. Blast! He'd forgotten to put on a coat and mittens. It was going to be tricky if they didn't show up soon. He could hear Anne's voice talking excitedly into the telephone from upstairs and he blew on his hands to warm them. Suddenly the dog, out in his kennel, barked. Andrew peered into the snowy darkness and listened. His ears caught the low purring of a motor over the diesel chugging in the adjoining barn. He could just make out a dark moving shape across the field. A car was coming down the lane with its headlights extinguished.

The car drew to a halt at the entrance to the yard and turned round. It then backed into the entrance. Three figures got out and began creeping towards the buildings. Andrew forgot how cold he was and peered into the darkness. He heard men's muttering voices above the muffled puttering of the generator. There was a curse as someone tripped over a snow-covered flagstone, then the security light blazed out. There came a furious cursing.

"'Oo said the fackin' electric was cut off? Get them fackin' boards off the fackin' winders!"

"Some fucker's got a genny runnin', that's why."

"Find the bastard and kill it then, prat!"

"Get a bleedin' jemmy to them winders, quick!"

"All right fer you ter stand rahnd givin' fackin' orders. Get a fackin' move on!"

There was a sound of running feet followed by the noise of a car boot opening. The feet came back. "'Ere y'are. Try this winder, it's near the bleedin' front door." There was a clank as something heavy was thrown on the ground.

Andrew saw three balaclava wearing figures clustering by the front door. One of them started hammering on it. "We know you're there Ellison. Better come out, or we'll smash our way in." Another voice roared "Ellison!"

Andrew sidled round the barn door and called "What do you want? Who are you?"

The three men swung round and peered across the yard into the glare of the security light. The tallest of the three called back "we wants Andrew Ellison."

"I'm him. What do you want?"

"You've bin stickin' your nose into fings what don't concern you. I fink we ought to 'ave a little chat." The three of them began advancing across the yard, blinking in the strong light. One carried a crowbar; the other two had baseball bats in their hands.

Upstairs Anne was talking desperately into the telephone. "They're here now. Three of them in the yard... What... Five minutes... I don't know if we can keep them that long. They're trying to get hold of Andrew. Oh, please be as quick as you can... Oh God!" Her words were interrupted by a shot.

Andrew was in darkness and the three were perfectly visible to him. He raised the shotgun and fired upwards at the roof of the house. An avalanche of snow descended just missing the three, who stopped, as if rooted to the ground.

"The next one of you bastards to move gets it" he called. "I shan't shoot to miss next time." He swiftly broke the gun open, ejected the cartridge and placed another in the breech. There was consternation in the ranks of the invaders

"No one said nuffink abaht shooters. I'm aht of 'ere"

"Stay where you are 'Enry. You ain't goin' nowhere."

"You said it was just goin' ter be a spankin', not a fookin' shoot out."

"Shut it, the pair of you!"

Andrew came slowly out into the lighted yard holding the shotgun level. "The best thing you lot can do is to sod off fast. Who sent you? Flower? Burson? Dooney? I want an answer, and bloody quick. Otherwise you're going to find out about artificial limbs."

"Don't shoot, guvnor" called the taller man, who seemed to be the leader. His voice sounded pleading.

"You were all very anxious to do me some GBH just now. Why shouldn't I?" A red mist seemed to be forming in front of Andrew's eyes. He collected his wits with a jerk. His anger at the intrusion of these violent thugs into his life had been increased by their apparent craven cowardice in the face of a determined enemy. With an effort he recovered his calmness. He stopped, facing them across the yard.

"Put your things down, on the ground. Move!" he shouted.

Suddenly one of the men made a run for it. He dashed towards the car. Andrew fired over his head, shot pattered in the branches of the tree which stood by the gate, bringing down more snow. The man veered off, away from the car. As he did so, car lights appeared over the crest of the hill at the top of the lane.

"You'd better put your hands over your heads and face the wall" called Andrew. The two turned, raising their hands. Andrew broke the gun again, ejected the spent cartridge, reloaded, then said "There's a barrel for each of you if you so much as move."

A police Range Rover swept into the yard. Three policemen in flak jackets tumbled out holding machine carbines.

"Freeze, the lot of you! Drop that gun!"

Andrew obediently dropped his gun on the ground. Two policemen ran to him and ordered him to lie face down in the snow. "I say, this is not very friendly" he protested.

"Shut up!"

Another car pulled up. Doors banged, but face down in the snow, Andrew was unable to see what was happening. Someone walked over to him and there came a loud peal of laughter.

"All right, Mitchell, let him up. Let me just unload the gun" said Kate Hollis's voice.

Andrew struggled grimly to his feet. "Great! One of 'em's got away."

"Not for long, I dare say. Yes, Mitchell, he's on our side. Don't worry, you weren't to know." She chuckled again. "It did look funny from where I'm standing." She bent down and helped him to his feet. Andrew's normal good humour began to reassert itself, PC Mitchell, a burly young man in his mid-twenties grinned as he helped Andrew dust snow off his face, trousers and jumper. The two men in balaclavas were being ushered away to a car. Anne came running out of the front door.

"Oh, Andrew, thank God you're all right." She flung her arms round him. Kate watched with her eyebrows ever so slightly raised. Andrew said "Nobody's hurt, thank goodness, but there was a bit of noise."

Detective Inspector Marriott came across from making a radio call in the car. "We're putting up a helicopter with infra red. That should sort matey boy out. Oh, hullo. I take it you're Mr. Ellison. I hope that gun is licensed?"

Anne said angrily "It's mine, I use it around the barns. Do you want to see the licence right now?"

The DI smiled at her. "All right Madam. Mrs. Clarke I presume. If the gun is legal and legally kept, you have nothing to worry about on that score."

A fearful racket grew overhead as a helicopter came sweeping across the valley, a searchlight was trained on the ground as the machine slowed and hovered above the farm. Over the racket Andrew called "can we go and check my boat?" Marriott nodded, and indicated to PC Mitchell that he should go with him.

The two walked round the back of the barn towards the wharf, Mitchell sweeping the beam of a large torch this way and that. Above the beating of the helicopter they could hear the sound of a two-way radio conversation between the aircraft and the ground, but it was impossible to distinguish words. Andrew, still buoyed up by the adrenalin that had been racing round his system since the lights first went out, led the way towards his boat. *If that thug had got aboard, he would smash him senseless with or without the presence of a constable* he thought, then once again, got a grip on himself and calmed down.

Romford lay, still locked in the ice, her chimneys smoking slightly, apparently untouched. Mitchell suddenly said "look there!" and pointed, focussing the torch on the spot with his free hand. A trail of single footprints led towards the canal bridge. Cowering in the arch, on the towpath side was the figure of a man. Mitchell gave Andrew the torch and lugged out his radio. "Mike India to Control" "Come in Mike India."

"Fugitive is beneath Bridge to the right of the farmyard."

"Roger Mike India. Can you see him from where you are?"

"Yes. He's trying to keep out of view of the helicopter."

DI Marriott's voice came over the radio. "Stay where you are Mike India, and don't repeat don't allow anyone else to tackle fugitive."

"Understood, Sir." The radio went dead. "You heard that, Sir?" he said to Andrew, "They don't want anyone other than us getting stuck in."

"All right. I'll stay here." Already his anger was abating and he felt a little ashamed of his feelings of a few moments before. He watched as three policemen in flak jackets ran across the bridge and down the far slope to the towpath. The man in the bridge saw them and began to run along the towpath. The helicopter clattered overhead. The crew had him now in their infrared video camera and were directing the chase from above. The fugitive looked back over his shoulder, saw the policemen burst out of the bridgehole and jumped onto the ice to cross back over the canal. Andrew swore under his breath. Mitchell had the same idea and began moving parallel to the canal. "How thick's that ice?" he asked.

"I wouldn't trust it myself. Especially under those trees. It was broken three days ago and there's been no hard frost since."

"Bloody Hell! He's taking a chance then."

The man had got half way across by now and was heading for a spot where a hedge would cut off his pursuers on the farm side. "Don't try to cross" Mitchell yelled to his colleagues on the other bank, "it's dangerous." Even as he spoke, there came a cracking sound. The man on the ice gave a yelp of fear as he felt it give under his feet. He paused for a moment and as he did so there came another crack and the ice on which he stood tilted. He scrabbled wildly, trying to keep his balance, then another piece broke off and he went into the icy water with a scream. Andrew had already taken his spare mooring line from under the canvas cover and was staggering through the snow as fast as he could behind the massive form of PC Mitchell. The man was screaming in terror now as the icy water began to seep through his clothes.

At the second attempt Andrew got the line to him.

"Put the loop round under your arms" he called, but the man was too frightened to listen. Andrew looked upwards. There was no chance of the helicopter getting him out; there were overhanging trees and an electricity cable overhead.

"Here" said Andrew to Mitchell "hang on to the end of this."

He put the rope into the hands of the amazed constable, stripped off his jumper and, holding on to the other, plunged onto the ice towards the fugitive. There were several unpleasant sounding cracks as he moved towards him, then he lay down and, spreading his weight as much as he could, crawled towards the man.

"Help me! Help me!" sobbed the man, as if Andrew had no intention of so doing. He crawled to the very edge of the ice and caught the man's hand. "Keep still, or you'll do for us both" he snarled at him, and succeeded at the third try in passing the loop under his armpits. He took hold of the man's hand and called to Mitchell to pull the rope. The man's body came shooting upwards like a landed fish; Andrew wriggled backwards as the ice cracked under their combined weight.

There were more policemen now on the bank pulling steadily on the rope and the pair slowly slid to the bank. DI Marriott helped Andrew to his feet as Mitchell coiled up the rope.

"Well done Ellison. Are you all right?"

"I've felt worse." He caught a glimpse of both Kate's and Anne's faces in the crowd. Anne said, "You'd best get straight inside and have a bath and change, you'll catch your death."

The man that he had rescued nodded weakly at him. His balaclava was gone, he looked thin, pale and pathetic with a heavy red towel draped round his shoulders. "Thanks, mate," he said. Andrew stared. He looked familiar, suddenly he recognised him. It was Mark, the skinhead who worked for JD Properties Ltd.

Chapter 15
Rifts in lutes

Mark Hawley sat painfully up in bed. There was a policeman on a hospital chair beside him, who grinned sympathetically at him. He was in a curtained off ward in the General Hospital. Memories of last night were flooding back and he shivered at the thought. He remembered running along the towpath and crossing the ice. He remembered the sudden shock of going through the ice, then it was all a blur. There was the elderly man, whom he was certain he had seen before, catching hold of his arms and pulling him through and onto ice, then he was being wrapped in blankets and put in a helicopter, then into an ambulance, then it was all dark until he woke in this hospital ward. He shuddered violently. The policeman leaned forward and touched his arm sympathetically. "All right, sunshine. At least you're alive and kicking."

Hawley looked at him dazedly. "Where the 'ell am I supposed to be?"

"Hospital, son. And bloody lucky you ain't in the mortuary department with the pathologist doing an autopsy. Mild hypothermia, that's all."

"Who was it pulled me out? I don't remember anything after I went through the ice."

"It looks like the guy you was going to do over got you out. If it'd been me," said the policeman cheerfully; "I'd have left you in there. He must be bloody mad. Inspector Marriott's been in and had a look at you all ready. I dare say he'll want to ask you a few questions. Oh, hullo, nurse. The patient's fine."

A young probationary nurse wearing a stud in one nostril came into the curtained off area, hearing the voices. She somehow looked familiar to Mark. She laid her fingers on her lips and said

"Sssh!" Behind her an older man, slightly built, in his forties, with thinning hair and wearing a white coat also entered. The man said, in a soft voice, "thank you officer. Would you mind if we just examine him in private. The nurse will pull the curtains if you'd just wait outside a moment or two."

So saying the nurse drew the curtains and Mark, his eyes popping, found himself confronted by his boss, Jack Dooney. Dooney grinned sardonically at him and said, "talk fast, boyo. We've not got a lot of time. Who sent you to de widder woman's farm again and why?"

Sunlight was glancing off the snow-covered roofs of the red brick houses in the quiet close. The wheel tracks of the early morning tradesmen and the postman were still visible in the uncleared ruts where the snow had not yet thawed. The large black Mercedes crunched through the ice, sending spurts of slush across the pavement. Jack Dooney grunted as he spotted the gateway that he was looking for. He had had a most illuminating conversation in the General Hospital, and there were more than a few questions that he wanted answering. He swung the Mercedes into a driveway, stopped, got out, carefully locked the car with a zapper, looked round warily but quickly, walked to the Georgian style front door and pressed the bell. Almost immediately the entry phone squawked at him. He said "Jack Dooney" and the door was immediately opened by a burly man wearing a rather tight fitting suit. The burly man ushered him into the house.

As the door closed behind him, Dooney glanced quickly about him. It was his nature to do so every time he entered a strange house. It was a trick he had learned years ago when training, and it had always paid off. He observed the electronic alarm system, the entryphone and the spyhole in the door. He noted that all doors leading off the entrance hall were closed, maybe locked. The door by which he had entered had a deadlock. The burly man bade him follow and led him into a large, pleasant room with a picture window looking out across a garden, which looked as well kept as anything might do under a carpet of snow. At the end of the garden a stretch of water, iced over, led to the gardens of other similar houses. The room was furnished with a cocktail cabinet, a TV set with a very large screen, several large easy chairs and two sofas. On the floor beside one of the chairs was the current issue of *Searchlight*. Another bulky man, wearing jeans and a tee shirt with trainers on his feet, was lounging on one of the sofas watching football on satellite TV. He had a round face, small, shoe button eyes and a cherub's mouth. Beside him sat a woman in her late twenties with blonde hair and a startlingly curvaceous figure that the bathrobe that she was wearing barely concealed. She did not get up but the man rose from a chair to greet him. As he stood up he towered above the diminutive Dooney; his shaven head gleamed in the glow of a ceiling spotlight. He held his hand out, but Dooney did not take it. He considered such niceties a waste of business time. Instead he said, somewhat formally, "I'm here on business, Burson, not a social call."

Burson looked slightly pained, then, waving Dooney to a chair said "what's it all about then, Jack?" He had the faintest trace of a Birmingham or Black Country accent.

Jack Dooney had long lost such an Irish accent as he may once have had. Normally only an occasional hard 'T', and a softness of tone betrayed his origin, but when it pleased him he could adopt the harsh accent of his native Dublin. It sometimes helped if people thought he was the Gombeen man from the Northside. Today it pleased him to play this card.

"I'll give yez fockin' Jack. Dere's one o' my boys fockin' half dead an' two o' yours singin' to de polis. Dat's what it's all about!"

Burson's eyes popped. He poked the woman in her ribs and said, "Outside, Doll, your Uncle Roland's got some business to talk." The woman scowled, but got up and flounced out of the room gathering her bathrobe round her as if defying Dooney to ogle her. Dooney however had no eyes for such things. "Just us two toget'er if ye plaze."

Burson waved the other burly man out of the room, then said in a low voice "what the Hell are you talking about?"

Dooney told him. When he had finished Burson said "Jesus! I didn't know anything about it."

"Ye're tellin' me dat dem two fockers weren't yours?"

"They weren't mine as I know of. I haven't got anybody outside the smoke as yet. Honest, Jack, it's the truth!"

"Well, if dey weren't yours, whose de fock are dey?"

"Christ! I don't know." He reached for a telephone and dialled a number. Dooney heard the other end answer. "George? Roland. Anybody missing from our lot this morning? You don't think so? Well bloody well check will you? I want a full roll call in five minutes." He slammed the receiver onto its rest. "Anyway, how come you know about it?"

"I've got me sources. Just as you have."

"Yes, I suppose so. Have a drink? Smoke?" he pushed a box of cigars towards the Irishman.

"T'anks, but no. I t'ink ye'd best be doin' some hard brainwork. What I want to know is, why de fock were your men, or whosoever dey are, pokin' about at dat farmhouse? And how did de fockin' peelers know dey was dere?"

"I'm buggered if I can think. What farmhouse? Who did you say they were supposed to be after?"

"Focked if I know. Does he owe yez money?"

"Does who owe me any money?"

"Don't play fockin' games wid me. De fella at de farm house."

"Straight up, Jack, I haven't the slightest idea who or what you're on about."

It was Dooney's turn to look surprised.

"Well, if ye're talkin' de trut' now, who are de ot'er fellas?" The telephone buzzed. Burson picked it up, "Roland." There was a space as the telephone crackled a conversation. "Two missing, and Flower's been trying to find me? Right." He put the instrument down with a bang and pursed his cherubic lips.

"I'm just thinking that one of our friends in the Met has got out of order. I think he might just have earned himself a bit of a spanking."

"Look, Burson" said Dooney softly, all traces of the Jackeen accent had gone. He exuded an icy menace that made Burson shudder inwardly. "If anything goes wrong with the delivery date for Carrickfergus, you're going to pay the bill. If your man needs a bit of correction, that's your affair, but I don't have my men near drowned for a game. You can tell him from me that Jack Dooney's not a happy man. I also suggest you leave Caroni alone until after the delivery date. I don't want your gangsters' feuds gettin' in the way of things. Do you understand now?"

"Yes Jack" said Burson, weakly. He was not accustomed to being ordered about, nor threatened. One of these days he'd make this smart arsed Paddy eat his bloody words, but for the moment he had to go along with it. Meanwhile there were a few loose ends to be tied up.

Dooney smiled for the first time since arriving at the house. He rose, turned on his heel, his eyes caught sight of a portrait photograph of Sir Oswald Mosley in Blackshirt uniform and he gave a mocking smile in return, then strode past Burson's minder and opened the front door himself. The minder had seen his smile. "Don't you fink it's a good picture?" he asked coming up behind Dooney.

"Oh, I've no doubt t'at he was t'e fine talker" he said, reverting to his Northside accent, "but never a patch on Michael Collins. Yez really ought to get a better lock" he said by way of farewell. As he drove away he pondered on the fact that things could have been a great deal worse. It was a stroke of luck that he'd had that tip from his informant in the police that Mark had been taken in to hospital last night. It was not likely that the police would know that he had once been a medical student at Trinity, Dublin, so impersonating a doctor was not difficult, even though Willis' assistant, Tracey, was not altogether convincing as a nurse. It looked as though Burson had blundered badly in his choice of bent policemen. Meanwhile he saw no reason to enlighten him as to who Mark had been sent to silence. He owed Joey Caroni a good turn, and if Ellison was a friend of Joey's, then he was not going to hand over a man who was prepared to risk his life for one of Jack Dooney's men to the tender mercies of Burson.

Roland Burson made a telephone call to a number in the East End. He issued rapid instructions then called "Wayne!"

"Yes Mr. Burson."

"Go and get the car out. We're going for a trip to London."

Detective Chief Superintendent Baskerville lit his pipe at the top of the flight of stairs. He blew a long cloud of smoke as he recovered his breath. At his age, he reflected, it did not pay to drink too much. It had been a good night though. When his retirement came along, he'd have to see whether he couldn't better it. A thin woman with bobbed grey hair passing him fluttered her hands as if to dispel the cloud and coughed disapprovingly, but Baskerville was oblivious to both her and the panorama of the town that spread out from below the windows. Puffing easily, like a steam locomotive that had surmounted a steep gradient and now faced an easy descent, he pushed open the door into the Special Group office.

Kate Hollis was alone, sitting in front of a monitor screen. She swung round as he entered. "Morning, Sir. Thank goodness you're here."

"Morning Kate" replied Baskerville cheerfully. "What have we got new today? Any of last night's bag singing?"

"Singing isn't quite the word, Sir. We've got a slight crisis on our hands."

Baskerville blew another cloud. "How so?"

"Inspector Marriott's just been on the 'phone. He missed you at home last night."

"Yes, so he would. I was at a retirement do in Birmingham, stayed up there rather than drive home, and my mobile battery's gone on the blink. Just got in. I heard about last night from the Chief when I rang in just now from downstairs. So what's the crisis?"

"The two that we picked up with Dooney's man. They kept stumm all night. Now they've just been identified. They're already known to us, thanks to the fingerprints, and they're Burson's men, but we don't want the press letting any cats out of the bag just at present." Baskerville sat down heavily in a chair. "Good oh! That's just what we want." He took a few more puffs, and then said "I think we'll have a complete news blackout. Let's have the 'phone, I'll clear it with the Chief Constable."

Roland Burson shifted his bulk in the chair. The man before him was not a pretty spectacle. His eyes were closed, there was a puffy swelling on his cheek, his lips ballooned over a couple of missing teeth. He found it difficult to stand because of the pain in his abdomen where he had been kicked. The cockiness had been driven out of Detective Sergeant Flower following a lengthy interview in a warehouse cellar. Flower's knees buckled under him, and he slumped on the bare concrete floor. Wayne, Burson's minder, jerked his hair to pull his face upright.

"You ain't finished yet, pal" he muttered. Flower moaned.

"You are not a very clever policeman" said Burson quietly. "You have made some people very unhappy. Now, I want to get this quite straight. You traced this guy by his car number. Nothing else?" Flower nodded.

"And then you thought you'd try to warn him off, and you got one of Dooney's men to take you to the farm? Yes? That's all?"

Again the bundle on the floor nodded. Burson got up, walked across to the groaning detective and kicked him hard in the stomach, causing him to groan louder. "You stupid bastard!" he shouted. "Two of my animals are in the bin at Northampton, Dooney's hopping mad because one of his men was nearly drowned, it looks like somebody's a squealer, and you've bloody well nearly given the game away to your mates in the local Old Bill. I am not a happy man. Not in any way."

He walked away, muttering. Then he turned to his minder. "He's no fucking use now. Get rid of him."

Flower licked his swollen lips and croaked, "If you get rid of me, you won't do yourself any good."

"You don't 'ear too well, mate" said Wayne. "Mr Burson's givin' you your P45."

From the floor, Flower gabbled desperately. "Listen, Burson... Ouff!" He broke off as Wayne kicked him in the ribs.

"Mister Burson to you, filth!"

Burson looked at him with disgust. "Well? I'm listening."

Flower raised himself on one elbow and gasped: "You'd best listen. Everything I know, along with a few documents which have got your name on, is sitting in a safe deposit. If I don't report in within twenty-four hours it'll be opened, and then the shit will really hit the fan. Not just for you, but for my bosses, and they won't be happy people either."

Burson had been about to leave. He paused. Perhaps he was just being a bit hasty. Flower could still be of some use, provided he had learned his lesson. Even if he were not bluffing, he could still play a useful role, but he had to be kept in order.

"Sit him up, Wayne" he ordered the minder. Wayne dragged Flower to his feet and sat him on a steel framed office chair. Burson strode over to him and pointed his index finger at Flower's eyes. "You are a very lucky little man that I'm in a good mood now. I'm going to let you go, and you're going to have to tell your mates that you had a nasty shunt in your car. We'll sort your car out won't we Wayne?" The minder sniggered. Burson went on, "You aren't the only person to have documents hidden away, know what I mean? So you'd better get back to your mates and get on with your job. I'd hate to think of the taxpayers wasting their money."

Flower had not risen to his place in the CID without being able to think quickly. Through the pain, he realised that Burson had been rattled by what he had just told him. One thing that Burson did not know, and had not asked, was the identity of the man whom he had sent the two thugs to visit last night. That was a useful piece of information that Flower proposed to keep to himself for the time being. He forced a smile onto his swollen face. Burson glared at him. "One more stroke like that, my son. One more, and you're dead. Got it?"

Flower nodded his agreement.

"Right" said Burson, "Someone's going to wish they'd never been born, 'cos when somebody grasses on me, they don't do themselves no good at all."

If the stupid prat thinks that someone has grassed on him, so much the better, thought Flower grimly, there was no way that he was going to enlighten him. What he had learned was that Ellison was a smarter guy than he had credited. He should have realised that a bent lawyer was someone worth respect.

"Have we got any further with Burson's passport?" asked Baskerville, putting down the telephone. It had not been an easy few minutes trying to explain to the Chief just why he had not heard about the presence of two London villains in his cells beforehand and why it should be kept quiet. Kate pulled out a drawer in the desk, taking out a file.

"Here we are, Sir. Roland Burson was born, according to his passport, in Birmingham in May 1942. I checked details with Somerset House, and the real Roland Burson died in January 1944 of whooping cough. Death Certificate provided. So Hannagan's adopted the identity of someone of his own age. The current Roland Burson claims to have been abroad working until 1974, according to the Inland Revenue. I've got his National Insurance Number from the passport office, by the way, Sir. His tax affairs seem to have been in order since 1974."

"Hmm! I wonder who it was whose body was in that car. It would have been too easy if it had been the real Roland Burson."

"I don't suppose we shall ever know, unless Burson tells us."

"We can't connect him with last night's affair I suppose?"

"Not yet, Sir."

"So how come that Burson knew about Ellison being at the farm?"

"I don't think he did, Sir. I think that the two that we've got hold of just happen to be thugs that are on Burson's payroll. I think somebody in the Met sent them. How else would they have been able to trace Andrew Ellison than by the DVLO records? They must have taken Dooney's man, Mark Hawley, along as a guide. It's not an easy place to find, especially in the dark, and he'd been there before."

"Had he? How do you know?"

Kate blushed slightly. "There was a report of an attempted break in before Christmas. We took no further action, since no damage had been done other than a broken window..."

"In that case, how do we...?" The Chief Superintendent interrupted, then trailed off enquiringly.

"Andrew Ellison traced Hawley and another man through JD Properties Ltd. who were leaning on Mrs Clarke at the time. He recognised him and got Mrs Clarke to confirm it. Somehow or other he got Dooney's company off her back. I'm not quite sure how he did it, but he told me how he traced Hawley. He's seen him again since, just before Christmas, driving Burson in Dooney's Merc."

"Ellison seems wasted as a failed lawyer. Now he's a local hero for saving Hawley from a watery grave. But you don't think that Burson had anything to do with last night's schemozzle."

"Not directly, Sir, no."

"So why were they there at the farm? What possible connection is there?"

"It's through an old friend of Ellison's who runs clubs and things in London. That's how we got the fingerprints. Burson, for some reason, is after controlling these clubs and has got at certain people in the Met."

"Is it a long story?"

"Yes, Sir it is, rather."

Baskerville settled himself down into his chair, refilled his pipe and said "Tell me. Start from the beginning, tell me exactly how

Ellison got mixed up in this Dooney business. I like a good tale."

When Kate had finished, Baskerville said "It just shows, you can never be sure of anything in this job. When I put you on to Ellison, I wanted you to get him to lead us to Shorland and possibly Burson. I never suspected this other connection. Still. It's a bonus. I just hope it doesn't prejudice Carrickfergus. Now then, let's go over to the interview rooms and see the birds that were brought in last night. We should have something to charge them with."

It was about this same time that Detective Inspector Marriott discovered in conversation with the constable at Mark Hawley's bedside that he had had visitors earlier that morning. "It's funny, Sir," said the constable, "but I've not seen either the doctor or the nurse who came in here first thing since. I'd know 'em again if I saw 'em, I know. The nurse had a stud in 'er nose."
An alarm bell began to ring in Marriott's head. He walked over to the Staff Nurse's desk. The nurse was a petite young woman with an intelligent looking face. She smiled enquiringly at him.
"Excuse me, nurse," began Marriott, "can you tell me if any of your ward nurses have studs in their noses?"
The staff nurse laughed. "Not on this ward. Why? Does it turn you on?"
"What about doctors? Have you got a slight, balding one, aged about forty to forty five?"
The nurse stopped laughing at the sight of Marriott's face. Marriott immediately took out his mobile 'phone and touched in a number. He caught Kate just as she and Baskerville were about to leave the office. Kate finished speaking, pressed the disconnect button and turned to Baskerville. "I'm sorry, Sir, but we seem to have got a leak somewhere in our midst. Dooney's already got at our witness in hospital."

Andrew carefully closed his cabin doors behind him. A thin stream of smoke was climbing steadily from the stateroom chimney. As he stepped ashore, the boat rocked slightly. It seemed that the frost was not gripping as tightly as it had done yesterday. A few yards up the canal, the hole where Mark had gone through yesterday had not refrozen and a gentle breeze was rippling the open water, which gleamed in the early sunrise. He walked past the scene of last night's excitement, there being nothing to show for it save the boarded over windows and an Electricity Board van belonging to the gang who were restoring the overhead supply. The invaders had thrown a length of light chain over the supply pole to short out the wires, and the subsequent mess was taking some while to repair. It was not yet eight o'clock and he thought it would be as well if he removed the window boards before Jane arrived and started asking questions. He had brought a screwdriver and an adjustable spanner with him, and set about unscrewing the coach screws that he had driven into the woodwork. Later on he would pop into Stony Stratford and get some putty to fill the screw holes before any wet got in. As he took down the board over the kitchen window, Anne came downstairs. She smiled somewhat awkwardly at Andrew, and then called out to him to come in.

Andrew stamped snow off his shoes and went to take them off. "Oh, don't bother" called Anne. "It's only snow."
She stood by the Aga and placed a kettle on the hob. "Coffee?"
"Yes please."
There was silence for a space, then they both began speaking at once, stopped, laughed, and Andrew said "after you."
Anne said "I really don't know how to start this, but last night..." she trailed off.
"I know, you were badly frightened, and it's all my fault."
"I wanted you to stay with me, in the house, but at the same time... Oh, damn, I just don't know what I want. Yes. You're right. I was frightened, but not that, so much as upset. I can cope with the fear, but having all those people invading my house. It somehow got to me."

Andrew took her hand. "Oh, Anne. I'm so sorry. It's all my fault. I'd no right to drag you into this horrible business."

"You seem to forget. I dragged you into it first. You first got mixed up with JD Properties Ltd. because you wanted to help me. Remember?"

"Yes. I know, but things have moved on since then. I really should have thought it through after I noticed the car tailing me the other night outside Joey's."

"Andrew, you did think it through. You prepared a trap for them and they walked right into it. It's not that that worries me so much as the thought that I might get driven out of here. It's been my life for so many years, I've buried my husband from here, brought up my children, and now circumstances are conspiring to drive me out."

Andrew squeezed her hand gently. "Look, Anne. You've been a good friend to me, and there's no way that I'll let this happen to you."

She smiled ruefully. "No, Andrew, I know that you wouldn't, so long as you were around. But I can't expect you to be hanging around here, just waiting to drive off the baddies. You've got your own life to live, and glamorous lady detectives to look after... No, let me finish, you know I don't resent Kate, I've got no right to do so."

But I think you do, deep down, thought Andrew, but did not say anything. Instead he was silent. It was no use complicating matters by explaining that he was by no means certain of his feelings in that direction. Anne too was silent for a space, then said, in a somewhat brighter tone "anyway it's no good trying to undo what's been done. I've decided, I'm going to go away for a while and get my thoughts back together."

"Well, if that's what you want, I'll gladly look after things here for you. Where do you think you might go?"

"Austria. Do you remember, I was thinking of going there ages ago, then we got all mixed up with Christmas and other things? I'm going to go skiing with an old girl friend of mine."

Why am I glad that it's a girl friend and not a man friend? thought Andrew, then, recovering himself quickly said "oh, yes. I remember. Hall im Tyrol. I went there years ago, when I was first married."

That afternoon Andrew tried ringing Kate, but she was not available to come to the 'phone, and although he tried several times, the best that he could get was a brief and breathless exchange in which she told him that she was completely snowed under with work, that she had taken a statement from Mark which seemed to get them little further, and that the other two had been charged with threatening behaviour and released on bail. They had since disappeared. Meanwhile a parcels van called at the farm leaving behind a small parcel addressed to Andrew and bearing the name of a local wine merchant. Andrew opened it suspiciously, half expecting to be blown up. It merely contained a litre bottle of Bushmills whiskey and a label with one word on it: "*thanks*."

Over the next few days there was a slow thaw, then there came a day and night of heavy rain. As if by magic the snow disappeared, the hole in the ice made by Mark got bigger and the wind rippled the water in it until the ice at the edges gradually rotted away. Another pool of clear water developed under the bridge and slowly increased in size until it met what Andrew, who was watching the process with interest and noting its process, had already christened 'Mark's Pool'. On the next Saturday morning Andrew woke to clear skies, a gentle westerly wind and the distant sound of a boat engine driving through what remained of the ice. The engine noise grew louder and soon Andrew was able to see the low down shape of a loaded working boat with the unmistakable figure of Jack Turvey hunched over the tiller beside a chimney that was sending a shimmer of pure heat above his head. He slowed down and drifted past the farm basin, then caught sight of Andrew and lifted his hand in greeting.

"All right, mate?" he called cheerfully as he slid past.

"Fine thanks" replied Andrew. "Where are you off to?"

"Ole' Jonesy sold all 'is load down at Boxmoor in that frost, so I'm goin' down wi' this to fill 'im up again."

"What's the going like?"

"It ain't too bad. Still a bit o' ice on some o' them big turns an' open bits like round 'ere. Stu lays at Braunston this week. I ain't seen no one else though, since I left Buckby yesterday." He smiled a smile that split his open countenance and flashed white teeth. "Mind you, that's 'ow I likes it. So long then mate, see you when I come back!" By now he was calling back from the arch of the bridge. He turned round and wound the throttle control wheel, the engine barked in reply, and the boat swam rapidly out of sight. Andrew leaned back contentedly against the warm doorway in which he was standing. The presence of Jack Turvey's massive solid figure, the way in which all the canal people seemed to work together, the cheeriness of it all, was somehow reassuring. There might well be villains like Burson, Dooney and Shorland invading it, but it was still a world somehow insulated against the contagion of such people, or so he devoutly hoped.

A little later, as he was thinking of going ashore for some shopping, he heard a voice calling him from the bank. Looking out he saw Sally Clarke standing on the wharf, wearing a skiing windcheater and waving. "Hullo, Sally" he said. "Just got home?"

"About ten minutes ago. Mum said you were on the boat, so thought I'd come and tell you the latest on Sir Colin."

"Come in, it's too cold to stand about."

"Thanks" said Sally, stepping nimbly down on to the boat. "Gosh, it's really warm in here. I'd forgotten just how snug a boat could be."

"Tea or coffee?"

"Oh, tea please, milk, no sugar."

Andrew went into the galley, filled the kettle and lit the gas.

"So what's new about our errant MP? Sit down. Make yourself

comfortable."

Sally dropped into the settee. "Well, you know that he and your wife have split up, I suppose?" Andrew nodded, "He's been spending more time than ever in Lupus Street," she went on "and he also regularly goes to a massage parlour."

"Maybe he does, but that doesn't necessarily make him a sex freak."

"It does when it's off Dean Street and has all sorts of dodgy adverts."

"He could always say he was carrying out research in the public interest."

"Gloria Lovejoy says different."

"Who her?"

"Oh, she's really called Sharon Briggs, but she works at the parlour and is a call girl as well. She wants to start her own hairdressing salon in Walthamstow, so my editor has agreed to pay her five thousand for her story."

"That's a bit below the belt isn't it?"

Sally's eyes flashed with annoyance. "Really, Andrew, you are too much of a Gent at times. Below the belt! Do you think having you put away for three years of whatever wasn't below the belt? Come off it! It's only what he and his like have asked for."

"Sorry I spoke."

Sally laughed. *That was when she looked so much like her mother* thought Andrew. "All right. It was perhaps a bit of a dirty trick, but he does deserve it. And don't go on about saying two wrongs don't make one right. At least I feel better for trying to expose the hypocritical bastard. Oh, thanks." She took the cup and saucer that Andrew offered her. "Anyway, what's been happening about the rotters who tried to do you over? Mum told me something about the high ding-dong here the other night. I gather she's a bit upset and wants out of it."

"You're dead right she wants out. She's talking about going off to Austria for a few weeks to get it out of her system. I can't help feeling she thinks it's all down to me."

"Um" said Sally, "I can understand you thinking that, but I don't think she holds you responsible. She likes you too much for that. I think it's another thing altogether, but she'll have to work it out for herself. She'd not thank me for interfering, don't forget I've known her a long time, all my life in fact!" The two laughed. "Anyway," she continued, "what's happened to the lot who tried to get you?"

"The one that I rescued has been released without a charge. I can understand that as a lawyer. It's difficult to see what criminal law he could be proved to have broken, unless it's an offence against the canal byelaws to bathe in the cut. Conspiracy? How do you prove it? Trespass? Well, maybe criminal trespass, but there again, what proof is there? Only my word against his. The other two have been charged with threatening behaviour and released on bail. They've not been seen in the area since, and frankly I should be very surprised to hear from them again."

"But how on earth did they know how to find you? They must have had access to police information...." she caught Andrew's eye as she spoke, and trailed away in mid-sentence "Oh, I see. There's naughty coppers at work are there?"

"Look, Sally, I can't tell you anything except this. The guys who wanted to part my hair and the ones who caused your mother grief last autumn are all part and parcel of the same thing, and there is some connection with our friend in Parliament. Beyond that I mustn't say more because it could prejudice investigations if the Press got wind of it and blew the gaff." He paused and listened. He opened the front cabin doors and stepped out, cocking his ear to the canal. "I'm sure I heard the sound of a boat's engine" he said, then after a pause "yes, I did. There's something coming." Even as he spoke, the boat moved with the forward swill of an oncoming craft.

Sally joined him in the front well and together they lifted up the canvas cover to look out. There was a distinctive popping sound coming from the Stoke Bruerne direction. Within a couple of minutes, the fore end of a boat swam into view. It was another working boat and looked somehow familiar. Andrew gave a little gasp as it drew nearer. It was almost certainly the 'dog boat', released from its imprisonment in the ice, like Jack Turvey earlier on. Andrew now recognised the figure of the man steering, a burly, bearded shape, his peaked cap pulled well down over his eyes. The boat was coming ahead at a tremendous rate and showed no sign of easing up as it passed the moored craft. Andrew suddenly ducked into the cabin. There was no point in letting the steerer see that he had been observed. Sally, a puzzled look on her face, joined him, letting the canvas well deck cover fall back in place. The boat continued past at a great rate, water swilling along the bank behind it. *Romford* jerked violently as the wash caught her. The steerer looked neither right nor left as he ploughed down the middle of the canal. The arch of the bridge caught and swallowed up the boat; the drumming of the exhaust faded swiftly.

Andrew had been watching the boat through a net curtained porthole. He turned to Sally with one of his queer, lop-sided smiles. "That was our friends who pinched the dogs. I'll be prepared to bet they're up to no good. Now then. If you want the chance of a story, I'll tell you what. If you like, we'll go shopping in Milton Keynes by boat and you can write about the experience. We might just turn up something worth writing about."
"Give me ten minutes" said Sally, jumping ashore.

In fact Sally was slightly longer, because neither she, nor Andrew had any idea of how long the job would take. Andrew merely had a hunch that he knew where Burson's retreat was from his perusal of the Land Registry documents, but he had never been that far along the canal before. It was difficult therefore making an arrangement which would enable Anne to get supper, and it was solved by Andrew's agreeing to ring her as soon as they were on their way home. Fortunately *Romford* was facing in the right direction, so no further time was lost in turning round. By the time Sally had found some warm clothes and suitable shoes' Andrew had the engine started and was ready to cast off. Anne came down to the wharf to see them off. She was not at ease, Andrew could tell, and told Sally to take care. "Mothers!" said Sally with a snort once they were out of earshot and through the bridge. Andrew said nothing. He sensed that Anne was unhappy at his taking her daughter into what was potentially the firing line.

It was a chilly morning, with a north easterly blowing across the valley towards them as they headed towards Milton Keynes. Hard edged clouds occasionally swept across the icy blue sky, but it remained fine. After working its way out of the little river valley, the canal came to the small village of Cosgrove. Andrew had been this far before on his foray to empty the cess tank and decided to make use of the same facility today. Sally walked ahead to get the lock ready while he did this and returned a couple of minutes later in a state of great excitement. Immediately below the lock there was a straight stretch of nearly a mile, and she had caught sight of their quarry in the far distance. Andrew had nearly finished the odorous business at the Sanitary Station and calculated that the 'dog boat' must be about twenty minutes ahead of them, but by the time he had brought *Romford* into Cosgrove lock it was out of sight. A bystander told him that it had been held up by Jack Turvey who had been delivering coal to a nearby wharf and had only just started when the second boat appeared. Andrew glanced at his watch as they left the lock. It was nearly twelve; they had some four hours daylight left.

Sally came and stood on the gunwale beside Andrew as they headed across the embankment towards the outskirts of Milton Keynes. Her eyes opened in alarm as, a few minutes later, they suddenly found themselves suspended some forty feet above the River Ouse in an iron trough with only a thin lip between her and space.

"Golly!" she said, "not really what I would recommend as a substitute for All Bran. Did you know it was like that?"

"No, I didn't" replied Andrew truthfully. "I've read the guide book, but it was not very clear about such delights."

The moment of terror however did not last long, and soon they were threading their way through the remains of the Wolverton railway works. After passing over another, modern, aqueduct over a main road, they found themselves apparently heading out into open country again. Sally went below and made a cup of tea and some sandwiches which they had as they wound this way and that through fields. The wind had dropped and it was turning into a pleasant winter afternoon. Andrew kept looking at his guide book, what had seemed only a short distance on the map seemed to take ages, but then the canal seemed to be finding its way back into an urban area again. This time though, apart from a very few older houses, it was a modern residential area. The houses seemed rather small at first, then, after they had been going about an hour and a half from Cosgrove, they both spotted their quarry.

"View Halloo!" called Sally, who had gone forward to the well deck, pointing to the right. Andrew had seen it almost at the same instant. A branch canal led off at right angles into a large pool with modern houses grouped round it. At the far end, the boat they were looking for lay tied up beside a pleasant detached residence. They could see the figure of the boatman standing by the garage talking to somebody. Andrew throttled down, wondering whether to sail in and investigate, then thought better of it. There was no point in upsetting the apple cart. If anyone recognised him, at the very least Burson and Dooney would be on the alert. Best to go past and appear to take no notice. They could always come back overland, or get pictures with a long distance lens. At least they knew where to look now.

Sally bobbed down into the cabin, emerging soon after with a camera. She clicked away as they passed the entrance to the branch canal. Nobody seemed to take any notice of her. As soon as they were out of sight Andrew slowed right down and drew in to the side. Sally came back to him along the gunwale.

"What happens now?" she asked.

"I'm going back to have a quick look. I'm absolutely certain that's the place that Burson rents from JD Properties Ltd. I've got a copy of the Land Registry plan in the cabin, and I'm going to check it."

There was a short length of concrete piling on the offside of the canal. Andrew steered alongside this and secured fore and aft to some convenient trees. He took a piece of A4 paper from a drawer in the cabin, then set off along the waste land which here bordered the canal. The canal basin was overlooked by a clump of bare hawthorn bushes, and by orientating the sketch map, which he had brought, he was able positively to identify it. He showed Sally the main points of resemblance, then the two scouted inland a short distance and found a footpath which led towards the houses surrounding the basin. It passed between two boarded fences and eventually led into a close. The houses were obviously four or five bedroomed, with large garages and spacious gardens at the front. Andrew assumed that the rear either led down to or overlooked the basin. They walked along the close and eventually found themselves outside the one that Andrew was sure was that occupied by Burson. There was no car outside and the garage door was shut, but there were lights inside. As they watched, they both saw a blonde woman pass in front of an upstairs window, but there was no other sign of life.

"I think we'd better push off" said Andrew.

"Just a sec" said Sally, clicking away with her camera. "You never know when they'll come in useful."

They made their way back to the boat, Andrew restarted the engine and untied. "According to my guide, the next turning place is about half a mile further on and handy for the shopping centre. I suggest we go there and I'll ring your mum when we're ready to start for home."

By the time that they had reached the turning place it was three o'clock. They both decided that if they were to go shopping it would be dark long before they reached home, so they began to retrace their course. As they neared the entrance to the basin, Sally waved to Andrew to slow right down. He did so and she took a series of pictures using the telephoto lens. As she was doing this there came an angry shout from the basin.

"Oi! You! Sod off! This is private property!"

The big bearded man was standing in the cabin doors of his boat waving angrily at them. Andrew waved pacifically back and Sally put her camera away. Andrew turned the speed wheel and the engine began to accelerate. The stern dug into the water and the basin faded away astern. Sally brought another cup of tea to the stern for Andrew. "Somehow, I think he's a little camera shy" she said.

Chapter 16
Old Comrades

Kate Hollis yawned and stretched herself luxuriously on her sofa. She flicked the TV control and killed the programme. It was her first Saturday night off since before Christmas, and there was absolutely nothing worth watching on any of the channels. It would have been pleasant to have gone out for the evening with Andrew, but she was getting worried about the relationship. He was a genuinely nice guy, but she did not wish things to proceed further, and at the same time she feared that he did. Sooner or later, and the way things were going, it would be sooner, the Carrickfergus thing would be finished and wrapped up and she would have to tell him that his usefulness was over. Kate was not a squeamish person, she had been in her job too long for that, but she genuinely liked Andrew and was not anxious to hurt him. She was just wondering whether or not to get changed and go out to the village pub for a chat with some of the locals, when the telephone rang. She picked it up and was not displeased to hear Andrew's voice at the other end. After a few seconds' conversation, she realised that she was not going to have a peaceful evening after all.

"Can I come over? I'll put everything on the laptop and send it down the wire to the boss."

When Kate arrived less than twenty minutes later, she had the laptop ready and a modem to connect to a mobile 'phone. Andrew gave as full an account of the matter as he could recall.

"What's he up to with the boat, do you think?" he asked when he had finished.

"Well, he must be moving something that's bulky or else valuable. You know more about this sort of thing than I, but I would imagine that it's not easy to hijack a canal boat, and you can move about the country pretty well unobserved."

"Yes, that's true, but the dog stealing shows that it's not quite as unobserved as some people think. The likes of Stu don't miss much."

"Don't talk to me about that any way. It looks as if the CPS is only going to let the RSPCA prosecute for cruelty. They say there's not enough evidence to make a theft charge stick. I sometimes wonder if lawyers live in the same world as everyone else."

Andrew raised his eyebrows and Kate laughed.

Andrew made coffee and they sat together on the sofa. Kate was just wondering whether to broach the matter of ending the relationship but to remain friends, when the boat gave a sudden jerk. She cast a puzzled look at Andrew.

"There's a boat coming" he said.

"What, at this time of night?"

"It's only half past eight." Andrew went to a porthole and looked out. The underside of the bridge arch was lit with the glow of a headlight. He darted to the main cabin light switch and immediately plunged the boat in darkness. "I think it's our man. He's certainly going fast enough."

Kate peered through the adjacent porthole. The fore end of a boat swept into the bridge, a bubbling wave of white water preceding it. *Romford* tugged hard at her mooring lines as water was dragged out from beneath her, and she lurched hard as the lines snatched tighter. "Speedy bloody Gonzales!" muttered Andrew, "Where's his water skier?"

The boat came abreast of the watchers, did not slacken speed and drummed past. It was impossible to see any details of who was steering, but Andrew was almost certain that it was the same man whom they had seen earlier.

"I know!" said Kate. "How long will it take him to get to the locks at Stoke Bruerne?"

"At that rate, about forty five minutes."

"Why don't we nip up there and take a look? If we go down the road beside the locks we could pretend to be a courting couple in a car, and light him up. He must be up to some sort of no good travelling at that speed at this hour."

"Do we have to *pretend* to be a courting couple?"

"Ooh! You are awful!"

In spite of the speed at which the mysterious boat was being driven, it was nearly an hour later that it arrived at the locks. Kate and Andrew had plenty of time in which to choose a strategic place where they could observe the locks from within Kate's car. There was a wide area of hard standing by the second lock where they could park facing the lock at right angles and observe matters. They had been waiting some ten minutes in this vantage point when they both saw a figure with a torch making its way towards the lock along the towpath. The figure came beside the bottom gate, pushed it open and stood waiting. A headlight came creeping up the pound towards the lock. It went out of sight behind the lock wall, but the watchers in the car could see the glow lighting up the lock walls immediately in front of them. The figure with the torch pulled the gate shut and another figure with a torch came clambering up the lock ladder out of the empty chamber. Andrew and Kate embraced one another as a beam of light flashed over them momentarily, then passed on. They heard the rattle of paddle gear and the thunder of released water, as the lock began to fill. The second figure lit a cigarette as he hunched over the top gate watching the water rushing in, and his face was very briefly illuminated. Slowly, agonisingly slowly, the levels equalised and the second figure came walking back along the lockside. He stepped on to the stern deck of his boat, now level with the copings, and began to rev his engine to push the gate open. The dark shape of the boat began very slowly moving forward. Andrew squeezed Kate's hand. "Now!" he said.

The twin beams of Kate's car headlights blazed out, throwing the boat and its steerer into sharp relief. The steerer turned and gaped at the car, blinking as the lights blinded him. There was no doubt.

Both boat and steerer were the same as Andrew had seen at Burson's house earlier that day. Kate started her engine and reversed away from the lockside. "We'll let him think he's disturbed us, rather than the other way round" she said as they sped back to the main road.

Next morning Andrew rang Stu. Stu promised that he would keep a look out for the boat. He was currently tied up at Braunston, but he'd speak to one of his mates at Buckby, just in case the boat should head north from Norton Junction on to the Leicester section.

"I thought that that way was closed for repairs" said Andrew.

"Not any more it ain't. They finished the job early, and the contractors have gone on to another job. Same as happened down the Arm."

"What, the Northampton Arm?"

"Yes, mate. They was going to replace a culvert under the cut, but when they got the water out last week they found the brickwork was OK, so they decided to spend the money on summat else. They're opening it up again next week."

"So your pal Roberts could have taken his boat to Braunston after all."

"Well, I suppose he could 'a' done. But he tells me the kid what you put on the boat's looking after it all right, so he ain't that bothered. By the way, that bit of advice you give me before Christmas was all right."

"I'm glad to hear it."

"Yes. My Ex has stated to get all reasonable again. I think we're going to settle things OK now."

"Oh, good!"

"I'm in your debt mate. Leave it with me. I'll get back as soon as I hears anything about that chap with the dog boat."

Stu rang back about an hour later. He had interesting news. His mate was working at Watford locks that morning and on going to work just before eight o'clock, had found a boat tied up below with the crew apparently asleep. He took the padlocks off the locks and went about his business and about an hour later had found the boat and its crew of a man and woman just entering the bottom of the staircase locks. There was no name on the boat, but Stu was certain that it was the one they were looking for.

"Y'see Andy, you saw him last night at the sixth lock of Stoke, when? Half past nine? Right! He'd have been at the top lock about half past ten, that makes him half past two this morning bottom of Buckby, four o'clock at the top and five at bottom of Watford. He wouldn't go no further, 'cos the locks is locked up till eight o'clock. If he'd have come down Braunston we'd have seen him. On top of that I had a word with my mate Ron at Buckby. They don't lock up there at the moment and he said somebody come up the locks in the night leaving all the gates open behind him, and he's had to refill two pounds this morning."

Andrew found this complex waterway reasoning a little hard to follow and had to ask Stu to repeat bits, but eventually came to admit that Stu was most probably correct.

"So, what's he up to, Stu?" he asked.

"You got me there, mate. He won't get down Foxton, 'cos that's stopped until March. Maybe he's going to the top o' Foxton or to Welford."

An idea struck Andrew. "Where could he meet a car or van to unload anything?"

"Now you're asking mate. It's dead lonely country up there, no end of little road bridges and quiet places where you could meet someone, 'specially this time of year. You don't see nobody from one week's end to the next in them places. But if I was going to get rid of summat to a car, I'd go for somewhere round Elkingtons or North Kilworth. You can tie up there, someone can meet yer and it'd all be over in five minutes. You're only talking of half an hour by car to Coventry or Leicester, even less for somewhere like Market Harborough or Kettering or Northampton. What d'you reckon he's got on that he wants to be rid of?"

"I'm not sure. I'm certain it's not dogs though this time. By the way, I think I've found out where he was going to put those dogs off. There's a place in Milton Keynes and one of the suspects has a house backing on to a basin there."

"Oh ah. I think I knows the place. Round the Fenny Pound, by them new houses."

"Probably, yes. I think he's taking something that's small and valuable. It didn't look to me as if the boat was very deep in the water."

"Well, why the hell's it goin' by cut? What's the point of rushing about all over the place when it's got to end up on a car or wagon anyway?"

"I'm not exactly sure, but I think that what's being carried is something that they want to be as little noticed as possible. Also nobody will notice if stuff gets moved out of the back of the place by boat, whereas too many comings and goings by cars or vans get noticed by neighbours and maybe even the registrations are noted."

"Yeah, but it's just the same on the cut. We notices it, don't we?"

"Oh yes, but I'm not sure that whoever is doing all this to-ing and fro-ing realises that we do. I think the job, whatever it is, is being set up by someone who doesn't know very much about how the towpath telegraph works. You see, your man with the dog boat. He's not a born boater is he?"

"No, he sure ain't. I've only seen him about since we had that run in with him before Christmas. He ain't a proper boatman."

Had Andrew or Stu known it, their joint analysis of the situation was not far wrong. At two o'clock that afternoon, at a lonely bridge on a quiet country lane near Husbands Bosworth, up in the lonely Wold country that forms the boundary between Leicestershire and Northamptonshire, the boat in question made a rendezvous with an unmarked hire van. It was just over two miles as the crow flies from one of the places that Stu had predicted. The driver and his mate scrambled down the bank on to the towpath where the boat was tied up. The driver knocked twice on the cabin side and the bearded man appeared. A few words were exchanged, the covers were thrown back and two wooden boxes were brought from under a pile of coal sacks. The driver and his mate took one apiece.

"What happens if I drop the focker?" asked the mate. His voice had a trace of Belfast in it.

"Don't worry! It ain't armed yet" laughed the driver, "if it were, I wouldn't be carryin' it over them bumps in the lane."

The bearded man watched them carry the boxes up the bank. The woman with the North London accent came out and watched too.

"Right, sweet 'eart" said the man, "we're off. We'll turn at the next windin' ole an' get back to North Kilworth. You can get some shoppin' there, accordin' to the book."

"I should bloody well 'ope so. I'm fed up wiv this job. I wants some bloody sleep."

Andrew made himself some sandwiches and a cup of tea. He was just wondering whether or not to ring up Kate and ask her out for a meal that evening, when the telephone rang. It was Pamela.

"Andrew, Darling. How are you?" Andrew was not at all sure that he wanted to be gushed at, especially by his ex-wife, but he replied civilly enough: "Hullo, Pam. What can I do for you?"

"Now who said I wanted anything from you?"

You'd not be running true to form if you didn't thought Andrew, but merely said "I just guessed, that's all."

"You clever old thing. Well, what I was ringing about was that I wonder if you could possibly help me. I'm starting divorce proceedings against Colin, and of course he acted for me when we were divorced, remember?"

Shall I ever forget? The devious, twisting bastard! Andrew thought, but merely said "yes, I remember."

"Well, you may remember, there was a schedule of my property drawn up at the time, but of course Colin's solicitors can't find it, and they say it never existed."

"I'm glad to know his professional advisors run true to form. But yes, I do remember the schedule being drawn up and agreed, although I was not exactly in a position to do much about it myself."

"Don't rub it in Andrew. I don't exactly feel ecstatic about what happened between us."

"Sorry, Pam. Go on."

"Didn't John Watson act on your behalf at the time?"

"He did. That's why I'm not completely destitute."

"Oh dear! This is getting very difficult."

"It doesn't have to. But you must forgive me if I chortle now and again."

"You're not as big a beast as you try to be, you know that Andrew! What I wanted to ask you was. Could you be a darling and see whether John still has that schedule, and send me a copy. I'll pay any expenses."

"Pam, if it will torpedo that stinker, I'll do anything you want. Now then, how's Jane?" They settled into a family conversation almost as if nothing had ever come between them.

"Yes, of course I've still got the schedule" said John Watson when Andrew rang him at his house later that afternoon. I'll look it out for you when I get into the office tomorrow and send you a copy."

"You might as well send it straight to Pamela, she's staying at my daughter Jane's." Andrew gave him Jane's Ealing address and John muttered as he jotted it down.

"Oh yes, before you go" said John, "I've been meaning to ring you and tell you. I bumped into an old friend the other day."

"Really? Who?"

John Watson laughed a dry, accountant's laugh. "I had to go to the Royal Hospital, Chelsea last Tuesday. We've been helping their auditors out with a few things. Anyway, I went to see the bursar and when I came out into the courtyard afterwards, who do you think I bumped into?"

"I haven't the faintest idea?"

"You may recall a conversation we had a few months back when you said if there was no justice in this world Company Sergeant

Major Dunton would be a Chelsea Pensioner? Well you were right. There he was, large as life, resplendent in red coat and cocked hat. He recognised me straight away."

"Not that old bastard!"

"The very same. He came straight up to me, back like a ramrod, stood and looked me straight in the eyes and said 'Mr. Watson, Sir!'

I bloody near fainted. The last time I'd seen him was after we'd passed out of Mons OCTU. It must have been when we came back from Cyprus and he was about to be posted to Germany. I never thought I'd come across the old bugger again. Do you know, he remembered both you and Joey Caroni."

"Well, well, old soldiers never die."

"No. He seems to have done well for himself somehow, because he was telling me that when he retired from the army in the early eighties, just before the Falklands business, he was able to set himself up in a sub post office somewhere. He'd have still been there, but his wife died and all his children had grown up and left home, so he applied for a place at Chelsea. I'll tell you what. He may have seemed an old bastard to us when we were doing basic training, but he seems a decent enough old stick now. He asked after you, because of course he still remembers that affair in the Troodos Mountains. When I said you had become a solicitor he looked at me a bit funny. 'I thought Mr. Ellison would be too straight to do that' he said. Funny old boy really."

"Was he in Germany long?"

"Several years I gather. At Sennelager mainly. He ended up a WO 2."

Somewhere a bell began to ring in Andrew's mind. Colin Shorland's CV had something about Sennelager in it he was absolutely certain.

"And you say he's still at the Chelsea Hospital?"

"Large as life and full of beans."

After he had finished talking to John Watson, Andrew sat stroking his chin for a while, and then rang Kate. He asked her if she could check service records for ex-WO 2. Dunton, retired about 1983. Within the hour she rang back to say that Dunton had been stationed at Sennelager during the period March 1959 to March 1965. Andrew pursed his lips and whistled.

"I think we may have found a useful link. You see, he's my old Company Sergeant Major. I remember him being posted to Germany just about the time my Service finished, I was on a three year short service commission, and he seems to have been at the same posting as Shorland, who was there as an officer in the Pay Corps. I just think that I'll slip up to Chelsea tomorrow and go and look up an old comrade. It's a long shot, but it's worth trying."

Andrew had got the Bursar's telephone number at Chelsea from John Watson, so it was not difficult to ascertain that, yes, Mr. Dunton was in residence. No, it was not possible to speak to him at the moment because he was out, but he would certainly see that a message was left for him.

Andrew found a parking space in front of the Chelsea Hospital. Perhaps because it was still late January there did not seem to be that many visitors in London and the Hospital Visitors' car park had several spaces. He gratefully slid in, got out, locked his car and, without realising that he was doing so, straightened his tie and glanced at the polish on his shoes. The appointment had been made by the Bursar's secretary so he had not spoken to Dunton, yet, after forty years or so, he till felt a twinge of unease that he might be barked at and put on a charge for being 'idle', which, as he recalled, was the greatest sin in Dunton's book. He walked through the great doorway and found the Reception Desk. The girl spoke into a telephone and then asked him to wait a moment; Mr. Dunton was on his way. Andrew wondered whether he should take a seat and decided against it, then the door opened and in strode the resplendent figure of his old CSM. He was a trifle over six feet tall, very slightly stooped, his bare head silver, and his black trousers spotless, as was his red coat and the cocked hat which he carried under his left arm. He strode directly towards Andrew, held out his right hand and said "Mr. Ellison, Sir. How are you?"

Andrew took his hand. The grip was firm and positive. He might be old, but he was still a powerful man.

"Lovely to see you, Mr Dunton. You're looking wonderful."

The old soldier beamed at him. "You're not looking so bad yourself, Sir. I'm very glad Mr Watson remembered me to you. We were all very proud of you, you did well Sir, and Corporal Caroni."

"It was all thanks to your training. We were far more scared of you than we were of any enemy!"

Dunton laughed. "That's just how it should be Sir, just how it should be."

"Well, there's not a lot of point in us standing here. How about a drink?"

"Very good idea, sir. There's a good pub just round the corner."

"Take me to it. I owe you at least one drink!"

Dunton took a long pull at a pint of Fullers *London Pride* and licked his lips appreciatively. "Very good of you, Mr Ellison. Your good health."

Andrew raised a pint of shandy in reply. Fixing his eyes on Dunton's face he said "I'll be absolutely straight with you, Mr Dunton. I'm very glad to see you, but not only because we were old comrades, but because I think you may be able to help me in some enquiries that I'm making."

"And what may they be Sir?"

Andrew paused a moment, then said "I think you knew a Mr. Shorland once. A Second Lieutenant, later Lieutenant in the Pay Corps."

A shadow passed across Dunton's face, then he replied, "I may have done. But you see Sir, when you've been in as long as I was, you get thousands through your hands, even officers, let alone other ranks. Only if they've made good or real bad do you remember them. You made good, Sir. You was a credit to your Regiment."

"Would it surprise you to know that I've been to prison?"

Dunton's face was impassive. "You Sir? Prison? I don't believe it."

"You can take it from me that it's the truth. I also have reason to believe that Shorland helped to put me there. Another pint?"

"Thank you, Sir. I don't mind if I do. You say Lieutenant Shorland put you there?"

"Yes." Andrew crossed to the bar and ordered another pint. When he brought it back, Dunton was gazing at nothing, with a puzzled look on his face. He thanked Andrew absently, raised the pint to his lips and took a pull, then suddenly seemed to come back into focus.

"What was it you done, Sir?"

"Three years. Misappropriation of Trust Funds. Not very dramatic. Nobody lost any money, but Shorland took my wife, I lost my job, my money, my house, my family. I can't prove it, but I believe Shorland set me up."

"If he did, you wasn't the only one."

"You did know him then?"

"Oh, yes. I knew him. I wasn't sure what you was after. But you see Sir, I reads the papers. I knew you'd gone inside, because I read about it at the time. I don't forget someone who was a credit to the Regiment, and when I saw it, I says to myself 'Les' I says, 'I don't believe Mr Ellison could do a rotten trick if he tried. That's what I thought Sir. And when you came straight out with it that you'd done bird... been to prison, I mean, I thinks to myself, you didn't have to tell me that. I'm grateful for your honesty, Sir."

"Thank you. But tell me about Shorland."

Dunton took out a small snuffbox, offered it to Andrew, who declined, took a pinch, blew his nose loudly, and then said, "It was after you come back from Cyprus. I was posted to the Second Battalion in Germany."

"Sennelager wasn't it?"

"That's right Sir. I was posted there to replace a Company Sergeant Major who had been discharged sick. It was what you might call a cushy number. In them days, there was a load of us NCOs who'd seen war service in North Africa, Italy, Germany, Korea and that, and we used to get these cushy postings as a sort of consolation prize. See our time out, like. Well I'd still got five years or more to do, so I wasn't grumbling, but we was always on the look out for ways of helping ourselves settle down in Civvy Street, like. Well, this baby officer, Mr Shorland, he comes out to us from the UK to help run the pay office. One day he finds that some of the Company's stores are, shall we say, a little under strength. Well, of course they was. There was plenty of Jerries who'd buy buckshee stuff off you. We all did it. Mr Shorland though, he says to me, 'Sar Major', he says, 'you're wasting your time with these fiddles.' 'I don't know what you means Sir', I says. 'Don't give me that old malarkey' he says. 'I know a much better way'. Well, the upshot was, I was responsible for sending stores back to the UK to Ordnance for replacement. What he wanted me to do was to let him send all sorts of things that you couldn't get hold of at home in them days, Swiss watches, American cigarettes, Jim Beam whisky, all sorts, back to the UK in empty containers of stores. Dead simple. He had a contact at the base at Aldershot, who was in the depot where I used to send the returned stores. We used to send used shell cases back to the UK after the Gunners 'ad fired 'em on the ranges, and they was ideal for the job. I remember the contact too. He got caught in the end, went to prison and then got killed in a car accident. Lance Corporal Hannagan he was, Ordnance Corps attached to the Depot."

"So, you were really just anticipating the European Union, by establishing your own Free Trade Zone?"

Dunton laughed. "I suppose you could put it that way Sir, but I soon found that it wasn't quite as straightforward. You see, most of the stuff was stolen."

"How did you know?"

"By the markings. A lot of it was from the American PX Stores. It can't have been bought legally. I weren't too fussed with doing the Americans, after all, they hadn't been too fussed about helping us, till after Pearl Harbour at least, but then I finds that there's other things going across to Aldershot."

"Other things?"

"You know, Sir. Drugs. Heroin and that. I didn't want no part in any of that sort of thing. I told Mr Shorland that I wanted out and he got a bit nasty. He'd opened an account for me in the local Sparkasse Bank, and all the payments I got were paid in there, but he told me that the greater part was in sterling in the UK for me to collect when I left the Army. He threatened to drop me in it if I didn't go along with him. Mind, I can't really grumble too much, because there was enough in my German account for me to buy a house out there. I've still got it, and it pays me a nice little rent every month. In them days, there was Exchange Control, and it wasn't too easy to move money from one country to another, so I kept my part of the German share over there. What did for the whole job was that Hannagan got posted to Germany himself, so we lost our UK contact. Mr Shorland finished his time and went home. When I was discharged in 1981, I went to see him. He was a solicitor in the City then."

"I know. He was my partner."

"Was he now?" said Dunton raising his eyebrows, "I wish I'd have known that at the time. I'd have come straight to see you. I went and asked him straight out about my share, and he laughed in my face. Told me I was lucky not to be in the Glasshouse, and kicked me out. Well, I wasn't too put out, because I'd got a bit put by and a Gratuity, so my missus and I bought a sub Post Office. But then she died, nearly five years back, and I couldn't manage it all on my own, so I had to sell up. All the family's grown up, and I thinks to myself, 'Les' I thinks, 'that Mr Shorland hasn't done himself too badly. He's an MP now, and maybe he could give me a bit of a helping hand, like'. So I goes to see him again, and he gets right shirty with me, and tells me to get out of the office and never come back. But, do you know Sir. If that was your office as well as his, he had some bloody funny clients. As I'm going out, who should I see in the waiting room but Lance Corporal Hannagan, what had been dead ten years."

"Hannagan? I never remember a client of that name."

"Probably not, Sir. Because that weren't what he had on his brief case. I saw him clear enough, but he didn't recognise me. Why should he? I was only in the same camp as him for a couple of weeks, but you see Sir, I never forget a face. You don't if you've been an NCO as long as I was."

"And what was on his briefcase?"

"The initials RTB. Now, if you're as well dressed as he was that day I saw him, you don't go borrowing or pinching someone else's briefcase, do you?"

Andrew leaped to his feet and clapped Dunton on the back to the amazement of a young couple sitting just behind. "Mr Dunton, you're a genius. This deserves at least another drink. Come on! Get it down!"

Dunton needed no further bidding to swallow his pint, which he did with a rapidity born of many years of frequenting Sergeants' Messes. Andrew could hardly believe his luck. Without a doubt Lance Corporal Hannagan had been reincarnated in some fashion as Roland Burson. What an amazing run of circumstances it was that had brought him and Shorland in contact with Dunton and Hannagan, or was it? Was it fate, or was there some strange influence that was to throw them all together all these years later? He returned from the bar with another pint, which the retired warrior supped appreciatively.

Would you be prepared to make a statement about all this?" asked Andrew. Dunton's face was impassive.

"Now see here, Sir. I've got a place at the Hospital because of a good service record. Now I'm not the only person in there who's bent the rules now and again, but there's ways of bending rules that the Army puts up with and ways that it don't. I wouldn't want to lose my place at the Hospital through all this coming out.

You see, the Army don't mind too much about watches and booze. Nearly everybody done some of that, but drugs is different. I've got a Grandson been into taking stuff. He's been in and out of prison, for stealing, beating people up, all because he's hooked. It's the likes of Mr Shorland who helped get him that way by finding the stuff for him to take. So I'll tell you what, Sir. You were always a good soldier, and a good officer and a gentleman. I may look old and silly, but I ain't as daft as the likes of Mr Shorland think. I kept records of some of our transactions years ago, and I've still got them. I won't make a statement, but if you'll give me your word as an officer and a gentleman that my name'll be kept out of it, I'll tell you where you can get hold of them. They're not far away, in a Safe Deposit box in the Kings Road."

The Securities Clerk at Barclays Bank was a young woman. Andrew reflected on how times had changed. As an articled clerk he often had to visit bank deposit vaults to obtain securities and the clerks then were generally crusty old men with drooping moustaches. She showed Andrew and Dunton to a seat, and reappeared a few minutes later with a small tin box, which she unlocked for him with a flourish.

"According to this list, there's a packet relating to a house in Germany, an Endowment Policy and a file" she said, opening the lid. Dunton nodded his agreement. Inside were three packets that seemed to tally with this description. Dunton lifted out a buff file with War Office markings on it.

"I kept this, when it was changed to the Ministry of Defence," he said, opening it up. Inside were a number of carbon copy dockets. "I used to keep an extra carbon copy you see. Here you are, they're all for consignments of returned stores to the UK Depot, and here's Mr Shorland's signature, and Lance Corporal Hannagan's at the other end. The documents were returned to me by post, see the date stamp there Sir? That's when I got them back and filed them. But I only filed one copy. I kept the third myself, and you see what I've wrote on them?"

Andrew put on his glasses and peered closely. In neat pencil writing on the first one was the legend:

"*Cigarettes, Lucky Strike, 50 packets X 12.*

Cigars, King Edward, 50 packets X 6.

Stockings, Nylon, ladies, 15 Denier, pairs 150.

Watches, Swiss, 25.

Whiskey, Jim Beam, 2 cases X 12"

"And that was the consignment?"

"It was, Sir. And so it went on. I recorded the consignments going out for over two years, until about 1962 or so. The dates are there. You can check them with Mr Shorland's Service Record, and Lance Corporal Hannagan's, and I dare say the Defence Ministry's still got the originals somewhere. If you go towards the end, Sir you'll see I've recorded shipments of heroin."

"Well, if you don't object, I'll make photo copies of just a few, and we'll take it from there. You realise that the authorities could get an order for the whole lot to be disclosed?"

"Oh, yes Sir. But that won't happen will it? I've got your word on it."

"Yes, you've got my word."

Andrew turned to the Securities Clerk. "If we could borrow your photo copier for a few minutes, I would be very much obliged."

Stewart Roberts, better known as 'Stu', eased off the throttle as he brought the pair of boats into the bridge at Norton Junction, where the canal to Leicester leaves the main line of the Grand Union. He threw off one cross strap, motored hard ahead for a second or two to throw the butty boat to the right, and threw off the second strap. The heavy bulk of the empty boat came booming up beside him in the narrow channel, he took the fore end string as it went past him and walked forward holding it and keeping the boats parallel. He glanced at his watch. It was just five and the sun was setting. No point in going beyond here tonight because it would be dark in an hour and goodness knows what the pounds down Buckby locks would be like today. He'd met no traffic and doubted if anything had come that way in front of him. Emma steered the butty boat alongside, and caught the sterns together as he secured the fore ends. Now the boats were firmly abreast and could be steered as one unit by one person. Emma jumped on to the stern deck of the motor boat and took hold of the tiller. She reached inside and tweaked the gear wheel into ahead. Slowly the two boats moved out of the bridgehole. Stu came walking back along the gangplanks. "We'll go above the lock" he said, "there won't be a lot about tonight."

"As you say" replied Emma. Stumpy the dog, standing in the well deck of the butty with his paws resting on the ash strips, dropped his jaw and let his tongue hang out approvingly as she steered round the bend, past the junction with the Leicester Section and coasted towards the towpath immediately above the lock. They tied up, sent Stumpy ashore for a run, had supper and were settling down to watch the television before going across the lock gates for a drink when Stu suddenly cocked his ear. Almost at the same moment Stumpy jumped into the well deck and gave a quiet bark.

"What is it?" asked Emma.

"Summat's coming" Stu replied, "off the Leicester Cut I reckon, and he ain't half going!"

Stu pushed back the cabin slide, sat on the cabin step by the range and listened. By now Emma, standing beside him, could also make out the noise of a modern high-speed diesel engine seemingly being driven hard, but some distance away.

"Look there!" whispered Stu. A beam of light was lighting some boats tied opposite the entrance to the Leicester Section, then, as they watched, a headlight came shooting out of the branch canal and began swinging round towards them. They heard the steerer of the boat open his throttle wider to force his stern round, and heard a dull bump as the boat struck one of the craft tied near the junction.

"Good job no one ain't on them boats" said Stu, "or he'd be getting some lip now."

The headlight came boring down the canal towards them, making no effort to slow down in spite of the numbers of moored craft along the bank. Emma felt their pair snatch at their mooring lines as the swill caught them. At the last minute, the boat shot beside the moored pair and went astern noisily. Its fore end slammed sideways into Stu's motor boat as it stopped. Stu stood up beside Emma and looked at her in astonishment. A female figure jumped off the fore end of the intruder's boat and wound up both ground paddles of the lock.

"It's the dog boat" whispered Emma.

"I knows that, what I wants to know is what the bloody hell he's playing at," muttered Stu angrily.

A harsh voice boomed out of the dark "Open one gate. These bloody barges are blocking the canal up, but I'll get by them somehow."

"Bloody barges are we?" snorted Stu. "We'll see about that boogger!" He stuck his windlass in his belt and leapt ashore.

"Stu!" called Emma anxiously, "leave it!" But Stu was deaf to her pleas.

The lock had been nearly full before the boat arrived, so by the time that Stu got to the lockside the woman had opened the gate opposite and the boat was nosing into the chamber. Stu wound the paddle down on his side, tucked the windlass back in his belt and leant against the downhill side of the balance beam to stop it swinging open. The steerer of the boat ignored him, so, when the gate had been closed, Stu crossed over and came up beside him.

"What's the rush matey?" he asked

"Just keep your fucking nose out of my business, right?" was the reply.

"Come on now, mate, there's no call to be like that..."

The man sprang ashore. He was a big built man and he took Stu by surprise. He seized the lapels of his coat and said "Look, you nosey bloody bargee. I'm about my own business. You stuck your bloody nose into my affairs before, now just keep it out."

"All right, all right, steady on, mate" croaked Stu, "but you don't have to smash half the cut up while you're about it."

"Shut it!" He shook Stu violently. The woman had meanwhile been edging round behind Stu. Emma could just make out her figure in the glow of the pub's outside light. She had her windlass in her hand, and caught the man's eye. He gave a slight nod and the heavy windlass crashed down on Stu's skull. Blackness settled over him and his legs crumpled. He fell on to the grass of the lockside.

"Get them bloody paddles up and let's bugger off out of here," said the big, black bearded man.

Emma came running across the gates. The boat was sinking in the lock, the big man jumped up on to the lockside carrying a length of rope. He grabbed her as she bent over Stu, slapping his hand across her mouth to stop her calling out. "Come here, sweet 'eart!" he called. The woman came back from the bottom gates.

"She's the interferin' bitch who got us done at Stoke that time" she said, shining a torch into Emma's face as she twisted and writhed impotently in the big man's grasp.

"They've stuck their snouts in once too often. Gag 'er"

The woman pulled a handkerchief tight round Emma's mouth. "Right, now we'll tie the little cow up. And 'er bloke too."

The man trussed Emma securely, and then threw her over his shoulder.

"I know where she'll be safe" he said, and clambered back up on to the top gates. He crossed over, walked back to where the pair of boats lay and rolled her over the gunwale into the empty hold. Emma's body thudded on to the floorboards. She rolled about, groaning, but was unable to get up. The man came back across the gates with a length of thin blue plastic line that he had seen under the butty boat's cratch, and trussed and gagged Stu similarly. He took his inert form and lugged it similarly across the gates and dropped it into the hold beside Emma. By now the lock was empty and the bottom gate opened. He clambered down the steel ladder on to his own boat, put the engine ahead and steered out. Although it was early evening and outside a pub, nobody had seen and nobody had heard anything of the incident.

Emma groaned and wriggled in the bottom of the boat. It was pitch dark, and she could not see anything. It was bitterly cold and she only had the jeans and tee shirt on that she had been wearing in the cabin. Suddenly she heard a thump and the pattering of small feet. Stumpy had jumped into the boat's bottom and was nuzzling her with his cold, wet nose. He nuzzled Stu and gave a short, puzzled bark. He then licked Emma's face, and in spite of herself she found herself wondering if he had been licking his bottom just before. He then went to Stu and licked him, making little whining noises. He then scrabbled his way up the side of the boat and jumped on to the towpath. He trotted towards the lock and through the gate to where his friend the lockkeeper lived. He scratched and whined at the lockkeeper's door, setting off the lockkeeper's own dog. After several minutes the lockkeeper's voice shouted "Shut up!" and his own dog stopped barking. The lockkeeper was trying to watch the early evening news and hoped to catch the weather forecast that came at the end. His dog continued to whine. "What is it, old chap?" he asked, getting out of his chair. The dog gave a quick bark and ran towards the front door. The lockkeeper took a heavy iron poker in his hand and went to the front door. He heard scratching and whinings from the other side, put on the hall and porch lights and carefully opened the door. Stumpy looked up at him with appealing brown eyes, wagged his tail and ran towards the garden gate, whimpering. "Stay!" ordered the lockkeeper to his own dog and closed the door behind him. Stumpy ran backwards and forwards from the gate. "What's the matter then, boy? What's the matter?" said the man, bending down to stroke the dog's head. The dog ran towards the gate and sat there, his tongue hanging out. "What's up, boy? Where's your master?" said the lockkeeper, moving towards him. The dog ran off to the right along the towpath. *The boogger's trying to show me summat* thought the man, and followed. The dog ran towards his boats and stopped. The lockkeeper could just make him out in the shadow thrown by his front door light, he was standing on his hind legs with his muzzle level with the motor boat's gunwale. The man turned and went back into his house, the dog ran back to him, barking, but he need not have worried. The lockkeeper had only gone to fetch a torch from inside the door. Almost immediately he was back and walking along the towpath towards Stu's boats. The dog once more stood on his hind legs, his paws on the boat's gunwale. This time the lockkeeper shone his torch inside and swore aloud. There were two trussed bundles lying under the cratch that looked like bodies. In an instant he was over the side of the boat and stooping under the cross beams to reach the bundles. His torch beam fell on the gagged face of Emma, who made grunting noises and wriggled. Out came a clasp knife and cut Emma's bonds and then he undid the gag.

"Oh, Jack, thank God!" she said, before collapsing in a dead faint.

Kate Hollis had nearly finished her piecing together of the Carrickfergus jigsaw. She looked at her watch; it was nearly half past seven, and she could be finished and done by eight if she had good luck. Then she would go home and have a long, luxurious bath, followed by a Chinese takeaway for one. She felt somewhat guilty over the matter of Andrew, he was after all a very decent guy and good company, but soon she would have to come completely clean with him, and, God knows, that was going to hurt him. She knew that, in spite of his exterior poise, he was a very vulnerable person, and one who was not going to take kindly to the news that he had been used. The ringing of the telephone interrupted her reflections; she snatched it off its hook.

"Kate Hollis" she said automatically. It was Inspector Marriott at the other end.

"Kate, we've just had a queer report in from Daventry of an aggravated assault on two of Ellison's mates. I'll get Daventry to fax you a copy, but the gist of it is, that they were both found by the lockkeeper tied up and gagged and unconscious in a boat at

Buckby about half an hour ago. At the moment they're on their way to Northampton General in an ambulance. Can you find Ellison and let him know? It may be nothing significant to our case, but he ought to know."

Andrew, feeling much gratified with his day's foray to London, had returned to the farm. There was no sign of Anne, and most of the lights were out, so after parking his car, he decided to spend the evening looking through Dunton's lists before giving the good news to Kate. He was about to uncork a bottle of Fitou and settle down to his task when the telephone rang. Within two minutes he had made up the fire, grabbed a coat and was in his car heading for the hospital. He found the Accident and Emergency Department, parked his car and ran inside, his brain still whirling. Kate was waiting in the foyer, and guided him to a ward where the two boaters were being cared for. Emma was sitting up in a chair, pale and shaken, but drinking a cup of tea and otherwise none the worse. Stu, his head in bandages, was lying propped up in bed, his eyes barely flickering. Detective Inspector Marriott and a policewoman were by the bed, along with a nurse. Marriott nodded a greeting to Andrew.

"Well?" asked Andrew.

Emma smiled weakly. "He's going to be all right, but he's under sedation."

"What happened?"

"Shall I tell him?" asked Marriott. Emma nodded again. She had already told the police everything that she could, and did not feel up to going all through it again.

Marriott briefly explained the circumstances. Andrew's face darkened as the tale unfolded.

"The vicious bastards! They've got to be stopped! They can't have got very far. Why, they're probably still going through the locks now!"

Marriott gently took him by the shoulder and whispered "not here, outside. OK?"

Andrew touched Emma gently on the shoulder. "Don't worry, Emma. I'll make sure they catch the swine."

Marriott and Kate were both standing in the corridor. Marriott said "don't worry. We'll nail them all right, but I think there's more at stake than a bit of GBH. We'll get the boat turned over after it leaves Milton Keynes next time and catch him with whatever it is he's been carrying. What we've got to do is to let him run this time, a sprat to catch a mackerel if you follow me."

Andrew sighed. "I suppose you're right. But what if he'd killed Stu? Would you have let him run, or brought him in tonight?"

Kate said "You'll just have to take our word for it, Andrew. Even if he'd killed Stu tonight we'd have let him run. There's much bigger things at stake."

"Bigger than a human life?"

"Bigger than several human lives. You see, we have reason to believe that national security is involved. I can't say more."

Marriott nodded, grimacing. "She's quite right. At this stage I can't tell you anything, but we need your assistance."

"How? Why should I help you? Remember I'm a convicted criminal!"

"Andrew!" said Kate with asperity, "just shut up for once and listen. You could do yourself a lot of good."

Andrew felt himself calming down. He felt ashamed, but this assault on a couple from whom he had had nothing but kindness and friendship had angered him more than anything that had happened since his sentence. "All right" he said, sighing again. "What do you want?"

"Not here" said Marriott, "outside."

The three of them climbed into Marriott's car, Marriott sat in the driver's seat, Andrew in the passenger seat, Kate in the back. "Look, what we need is for you to coordinate a watch on the canal" said Marriott. "You and your pals know how long it takes to move from place to place, we coppers could be lumbering about in the dark and still miss him. The boss wants him to..."

"The boss?" interrupted Andrew.

"Detective Chief Superintendent Baskerville. You've met him" put in Kate.

"All right. I'm with you."

"Good. The boss wants him to be given a run, then we can follow him, see where the stuff's going to and then feel his collar."

"Yeeess," said Andrew, "I can buy that. So what do you want me to do?"

"Well thanks to your following him last Saturday, we know where one of his pick up points is. Now, all we are asking is this. Just keep observation, don't tackle him, like your pal Roberts did tonight, but report to us."

"I shan't be able to do it all myself, I'll have to get assistance, but I think Stu's mates will help. In fact I'm certain they will."

"As long as they can be trusted to keep quiet about it."

"Have no worries on that score. If she's well enough now, we'd better start with Emma. By the way, I've got some hot news for you about Shorland and Burson. Do you want me to give it you now?"

Kate was already setting up her laptop and modem.

"Off you go, Andrew. Let's get it on file."

Chapter 17
Carrickfergus

Kate picked Andrew up from the farm just after one o'clock next afternoon. She said very little as they drove into Northampton, and Andrew began to wonder whether things had gone quite as smoothly as had been hoped. She pulled up in a side street close to the town centre, and led Andrew to what looked like an old warehouse building but bore the title of the County Libraries Department on a plate by the door. She spoke into a security entryphone, the door clicked open and she indicated a flight of stairs.

"Here we are, I'll leave you alone with the Boss." Kate stopped at the top of the stairs above the library store and gave a discreet rap on the door that led off the landing.

"The Boss?"

"The Boss. He's the one you really ought to talk to. In you go." She pushed the door open, a strong whiff of Tom Long rolled out into the passage. The voice of Detective Chief Superintendent Baskerville boomed out from inside "Come in, Ellison. It's time we put cards on the table."

Detective Chief Superintendent Baskerville leaned back in his chair, took a pull at his pipe and blew out an appreciative cloud. He offered Andrew a whisky, which he refused, saying that he had to drive, but that he would appreciate a coffee.

"Quite" said Baskerville, picking up the intercom. "Black or white?"

"White, no sugar please."

Baskerville ordered the coffee from Kate and turned to Andrew. "You realise that this is all pretty irregular. I suppose you could be a sort of supergrass, except that I'm not so much asking you to grass as to assist."

"I'm pretty sure you've been setting me up for a couple of months."

"Yes, and no. I have to admit to you that I twigged who you were as soon as your parole details were passed to me when you came. You see we were asked by the Home Office to investigate certain irregularities in the Met last autumn, and Shorland's name came up then. I knew he was a partner in a firm of solicitors, and when I saw in your antecedent history that you had been a partner in the same firm, I was interested. It was a very lucky coincidence as far as I was concerned. Then, lo and behold, up you pop involved in an incident involving Dooney's property loan scam. We knew all about that, but there was not much we could go on. Before we could turn round, there you were again catching a dog thief whom we suspected as having links with Burson. Couldn't keep you away from the front line it seemed."

"Coincidence can be a strange thing."

"Take it from me, it was coincidence at first. I had noted your presence, but it took my nimble witted Detective Sergeant to match it all up. You've got her to thank."

"Thanks for nothing" Andrew was unable to keep the bitterness out of his voice. "You sure made a monkey out of me."

"Don't be too hard on the lovely Kate. She's a dedicated policewoman."

"Too bloody dedicated."

"Her private life is her affair, you are, after all an adult, and I take it, a consenting one?"

Andrew was silent. He felt dirty and used. A wave of blind fury swept through him at Kate's duplicity, and then subsided as his logic began to reassert itself. Things could have been worse, and he felt sure there was some genuine feeling between him and Kate. Baskerville was continuing. "..been more than useful to us, and I shan't forget it."

Andrew snatched his mind back into gear. "Sorry, I didn't catch what you said."

"I said you've been more than useful to us, and I shan't forget it.

You see, you have been our extra eyes and ears. I can't say too much, but things have come to a head recently. Our sources outside the Force have caused us to become much more security conscious, and you have provided us with valuable leads."

"Well, since I seem to be implicated right up to my neck, I think I ought to be put a little bit more in the picture. If you want me to help you further, I ought to know what I'm looking for."

Baskerville's pipe had gone out, he fumbled for matches and relit it, looking quizzically at Andrew through the smoke. At length he got it to draw to his satisfaction and said: "As an ex-solicitor you can be trusted to keep confidence, I take it."

"Of course."

"Do you regret losing it all?"

"Of course I do, but that's in the past. I'm looking to the future and my future is here, with people I like and love, even if they do misuse my emotions. I can't go back."

"Even if your conviction was quashed, and you were exonerated?"

"That's most unlikely. And even if it were, I've had enough of the City and all that rubbish."

"You could practise in the country, you could help your new friends if you wanted."

Andrew said nothing. Secretly he damned Baskerville for putting his finger on the very nub of his aspirations. With qualifications, he could be so much more help to the likes of Stu and Jane.

"Anyway", said Baskerville, "that's another ballgame. Can I have your word that you can keep a confidence?"

"Yes, I suppose so. I mean, of course you can."

"Good man. Ah, here's the coffee. Thank you Kate." He smiled at his assistant. "Mr Ellison and I are getting on like a house on fire. You can go off duty if you want, I'll be in touch with you later though." Kate slipped out of the door before Andrew could so much as catch her eye. Baskerville stirred his coffee. "Right. Now Kate tells me that you have heard the name Carrickfergus."

"Yes, my son heard it at Colin Shorland's. My ex-wife also mentioned it to me."

"Right. Carrickfergus is a code name, as no doubt you've guessed. It's the name of a plan by which a certain terrorist organisation intends causing a political crisis. It involves the assassination of certain figures and the bombing of selected targets. I need hardly tell you that Irish matters figure largely in it."

"The IRA you mean?"

Baskerville chuckled, blew out another cloud and shook his head.

"The IRA gets blamed for everything, but in this case they are not the prime suspects. Do you know where Carrickfergus is?"

"Somewhere in Northern Ireland."

"How good is your history? Know anything about 1688?"

"The 'Glorious Revolution', William of Orange, and all that. I did it for History 'A' level forty years ago."

"At least you know something about it, which is more than can be said of ninety nine point nine per cent of the population of mainland Britain. Now then, what did William of Orange do after he chased James II off the throne?"

"He put down a rebellion in Ireland didn't he? The Battle of the Boyne, 1690."

"Good. And the anniversary of the Boyne is a day of celebration for the Protestants of Ulster. So, now can you tell me where Good King Billy landed when he went to Ireland?"

"No, my studies did not go that far. I'm more into the constitutional history of that time."

"Very laudable for a lawyer. I'll tell you. In August 1689 the troops of William III, alias William of Orange, alias Good King Billy, led by Count Schomberg, landed in Ireland on Belfast Lough near a place called Carrickfergus. I only found this out myself when I went to the library and looked it up. Apparently it was an old Norman castle that was the stronghold of the early Protestant settlers there, and it was occupied at the time by the Catholic Jacobites. It was the first place to surrender to William's army in August 1689, so it's got a good deal of symbolic significance. The codeword symbolises a Protestant hit back."

"Protestant?"

"Yes, Protestants. The plot is a Protestant one, or perhaps I should say a Unionist, or loyalist one. Everyone in this country thinks that it's the IRA who do all the bombings and shootings, but the Protestants don't take it lying down. Now most of them are decent folk who hate the violence, just like most Irish Catholics, but there's a hard core of dangerous bastards. You've heard of our homegrown racists and troublemakers, the skinheads and football yobbos who wave the Union flag and shout 'coloureds out'? Generally they're just a noisy bunch of airheads, but not all of them are. There's a strong movement throughout Northern Europe and the US of white supremacists. They hate all coloureds, Jews, Catholics and Slavs and their number one pin up is Adolf Hitler."

"I've come across a few of them in my time. There were more than a few in prison. I've always suspected Burson had such sympathies."

"And you'd be dead right. That's where Sir Colin Shorland and his ultra-right politics comes in. You know he's a prominent anti-Euro MP, well he's also mixed up with the extreme Unionist side of the Anglo Irish Peace Accord."

"My ex-wife told me something about this."

"Umm! How much does she know? Does she know of his involvement with 'the Loyal Order of William'?"

"Why don't you ask her yourself?" Andrew saw Baskerville's eyebrows go up and his eyes harden. "Oh, all right then, I take your point. Pamela is nobody's fool, but she has no interest in politics beyond what hat she should wear at a Conservative Garden Party. I daresay if Colin had come in and said 'can we have dinner early tonight dear, I'm speaking at a Ku Klux Klan meeting' she would have merely asked if he minded something cold. No, from what she told me the other day when we had lunch, I'd say she knows nothing. She knew of the Anglo Irish Peace Accord because she went to Ireland with him when he went to meetings. And she did somewhat disapprove of his more extreme politics. Middle of the road Tory, that's Pamela's politics, so far as she has any at all. From what she told me about Carrickfergus, it meant nothing to her either."

Baskerville grunted and relit his pipe. "This whole affair is intended to throw the Irish Peace Accord movement off course. There is a chance, just an outside chance, of the IRA declaring a genuine cease fire, and if they do, the extremists of both sides will lose the power that they have over whole sections of Belfast and Derry. Neither side wants that. The Unionist extremists are prepared to play the patriot card, you know, wave the Union flag, do down the Republicans and so forth, but if they strike a hard blow at the Republican cause outside the six counties they'll do more. They'll stop the peace movement in its tracks. The Garda in the Republic and our Special Branch are aware of this, and that's why we want to break Carrickfergus up before it even starts."

"And Burson?"

"He and his lot are their English paymasters. The VAT scam, the drug dealing, the protection rackets are all what he does best, and it fits in with his perverted notions of politics. If we close him down and seize his assets, we cut off Carrickfergus's lifeblood; if we break it up and arrest the suspects we merely prune it. It will grow again in the prisons and outside, but without money, it's a hollow threat."

"What about Dooney?"

For the first time Baskerville laughed aloud. "I think there's something you ought to know about him before we go any further."

When Baskerville had finished speaking, Andrew found himself smiling in spite of himself. Baskerville grinned back at him, his face gargoyle like, wreathed in tobacco smoke.

"I'm glad we seem to share a certain macabre sense of humour, Ellison."

"Does Burson know?"

"Nobody knows except a very select few, and that does not include Sir Colin Shorland. Now, this brings me to the whole point of this conversation. I have one more favour to ask of you before we wrap the whole thing up."

"And that is?"

Baskerville got up and paced across the room. He peered through the window at the town centre outside, took a few more puffs, then turned and faced Andrew across the room.

"I want you to go and take a message from me to Sir Colin."

"Tonight?"

"Tonight. There's no time to lose. He's at his home near Dorking."

"Why the Hell me?"

"Ever seen the film *Zulu*?"

"Yes, but what's that got to do with it?"

"Just before the impis attack Rourkes Drift, there's a little scene where a scared boy soldier asks the CSM the same question, and he replies *'because we're here, son, because we're here'*, and that's my answer to you too."

"But, I do have a choice, the South Wales Borderers at Rourke's Drift didn't."

"True, but I think I know what sort of a man you are. I don't think you're the sort who chickens out easily."

"Thank you for nothing. But what's in it for me?"

"Not much, but you might like the satisfaction of seeing him squirm after what he's done to you."

Andrew chewed his lip. *Blast Baskerville*, he thought. *He's a much brighter copper than I'd given him credit for. I can see why Kate enjoys working for him.* Baskerville meanwhile puffed placidly, looking at him over the rims of his spectacles. "All right. I'll do it. I feel I owe it to myself."

"Good man. I'll tell you now you've agreed. If you want me to, but only if you want it, I'll use my best endeavours to get your conviction and sentence quashed. I deliberately didn't offer that as a carrot."

"I'm obliged to you. That's something I've still got to think about. Meanwhile hadn't you better give me a full briefing about what you want me to do?"

"Right. This is what I want you to do. Remember time is of the essence, I have every reason to believe that the whistle may blow within the next twenty four hours."

In an office off one of the ornate Victorian 'Corridors of power' in the Palace of Westminster, a rather uncomfortable interview was taking place between Sir Colin Shorland and his Chief Whip. The Chief Whip was gazing, somewhat distastefully, at the front pages of several tabloids. One read 'TORY MP'S SECRET LOVE NEST' another 'NAUGHTY! NAUGHTY! SIR COLIN', and a third 'ONCE A KNIGHT IS NOT ENOUGH'. The Chief Whip, a slim, silvery haired man, attired in an elegant Savile Row suit, looked over the top of his half moon spectacles at the subject of these witticisms who was shifting uneasily in his leather chair.

"It wouldn't have been quite so bad, had you not featured in the recent Honours List, Colin, for 'services to the Conservative Party'. It's going to be the very devil keeping the Press off your back. What really concerns me are these allegations that you have been seen consorting with criminals in public places. The Opposition are already scenting scandal. I think it would be for the best if you were to be completely frank with me. Whisky?"

Sir Colin nodded and gratefully accepted a large single malt from the Chief Whip's decanter. He licked his lips, then sipped at it before replying "of course, the whole thing has been blown up and taken out of context."

"I'm sure it has, but let me hear your side of the tale."

"There's not very much to tell, I'm afraid. Mandel is an ex-constituent of mine, and I may say, a loyal supporter, we met for a few drinks the other night at Langans."

The Chief Whip was silent. He did not reveal that he had recently had a long conversation with his friend in the Press Council, who had revealed that there was plenty of evidence to connect Sir Colin with visits to a massage parlour run by Barbara Moss, Mandel's other dinner guest, and that HM Customs and Excise were only waiting their time to pounce on the other couple who dined that night at Langans. It was only going to be a matter of time before the truth was forced out, and if this fool were going to try and brazen it out in the House, then things would be even worse.

After a few moments he spoke, deliberately, softly, but firmly. "And you have nothing more to say? Nothing about your visit to the Chicago Rock Club in Finchley with Barbara Moss and at least two known violent criminals who are also members of the United British Front?"

Sir Colin opened and shut his mouth, but no sound came from it. "I take it you do not deny it?" Sir Colin nodded dumbly; he swayed in his chair and nearly collapsed. The Chief Whip looked at him almost kindly. "I'm very sorry, Colin, but the Government can't afford you. You realise we're only hanging on by the skin of our teeth and if the Ulster Unionists get wind of anything, all your best efforts will do nothing for your friends on the right of the Unionists, and they may well vote against us in the House. I realise that if you leave us, our majority is going to be even less, but I'm afraid that the PM feels that that will be the lesser of two evils. It will certainly be better than facing a by-election which we would certainly lose."

"Just what are you trying to tell me?" said Shorland angrily.

"Merely that it is best that you resign the Party Whip and sit as an Independent. The Party of course will not be ungrateful if you go quietly. On the other hand, I need scarcely remind you that the consequences of your attempting to brazen things out will be serious indeed. I'm afraid that we shall have no alternative but to compulsorily withdraw the Whip. You may still sit as an Independent, and if you continue to give us your support, we shall be very grateful. Beyond that, there is no more that I can offer."

Shorland glared at him across the desk. "You smooth talking bastard!" he spat. "You realise that this is going to blow up in your faces when the Loyal Order of William gets to know that their representative round the table has been scuppered? If there's any violent backlash, you are going to be responsible!"

"I think we'll cross that bridge when we come to it, Colin. Now, hadn't we better calm down and draft a Press Statement as a damage limitation exercise?"

Andrew found Sir Colin Shorland's house without much difficulty, although it was long after dark when he arrived. He remembered his way round the Dorking area from his previous life, for Pamela had several friends in the area and they often would drive over from Lipscombe to meet them. He had also played several rounds with Shorland at a local golf club in the days when he had thought that such things mattered in business life. The house lay on the Reigate side of the town, detached and behind gate pillars. Joe, his son, had given him full directions over the telephone, so when he swung right on to the minor road, he soon found the entrance as Joe had described it. Brick pillars flanked the gateway with terra cotta gryphons standing on each one. *Pretentious ass!* thought Andrew, then realised that it was probably the conceit of a previous owner, but one of which no doubt Sir Colin approved. A drive wound upwards through laurel and rhododendron bushes, Andrew's headlights picking out the wire of a tennis court on his left, then he found himself following a curve towards the imposing front door of an Edwardian brick built mansion. A security light flared out. Andrew stopped the car, parked and walked towards the door. There was a light in the hallway, showing through an art nouveau fanlight. Andrew pressed the bell. An entry phone rasped beside him, asking who he was. "On business for Roland Burson" he replied. There was a buzz and the door unlocked. He stepped through to be confronted by Sir Colin Shorland himself in a white dinner jacket and bow tie.

"Good evening, Colin" said Andrew. "I think we need to talk."

Sir Colin Shorland gaped at Andrew. "Ellison!" he gasped at length. "What the hell do you want?"
Andrew looked critically at him. The years had not been kind. He had put on a good deal of weight, his head was almost completely bald and there were pouches under his eyes.

"I told you. We need to talk."

"About what? Look, Ellison, I'm a public figure and a busy man. What's past is past, and if it's any consolation to you, Pamela's left me."

"Oh, I know all about that" said Andrew breezily, "No, old boy, we need to talk about Carrickfergus."

If Andrew had burst a paper bag behind his back at that moment, Shorland could not have looked more surprised. He almost staggered, and his eyes popped. "What are you talking about? I don't know what you mean. Look, who the hell do you think you are, you bloody jailbird, bursting in here and..."

Andrew cut him short. "Save your breath, Shorland. I know all about it, including all about your assignations in Lupus Street, and your connection with the Anglo Irish Accord, so shall we stop bluffing and then you can ask me in to sit down like the proper Gentleman you would so much like to be?"

"All right, you'd better come in" said Shorland with bad grace, waving Andrew towards an open door leading off the hallway.

The door led into a large and comfortable study with parquet flooring. The walls were lined with shelves containing legal volumes, Court Reports, Halsbury's Statutes, Hansard and similar works of reference, much the same as any successful solicitor's office. There was a large, leather topped desk with a computer and screen, a comfortable looking swivel chair, two club chairs, several filing cabinets and a log effect gas fire blazing cheerfully in an Edwardian looking fireplace. There was a decanter of whisky and glasses on a tray on the desk. Shorland picked up the decanter and a glass. "Drink?"

"No thanks, I'm driving" replied Andrew. Shorland motioned him towards a club chair, while he himself sat in the swivel chair at the desk.

"Well?" he demanded, "What's your business with me?"

"I'll come straight to the point, Colin. I want a full confession from you."

"WHAT!!" Sir Colin's face was scarlet, and he nearly dropped his whisky. "How dare you! What the Hell are you drivelling about? Confession? Bloody Hell! Surely you're the one to make a confession. You're the one who got four years for fraud, remember?"

"Well now" said Andrew equably, "that's as may be, but you see, at least I've served my sentence. What I need is a full confession from you about your relationship with Joseph Hannagan" (Andrew was gratified to see Shorland start at the mention of his name) "alias Roland Burson, wanted by the police for questioning on suspicion of murder of a person unknown, also for conspiracy to pervert the course of justice, demanding money with menaces, fraud, and conspiracy to carry on war against the Queen in her own domain. I think there may be other charges, but those will do for the moment."

"You know as well as I do, Ellison, Burson was merely a client of mine. A purely business relationship. If you think you are going to blackmail me, or try to destroy my political career with these insinuations, you've got another think coming. In fact you're too late. I've just come back from the Chief Whip's office. All these sleazy allegations you and others are making about me are all just lies. Show me the proof of any of it!" He took a gulp at his whisky and refilled his glass. Andrew said nothing, he sat in his chair with an impassive face, but reached into his inside jacket pocket for an envelope.

Shorland continued: "There's a Press Statement gone out tonight refuting all allegations made against me in the press, I daresay you'd have seen it on the television late night news if you hadn't come gallivanting out here on a fool's errand. You're finished, Ellison, and you know it. If you think that by blackening my name you can somehow crawl back into respectability, you must be sillier than I thought you were. The Law Society'll never accept you back, and I'm in a position to make damned sure that you won't even get a job as a process server for the West Cornwall County Court!" Shorland laughed at his own wit.

Andrew smiled "I'm glad to see your sense of drollery has not left you. Now then. Since you claim not to be connected with Burson, other than in a professional sense, I wonder what professional matter was being discussed at the Chicago Rock Club in Finchley last week. I think you should look at these photographs. Not only you and Burson together, but two others wanted by the police."

Shorland goggled at him. "Where did you get those pictures?" he croaked. "How do I know they're not fakes?"

"Quite simply. You see those rather distinctive glasses, marked *Chicago Rock Club* in front of you?" Shorland snatched at the photographs, "Now, now! Manners please! These are of course copies. They're very distinctive aren't they? Only exist in the Chicago Rock Club, because the owner, my old friend Joey Caroni has them specially made. You'll be interested to know, your fingerprints appear on at least three of them, so do Burson's, sorry Hannagan's."

"You're bluffing, Ellison. Nobody's got my fingerprints. I've never been in trouble with the police."

"Quite so, but the prints are identical with those on a cigarette case given to you by my ex-wife, and left in Langans Brasserie two weeks ago, an occasion which you may recall, for you were accompanied by your research assistant Janet Thomas, and a mutual acquaintance of ours, Jack Reeves, a solicitor who is suspected by the police of acting as a courier for Burson and others."

"You bastard" hissed Sir Colin.

"Flattery will get you nowhere, but I'm glad that you realise that you are not alone in being one" said Andrew smoothly. "Now, we'll quit the pussyfooting about and get on with the real business. You see I'm working for the police... Oh, no! Not the ones in the Metropolitan Force whom you've coerced and bribed to cover up your dirty business, but ones in what you doubtless regard as an unimportant County Force, asked to investigate by the Home Office on the urging of Special Branch. I'll tell you straight now. They know all about your involvement with Carrickfergus, about how you were nearly done over at Heathrow last summer, about how you and Hannagan, sorry, Burson, have conspired with other right wing extremists to disrupt the Anglo Irish Peace Accord. They know all about the connections with the League of White Supremacists and the Loyal Order of William, and they are making a number of arrests as we speak. No, there's no need to play the injured innocent any more." Shorland had been trying to rise from his chair, but subsided again at Andrew's words. "There are more than enough pieces of evidence to connect you with all these people, and they have enough on you to ruin you ten times over. I don't seem to recall when the last Tory MP was charged with treason but I do remember that Sir Anthony Blunt was stripped of his Knighthood for betraying his country, and Sir Roger Casement was hanged..."

Shorland slumped in the swivel chair. His face was now ashen. He breathed a deep sigh and drained his glass. He raised his eyes and Andrew saw a pleading look in them. "So, you've got a hand with the aces. What am I supposed to do?"

"Just in case you think I'm bluffing, I'm holding a joker too. Your associate, Dooney", Shorland gave another involuntary start, "is perhaps more consistent than all the rest of your half-baked associates. You know of course that he's arranging for the funds to be laundered for the Loyal Order, and all these VAT scams, and the drug dealing, and the gold smuggling, and the protection rackets that are financing the great right wing coup, which will start in Ulster and proceed to the Mainland. And you doubtless hope that your links with the German Neo-Nazis and the Flemish Separatists and the Austrian South Tyrol freedom movement and Uncle Tom Cobley and All in European nutcases will encourage a Europe wide revival in fascism..."

"You're damn' right I do" said Sir Colin hoarsely. "Oh yes, you can shut me up, but there's lots more behind me, don't you worry. Yes, your mealy-mouthed democracies may think that they've got the upper hand, but the only strong Europe will be a Europe of the right. You just wait and see, Ellison, the scum that pollutes our cities and public life, Irish, Turks, Asiatics, Caribbeans, Jews; they'll all have to come down in the end. We'll finish the job that

Hitler didn't, a scum free Europe, and a Europe free of the power of the Vatican. Look man, you're the same generation as I am; didn't our parents let themselves get bamboozled by the Jews and the Vatican into fighting for Poland? And to what end? So that Bolshevism ruled for forty years in the east. And when Bolshevism failed, what was there waiting in the wings to fill the vacuum? The bloody Catholic Church. The bloody Pope's a fucking Pole isn't he? Look at every Third World country in Africa or South America. Who lords it over the shanty towns? Who controls the Mafiosi and their like? The Catholic Church. Look at every slum ghetto in this country, if it's not crawling with foreigners, it's overrun with Irish Catholics. What a race of evil, corrupt, backstabbing bastards they are too? Look how they stabbed us in the back in 1916, look how they refused to help us in 1939! All the way through history it's been the same with the Irish Catholics, 1641 they helped start the Civil War, 1688 they were allied with Louis XIV, 1798 with Revolutionary France..."

"And in 1815 they died in their thousands at Waterloo, they stormed the Alma for us in 1854, they died in their tens of thousands at Thiepval in 1916 and Passchendaele in 1917. You're talking pure and unadulterated bollocks, and you know it. The last place I came across such unmitigated twaddle was when I read *Mein Kampf,* when the bog roll ran out in the ablutions at Aldershot and they had to use something cheaper. For a so-called intelligent man, you amaze me. Perhaps you also believe in fairies. Even if you don't, you've got to believe in a leprechaun called Dooney."

"Well, at least he's sound."

Andrew threw back his head and laughed. "Sound. Oh yes, he's sound all right. But not as far as your lot are concerned. Do you know who he really is? His real name is Cathal O'Riordan and he's a Brigade Commander in the Provisional IRA. And you, my old partner, are on his hit list. That's why I've come tonight to offer you a deal."

Sir Colin's eyes stared, drained of all emotion. His shoulders slumped and his head dropped. "You're lying, Ellison. You're trying to trap me!" he muttered.

"I can assure you, I'm not. If you want proof, you only have to ring this number. It's a special one at the Home Office, and they are expecting you to call. You don't have to believe me, but it will be better for you if you do."

Shorland grabbed the piece of paper that Andrew held out to him. He dialled the number and the telephone was answered almost instantly. He said in as authoritative a voice as Andrew had heard all evening, "Sir Colin Shorland here. I'm making some enquiries about a Mr. Jack Dooney. What? My number? You need to check? I've never heard such a nonsense in my life! Look here, I'm a Member of Parliament. Very well, ring me back on this number." He gave the number of his telephone then put the receiver down. "Bloody pen-pushing office rats. They want to check that I'm who I say I am."

"You can hardly blame them for that" said Andrew.

After about a minute the telephone rang, Shorland snatched it from its rest. "Sir Colin Shorland here."

There came a burble from the receiver, and Shorland's face changed slowly. The colour drained and he replaced the receiver wordlessly. After a while he spoke, slowly and with all his old bombast gone. "You were right. Dooney is an IRA man. What is your offer?"

"I am empowered to make you the following offer, but there is nothing in writing. If you will give me your most solemn undertaking that within twenty-four hours you will use your best endeavours to call off Carrickfergus and to deliver to my hands a full statement of your dealings with Hannagan, duly sworn before a Commissioner, you will not be arrested and will be given a clear run to any non-EU or English-speaking country and no extradition proceedings will be taken. The alternative is that you must take whatever the law directs."

"How do I know you won't double cross me?"

"You don't" replied Andrew with a smile, "but I'm your best

chance of freedom. Oh, I forgot to mention, ex-Company Sergeant-major Dunton wishes to be remembered to you. We had a long chat the other day about old times; he did ask me to mention to you a matter of some property. Would it be asking too much if you were to square him up at the same time?"

"Damn you, Ellison! Damn you and your self-righteous bloody ex-wife! Always the bloody hoity-toity middle class snobs weren't you? Well, I didn't have any rich daddy to send me to Cambridge, or buy me a commission in a line regiment. I had to work my way, didn't I? And the likes of you always smirking behind my back. The Grammar School oik with ideas above himself. Oh yes! I've had it all. And now, of course, you and your bloody *bourgeoise oblige*, you get even Dunton to betray me. Shit scared of him you all were when you were swaddies, now you can lord it over him."

"Really, Colin, you have an endless capacity for self delusion. You didn't work your way to University; you bribed your way there. You fiddled and cheated your way there, using the likes of Sergeant-major Dunton, and Corporal Hannagan too, except that he was too smart for you and used you instead. He was too smart for me as well, and for Joey Caroni, but now it's all over. I wouldn't want to take away anything that you earned honestly, but just think. Everything you've got has been got by smart talking, cheating, bribing and doing it any other than by the straightforward way, and that includes taking my wife. Apart from the favour you did me there, I've got nothing to thank you for, only three years out of my life which taught me that the likes of you are not worth the wind that you eject from your capacious backside." Andrew got up out of his chair. "Just think over what I've said. You've never done an honourable thing in your life, but you've got one chance. I shall be back at this time tomorrow and shall expect to see your statement. I shall have the police with me, and a Press photographer. If I get what I want they'll do nothing. You have my word on it. Don't try to run for it tonight, they're watching all the airports and ferry ports for you, they're even watching in the lane outside, so you'll just make things worse if you do. I wish you a good evening."

"Ellison." Shorland's voice was calm now. When he spoke it was in an almost diffident manner. "I suppose there's no other way out? I've got no power to cancel Carrickfergus. If it happens it is out of my hands. God! I've never wanted the bloodshed, but those psychopaths of Burson's can't wait."

"And how were you going to bring about your revolution and ethnic cleansing without it?"

"By democratic and legitimate means."

"Oh, I see! Just like Hitler did in 1933. And when did you propose to bring in the Final Solution?"

Shorland was silent. Then he said in a low voice "it's no good, Ellison. I've already tried to stop it. The Ulstermen won't listen. They've taken so much from the Republicans that they won't stop now. They have promised to activate Carrickfergus tonight."

The anger left Andrew's voice as he saw the fear in his enemy's eyes. He spoke more gently. "Look, we're both lawyers, we're used to getting our clients out of every sort of jam. I still don't see any other way that you can get out without making things ten times worse."

Shorland was silent again for a moment, then he rose and held out his hand. "I don't suppose you would wish to shake hands with me, but, in a way I'm grateful to you. Yes, I see the way out and you've shown me. Thank you."

There was no feeling of triumph in Andrew's heart as he took the proffered hand; the words of Christopher Marlowe came into his head *"Cut is the branch that could have grown full straight."* He no longer saw a pompous fraud, but a beaten and dejected foe. Pity tried to well up in him, and he fought it back momentarily. Where was Shorland's pity when he had been sentenced? Then the realisation that he was not Shorland, but himself, with different values and feelings, came back and he knew pity as well as contempt for the wretched man before him. He shook hands wordlessly and turned away. He did not look back as he made his way to the front door.

Outside, Andrew made a brief call to Kate, and then drove back to Northamptonshire in a curiously unelated mood. There was little traffic about, and he made good time. It was soon after midnight when he turned in to the lane leading to the farm. Kate's car was parked in the yard; she flashed her headlights at him as he drew up. He got out, locked the car and walked over to her.

"There's a lot to tell. Let's go on the boat," he said, heading off towards his mooring. Kate followed at a distance. Once aboard, Andrew raked the fire into life and put a kettle on. Kate sat in a chair beside the stove while Andrew bustled in the galley. Bit by bit she extracted the details of his conversation with Sir Colin. She made a call to DI Marriott on her mobile and reported.

"What made you do it?" she asked at length.

"Difficult to say. I suppose I wanted revenge. Yes. I really wanted to see him put through some of what he's put me, and other members of my family, through, yet at the final analysis I didn't have the wish to put in the final boot. Perhaps it's because he's such a pathetic coward. After all, if he'd had the guts to stand up to Burson, he wouldn't have been in this mess. Anyway, I'm sure he's going to play it your way..."

"Not mine, Andrew, Chief Superintendent Baskerville's. If it were left to me I'd make the bastard face up to what he's done."

As Kate was leaving the farm, she received a call from DI Marriott. "Don't go to bed yet, Kate. Get yourself something to eat and come in to the office. If Carrickfergus is about to blow we're going to be busy soon."

The Green Grass Social and Community Club in Braunstone, a suburb to the south of Leicester, was doing well tonight, the manager thought, as he cast his eyes over a sample of the till receipts. There was a good crowd of lads in from a Motorway contract; there was a dinner for a hosiery firm's employees taking place, although that had been a bit of a nightmare to organise with no pork and Halal meat, but Mr Mohammed had come up to his office and told him that he was pleased with it all; he had got in an Irish group to give them some diddley-diddley music and a few songs, and he had already seen Father Heeney, the young Catholic priest from The Sacred Heart down the road, having the odd glass at the bar with some nurses from the General Hospital. Perhaps he should have a word with Sean the barman to keep an eye on some of the big Guinness drinkers. There had been a bad scene last Saturday when some of them had taken a little too much, and a shouting match had developed between some of the Republican boyos and some skinheads. He had managed to get them ejected by the bouncers without too much trouble, but a scrap had started outside. On Sunday morning he had found the slogan "IRA TRATER SCUM" daubed on a fire door and it had taken all morning to get it scrubbed off. If the boss had seen that, there would have been hell to pay. For the same reason, he had ordered the doormen to scrutinise closely anybody known to be dealing. The big problem with the youngsters was Ecstasy, because they took it into the club hidden anywhere, and you couldn't insist on stripping everyone down to their underwear on entry, though, how else did the authorities think you could stop them bringing it in? He relied on CCTV and a sharp-eyed security staff to pick up anyone dealing, because, whilst he didn't give a damn about how bombed out they made their stupid selves, anything that might look like drug related crime in the vicinity of the club was bad news, not just for him, but for the boss.

The manager walked over to the bar to speak to Sean. It was ten thirty now and the club was filling fast with drinkers from the pubs in the City. On the stage the leader of the musicians knocked his hand across his microphone and said "One, two! One two", coughed nervously and then announced the next number. "For all those, from the ould country, here's a few to get yer feet tappin'." A fiddle player began and then his colleagues with guitar, bass, melodeon and bodhran joined in. A burly young man gave several loud whoops and began to jig, two nurses straight away started to dance in the Irish style, back upright and knees lifted, trim ankles flying. Even Mr Mohammed's workers found themselves tapping their feet and drumming their fingers on the table in time. Sean the barman grinned at the manager "Eat your hearts out Riverdance" he said, placing two pints glasses under the Caffreys beer dispenser and turning on the tap before reaching for a third glass.

The explosion took place at that moment. The electric clock behind the bar stopped at precisely 10.35 pm and was picked up hours later by the forensic team. The manager suddenly saw a brilliant flash of white light with a purple centre, and just had time to begin to think that this was not part of the disco effects before he was blown bodily through the partition wall of the bar. Sean was saved by the fact that he had just bent below the bar and it took both the main force of the explosion and protected him from the collapsing ceiling joists. The two nurses were killed instantly, their bodies lay beside that of the burly young contractors' man, naked but in one piece. The young man's legs were lying ten feet away on the stage, the bodhran player's instrument was spattered with his blood.

In the darkness which followed, there was an instant of silence, followed by moaning and screaming. Somebody struggled to his feet and lit a cigarette lighter. From outside came the screeching and hooting of car alarms set off by the shock. Water from a shattered main pipe dripped onto the dance floor, one of Mr. Mohammed's women workers lay sprawled across the shattered table and the water soaked into her torn sari. Among the wreckage, people began to struggle to free themselves, clothes torn, faces blackened and cut. Father Heeney, his hands shaking, managed to administer comfort to a sobbing woman whose husband had just that minute gone to the bar to place an order. In the distance, the sirens of the emergency services began to sound. A man's figure clad in a kapok padded top coat walked hurriedly away from the telephone kiosk further along the road, from where he had been watching and climbed into a car parked round the corner in a quiet residential road. Ten minutes later the BBC's Newsdesk at Pebble Mill, Birmingham, received a call from a mobile 'phone. The operator managed to record part of the call in which the caller, speaking with a Northern Irish accent, claimed responsibility for the bombing and gave the codeword *Carrickfergus*. What the man in the kapok padded coat did not know was that he had been picked up on the club's CCTV as he walked in carrying a grip, which he had left under a table near the stage.

Superintendent Baskerville was in bed at home when the telephone rang. He sleepily flung out his hand and put the instrument to his ear.

"Baskerville."

Marriott's voice was at the other end. "Sorry to disturb you, Sir, but I think Carrickfergus has started. We've just had a report that an Irish Catholic club in Leicester's been bombed."

"Christ! Sorry Mabel, it's Marriott." This last was to his wife who had sat bolt upright in bed. "Look, Inspector, give me ten minutes and I'll be over. Where are you? At the office? Good. Is Kate about? Right, get her over. While you're waiting ring this number and fax them the search warrant for that flat in Harlesden. Yes, it's a Special Branch number, they'll fix up the London end for us. I'll see you."

He flung the receiver down on its rest and rolled out of bed. Mabel looked reproachful.

"All right, old girl. It's not going to be for much longer, then we'll be able to have a full night's sleep every night."

"I suppose I should be used to it after forty years, but it still sends the shivers down my back."

Baskerville was lugging on his trousers with one hand and doing up his shirt with the other. "Don't worry. I'll give you a ring as soon as I can see where we're going. Blast! Where the hell's my socks?"

"In your sock drawer, dear. Have you found a clean pair of pants?"

"Bugger the pants. I'm off" Baskerville found a tie and threw it round his neck, he grabbed a rolled up pair of socks, slipped his bare feet into his shoes and ran out of the door. Mabel heard the front door bang then lay down and turned on her side. Within a minute she was asleep.

It was a somewhat dishevelled Detective Chief Superintendent that found his way to the top floor office above the library store. While Marriott gave him a rundown of the latest information he put his socks on, tied his tie and shoelaces so that when Kate arrived soon after he was at least presentable. Kate had been briefed over the telephone by Marriott as she drove in, so no time was wasted in further talk. Baskerville rapped out a stream of orders for arrest and search warrants, most of which were ready and waiting. His two assistants transmitted them in a constant stream of calls and faxes. All over the Midlands and the London area preparations were made for a concerted swoop at six thirty. The man in the kapok padded coat was just one of the persons whose home was on the list for raiding. A call was also made from a public call box to Jack Dooney's ex-directory number.

At three a.m. Dooney called a number in Liverpool "It's blown" he said "I want Fergal and the other two first thing at my office. Half five sharp!"

There was barely the trace of an Irish accent as Jack Dooney gave his orders. A trio of men had joined him in the manager's office behind the facade of JD Properties Ltd. in the centre of Northampton. One man wore the mackinaw jacket and jeans of a contractor's man, the other two were well, almost sharply dressed. Dooney himself wore a heavy tweed suit and brogues, check shirt and tie and would have passed for a cattle dealer at the nearby market. He finally finished. The man in the mackinaw jacket lit a cigarette, cupping his hand round the lighter flame, and blew a cloud of smoke. He had the slow voice of a Kerryman, but his manner belied it.

"The device," he grinned as he said the words, "is available. Do we have the orders to use it?"

"We do indeed," said Dooney, gazing at the tips of his fingernails. He was silent for a short space, and then continued "we have no option if we are to stop them in their tracks. Our man tells us that the excellent Mr. Ellison is on his way to Sir Colin as we speak if indeed he has not already been there. We can't stop him, but you all know where the important stuff is. It's my reasoned guess that Shorland will have tried to stop his mates in the North, so it is as well to let Ellison go his own way. He's not harmed us, and I have no reason to think that he will. Burson however, is another matter. He's the one we want. He's the paymaster who controls it all. Sir Colin is just his puppet and we'll deal with him another day if we have to. You're the expert, Fergal. It's down to you."

The Kerryman smiled a sad smile. "May God forgive me," he said. One of the other well-dressed men nodded gravely. "Orders confirmed to Brigade from High Command."

The four men shook hands and dispersed into the night. Dooney was last out and carefully locked the door. A police car came slowly down the street, two constables gazing from side to side at the deserted shop fronts, and Dooney waved cheerfully to them as they passed. He was well clear of the building, in fact twenty miles away, when Baskerville's men raided it some fifty minutes later.

Sir Colin sat in his chair motionless after the door banged behind Andrew. He sat staring into space for a long time, then he sat up, drained the last of the decanter, logged on to his word processor and began typing, slowly at first, then faster and more confidently. It was gone three in the morning before he had finished. His head dropped on to his chest and he fell into a deep sleep in the chair. When he woke it was broad daylight. He felt as if a cloud had lifted from his head. He knew exactly what he had to do, and made himself a cup of coffee in the kitchen. He switched on the television and caught the breakfast time news. There were pictures of a wrecked night club in Leicester, and he felt fear clutch at his heart. The presenter was saying: "...the bomb has all the hallmarks of an IRA bomb, but there has been no acknowledgment by them. The fact that the club was frequented by Irish Catholic workers as well as by Asian people lends credence to an unconfirmed report that a militant Ulster Protestant organisation may be involved. BBC sources claim that a telephone call was received last night from a Northern Irish group who claimed responsibility."

He sat, unmoving as the report prattled on, Ulster Unionist politicians appeared expressing genuine horror but Sir Colin saw them not. At length he glanced at the clock. It had just gone nine. He switched the TV off, picked up the telephone and punched in the number of a Commissioner for Oaths.

Chapter 18
Completion statement

Andrew woke about half past seven. Sun was streaming in through the porthole. He glanced outside to see a perfect late winter's day of blue sky and sparkling frost. After breakfast he washed up, then strolled across to the farm to feed the dog and to take in any post. From across the valley came the steady drone of a tractor at plough, he could just make it out as it turned at the headlands of the field, along with its skein of gulls swooping behind. He was reminded of the day that he first looked out of the farmhouse window, presumably the sun was about the same strength again. Then it was early November, now, he realised with a start, it was the end of January. Crocii and snowdrops were showing in Anne's garden, and green shoots of narcissi were everywhere. Perhaps there was such a thing as a promise of rebirth; it was too bad that there was such an empty desolation in his heart. For the first time he realised that he loved Anne and that he missed her terribly. But she was gone, he was sure of that. The siege of the farm had broken something between them, and there was no way that Kate Hollis could replace it, much as he liked her. Still, one useful piece of information was now his, thanks to Kate. She had informed him last night that one of the sets of fingerprints on Joey's glasses matched those on a baseball bat found in the flat at Harlesden that had been raided earlier that day. The same bat also had hairs and blood on it that matched the DNA samples taken from Fiona. The fingerprints were of Wayne Kinsey, who was a known associate of Burson, who had convictions for violence and was a known member of a right wing group suspected of racist attacks in North London. At least he had Fiona's attacker, and some solid forensic evidence. It would take some putting together to make a watertight case, but at least he could justify Joey's trust. On the other hand, perhaps it would be premature to tell Joey too much, just in case he took the law into his own hands.

The Special Branch policeman on duty in the lane outside Sir Colin's house yawned and stretched out his legs in the back of his car. He had been there all night and had seen nothing beyond Mr. Ellison's car drawing in to the drive and then leaving soon after eleven o'clock. Now it was broad daylight, it was bloody cold, and above all he needed his breakfast and a pee. The paperboy had gone up the drive at seven fifty two and had left at seven fifty six. The milkman had delivered in his milk float at eight twenty and left two minutes later. A woman driving a Fiesta had driven in at eight forty five, presumably some sort of daily help. He yawned again and gazed dully at the bright winter sunshine. The play of the light about the bare branches meant nothing to him; all he wanted was breakfast, bed and a pee. Not necessarily in that order. Suddenly he froze. A car was coming down the drive. He recognised the number plate as being that of Sir Colin's Toyota. He quickly put up a newspaper in a clumsy attempt at disguise, and Sir Colin waved to the man sitting on the back seat of his car reading a three day old paper as he passed. The policeman got out as Sir Colin vanished down the road, and jumped into the driving seat. He switched on his radio and gave his call sign. His control centre came back instantly.
"Suspect driving towards Dorking. Am tailing him." He pressed the self-starter, clutched in and shot off down the lane.
"Roger, Tango Echo."
Sir Colin evidently was not in too much of a hurry. He soon caught him up on the outskirts of the town. Traffic was brisk, mums were coming home after the school run, traders vans and lorries were about their first deliveries, but he managed to follow Sir Colin to a car park adjoining a firm of solicitors. Shorland got out of his car, went into the building and, before the policeman could park his car and follow him, was coming out and getting back into the

Toyota. Desperate not to lose him, the policeman dodged back into his car only to see the Toyota backing out of its place and heading back whence he had come. He reported this over the radio and followed him back up the hill to the lane where he had watched all night. He parked in his old spot as Sir Colin swept back up the drive.

"Tango Echo to Control."

"Come in Tango Echo."

"Suspect has returned home. Am going in to take a closer look."

"Roger, Tango Echo. Just keep yourself out of sight."

The policeman carefully locked the car and, bending almost double, ran into the shrubbery that lined the drive. Keeping to the shrubbery he avoided the tennis court on the other side of the drive and was able to get within a few yards of the house. He saw the cleaner's Fiesta parked near the rear of the house, and then saw the Toyota parked outside a double garage. Of Sir Colin there was no sign, so he slipped across to the house under cover of the garage. Just as he reached the house wall he heard a loud bang. He heard steps inside the house crossing parquet flooring, followed by the sound of a door opening, followed by prolonged female screaming. Abandoning all pretence of secrecy he ran to the front door, which was unlocked, thrust it open and found himself in the hallway. The screaming was coming from within a doorway on the left. He tore across to it and then said "Christ!" very loudly. Sir Colin Shorland was sitting in his swivel chair with a shotgun, its butt on the floor and its barrel in his mouth. The top of his head and his brains were plastered over the ceiling above him.

Kate broke the news to Andrew as he was washing up after a late breakfast. Andrew hardly said anything before he put the 'phone down. He found the news difficult to comprehend. Only twelve hours ago he had been talking with Colin Shorland, now he was dead. It didn't make sense, but he supposed that he had left him with little option to do otherwise. A terrible feeling of the enormity of what he had done came over him. He had effectively been Shorland's executioner. Now, Kate said that her boss wanted him to meet them down in Surrey to examine any evidence that might be turned up. *Oh God!* He thought. *Is there ever going to be an end to this awful business?* He very reluctantly put the boat straight, locked the cabin and went to his car to drive back to Surrey. The journey down the M1 and round the M25 passed in a sort of daze.

It was with distaste that he recognised Kate's car among the others on the drive outside Shorland's house. He knew now that he hated himself for letting her use him, he hated himself for his weakness in succumbing to passion for her, and he hated himself for his dithering about and losing Anne. Funnily enough, he realised, he did not hate her. Kate and Baskerville were waiting in the hall talking with a uniformed constable. They nodded a greeting and he followed them into the study. Shorland's body had been removed to the morgue, the shotgun had gone to forensic at Guildford, but nothing else had been touched. It looked exactly as Andrew had left it last night, with the exception he noted with an involuntary shudder, of bloodstains and fragments of bone and hair on the ceiling.

Kate made her way straight away to the answerphone and pressed the message button. The machine clicked and whirred and then began to regurgitate the messages of the previous day. The only one of any interest was one with a Northern Irish accent, but it only seemed to relate to Shorland's normal Parliamentary business. While Kate was playing the messages back, Andrew's eye wandered to the desktop. His eyebrows lifted and he pointed silently towards it. Baskerville, unlit pipe in his hands, nodded.

Lying on the desktop were several sheets of laser-printed paper. Baskerville picked the top one up. "This looks interesting." He read a few lines, and then put it down with a strange expression on his face. "I think this is something that you ought to read,

Ellison. I think it's going to tie up a lot of loose ends." He held the sheaf of papers out to him.

Andrew shrugged. "Not for me now. I think I know all there is to know." He turned to Kate. "Carry on though, Sergeant and do your duty."

Kate sat down in the swivel chair, held the closely typed sheets under the light and read:

I, Colin James Shorland, Knight Bachelor, being of sound mind and not under duress, make oath and say as follows:

I was born in 1942 at Lincoln and was called up for National Service in 1961. In December 1962 at the age of 19, I was awarded Her Majesty's Commission in the Royal Army Pay Corps. I was stationed at Sennelager in West Germany, where I was in charge of the accounts for an infantry battalion and its supporting units of Royal Artillery and service Corps personnel. It was there that I made the acquaintance of Company Sergeant Major Dunton. CSM Dunton explained how it was possible to smuggle contraband articles into the United Kingdom by secreting them inside items of military equipment which was being returned for servicing or upgrading. In particular cases of spent shells, which were returned to RA depots, were used. I managed to obtain money to finance the further purchase of alcohol and tobacco by transferring sums temporarily from various military funds. After three successful shipments it was no longer necessary to use this method, and Dunton and myself financed subsequent ventures out of profits. Our contact in the UK was based at Aldershot and was Corporal Joseph Hannagan RASC. I identify Corporal Hannagan as the man now known as Roland Burson. Dunton and I operated this venture until I was discharged from the army in June 1964, having completed my term of service. Dunton had made sufficient money to purchase property in Germany, and I was able to finance my studies in law at Cambridge and to buy a house in North London with my share. The commodities that we traded in were alcohol and tobacco. At no time did we trade in narcotic substances.

Some time about October 1965, Joseph Hannagan approached me at

Cambridge. He told me that he had left the Army and was down on his luck. He threatened to reveal my involvement in smuggling unless I gave him money. I persuaded him that I could also reveal information about him that he was unaware that I possessed, and we compromised by my lending him one thousand pounds to finance a deal. He subsequently repaid the money and I lent him various sums over the ensuing years, all of which he repaid with interest. I do not know what the money was used for and did not ask at the time.

I qualified as a solicitor in 1970 and worked as an assistant in various firms, specialising in Company Law. During this time I frequently met Joseph Hannagan, who claimed that he was working as a business agent. I did not check his credentials, but continued to finance sundry deals until I heard that he had been charged with several offences relating to demanding money with menaces. After this I told him that I could no longer deal with him. He was sentenced to two years imprisonment and tried to make contact with me from inside prison. He knew that, as a solicitor, I would have privileged access, but I refused to see him. Earlier in the year 1973, I had entered into partnership as a Solicitor of the Supreme Court with Andrew Douglas Ellison and others in the firm known as Pringle, Ellison and Company.

On his release in 1973 he again made contact with me and succeeded in blackmailing me into acting as his solicitor in the following way. Soon after his release from prison, Hannagan was reported killed in a motor accident. I was relieved at hearing this news, feeling that I was rid of an unwelcome incubus. I found a will amongst his personal documents which were still in my possession, in which he left all his personal effects to one Roland Burson, at that time supposedly domiciled in South Africa. I acted on behalf of his estate, and made contact with Burson at an address in Johannesburg. There were no other relatives, and I duly paid the residue, which was mainly the proceeds of life Assurance policies amounting to some fifty thousand pounds, to the legatee. As Trustee of the estate I wrote and asked Burson for proof of his identity and he sent me a passport and an official copy of his birth certificate from South

Africa. Only after the whole matter was concluded did Hannagan reappear and introduce himself to me as Roland Burson. He found the way in which he had duped me to be highly amusing. He has continued to use that name ever since.

From then on Burson, as I must now call him, had me under his influence. He always threatened to expose me as a fellow conspirator of his both from Army times and after. He warned me that I could face charges of conspiracy to defraud Insurance Companies if he was unmasked. When my partner Andrew Ellison defended Guiseppe Caroni on a charge of murder in 1977, Burson was extremely angry and tried to get me to use my influence with my partner to drop the case. I now know that Burson was attempting to remove Caroni as a business rival and had suborned two police officers in order to secure his conviction. I also know that Burson or one of his assistants killed the murder victim, Moses Levy, a bookmaker, because he boasted of the fact to me one night when he was drunk.

Because I was unable to prevent Andrew Ellison defending Caroni, and because he was acquitted, Burson swore revenge upon both of them. Some years later Caroni was sent to prison for tax evasion and irregularities. I was responsible for providing both the Inland Revenue and HM Customs and Excise with false information that secured his conviction and I freely confess this now. The details of deals and transactions in property and shares were forged and sent by me anonymously to the authorities concerned after the death of Mrs. Caroni, whom I knew was the only person to have full knowledge of his affairs. I have no reason to suppose that Caroni is any other than an honest man.

So far as Andrew Ellison was concerned, Burson wanted him out of the way for his part in preventing the take over of Caroni's business enterprises in 1977 for the purposes of laundering money from Burson's enterprises. I was unable to do much about this until the mid 1980's, when I became enamoured of his wife Pamela. I had always been attracted to her, and I now discovered that the attraction was mutual. She is an ambitious woman, both in the monetary and social senses, and she was dissatisfied with her husband's progress in these matters. He was an extremely successful lawyer professionally, but had not achieved the financial eminence that Pamela desired. Because of my dealings with Burson, there was no shortage of money in my case. I therefore used my influence with Pamela to persuade Ellison to overreach himself during the financial boom of the 'eighties by property and share speculation. When the inevitable crash came, I assisted him in recovering his financial position by borrowing from trust funds. However I was able to conceal my part in this and when the Law Society auditors discovered it, I was able to maintain that it was all Ellison's doing. The subsequent trial and imprisonment of Ellison and his professional disgrace at length satisfied Burson, for revenge is a dish best eaten cold. I felt that the seduction of, and eventual marriage to, his wife was a satisfactory outcome for me. On reflection I can see that this was the pinnacle of my career, although I have apparently been more successful since.

My political career had meanwhile prospered and once I had been returned to Parliament at a by-election, I tried to shake off my contact with Burson. Unfortunately he proved difficult to dislodge. I became associated with the Anglo Irish Peace Accord movement through one of my constituents, and it was not long before Burson discovered this and began applying his pressures again. I now know that he was in direct contact with members of the Carrickfergus Unit, which is an extreme and secret Protestant para-military group whose aims are to disrupt the workings of the Peace Accord. I have since found myself in the impossible position of attempting to obtain political concessions for this group and at the same time maintain a position of neutrality in public towards the Republican/Nationalist elements on the Peace Accord committee. I was awarded my Knighthood on account of services rendered to the Accord, and Burson and his accomplices know this and have used their powers of blackmail to the utmost.

Because I was unable to deliver certain concessions following a conference in Dublin last summer, I narrowly escaped an assassination or kidnap attempt at Heathrow on my return to England. I recognised a known Protestant gunman watching me as I retrieved my baggage. He looked as if he could be pointing a firearm at me under cover of a briefcase. I could not inform the authorities for fear of exposure, but I managed to feign a heart attack and was taken out in an ambulance. The man disappeared in the confusion. My wife, Pamela, was with me and was very concerned, but I did not dare tell even her of what was happening. Since then my constituency and private telephones have been continually plagued by threatening calls warning me to deliver political concessions before 31st January or face the consequences. This has placed a great strain on my marriage, which had not proved as successful as I had originally hoped. I have since found comfort and solace in the person of a Parliamentary colleague, Janet Thomas, and my wife has left me. This has proved a blow to my public ambitions, for a supportive wife is an incalculable Parliamentary asset. I now know that my meetings with Miss Thomas have been logged and that I face media exposure as a result. I also know that my involvement with other associates of Burson is likely to be made public, but above all, I know that nothing that I can do now will prevent a ruinous and murderous outbreak of political violence in both the Irish Republic and the United Kingdom orchestrated by the Carrickfergus Unit.

In these circumstances, there is little point in my continued existence. I have wronged many people in my life, in particular Andrew and Pamela Ellison. It is too late to make amends, and goodness knows how many innocent people may be killed or die because of what has been plotted. I now see that Roland Burson is an evil and calculating man who has ruined many lives. I am not prepared to stand by and see him ruin any more. In a locked drawer in my desk at my office will be found details of deals involving explosives and firearms on behalf of the Carrickfergus Unit, together with full particulars of the drug deals and VAT frauds with bullion that have financed the operation. These details are contained on computer disks, which are labelled "Sundry correspondence." I would also ask the reader of this letter to forward the attached envelope to Sgt. Major Dunton, c/o the Royal Hospital, Chelsea. It contains nothing of relevance to current matters, but it will settle a long-standing debt.

I have made my peace with Ellison in person, I would have liked the opportunity of doing so with Pamela, but time is running out. Doctor Faustus has received his summons.

Sworn before me, this twenty ninth day of January 1995.
Kenneth Dobson,
Dorking, Surrey.
A Commissioner for Oaths.

Kate finished reading and sighed. "We shall have to take possession of this and produce it for the Coroner. Don't you think Mr. Ellison ought to have a photo copy Sir?"

Andrew grimaced. "What's the point? He's dead now. At least he made his peace with me and kept his word at last. It's odd that, about Faustus. I thought the same thing when I left him."

"Andrew! You are sometimes infuriating! Don't you see? Here's your big chance to clear your name and undo all the wrongs you've gone through, and you don't take it?"

Baskerville gave a diabolical grin as he lit his pipe. "You seem to have an advocate in my team, I really can't think why. But never mind, go on man, take it while you're offered it. It's the best chance you'll ever have to set things straight."

Andrew smiled his lopsided smile. "I know, I know. Do you think I haven't thought all that through? But at my time of life, what on earth is the point of looking backwards? I've made my new life, and I don't want the old one."

"Oh rubbish!" Baskerville snorted. "Look, you've been of tremendous help to us in clearing everything up, and don't think I'm not grateful, because I am, but I've bent a lot of rules today to get you here. It's only because DI Marriott has an old pal in the Surrey force who owes him a favour that we've been given the go ahead by their Chief Constable to come in here, so for Christ's sake, swallow your pride and take the opportunity while it's there."

Kate said "Look at how you've been able to use your skills to help people like Stu and Gary. Just think how much more useful you'd be if you were a real solicitor again. You don't have to go back into City practice. For my sake, Andrew, just try for once in your life to be positive about yourself. And if you can't do it for me, then what about Anne Clarke? What about your children? At least, take a photo copy for your family records before I have to make it disappear into police records."

Andrew was silent for a while, then said: "All right! You win. I'll take a copy. But that's all for the moment."

Kate smiled briefly. "Good. I'll make a copy and let you have one." Baskerville held out his hand. "Thanks, Ellison. I'll do my damnedest to see the authorities keep my side of the bargain. Now, I must be getting down to your old City office. I fancy there's enough there to put Burson away for a good long stretch, if not Dooney. I'll see you there Kate." He puffed a contented cloud of smoke, turned on his heel and strode out. Andrew heard his car start and drive away. Kate took the tape out of the Answerphone and sealed it in a plastic envelope, turned and was about to open the study door, then paused. "What are you going to do now, Andrew?"

"Oh, I suppose I shall go back to the boat and try to forget the whole business. I've still got a promise to keep to Joey Caroni. But you're not going to need me as a witness any more, are you?"

"Right then." She went to the door and called "OK constable." The uniformed policeman who had been waiting in the hall came in. "Thank you, constable, we're just leaving." She turned to Andrew as they stood in the hall "Keep in touch. See you soon, bye!" She gave him a peck on the cheek and vanished down the stairs from the front door. Andrew heard her car door slam and the engine start. There seemed to be a terrible emptiness in him somehow.

The man known as Roland Burson put down the telephone and swore under his breath. He crossed the room to the doorway and called for Wayne. The girl lounging on the settee and watching Sky TV did not look up as he passed, but suddenly the television was switched off and she found herself sprawling on the floor beneath the overturned settee. Her doe eyes flashed angrily at a red faced Burson towering above her. "What you do that for?" she whined.

"Get up, you cow!" snarled Burson, then grasped her by her shoulder and jerked her up.

"What's it all about, Rowie?"

"What's it all about? You lying little bitch. I'll tell you what it's about. It's all about who's been singing to the filth."

The girl began to snivel "I don't know what you mean, honest Rowie. I loves you, don't I?"

Burson slapped her hard round the face. "Don't give me that crap!" he shouted. "You've been talking out of turn."

"No I ain't Rowie. I ain't talked to no one."

"Well some bastard has."

She was sobbing now, a red weal across her cheek, and struggled to her feet. In between gasping sobs she cried "Rowie! I ain't never done nuffink. I don't know what you means."

"Shut up, and stop your bloody snivelling before I give you something to snivel about!"

Wayne came in the door, in tee shirt and jeans. "What is it boss?"

"Some fucker's blown it. Sir Colin fucking Shorland's topped himself. That prat with the boat what you said was all right's sung away to the law, and do you know who it was that Flower was trying to shut up?"

Both Wayne and the girl looked dumbly at him. "It was that bastard Ellison that I got put away, Shorland's partner. Now why wasn't I told he was around again? Ellison knows everything. I'll tell you what Wayney boy. When I get this lot sorted, he's due for a proper spanking."

"Oh, come off it, boss. 'E can't know everything. Maybe 'e knows about the VAT business, and the dog scam, but 'e can't know about the rest."

Burson smiled grimly "Can't he now? Well, our mates in the Met reckon he does. He's got enough to put me on a murder charge; he's got enough to send Flower down for ten years. He's taken photos of this very house right under our noses, he's got Dooney's number, and what's more Sunshine, he's got enough evidence on you to put you away for a long time for GBH on Caroni's missus, and don't forget he's a brief by trade, so it'll all stand up in court. The law searched your flat in Harlesden last night."

Wayne had gone very white during this recital. "How the bloody hell did he get all that?"

"I ain't too sure yet, but I think someone's grassed us all up, don't I Karly?"

The girl nodded. Wayne's jaw dropped "What? She done it?"

"I ain't done nuffink. I don't know what you're talkin' about" she sobbed.

"Shut up, you lying little bitch. Just piss off out of it before I get really upset" snarled Burson.

Karly picked up a few of her things that were lying about and crept to the door. "Honest, Rowie, I don't know nuffink."

"Get out!" shouted Burson. "I want you out of this house in five minutes. I never want to see your face again! Got that into your thick head, have you?"

Karly fled, sobbing.

"Right Wayney boy. We've got to work fast. We're out of here in ten minutes. There's a charter flight from Luton in less than two hours and we're going to be on it, my old Son. You go and chuck some things in a case, use the second set of passports. I'll do some phoning. We ain't got a lot of time before Old Bill comes and wants to ask us to assist with inquiries. You got that car o' Dooney's back from the service yet?"

"It come back first thing this mornin'."

"Right! Let's get on with it."

It took Burson somewhat less than five minutes to make the necessary telephone calls and Wayne slightly more to cram everything that the two would need into four suitcases. Burson opened a wall safe, and took out a bag containing diamonds and high denomination US dollar bills. He tossed them into a grip and ran to the side door of the house, slamming it shut behind him. Wayne had already loaded the other cases into the Mercedes and had started the engine. Burson climbed in the passenger side.

"Well done, my Son. Looks like we've got a clear run. I've got tickets to Tenerife and we gets a plane from there to Brazil tomorrow, right!"

"Right, boss. You're magic you are."

"I know! Now let's bugger off before John Law turns up. We're a couple of business associates called Jones and Robinson, going to Tenerife for a bit of a break. Got that? Our man said we'd have twenty minutes at least, and there's less than five of them left."

Wayne clutched in gently and the big car purred away from the carport. He swung out into the close. Nobody was stirring, and there was no sign of any police cars yet. Only Karly, her vacant looking face streaked with tears, stood in the close and watched dumbly as they swept past. Wayne accelerated down the close towards the main road, narrowly missing a man in white plumbers' overalls who was trying to get into his van at the end of the road. He turned right, towards the sharp incline which led towards the main road out of the city that crossed the canal nearby on a high viaduct. Burson glanced at his watch, five minutes to the M1 motorway and twenty minutes to Luton Airport. They were as good as home and dry. At that moment, as the car tipped upwards, a small steel ball in a glass tube taped to the frame under the driving seat rolled back and made an electrical contact.

Andrew found himself driving home in a more disorientated mood than he had felt since his release. He found his way to the M25 and the M1 on automatic pilot, his brain numb. It was not until he had got back aboard the boat and poured himself a hefty whisky and water that his mind began to clear. He turned the television on and settled down in his favourite chair to watch

University Challenge. Just before the programme came on he idly noticed words running across the bottom of the screen. He suddenly realised that they spelled out a message. NEWSFLASH. TWO MEN REPORTED DEAD IN CAR BOMB INCIDENT AT MILTON KEYNES. He thought *this must be something local* and forgot about the matter until *News at Ten* came up on the screen. By now he was into his third Scotch and felt reasonably detached as Big Ben bonged out and the title rolled. Trevor Macdonald intoned, "Two men die in a car bomb attack in a quiet residential neighbourhood" and then went on to announce the rest of the evening's headlines. There was just a brief shot of police car lights flashing and wreckage before the next news item came up. Andrew was interested now, and watched to see if he could identify which part of the New City was featured. Macdonald came back to the item. "News is still coming in about a car bomb attack in Milton Keynes in which two men died earlier today. Police sources say that the attack bears all the hallmarks of an IRA bombing, but no official confirmation has been received from Republican sources. No comment has been made as to whether this was a reprisal for the bomb attack on an Irish club in Leicester last night in which five people were killed." The camera then panned over the darkened wreckage and startled looking bystanders. A shaken looking man in the local casualty department wearing plumber's overalls told the camera that he was just about to get into his van to drive to his next job when he saw this big Mercedes pull out from a house further down the road. It passed him and drove up the hill towards the canal bridge. As it pulled up at the road junction there was this huge explosion and he was blown flat. The camera showed shattered windows and stripped roofs illuminated by searchlight and what looked like some loose currency notes lying beside the wreckage. There then followed a piece by ITV's Ireland correspondent as to whether, if this was an IRA attack, it signified a new shift of violence to the mainland, and could be some sort of retribution for the Leicester bomb, but since the identities of the two dead were not yet known, it was difficult to see what the motive was. It was only when the camera picked out the number plate of the wrecked car, that Andrew realised who the victims were.

It was raining in North Wales and for the last fifty or more miles along the A5, the windscreen wipers had been continually sweeping back and forth. The three occupants of the stolen car said very little as they sped through the darkened hill country. The car radio, tuned to BBC Radio 4, gave them the occasional newsflash. They were past Betws-y-Coed when the newsreader announced that they had just received reports of an explosion in Milton Keynes in which two men were believed to have died. The driver gave a low whistle and said in a soft voice "Good goal, Fergal."

"Ah, so it was." Fergal crossed himself "may the Lord rest their souls."

Jack Dooney, sitting in the passenger seat, said, "Father Liam will hear your confession. He's a sound man."

Little more was said until they arrived at Caernarfon Quay soon after midnight. The car was carefully parked in a tourist car park after a careful wipe over of the door handles and steering wheel. The three slipped across the quay, down a ladder and were soon aboard a motor sailer. A man's voice came quietly from the wheelhouse. "We'll be leavin' right away, while the tide's makin'. Get yerselves below and have some sleep now. There's tea bein' made for yous."

"Sure, and it'll be a good breakfast in Wexford for all of us."

The motor sputtered into life. Somebody ran forward and cast off the bow warp, the stern was already free. A Welsh voice called from the quayside "Safe journey, *bach*."

No reply came from the yacht as it slipped out of the harbour, headed South of West out of Menai and then set course for Wexford Harbour.

Next morning Andrew was late rising. He had the most appalling headache, which he put down to the half empty bottle of whisky on the table in front of the fireplace. He groaned as he looked at himself in the mirror, took a couple of aspirins and an Alka-Seltzer and made himself some breakfast. He was not quite sure whether he had slept or not, or whether he had dreamed about a bomb in Milton Keynes. After making himself some toast he dressed, drove up to the village for milk and bought *The Times*. He scarcely gave it a glance until he was back aboard the boat. Then the screaming headlines caught his eye and he read the news story of the bomb outrage in Milton Keynes. The story told him little that he did not either know or could have deduced, but after he had read it he rang Joey. Joey sounded incredulous.

"It ain't 'im fer Gawd's sake?! Well I'm buggered! I don't suppose no one'll cry much abaht 'im. An' the uvver one was the bastard what done Fiona over was it? Andy boy, I'm an' 'appy man this mornin'. You've got ter come up an' stay wiv me while we celebrate. Anyfink you wants pal! Anyfink you wants. 'Ullo! 'Ullo! Andy? What's up pal?" But Andrew had rung off. The fruits of victory tasted too bitter for him to enjoy Joey's pleasure.

At much the same time Detective Chief Superintendent Baskerville emerged from a room at the Home Office with a jaunty step. There had been a full attendance there, the Metropolitan Chief Commissioner, his own Chief Constable, the Home Secretary and his shadow and two senior civil servants. Already the telephone lines were crackling to various London police stations, warrants had been sworn out and press releases prepared. There were going to be a number of sudden arrests and early retirements over the next few days. The Chief Constable caught up with him in the passage. "So, Jack! Well done all round! I think we both deserve a drink."

The Chief Constable was fifteen years younger than his Detective Chief Superintendent, and had for some time felt that it was time old Jack Baskerville was pensioned off, but he had to admit that the old boy had pulled it off in style this time. A major political crisis averted, a police corruption issue neatly buried, a whole can of Irish worms safely resealed, and two villains removed from his own patch without the expense of a trial. The politicians would be delighted. He had already received intimation that he would be in line for being a Commissioner; buying old Baskerville a drink was the least he could do.

They found a quiet bar off Queen Victoria Street. The Chief Constable enthused for several minutes over his half of bitter, then Baskerville, now well into his second pint of London Pride, abruptly said: "look, Sir, I'm just about finished. I've only got two more months to do, but I would like to see my team looked after. They agreed to come on this case and took a big gamble with their careers. And there's one other thing."

"Yes?" asked the Chief Constable, rather testily. He did not want Baskerville to think that he was God, in spite of everything.

"I'd like you to see if you could bring some influence to bear with the Lord Chancellor's Department."

Jane was flashing a duster round the sitting room when Andrew called in to say goodbye. She stopped and gave him a small package that had arrived in that morning's post. It had Kate's writing on it and he absently thrust it into his pocket. Jane seemed genuinely upset when Andrew told her that he was leaving for an indefinite time.

"We'll miss you, me ole doock, an' Gary will an' all."

"Oh, I shan't be too far away. I'll probably call in and see you before too long."

Jane looked serious. "It ain't my place I suppose to say this, but I reckon you'd be daft if you didn't keep in touch wi' Anne. You don't want to take too much notice o' what she says about wantin' space. If you asks me, that's a load of ole squit. I been on me own now fer ten years, an' I know 'ow lonely you can get, an' if it were me an' a good lookin' feller like you turned up, I'd be there straight off. Mind, you can get set in yer ways, an' she's been on 'er own a few years now." She stopped suddenly. "There. I've been an' shot me gob off, an' it ain't no business o' mine. I'm sorry."

Andrew smiled and touched her arm. "You're a good sort, Jane, and I don't take any offence. But thank you for telling me that. I shan't forget it."

"Ah well. I 'ad a card from 'er yesterday. She's comin' back next week, so you'd best think it over."

"Thanks Jane, I will."

Andrew had checked all his oil levels and the engine was prepared, so on returning from the farmhouse he started up and made ready to leave. The winter morning was bright and promised a few hours of pleasant weather. He would explore further south for a day or so, leaving his car to await his return. There were several places from which he could get a train to Euston, according to the guidebook. He shoved the fore end of the boat out into the channel and set off under the bridge. When he came to Cosgrove village he tied on moorings at the bottom of a pub garden and made himself a cup of tea. He thought he would walk up after dark and treat himself to a meal. As he sipped his tea, a thought struck him. He rummaged in his pocket and took out the packet that Jane had given him. He tore the little package open, his hands trembling slightly. There was no letter, but it contained a compact disc and a silver watch chain. He gazed at them dully. Perhaps he had been a bit too hasty in his dismissal of Kate. He picked up his mobile and rang her works number. A recorded message informed him that this number was no longer in use.

A passer by walking a dog on the towpath told him that there was a shop in the village, so a little later he made his way up the narrow street beside the pub and duly found it. Among his few purchases was a copy of the local Northampton evening paper which he duly read over another cup of tea as the light faded. A small by-line caught his eye and he read "Promotion for Northants Police Officers." Tucked away at the bottom of an inside page was the news that Detective Inspector Marriott had been promoted to Chief Inspector and that Detective Sergeant Hollis had been promoted to Detective Inspector and transferred to the Kettering Division with immediate effect. Andrew sighed. The setting sun struck through the porthole and settled on the music centre. He turned it on and inserted the CD. After a short while, it began to play *"Just one of those things."*

Andrew listened to it right through, sighed once more, then picked up the mobile and rang Pamela's number.

CODA, by Editor (see Foreword)

When Andrew woke the next morning after a restless night, the rain was falling noisily on the boat's roof, so he decided to stay where he was with the hope that the rain would ease. He then thought that as the canal was now open through to London after the long stoppage, he would go further that way, see his children again and perhaps explore more of the canal system whilst trying to forget about Anne.

He would also be able to see DCI Baskerville, who had kept his word to have Andrew reinstated as a member of the Law Society. Although Andrew had had no intention of returning to London practice, he realised that it would be very useful to his new friends for them to have a 'waterways solicitor'.

Andrew passed the rest of the week exploring Cosgrove, the horse tunnel under the canal and the remains of the old locks down into the River Ouse. A few days later, as he was eating a late breakfast, he realised that Anne was due back that morning and, as he thought about Anne he wondered sadly if he would see her again. He decided that now he must set off, even though it had started raining heavily once more.

Andrew went through the now familiar routine of starting the engine and untying the boat and, not without misgivings, he moved off in the direction of Fenny Stratford.

As Andrew approached the bridge by Wolverton station, he saw a figure sheltering under the bridge, with a small bag at its side. At first he wondered if this person was connected to the recent incidents, then to his astonishment he recognized Anne, bundled up in a waterproof coat. As he drew near, she spoke, "Hello Andrew." she said quietly, "Jane told me that you had gone and she had heard from Stu where you were tied up. I arrived back less than a couple of hours ago and saw your note; when I got to Cosgrove somebody told me that you had just left. I could not let you leave without trying to see you."

"I had hoped to see you too." replied Andrew. "It's simply that I could not stay there any longer on my own."

Hesitantly, Anne said softly, "You need not be on your own again, you once told me that your boat was just big enough for two. If you think I will fit in, would you let me join you?"

"B-but what about your house and the farm?" gasped Andrew, reluctant to believe what he hoped she had said.

"Jane is looking after it all, and now I am here. May I step on?" With that, Andrew took Anne's bag and helped her on board. He pushed the gear rod into ahead and wound up the speedwheel, then, despite the rain still lashing down, they stood close to each other on the footboard as they headed off towards London with renewed hope in their hearts.